CRAF

3 1 OCT 2011

− 7 NOV 2011

1 9 NOV 2011

- Please return items before closing time
  on the last date stamped to avoid charges.
- Renew books by phoning 01305 224311 or
  online www.dorsetforyou.com/libraries
- Items may be returned to any Dorset library.
- Please note that children's books issued on
  an adult card will incur overdue charges.

Dorset County Council
Library Service

DL/2372 dd05450

THE DEEP DARK SLEEP

Craig Russell

First published in Great Britain in 2011 by

Quercus
21 Bloomsbury Square
London
WC1A 2NS

A CIP catalogue reference for this book is available
from the British Library

ISBN 978 0 85738 180 4 (TPB)
ISBN 978 0 85738 181 1 (HB)

10 9 8 7 6 5 4 3 2 1

Typeset in Swift by Ellipsis Digital Limited, Glasgow

Printed and bound in Great Britain by
Clays Ltd, St Ives plc

For my mother, Helen

PROLOGUE

Gentleman Joe Strachan, it would seem, had slept the deep, dark sleep for a long time.

Gentleman Joe had slept the deep dark sleep while I had been up to my knees in mud and blood in Italy; while the Luftwaffe had growled high above him on its way to rearrange Clydebank's town planning; while Stalin, Roosevelt and Churchill had carved up Europe between them and had given an idea to Glasgow's crime bosses, the Three Kings, about how they could do pretty much the same kind of carve-up with the Second City of the British Empire. The fireworks at Dresden, Hiroshima and Nagasaki had also done nothing to disturb Joe's slumber.

Even the constant toing and froing above him – the propeller churning of the vast Clyde-built ships or insolent tugs – had failed to stir him.

For the deep, dark sleep that Gentleman Joe slept was the undisturbed rest one only found at the bottom of the Clyde after somebody lullabied you to your final slumber with a solo for blunt instrument, tucked you up nice and cosy in some shipyard chains, and slipped you over the side of a midnight rowboat in the middle of the river's deep channel.

But, as I say, I spent the war years as ignorant as everyone else about Joe's repose. I just wish I had stayed that way.

CHAPTER ONE

I, for one, was someone for whom the whole idea of dredging up the past was particularly unappealing: being of that generation given especially colourful pasts courtesy of the little party thrown for our benefit in Europe and the Far East. My own history had been particularly gaudy, and I had to admit to adding more than a dash or two of extra colour myself over the years. I had once seen a movie about some guy who woke up in the middle of nowhere and couldn't remember who he was or where he was from and this lack of autobiography troubled him immensely. Me, I would have given a lot to have had that kind of amnesia.

The dredging up of Joe Strachan's past had been literal rather than metaphorical. The River Clyde must have been about the busiest waterway in the world, mainly because – wherever you were on the world's seas – any luxury liner, cargo ship, warship, tub or rust bucket you saw bobbing past carried the mathematical probability that it had been conceived and born on the Clyde. And that meant that the riverbed along the navigation channels had continuously to be kept wide and deep by a constant grime-dark procession of scouring dredgers.

So when a tangle of skull, bones, a few rags and a gold cigarette case were hauled up in a conveyor bucket through roiled waters to the surface of the Clyde, then it really had been a literal dredging up of the past; a past that would have been best left exactly where it was.

Dredger crews on the Clyde were a pretty phlegmatic lot; they had to be. Their haul was mainly the oily, silty muck that clogged the bottom of the channels and had an odour to offend a dung beetle; but it also included everything from fossilized tree trunks and giant elk antlers from a long-inundated ancient forest, to bedsteads, pieces of ship's engine, aborted babies in weighted Gladstone bags, dumped murder weapons, and anything else that could be jettisoned from a passing craft.

The late Mr Strachan's were by no means the first mortal remains to be recovered from the Clyde and they certainly would not be the last. But there was a significant difference between the floating corpses retrieved from the surface by the Glasgow Humane Society and the City of Glasgow Harbour Police, and those brought up from the river bottom by the dredger crews; and that difference was all about *intent*. For a body to sink and stay sunk involved ballast, usually pockets filled with stones or a wrapping of chains. The bodies the dredgers brought up were the bodies that had been meant to stay lost.

Like Gentleman Joe's.

I could imagine the scene: the dredger's crew taking a

moment to decide what to do as the still anonymous Joe beamed a bright skull grin at them from the greasy black mud of the bucket. There had probably been a debate about whether to toss the bones back into the river; there would certainly have been a tussle over the gold cigarette case. But my guess is that someone on that tub had been long enough in the tooth and had enough sense about him to think that the initials *JS* on a hunk of gold might just spell a lot of trouble. In any case, the decision was made to inform the City of Glasgow Police.

The initial discovery of the remains was something that had passed me by; me, and the vast majority of Glasgow's population. It had only warranted a couple of lines of red print in a late news column of the *Glasgow Evening Citizen*. Significance, you see, is something that tends to attach itself to things or events after the fact. To accrue. The significance of the bones, their resting place, and the monogrammed cigarette case remained disconnected for a few days. After all, it wasn't uncommon for human remains to be found in the Clyde. More than a few tipsy fishermen or smog-blinded patrolling coppers had misjudged the long walk/short pier equation; capsized tugs and the odd shipyard launch disaster had also helped populate the river's currents. And, of course, the city's enterprising underworld made full use of the river's capacity for concealment.

As for me, I had a lot of other things on my mind in that September of Nineteen fifty-five. It was the end of the hottest Glasgow summer on record which, admittedly, isn't a big claim – like being Yorkshire's greatest lover, the cheeriest person in Edinburgh, or Aberdeen's most generous philanthropist – but the summer of Fifty-five had literally outshone the previous summer and temperatures had, according to the bemused local press, become hot enough to melt tarmac. Whatever the statistical truth about the temperature, I remember that Glasgow summer as sticky and acrid: the thick viscous air smelling like hot metal and the bright sky black-streaked with the dense granular smoke from the factories and shipyards. Whatever the weather, Glasgow's element was carbon, and in the open street you felt like you were walking through the hall of a foundry.

And now the season was changing. Summer was becoming autumn, which it rarely did in Glasgow: the climate of the West of Scotland was famously mitigated by the Gulf Stream and the weather generally varied only from slightly warmer and wet in the summer to slightly cooler and wet in the winter. Glasgow's smoke-belching heavy industry also lent the city a unique, season-fudging urban climate, and autumn normally confined itself to the calendar and sodden, adhesive, grey-brown clumps of leaves clotted over street drains. But this year, because it had been preceded by a summer to notice, autumn was a presence felt.

Glasgow's founding city fathers had been a benevolent bunch, deciding to alleviate the cramped tenement squalor to which they had condemned the majority of Glaswegians with large, open parks. This had been the first year that I had noticed a blaze of autumn reds and golds in the trees.

There again, a lot of things were different that year.

For the first time since I rented my Gordon Street office, I was using it as my main place of business. I had just tied up three divorce and one missing person cases, and I provided security on a weekly wages run for one of the shipyards. I was particularly pleased with this last contract. Jock Ferguson, my contact at the City of Glasgow Police, had vouched for me; which was quite something, given that he was aware that I had been known to associate with the likes of Handsome Jonny Cohen or Hammer Murphy, both leading lights of the bala-clava-wearing set. But Ferguson and I were part of that grim post-bellum freemasonry who recognized each other as having gone through the mincer in the war. I didn't know what Jock's history was – and would never ask, as he would never ask me – but I knew it was more Dark Ages than Enlightenment.

Like mine.

I also knew that Jock Ferguson reckoned me to be straight – well, *comparatively* speaking. There had been a time when I would have vouched for Jock with similar confidence. I had taken him as one Glasgow copper I could be sure wasn't on the take or otherwise double-dealing; but my faith in him had taken a knock a year or so back and anyway, even at the best of times, I wasn't the most likely to see the good in people.

The most important thing in landing the wages-run contract was that I had made a real effort to stay out of the way of the Three Kings: Cohen, Murphy and Sneddon, the triumvirate of gang bosses who ran everything worth running in the city, even if the peace between them was as tenuous as a showgirl's chastity. The jobs I had done for the Three Kings had been more than a few and often less than legal.

But it had gotten me started in Glasgow after I had been demobbed and the work had suited me more back then, still under the shadow of the mountain of crap that had built up behind me during the war.

But now, I hoped, things were beginning to change. *I* was beginning to change.

I had, however, made a point of making it known to those to whom it should be made known that I was running the security for a particular company's particular wages run, and that I could develop a particularly good memory for faces if anyone tried to stick us up. So my message was hands off my run. Or else.

I'm sure my warning had Glasgow's three most feared crime bosses quaking in their handmade Loake semi-brogues. I had actually half expected, and dreaded, a proposition of the blind-eye-turning sort, but none had been forthcoming. Like Jock Ferguson, each of the Three Kings knew I was straight. Comparatively speaking.

Anyway, like I said, the original discovery of a pile of bones in a dredging bucket didn't raise a ripple on the pond of Glasgow's collective consciousness. But a week later, it made a splash. A big splash. And the papers were full of it:

RIVER BODY IDENTIFIED AS WANTED
EMPIRE EXHIBITION ROBBER.
MYSTERY OF JOSEPH STRACHAN
DISAPPEARANCE SOLVED AFTER 18 YEARS.
PROCEEDS OF DARING 1938 EXHIBITION ROBBERY
STILL UNRECOVERED.

*

Now Gentleman Joe Strachan was before my time. But so were Zeus and Odin and I had heard of all three. The Glasgow underworld had more myths and legends than ancient Greece, and Gentleman Joe had become a towering figure in the folklore of those trying to turn a dishonest buck.

Reading the article reminded me that I had heard the name mentioned with hushed reverence over the years; but because my acquaintance with the Second City of the British Empire had only begun when I was demobbed after the war, Strachan had never been a visible figure in my landscape. However, I did know that there had been a spate of pre-war robberies, the biggest in Glasgow history, culminating in the Empire Exhibition job in Nineteen thirty-eight. All of which had been attributed to Gentleman Joe. Attributed but never proved.

What I had also heard was that if Strachan had hung around – and not at the end of a rope for a policeman's murder – then he probably would have been the Fourth King of Glasgow. Or maybe even the One True King of Glasgow; with Cohen, Murphy and Sneddon having to settle for fief-doms. But then there had been the spectacularly daring robbery, a copper lying dead, and Gentleman Joe was suddenly nowhere to be found. Nor was the fifty thousand pounds.

No one at the time had thought Strachan would be dead: rather that, in keeping with his now mythical-heroic status, he had entered the Glasgow gangster version of Valhalla. Which many took to be a luxury bungalow on the Bourne-mouth coast or somewhere similar. Probably called *Dunrobbin*.

All of which really had nothing to do with me and was of less interest.

Until I got a visit from Isa and Violet.

CHAPTER TWO

You never see it coming. Or at least it always seems to be that *I* never see it coming. Right up until Isa and Violet brought their shapely similitude into my office, my year had been going well. Very well.

I had a client list and a set of matching, balanced books that I could wave in front of the taxman and the occasional inquisitive copper to prove that my business was legitimate. Well, at least a lot more legitimate than it had been a year or two before. And the kind of cases I was working on made more demands on my wits – and not even many demands on them – and fewer on getting handy with some low rent Teddy Boy in an alley somewhere.

Which was good. Of late, I had been making a real effort not to get heated.

You pick up different things in war. A lot of men came back with venereal diseases caught from whores in Germany or the Far East, which they passed on unselfishly to their waiting wives, while others came back with trophies stolen from bodies. I came back with a hair-trigger temper and a tendency to express myself with great physical eloquence. Truth was, there had been times when I'd gotten more than a little carried away. Once I got started, it was difficult to stop. It was something that, when I'd been serving in the First Canadian Army in Europe, had been positively encouraged; but the authorities were decidedly sniffy about you using the skills they had taught you, now you were back in civilian life. The truth was that it was another good reason for curtailing my involvement with the Three Kings. It had involved me in a world I could understand at a time I could understand practically nothing else. Where everybody talked the same language: violence. And I was fluent.

So, whereas Sherlock Homes had used intellect and deer-stalker to crack cases, I had tended to employ muscle and blackjack. And to be honest I had enjoyed it just that little bit too much and I wanted away from it. Something had gotten broken during the war and I knew that if I wanted to fix it, I was going to have to steer clear of the kind of crap I'd been wading about in. The problem was, when someone like the Three Kings got a hold of you, they didn't like to let go.

But I had been making a pretty good fist of it; then Isa and Violet came to see me at my office.

Isa and Violet were identically petite, identically pretty, with identically large, blue eyes. Which was not surprising: they were identical twins. I worked that out as soon as I saw them. It's the kind of detail people expect you to notice when you're a detective.

And now Isa and Violet sat earnestly, and a little primly, opposite me.

I had, once before in my career, professionally encountered twins; but that had been an altogether different business. The last matching pair I'd come across had been Tam and Frankie McGahern. It had been an encounter that I had barely survived, so I had developed something of a superstitious aversion to matching siblings. But as Isa and Violet had come in and taken their seats, I had stolen a look at their identically peachy rears and had decided to become more pragmatic in my approach.

They introduced themselves, simultaneously, as Isa and Violet but had different surnames and I guessed there were wedding rings beneath the grey gloves. The twins shared the same pale, heart-shaped faces, small noses, bright blue eyes and full mouths, both of which had been encrimsoned in exactly the same shade of lipstick. They had their dark hair short and demiwaved, coming halfway down delicate ears that supported large domes of faux pearl. They even wore identical expensive grey suits, with tight-waisted jackets and pencil skirts that squeezed where I would have liked to do a bit of squeezing myself.

And, when they spoke, they finished each other's sentences without breaking the rhythm of what they were saying and without looking at each other.

'We heard you was . . .' began Isa. Or maybe it was Violet.

'. . . a private detective,' concluded Violet, or Isa, seamlessly.

'We need your help . . .'

'. . . about our father.'

'I suppose you've read all about him . . .'

'. . . in the papers . . .'

I smiled, a little confused. The truth was I had been a little discomfited by their arrival. They were both *very* pretty. Well, exactly as pretty as each other. And they were twins. The usual lustful scenario that would lurch unbidden into my imaginings when faced with a set of curves was subject to multiplication and I had to snap out of my speculation about what other tasks they might be disposed to take in turns.

'Your father?' I asked with a professional frown.

'Yes. Daddy.'

'Our maiden name you see . . .'

'. . . is Strachan,' they concluded in unison.

Even then it took me a moment to catch on; for significance to attach.

'The remains found in the Clyde?' I asked.

'Yes.' Another chorus.

'Gentleman Joe Strachan?'

'Joseph Strachan was our father.' The two pretty heart-shaped faces took on an identically harder look.

'But you must hardly have known him,' I said. 'From what I've read, Joe Strachan has been missing for nearly eighteen years.'

'We were eight,' said Isa. Or Violet.

'When Daddy had to go away.'

'We've never forgotten him.'

'I'm sure.' I nodded sagely.

When people pay you to find out things, sagacity is an attribute you should project at every opportunity. Much in the same way that when you visit a doctor you want him to exude an absolute mastery of his craft, despite the fact that the workings of the human body leave him almost as confused as everyone else. I wanted to impress the twins by saying, as they do in all the best movies, '*So you want me to find out . . .*' and then anticipate their request.

It wasn't working for me: I hadn't a clue what they could want from me, other than to find out who dumped Daddy in the drink. And that couldn't be it, because the police were all over that like a rash. There was, after all, the matter of a dead patrolling copper who happened to be at the right place at the wrong time eighteen years before. Whoever nudged Gentleman Joe over the side would know who tapped the beat bobby. The City of Glasgow Police were a less than cerebral bunch and if the case had been beyond them two decades before, I couldn't see them making anything of it now. And I would make even less.

'So what can I do for you?' I switched off the bulb of my omniscient sagacity for a moment.

They simultaneously lifted their handbags and placed them on their laps, snapped them open and took out identical wrapped wads of cash, placing them on the desk. The wads had made their handbags bulge and were now having the same effect on my eyes. The big Bank of England notes were crisp and new. And twenties: a denomination you would not exactly hand over the counter in a fish and chip shop. For a moment I thought this was an advance payment and from the size of the bundles, I saw myself working exclusively for the twins for the next three years.

'We get this every year . . .'

'On the twenty-third of July . . .'

'One thousand pounds exactly, each.'

I couldn't resist picking up a bundle in each hand, just for the feel of them, responding to an instinct similar to the one I'd had when the twins had first walked in.

'For how long?' I asked, bouncing the wads in my hands as if weighing them.

'Since Daddy left. Our mother got the money for us each year and then, when we were eighteen, it came directly to us.'

'Does your mother get any money for herself?'

'Mam passed on a couple of years ago . . .'

'. . . but before that, she got the same.'

'. . . a thousand pounds each year.'

'I'm sorry for your loss . . .' I said.

After an appropriate pause I blew a long, low whistle. 'Three thousand pounds a year is a very substantial amount of money,' I said. It certainly was, especially in a city where the average wage was about seven pounds a week. 'And it always arrives on the twenty-third of July?'

'Yes. Give or take a day . . .'

'. . . if it falls on a Sunday . . .'

'. . . for example.'

'Is that your birthdays?' I asked.

'No,' they said in unison and I could see identical reluctance on both faces.

'So what is the significance of the twenty-third of July?'

The twins looked at each other before answering.

'The robbery ...'

'... in Nineteen thirty-eight ...'

'... at the Empire Exhibition ...'

'Saturday the twenty-third of July was the day the robbery took place ...'

'Do you see ...'

'... our conundrum?' The twins asked between them.

I leaned back in my captain's chair and laced my fingers before me – sagely – while thinking of how much I really would like to see their conundrums. The truth was that I was struggling: I'd worked out that Isa and Violet were twins as soon as I saw them and felt that should have been enough Holmesian deduction for one day. I could see identical disappointment on their faces.

'We knew that Daddy had had to go away ...'

'... after all of that trouble ...'

'... but we knew he was looking after us ...'

'... by sending us the money every year ...'

And then it hit me. The discovery of his remains in the river meant that Gentleman Joe Strachan had been in a state of terminal repose for eighteen years and, as far as I was aware, there was no postal pick-up at the bottom of the Clyde.

'So you want to know who's been sending you the money, if not your father?'

'Exactly,' Isa and Violet said in emphatic unison.

'Unless it's not your father's remains they found ...' I said.

Two identical heads shook with identical grim certainty. 'The police showed us the cigarette case . . .'

'. . . we both recognized it right away . . .'

'. . . we remembered it clearly . . .'

'. . . and our Mam always said to us how Daddy wouldn't go nowhere without his special cigarette case.'

'But that's all there is to go on?' I asked.

'No . . .'

'. . . they found clothes . . .'

'. . . rotted to rags . . .'

'. . . but they were able to read the labels . . .'

'. . . and they were from Daddy's tailors . . .'

'. . . and our Da was always particular about where he bought his clothes . . .'

'What about dental records?' I asked. They both looked at me with blank confusion, which shouldn't have surprised me. This was Glasgow, after all.

'Our Da was tall . . .'

'. . . five foot eleven . . .'

'. . . and the police said the leg bones matched someone that height . . .'

I nodded. Five foot eleven *was* tall for Glasgow. *I* was tall for Glasgow and it was my height. I reluctantly handed back the wads. Isaac Newton had formulated the concept that every mass, from a coffee cup to a mountain to the Earth, had its own gravitational field: for me, cash always seemed to exert an irresistible force disproportionate to its mass. And as an object, I was anything but immoveable.

'I have to tell you ladies,' I said, 'that I don't think it's a good idea for you to walk around the streets of Glasgow with that amount of cash about your persons.'

'Oh, it's all right,' said Isa. 'Violet's husband Robert drove us here. We're on our way to deposit the money in the Clydesdale Bank around the corner.'

'But we thought we'd come and see you first.'

'Well,' I said, 'I suppose the starting point has to be the money itself. It would appear to be the only material clue we have at the moment. It arrives by post, you say?'

Another simultaneous nod, followed by another coordinated dip into the handbags which resulted in two empty brown envelopes presenting themselves on my desk. Each was addressed differently, but in the same hand. There was a London postmark on each.

'These are your current addresses?'

More harmonious concurrence.

'And you have had no contact with the sender?'

'Of course not.'

'So how did the sender find out about your new addresses? What about your mother? Whoever is sending these payments must have been told of your marriages. Could it be that your mother really knew who this is?'

'No. She was as surprised as we was . . .'

'. . . we both got married in the same year and the next packages arrived at our new addresses . . .'

'. . . with an extra five hundred each.'

'I have to say, ladies, that that sounds very much to me like the actions of a regretful absentee father. Especially when you take the significance of the date into account. You're both absolutely sure that it was your father they found?'

'As sure as we can be.'

'And our Ma said she never believed the money came from Daddy.'

'Oh?' I asked. 'Why did she think that?'

'She said . . .'

'. . . all along . . .'

'. . . that if Daddy had been alive, that wherever he was, he would have sent for us. To be a family.'

'Maybe that was impossible for him to do,' I said.

I didn't mention that I had also heard of Gentleman Joe's prowess as a bedroom swordsman: the twins were unlikely to be the only family he had.

'I don't mean impossible because he was dead, but because he couldn't risk coming back to Glasgow and the police tracing him. Three thousand pounds a year is a huge amount of money and I don't think, with respect, that you have a munificent but anonymous secret benefactor.'

They frowned and I simplified my vocabulary to a Glasgow level. Sometimes I can be too polysyllabic for my own good.

'So you're saying you think that it *isn't* Daddy they found in the river?' Isa spoke for them both, with an assertiveness I hadn't heard from either of them before. Maybe she was the older. Seniority in minutes and seconds counted to twins, I had been told. But maybe she was Violet.

'Truth is, I really don't know,' I said. 'Tell me, have either of you tried to trace back the packages to where they were sent from?'

'Until now we've kept very quiet about it . . .'

'. . . thinking it was Daddy . . .'

'. . . we didn't want to make waves . . .'

'. . . or do anything to lead the police to him.'

'That's understandable, I suppose,' I said; then, in a let's-be-absolutely-clear-about-this kind of tone, 'So you want me to find out who has been sending the money?'

'We do.'

'Even if that leads me to your father, who is wanted for the most serious crimes you can be wanted for?'

Identical frowns. Then an emphatic 'Yes.'

'Before we go any further,' I said, 'if that *wasn't* your father at the bottom of the Clyde and my investigations lead me to him, alive and well, then I will have to notify the police.'

They looked at each other, then back at me. 'We heard you was . . .'

'. . . discreet . . .'

'. . . that you and the police don't get on.'

'Did you?' I leaned forward. 'And who told you that?'

'We asked around . . .'

I studied them for a moment. Despite the cute ditzy twins thing they had going, they were after all the daughters of a legendary Glasgow gangster. I began to imagine where they had got character references for me.

'Turning a blind eye to the odd technical *infringement* of the law is one thing, ladies. But perverting the course of justice, misprision of felony or being an accessory after the fact in armed robbery and murder are something else.

Anyway, I'm not in the business of breaking the law,' I said with such conviction even I believed it.

'Our Daddy is dead, Mr Lennox . . .'

'. . . we want to know who is sending us the money.'

I took a moment to think about what they had told me. The penny dropped.

'So you want me to find who's been sending you the money because, if it isn't your father, then he or she has to have a pretty strong motive to part with that kind of cash. You think that maybe whoever's sending you the money is doing so out of guilt. If that *was* your father at the bottom of the river, someone must have put him there, is that it?'

When I said it, I said it as if it had been in my mind all along.

'We just want to know who's sending it to us.'

'Then what?' I asked. 'You call the police? I'm guessing you haven't been troubling the tax man about these payments. And the police come over all pernickety and bureaucratic when it comes to the proceeds of armed robbery. So what do you have planned? I have to tell you that if this is about some kind of personal retribution, then I'm not interested.'

'We just want to know who is sending it,' Isa repeated; this time there was a little steel in her voice and both heart-shaped faces again set hard.

'The postmarks on the envelopes are always London?' I asked with a hint of a sigh as they slipped the money back into respective handbags.

'Not always . . .'

'... sometimes Edinburgh ...'

'... and once from Liverpool.'

'I see ...' I frowned for effect before the punchline. 'I have to warn you that this may all become expensive, ladies. I may have a lot of travelling to do – all of which will be receipted and accounted for, of course. And it will take time ... whoever is sending you this money certainly values their anonymity. And time, I'm afraid, is money.'

'Is this enough ...' They both took out the cash bundles again and each peeled off crisp twenties, laying them, in turns, on my desk. When they were finished they had each laid six portraits of the queen before me.

'... to get you started?'

'You can let us know if you need more.'

I looked at the two hundred and forty pounds. The irresistible force had met with the moveable object.

'Let me see what I can find out,' I said and smiled my most at-your-service smile. 'I have to say, ladies, that I think you're paying me to look a gift horse in the mouth. You would maybe be better leaving things lie as they are.' But I had already picked up the twenties. I had decided that, given that Isa and Violet hadn't troubled the tax man, it would be diplomatic for me to do the same.

'We just want to know who it is ...' said Violet.

'... but we don't want them to know we know,' said Isa. 'Then we'll decide what to do.'

'That could be tricky,' I said. I thought of where this could all lead me and started to wonder if I should have made a bigger effort to be immoveable.

'I'm an enquiry agent. I make enquiries. People tend to hear when someone's asking questions about them. I suggest we take this one step at a time. Could I see one of the wrappers the money comes in?'

Isa obliged and handed me a paper band. It was plain, unmarked with a gummed closure.

'This isn't a bank's,' I said. 'The only way to trace this money would be to have the police check the serial numbers, but I guess that's not going to happen.' I punctuated my sigh with an obliging smile. 'Let me see what I can do. I'll ask around.'

'Thank you, Mr Lennox,' they said simultaneously.

'Do you have a photograph I can have of your father? I wouldn't need to keep it ... just long enough to copy it and then I'd return it to you.'

Isa, or Violet, shook her head. 'We don't have any photographs of Daddy ...'

'He never liked having them taken ...'

'Then, when he disappeared, the few photos there were of him also went missing ...'

'I see,' I said. Ghosts didn't steal photographs. 'Can you give me a list of people your father associated with before he disappeared?'

'We never knew anyone Daddy had dealings with ...'

'But there were the names we found ...'

'... behind the bureau ...'

'What names?' I asked.

'It was a list that Daddy had made ...'

'... years and years ago ...'

'... it had fallen behind the bureau ...'

'Mam found it when she was cleaning . . .'

'It had some names on it . . .'

'Would that help?'

'Anything that could give me somewhere to start looking would help,' I said, although I couldn't imagine Gentleman Joe committing a list of his Empire Exhibiton robbery co-conspirators to paper.

I went across to my office window while their heels were still clacking their way down the stairwell. Gordon Street below and the entrance to Central Station opposite were both thronging with people. Because it was before noon, there were no parking restrictions on Gordon Street and there was a car pulled up directly outside the entrance to my building. A brand new Ford Zephyr, all black and Hire Purchase shiny. A smartly dressed man stood leaning against the wing smoking a cigarette. He wasn't wearing a hat and I could see he had a full head of thick, dark hair. The suit looked expensive and must have been tailor-made to fit the shoulders that bulked beneath the material. He snapped away his cigarette and dutifully held open the door for the twins when they emerged from the doorway. So that was Violet's husband, Robert. I could tell, even from the distance of four floors up, that this guy was 'handy', as my shady business chums would say.

I found myself wondering how much of Robert's tailoring was paid for through the largesse of his wife's anonymous benefactor and how much came from earnings that spared the taxman effort. I couldn't see his face and therefore couldn't tell if he was someone I'd come across in my dealings with Glasgow's less salubrious social set.

After they had driven off, I sat at my desk frowning, without knowing what it was I was frowning about. Or maybe I did: I had spent a long time putting some distance between myself and the Three Kings. I still got the very occasional job from them, and it was difficult to refuse Willie Sneddon, Handsome Jonny Cohen or Hammer Murphy. Murphy particularly had a problem with anyone saying no to him, and had a temper that a psychopath would deem unseemly. It was blindingly obvious that this case, involving as it did the famous – or infamous, depending on your point of view of a sawn-off shotgun – Gentleman Joe Strachan, was going to suck me right back into that world.

But it wasn't even that: there was more to the nagging in the back of my brain. I frowned some more.

Then I took the cash the twins had handed me out of the drawer and counted it. Then counted it again. I stopped frowning.

CHAPTER THREE

Three thousand miles and a wartime before, about the time that Gentleman Joe Strachan's criminal career was already well underway, I had been an eager-beaver schoolboy in the prestigious Boys' Collegiate School in Rothesay, New Brunswick, on Canada's Atlantic coast, where Glasgow was far, far away. Mind you, no further away than Vancouver. One of the subjects at which I had excelled at school was History. Then, without pause or hesitation, I'd answered the King's call and rushed to defend, against a small Austrian corporal, the Empire and a Mother Country I had left before I'd been toilet trained.

The funny thing about the reality of war was that you suddenly lost your enthusiasm for history. Watching men die in the mud, screaming or crying or calling for their mothers, blunted your appetite for memorizing the dates of battles or for learning the glories of past conflict. If the war had taught me anything about history, it was that there was no future in it.

That was probably why, despite there being an impressive

wad of cash in my desk drawer, I put off delving into the history of Glasgow's most audacious robbery and the colourful if dangerous character behind it. It was true, of course, that I really needed the list of names that Isa and Violet had promised me before my delving could have any clear direction, but the truth was I knew where I could get started and I was putting it off for a day or two.

The day before the twins had turned up, I had received a telephone call asking for an appointment to see me. The male voice on the line had had that accent that was normally associated with Kelvinside: nasally and vaguely camp, with the tortuously articulated vowels that over-compensated to hide a Glasgow accent. I had lived in the city for a couple of years before I'd worked out that *Kay Vale-Ray* wasn't some obscure nightclub chanteuse, but referred to a company of mounted soldiers.

The voice spoke in multi-syllabically dense sentences and told me that it belonged to Donald Fraser, a solicitor, and that he would appreciate me calling out to see him at his office in St Vincent Street on 'a matter of not inconsiderable delicacy'. More than that he was 'unprepared to divulge telephonically'. I let it go and agreed to meet with him: as an enquiry agent, I had learned that some people desperately wanted to tell you their story – and their whole reason for contacting you was to tell you their story – but nevertheless needed time to open up; and they expected you to coax it out of them. I was rather good at it, and had often contemplated that my talents would have been equally well employed if I'd qualified as a doctor of venereal diseases. The truth was that I would probably have had to listen to less sordid stories.

In any case, I hadn't pushed Fraser for more information. The other reason was that he was a lawyer in a firm whose name I recognized. Being an enquiry agent, the city's lawyers were a key source of legitimate jobs. Mainly divorces, which under Scottish law required some upstanding member of society such as myself to testify that some other member of society had been upstanding when, where and with whom he shouldn't have been.

After Isa and Violet left, I had a couple of hours before my appointment with Fraser. I picked up the phone and asked the operator for Bell 3500, the number of police headquarters in Saint Andrew's Square, and asked to be put through to Inspector Jock Ferguson.

'Fancy a pie and a pint?' I asked him.

'What is it you're after, Lennox?' I could hear the chatter of a typewriter in the background. I imagined a burly, ruddy-cheeked Highlander in uniform tapping away with two fingers, tongue jutting sideways from his mouth, frowning in concentration.

'What do I want? The pleasure of your society, of course. And a pie and a pint. But don't pin me down too soon . . . I need to view the Horsehead Bar's à la carte options, first.'

'The Horsehead?' Ferguson snorted.

'For some reason I'm harbouring a grudge against my digestive system.'

'Aye . . . and mine, it would seem. Why don't you save us the indigestion and just tell me what you're after?'

'Just a chat. See you there in half an hour?'

Ferguson grunted his assent and hung up. Small talk was not his forte.

Scotland had two national pastimes, the only subjects that awoke profound passion in the Scottish breast: football and the consumption of alcohol. The funny thing was that they were as spectacularly bad at the first as they excelled at the second. Like the Irish, the Scots seemed to have a prodigious thirst woven through the fabric of their being. But being Presbyterian, the Scots felt the need to temper, contain and regulate anything that could be deemed pleasurable and make it run to a timetable. Midday drinking was therefore restricted by law to between eleven a.m. and two-thirty p.m. Bars were only allowed to open between five and nine-thirty in the evening. Sundays were dry.

There were, of course, all kinds of social clubs that found their way around the licensing laws but, generally, the Scots had learned to consume impressively large quantities of alcohol with breathtaking speed. So when I walked into the Horsehead Bar at one, it was shoulder-to-shoulder packed and the air was eye-stingingly dense with cigarette smoke. It was a typical Glasgow city-centre-pub lunchtime: mainly flat caps but a fair smattering of pinstripe. I saw Jock Ferguson at the bar and squeezed my way to him through the sea of drinkers. I washed up on the shore of the counter, resting my elbows on it.

'How's it going, Jock?' I asked cheerfully. And loudly, to be heard above the din of the other drinkers. We didn't shake hands. We never shook hands. 'Waiting long?' I noticed there was no drink before him. He had been waiting for me to buy the first round. I reckoned I'd be buying the second and third.

'A few minutes,' said Ferguson, again exhausting his repertoire of small talk.

Big Bob the Barman was behind the bar, wreathed in cigarette smoke and working the beer pumps like a railwayman pulling levers in a signal box. As usual, he had his shirtsleeves rolled up above his tattoo-swirled Popeye forearms. I caught his eye and he pulled two pints of heavy.

'Give us a couple of pies to go with that, Bob,' I shouted across the bar when he brought the beers.

'Okay,' said Ferguson, taking the first sip of his beer and savouring it for a moment. 'What is this all about?'

'Does there have to be a reason? Purely social. Maybe partly thanks for helping me land that wages run.'

'You've already thanked me.' Ferguson looked at me suspiciously, which, given that he was a Detective Inspector with the Glasgow City Police, was pretty much the way he looked at everyone.

'You involved in this Joe Strachan thing, Jock?' I asked as casually as I could. 'You know? Those bones dredged up from the Clyde.'

Ferguson put down his beer.

'Now, why would Gentleman Joe Strachan be of interest to you, Lennox? He was long before your time.'

'Well, he seems to have resurfaced. Literally. Or am I wrong? How sure are you that the remains are Gentleman Joe's?'

Ferguson twisted to face me full on. He turned up the volume on his suspicion and my wrists itched with a premonition of handcuffs.

'Okay, Lennox, now I know that this is more than idle curiosity. Whatever your interest in Strachan is, I would bury it somewhere very deep. This is a subject close to a lot of Glasgow coppers' hearts.'

'Oh, I understand that, Jock,' I said, putting on the ingénue act. 'But it's a perfectly innocent and reasonable question: was it Strachan or not?'

Ferguson sighed. 'Yes, the body was Strachan's.'

'It couldn't have been much of a body, after nearly twenty years at the bottom of the Clyde,' I said, again as casually as I could. Laurence Olivier wouldn't have felt threatened.

'There was enough to identify him. Now, do I have to repeat myself? Officially?'

'Take it easy, Jock. It's just that I've been asked to confirm that it *is* Gentleman Joe you've got in a shoebox at the City Mortuary.'

'And who's been doing the asking? I thought you were putting that shite behind you. You working for the Three Kings again? Listen, Lennox, I vouched for you with that job. If you're . . .'

I interrupted him with an emphatically held-up hand and an indignantly shaken head. 'No, Jock, nothing like that. I can't tell you who my client is, but it isn't any of the Three Kings and it isn't anyone remotely colourful.'

'Client confidentiality, eh?' Ferguson snorted. 'Just tell me that whoever it is isn't of interest to us.'

'Trust me,' I said disarmingly. 'The only records my clients have were recorded by Jimmy Young.'

'The twins . . .' Ferguson frowned for a moment, trying to pull their names into his recall. 'Isa and Violet?'

I looked at him blankly for a moment.

'I've got to learn to make my wisecracks more cryptic,' I said. 'I'm that easy to see through?'

'If you're not working for a crook, then it has to be family. And Joe Strachan's daughters are the only family that would give a shit. They have the advantage of not having had to grow up with Strachan. Listen, Lennox, be warned: drop this one and drop it fast. Whatever Strachan's kids are paying you, it's not worth it.'

'What's the big drama?'

'A dead copper, that's what. That and the fact that the name Joe Strachan carries a lot of history. Bad history. You've had dealings with Superintendent McNab in the past . . .'

'Willie McNab? You know I have. He's the president of my appreciation society, but he's not been forwarding my fan letters lately.'

'Aye . . . very funny. Let me tell you this, Lennox: if Superintendent McNab finds out you're sniffing around the Strachan thing, you'll be wearing your balls as earrings.'

'Why? What's his special interest?'

'Police Constable Charles Gourlay, that's what. The young policeman who was shot and killed by the Empire Exhibition robbers. You know McNab, and you know about his sense of eye-for-an-eye justice when it comes to coppers being attacked or killed.'

'The word *biblical* comes to mind,' I said. 'His sense of vengeance makes Moses look like he took it easy on the Pharaoh.'

'Exactly. Well Gourlay wasn't just any bobby on the beat. This was Nineteen thirty-eight and Willie McNab was a young PC himself. Gourlay was a friend. A drinking buddy at the Masonic Lodge and Orange Hall and Christ knows where else. Willie McNab took Gourlay's murder to heart, and it became a personal crusade for him to find Strachan and watch him drop through the hatch at Duke Street or Barlinnie. Now that Strachan has been found at the bottom of the Clyde, Superintendent McNab feels that both he and the hangman have been robbed of their chance to put things right.'

'But maybe it wasn't Strachan who killed the policeman. Maybe whoever did the copper, did Strachan too.'

Ferguson's expression darkened. 'Listen, Lennox, you and I have both seen our share of shite during the war. We both know what it's like to be in a place where life is cheap. But never, *ever* talk to me about the murder of a police officer like that again. No one *did* PC Gourlay. He was murdered in the course of his lawful duty, in cold blood by scum who knew he was unarmed and unable to defend himself. I'm not Willie McNab, but I do have loyalty to my fellow officers.'

'Okay, Jock . . . no harm meant.' I held my hands up. It was a stupid way for me to have put it. The City of Glasgow Police were a tight-knit bunch and touchy about their own. It didn't matter if your colleague was on the take, on the bottle or on the level: if he was a Glasgow copper you looked after your own first and foremost and expected the same in return.

'But you do see how it is possible, don't you, Jock? Strachan maybe wasn't the killer.'

'But he was behind the whole thing. Planned it, put the crew together, led the raid. He was in charge. Guilty before and after the fact. When that constable died there was a rope around Strachan's neck, no matter who pulled the trigger. Anyway, there was a witness. Said it was the tallest of the gang who did the shooting.'

'There was a witness?'

A couple of other drinkers jostled past Ferguson and he frowned. Our conversation had been half-shouted to be heard and Ferguson overdid a weary expression, but I guessed he was using the interruption to decide if or how he was going to dodge my question.

'The van driver,' he said eventually. 'He said there were five robbers. They all wore stocking masks, but one was tall and all the others were no bigger than five-six, five-seven. In my book that fingers Strachan as the shooter. So maybe there's no mystery to Gentleman Joe taking the deep, dark sleep: he put a rope around the neck of every man in that gang. Maybe they made him pay the price.'

'How do you know that it was Strachan at all? I thought that the identities of the Empire Exhbition Gang were all unknown.'

'Strachan . . .' Ferguson paused again, this time while Big Bob placed two plates in front of us, each with a small, round meat pie centred in a pool of viscous grease. 'Strachan went missing right after the robbery. Dropped out of sight. And Joe Strachan wasn't one to keep a low profile.'

'That's it? God, Jock, we now know that Strachan was at the bottom of the Clyde. That's the lowest profile I can think of. It could be a pure coincidence that he was topped about the same time as the robbery.'

'You're right, we don't know who the other gang members were. But that in itself points to Joe Strachan. He was a stickler for security. We could never get the bastard because no one talked about a job if they were doing it with Strachan. No one knew in advance what was going to be hit or when or who was in the team. If there's one thing I can say in his favour, it's that when it came to planning and executing big-haul robberies, he was the best. No one came close. Even if he hadn't gone missing he would have been at the top of a list for the Empire Exhibition job. A list of one. Anyway, the Empire Exhibition robbery was only part of it. The Triple Crown.'

'The Triple Crown?' I knew the story, but sometimes being an outsider to Glasgow helped: you could plead ignorance and people told you more than they had intended to.

'That's what the older boys call it. The ones with enough years under their belts to remember it. Three massive robberies, committed in fast succession, but planned right down to the last second and penny. And there's a very good chance that they're linked to a series of other, smaller robberies that took place a few months before. Trial runs, they reckon, to sharpen the team for the big ones.'

'And the biggest of the big ones was the Empire Exhibition robbery?'

'Totally different targets but carried out with the same

military precision. The first was the National Bank of Scotland in St Vincent Street. Twenty thousand pounds in wages and God knows how much else from the safe deposit boxes. Then a van on its way with wages cash to the Connell shipyard in Scotstoun – the kind of run you're doing now. The bastards actually wore police uniforms for that one. Thirty-two thousand. Then they hit the real jackpot: the Empire Exhibition. Fifty thousand.'

I blew a long whistle and probably looked more impressed than I should have in front of Ferguson. One hundred and two thousand in total was a massive amount of money, particularly in pre-war Glasgow. It was no surprise that everyone assumed that Gentleman Joe had done a disappearing act. It was, after all, the kind of money that could buy you a new, luxurious life anywhere and have enough left over to buy the silence of others. It was also, I realized, more than enough to post off three thousand a year from small change.

'And you're convinced it was the same crew?'

'Absolutely convinced. I don't want to badmouth your social circle, but I don't see Hammer Murphy or Jonny Cohen having that amount of brains or style.'

'Like I said, I don't have many dealings with them any more. And less as time goes on. But I know what you mean.'

And I did: Jonny Cohen's mob were the most successful when it came to hold-ups, but it was small-league stuff compared to what Ferguson had described. I noticed that he hadn't mentioned Willie Sneddon. Of the Three Kings, Sneddon was the one with the biggest ambitions. And the biggest reach. Sneddon had never been successfully convicted of a single crime, and his personal empire now had as many straight enterprises as crooked ones.

'Like I said, Lennox, there's a lot of history attached to the name Joe Strachan. And a lot of grudges and scores to be settled. If you know what's good for you, stay clear. Tell Isa and Violet that it really was Daddy sleeping the deep, dark sleep, then take the money and get clear of it.'

'But what if it wasn't?' I persisted. 'What if it's somebody else's bones you've got?'

'It's Strachan all right. But if it isn't, then that's even more reason for you to stay out of this business. If Strachan *is* alive, then you don't want to be looking for him and you definitely don't want to find him. Joe Strachan is a legend amongst Glasgow's scum. All of this "Gentleman Joe" crap? Trust me, I've heard all about the real Joe Strachan and read the case files: he was a merciless bastard of the first water. Just take my word for it, Lennox, stay out of this one if you know what's good for you. Some skeletons should be left in their cupboards . . . or at the bottom of the Clyde, for that matter.'

'Listen, Jock, I'm not interested in pursuing this any further than I have to. I just want to establish for his family that it was Joe Strachan they found. That's all.' I didn't make mention of the fact that I was also on the trail of whoever was sending large sums of cash to the twins. 'Just give me something to go on. Someone who might be able to point me in the right direction.'

Ferguson looked at me for a long time. That cold, empty stare of his. You could never tell if he was appraising you, seeing deep into your soul with his copper's gaze and unlocking your darkest secrets, or if he was simply thinking about whether he was going to have pork chop or fish for dinner.

'What I *will* do for you,' he said at last and wearily, 'is give you a name. But don't bring me into this, Lennox.' He took out a notebook and scribbled something on it with a stub of pencil.

'Billy Dunbar.' Ferguson tore the note from the pad and handed it to me. 'That's the last address I have for him. Dunbar was a peterman and occasional armed robber. He used to hang around with Willie Sneddon, way back in the days when Sneddon didn't count for much. Dunbar did ten years for an early job but never got caught after that. He was brought in after the Empire Robbery.'

'You think he was one of the crew?'

'No. He had a cast-iron alibi. I don't mean the usual I-was-with-my-aunty-and-uncle-just-ask-them type of cast-iron alibi. It was genuine. And there never had been any link between Joe Strachan and Billy Dunbar, but there again, there was never any link that we could prove between Joe Strachan and anybody else. That didn't stop a few in CID having their own ideas. The other thing about Dunbar was that he was making a real effort to go straight. But he was a name and a face .. . so, for a few hours, he had it hard.'

'I can imagine,' I said. With a copper dead, the mere inconvenience of your innocence wouldn't save you from the beating of your life if the police thought you had even the smallest scrap of information.

'You say he used to hang about with Willie Sneddon, before Sneddon became big game; what about Hammer Murphy? Was there any connection there?'

'Not that I know of. I think it's highly unlikely. Like Sneddon, Billy Dunbar's a true blue ultra-loyalist Prod. The only contact he was likely to have with a Catholic would be with a razor.'

'You say he's straight now?' I asked.

'Since before the war. Or at least as far as being caught's concerned. But, from what I've been told, Billy Dunbar wouldn't hold up a teashop these days.'

I nodded, dispelling the image of masked raiders escaping with twenty pounds in half-crowns and a crate of Darjeeling. Although the thought did cross my mind that teashops probably *had* been the target of hold-ups in Glasgow. Everything else was. Any business that handled cash was seen as fair game by the city's armed robbers. I had once met an ex-bank teller-turned-policeman who told me that one of the reasons for his career change was that as a copper he was much less likely to find himself looking down the barrel of a gun.

'He's maybe even out of Glasgow,' Ferguson continued. 'Someone told me some story about him being a ghillie on some country estate somewhere. Or a gamekeeper.'

'He must stand out from the others,' I said. 'I mean, he'll be the only gamekeeper with the barrels sawn off his shotgun. Anybody else you can think of that might give me a steer, Jock? What about the witness?'

A roar of laughter from a bunch of flat-caps behind us

swelled the clamour and Jock made out that he hadn't heard me.

'What about the witness you mentioned? The van driver?'

'I don't know his name offhand,' he said with a sigh. 'I'll get back to you with it. I'll tell you what, you should speak to Archie McClelland about it.' Ferguson referred to the retired policeman I had hired to ride security with me on the wages run. 'Archie was in the force back then. I've no doubt that he can tell you something about it. Now . . . I think you owe me another pint . . .'

I smiled resignedly and, shaking my empty beer glass, turned to Big Bob, who was at the far end of the bar.

I arrived on time for my meeting with Donald Fraser, the solicitor. Disappointingly, he was pretty much as I had expected from his voice: unremarkable and dour. He was tall and dull looking in the way only lawyers and bank managers managed to look dull, dressed in an expensive blue serge suit that was very carefully just out of fashion. It was also several cloth weights too heavy for the time of year and the elbows had glossed with too much desk leaning. Like his elbows, the dome of his skull seemed worn and his scalp shone through the thinning dark hair. The small, beady eyes that watched me through wire-framed spectacles had a look that I guessed was meant to be superior or intimidating. It didn't work. He took half a dictionary to ask me to sit down and I did, taking my hat off and hanging it on my knee.

'I was fortuitously supplied with your name by Mr George Meldrum, a colleague of mine,' said Fraser.

'I know Mr Meldrum,' I said, without adding that I was surprised that Fraser knew him professionally. Everybody knew George Meldrum by reputation, of course: he was Glasgow's most flamboyant defence lawyer and had represented some of the more colourful members of the city's underworld, his principal client being Willie Sneddon, one of the Three Kings. Meldrum was the kind of oleaginous creep who treated people like crap whenever he could get away with it, yet when in Sneddon's presence displayed an obsequiousness that would embarrass any self-respecting lickspittle.

'I appreciate his recommendation,' I said as if I meant it.

'Quite . . .' Fraser's tone suggested that it had been less a recommendation, more of a needs-must. 'Mr Meldrum assures me of your discretion. Particularly with regard to the more unsavoury aspects of some investigations.'

'I see,' I said, guessing that Fraser expected me to polish up my lead-and-leather sap. 'I hope you understand that I operate within the law at all times, Mr Fraser.'

'Of course,' Fraser said, emphatically and with a hint of wounded integrity. 'I would not expect anything less. We would not be having this conversation if I thought otherwise.'

'Why don't you tell me what it is you want me to do? The thing you didn't want to *divulge telephonically*.' I threw his twenty guinea phrase back at him.

'You're American, Mr Lennox? From your accent I mean . . .'

'No. I'm Canadian. Scottish parents but brought up in Canada.'

'Ah,' he said approvingly, as if he found the latitude of my childhood more commendable; there was a strong fraternal link between the Scots and the Canadians – as could be seen by the three-block queues of eager soon-to-be-ex-Glaswegians outside the Canadian Consulate in Woodlands Terrace. By contrast, the British generally had a distaste for the upstart vulgarity of Americans, particularly for the insolence with which they had saved Britain from defeat during the War, and then from bankruptcy after it. 'Like Robert Beatty, the actor?' said Fraser eagerly. 'My wife is something of a fan of Robert Beatty.'

'Not quite. Beatty's an Ontarian. I was raised in New Brunswick. Atlantic Canada.'

'I see,' Fraser said with a hint of disappointment. I had gotten the latitude right, but not the longitude. He opened a buff foolscap folder and slid a large, black and white portrait photograph across the desk at me. An unfeasibly handsome face grinned a one hundred-watt smile at me. I recognized the face right away.

'That's not Robert Beatty,' I said.

'No ... that's the American actor John Macready,' said Fraser, telling me something I already knew. 'Mr Macready is over here in Glasgow at the moment. He's been partici-pating in a film currently being made in Scotland. The filming has been mostly done in the Highlands: an adventure story, I have been led to believe. Mr Macready will be flying back to the United States at the end of the month or thereabouts, from the new airport at Prestwick. Until then, he is resident in the Central Hotel, which I believe is directly opposite your offices, Mr Lennox.'

'Where do I come into this?' I asked.

'My firm here is affiliated to Hobson, Field and Chase, a most prestigious law firm in the City of London. In turn, they represent the UK interests of the studio currently undertaking the production of the film, set here in Scotland, in which Mr Macready is appearing. I believe it is a film of a historical theme.'

'I see,' I said. 'What's his poison?'

Fraser frowned. 'I don't quite understand . . .'

'Don't you? I'm guessing that you're looking for a chaperone for Macready. My experience is that these people tend to need a governess more than they do a bodyguard. What's Macready's deal? Booze, prostitutes, pretty boys or narcotics? Or all of the above?'

Fraser looked at me with distaste, which I rather enjoyed and smiled back as insolently as I could. The beady-eyed lawyer needed me more than I needed him, I reckoned. He had been asked by someone he couldn't refuse to dip a toe into the gutter. And that, it was clear, was where he thought someone like me belonged.

'There is absolutely no need to be vulgar about this, Mr Lennox.'

'Oh I know I don't *need* to be . . . but I'm right, aren't I? You want me to nursemaid him till he gets his flight?'

The distaste in Fraser's eyes didn't abate. 'Actually, no. The studio has sent over two of their security people to do just that.'

'I see. Why do I get the feeling that I'm here to lock the stable door after the horse has bolted?'

'Your train of thought in relation to things like this seems rather well *informed*, Mr Lennox.'

'What can I say? I lead an interesting and varied life. I'm right, I take it: John Macready has done something questionable and he's under five-star house arrest until he can be gotten out of the country. In the meantime, you're looking for someone in the tying-up-loose-ends business. How loose *are* the ends?'

'Very loose, I'm afraid. Mr Macready is something of a *heart-throb* as I believe our American friends describe it. He has *sex appeal*, which is bankable at the box office. And he has a reputation as an incorrigible ladies' man and is regularly seen with some of Hollywood's most beautiful actresses on his arm.'

'I'm aware of that,' I said. 'But your reminding me of it suggests that this trouble Macready is in either relates to the truth of that reputation or its falsity.'

Walking over to a robust filing cabinet, Fraser unlocked it with a key from his pocket. He took out a brown envelope and handed it to me before retaking his seat behind the vast desk.

'I think you'll see that we are in a very delicate and very serious situation here . . .'

I took the envelope and braced myself before slipping out the photographs.

'My God . . .' I said, not enough under my breath for Fraser not to hear.

'Indeed . . .' Fraser's voice was filled with malicious satisfaction. 'I was very impressed with your cynical seen-it-all attitude, Mr Lennox, but I see it has its limits. I take it you recognize who is in the photographs with Mr Macready?'

I stared at the photographs. For a moment, I found it difficult to take it all in. The young, bent-over gentleman beneath Macready in the photograph was clearly not having the same trouble.

'I don't follow the society pages but yes, of course I recognize him. That *is* the Duke of Strathlorne's only son and heir, isn't it? I'm guessing that's one noble lineage that's run its course ...' I glanced through the photographs as quickly as I could. Not quickly enough to stop me feeling queasy. 'Blackmail?' I asked eventually.

'Yes. Or, in effect, yes. The person making the demands is not concealing his identity and is taking the utmost care to word things in a way that cannot be seen as a threat. And he is claiming that it is in the public interest that these photographs be made public.'

'Unless someone buys them from him?'

'Exactly.'

'I don't see *Picturegoer* or *Everybody's* running this little tableau with the headline "Hollywood Star Penetrates High Society's Inner Circle." The other . . . *party* in the photographs . . . surely he would have more to lose. Why isn't he the one being blackmailed?'

'The other *party*, as you put it, and his *people*, are unaware of the existence of these photographs. As yet. I think you can understand that the repercussions would be profound. And they have the power to ensure that no suggestion of this appears in the British press. But the American media would have a field day. I'm sure I don't have to point out to you that buggery and gross indecency are serious crimes. It would take a lot of nerve to blackmail a member of the Royal Family, even a peripheral member.'

Fraser scooped up the photographs from the desk and placed them back in the envelope.

'You understand, Mr Lennox, that you now have knowledge that very few people will ever be allowed to have. If you tell anyone what you have seen, I will rigorously deny the existence of the photographs – which, I assure you, will no longer be in this office – and, given the status of the other party in the photographs, you will attract the attention of individuals and organizations infinitely more dangerous than your current associations.'

It was the most long-winded threat I'd ever been subject to. But it was effective.

'Maybe I don't want to become involved,' I said. Truth was I wasn't sure that I did. 'This is more than a little out of my league.'

'I quite understand why you may feel that. I have been authorized to make a payment of fifty pounds to you, should you decide against taking this assignment. In return, I will require you to sign a declaration that you will not discuss anything that has passed between us today.'

'Fifty pounds?' I grinned. 'Please feel free to 'phone me any time you have a job for me to refuse.'

'If you take the assignment, however, I am also authorized to make a cash payment of one thousand pounds to you, with the understanding that another four thousand will be paid to you on recovery of the negatives. And we really would appreciate your professional help with this matter, Mr Lennox.'

I blew another of those long, low whistles that large sums of cash seem to elicit from me. 'Five *thousand*? I don't get it. Wouldn't you be cheaper paying the blackmailer off?'

'Do you really think that the ransom asked for these images is anywhere near five thousand pounds? These photographs could command heaven knows how much on the open market. And, of course, a blackmailer is a blackmailer, no matter how he couches it. I would not for a moment imagine that we would hear the last of it if we meet his initial demands. But even if no further demands were made, we could not be guaranteed that all copies and negatives had been destroyed. What we are paying you to do, Mr Lennox, is to hand over the money, secure the negatives and make sure all copies, other than those I have here, are destroyed.'

'And the blackmailer?'

'Quite frankly, Mr Lennox, we would wish the person responsible for these photographs to be made fully and unequivocally aware of the seriousness of our intent.'

'I see.' Fraser's halo of rectitude was slipping: it looked like I was going to have to polish my sap after all. 'I don't know what George Meldrum told you, Mr Fraser, but I am no hired thug. But I'm sure, given his other associations, that Mr Meldrum knows a great many people better qualified for that kind of work—'

Fraser held up a hand. 'This is not a job for a thug, Mr Lennox. I am assured that you are an ex-officer and a man of some intelligence as well as ... well, having a *robust* approach to your work. You have seen the photographs and understand the gravity of the situation. We need someone who can conduct themselves decisively but discreetly. Now, Mr Lennox, do I pay you fifty pounds or one thousand?'

I watched his forgettable face for a moment.

'I have other work on at the moment. Other commitments.'

'I expect you to forget about everything else until you have recovered all originals of these photographs.'

'That I can't do,' I said. 'I have a Friday wages run.'

'I'm sure you could find someone to stand in for you.'

'No. I handle the run personally. And I have another case that I need to pursue. I've also been paid in advance for that. It wouldn't make many demands on my time, but I can't drop it. I can still do this for you, depending on what leads you can give me, but I won't drop my caseload.'

I used the word 'caseload' instead of jobs a lot these days: it sounded professional. More like a lawyer and less like a plumber. 'Anyway, dealing with these other cases is my problem, not yours.'

'I'm afraid we would see that exactly as being our problem,' said Fraser.

'We?'

'The studio, my colleagues in London and myself, of course,' said Fraser. 'You will deal directly with me, Mr Lennox.' He leaned across the desk and handed me a visiting card. 'You can reach me on one or either of these numbers, twenty-four hours a day. If you have anything to report, I want to hear it right away.'

'Of course. Listen, Mr Fraser, I am more than willing to undertake this for you, but I repeat that I cannot promise to work on it exclusively.'

Fraser watched me for a moment with his beady lawyer's eyes.

'Very well,' he said, as if indulging a child, but in that moment I realized he had no choice. Whoever *we* really were, they were desperate.

'You say you have a name for this extortionist?'

'Paul Downey. He is a photographer. Of sorts. And, apparently, some kind of aspiring actor. He has dropped out of sight and has left instructions for all "bids for his scoop", as he puts it, to be mailed to a PO box at Wellington Street post office.' Fraser dipped into the file again. 'Here is his last known address and a photograph of him. Reasonably recent, I've been led to believe.'

I looked at the photograph. Downey was a young man in his early twenties, and had the Iberian Celtic look of a Glasgow Catholic: dark hair, pale complexion. He had a faintly girlish appearance with his black hair a little too long but not Teddy Boy style, largish, soft eyes, a weak mouth and a soft chin.

'Mr Downey is also a ...' Fraser left the word hanging in the air. 'He is also involved in that world.'

'I see.' I thought it over for a moment. 'And you say the other party in the photographs is unaware of their existence?'

'That is correct.'

'How long, exactly, is Macready going to be in Glasgow?'

'He has very little still to do in the way of actual shooting, but there are some other tasks he has to perform before he returns, technical issues and publicity matters. He is scheduled to return early next month. His flight is already booked on BOAC from Prestwick.'

'If I am to take this any further, then I have to talk to him. You do understand that, don't you, Mr Fraser?'

'I supposed you would, Mr Lennox. That's why I have drawn up this schedule of the remainder of his stay in Scotland. His personal assistant is Miss Bryson. Here . . .' Fraser handed me a sheet of paper. 'I don't suppose there is any way you could avoid the necessity of your discussing this directly with Mr Macready?'

'I'm afraid not. Those photographs you showed me weren't taken in a rush. I smell a premeditated set-up. Whoever took them knew what they were doing. And I guess that, knowing who Macready was *entertaining*, they have been fully aware of the stakes they've been playing. I'm going to have to ask Macready some *difficult* questions.'

'I know that this is of no interest or concern to you, Mr Lennox, but distasteful as any right-minded person finds that aspect of his life, it is my opinion that John Macready is a good man.'

'I'm sure he's a faithful pilgrim,' I said. 'From what I could see from the photographs he certainly adheres to at least one Christian tenet.'

Fraser frowned questioningly.

'It looked to me like he truly believes that *it is better to give than to receive.*'

CHAPTER FOUR

I wanted to find out more about Donald Fraser, and before heading back to my office I decided to telephone Jock Ferguson from a telephone kiosk on the corner of Blythswood Square. It was the regulation Glasgow 'phone box: its exterior inexpertly coated in thick red paint that was flaking where it had bubbled; its interior fuming with the regulation Glasgow call box odour of stale urine, forcing me to prop the heavy, spring-loaded door open with one foot. For some reason, Glaswegians had always been confused about how the word *urinal* differed lexically from *telephone kiosk*, *bank doorway*, *swimming pool* or *the back of the raincoat of the supporter in front of you* at a football match.

I was lucky and got Jock Ferguson at his desk. I asked him what he knew about Donald Fraser, which was nothing, but he said with a sigh that he would ask around. In turn, he asked why I was asking and I told him the truth: that Fraser was a solicitor in the city and wanted to hire me and that I just wanted to check Fraser's *bona fides* before I took the job.

Ferguson told me he would 'phone me back at my office later with whatever he could find out. He also made it plain that the next lunch I treated him to would have to be somewhere more upscale than the Horsehead Bar.

I walked back to my office. It remained unseasonably warm – and muggy, which seemed to be the only warm Glasgow did. Even in the middle of that summer's heatwave, it had been as if the city had opened up its pores and sweated itself slick. Something in this mugginess, however, hung in my nostrils and chest; that old warning feeling I always got when a smog was on its way.

When I got back, the afternoon mail had been delivered. One envelope contained a single, plain sheet of paper with a list of names. No signature, note or anything else to show who had sent it. Isa and Violet were perhaps not as guileless as they appeared.

Of the names, I recognized only three, and one of those happened to be the name at the very top of the list. For a moment I hoped that the Michael Murphy heading the list wasn't the one that immediately leapt to mind. I transferred the name along with all of the others to my notebook:

MICHAEL MURPHY

HENRY WILLIAMSON

JOHN BENTLEY

STEWART PROVAN

RONALD MCCOY

Five names. There had been five robbers involved in the Empire Exhibition job. But one of those five had been Strachan himself, and if the Michael Murphy on the list was the Michael

Murphy I was thinking of, then I couldn't see him having been one of that team.

During the twins' visit to my office, Isa – or Violet – had left me a telephone number and I called it. It was Isa after all. I asked if the Michael Murphy on the list was Hammer Murphy; she told me she didn't know for sure but it was possible. Her father had known Murphy.

'What was your father's involvement with Murphy?' I asked.

'Daddy knew all the Murphy brothers. I think they did some work for Daddy. Now and again. Mam said that that was before Michael Murphy became successful and important, in his own right, like. But Michael Murphy was round now and again. I don't remember him being at the house, but there again I was only wee.'

'And Henry Williamson?' I asked. The name had leapt out at me as not being typically Glaswegian.

'He was a good friend of Daddy's. I never met him either, though. From what Mam said, Daddy had known him for years. Since the war. The First War, I mean.'

'Your father served in the First War?'

'Aye. He was a hero you know.'

'I wouldn't have thought your father would have been old enough.'

'It was near the end of the war.'

'And that was where he met Williamson?'

'I think so.'

'Was Williamson involved in crime too?'

There was a short silence at the other end of the telephone; I wondered if I had offended her by reminding her of the origins of her father's wealth.

'I don't know. That's the truth,' she said. 'I don't think Mr Williamson was ever in prison, or anything like that, but I just don't know. He stopped coming around after Daddy went away. But they saw each other all the time before that.'

'Do you know where I can find him? Where he lives?'

'Not really. All I know is that Da knew him from the war. But I don't think he was from Glasgow.'

'I see . . .' I said.

I ran through the other names with Isa. A couple of them I knew, or realized I knew when she gave me some background information. All thieves and hardmen. I reckoned that there was a good chance, after all, that I was sitting with the names of the Empire Exhibition Gang in my hand. But could it really be as easy as that? In Thirty-eight, the police would have had exactly the same list of names, yet they never nailed even one of the robbers.

The only other name I had to ask about was John Bentley.

'I never knew him either. Mam said that he was just someone she had heard Daddy talking about to the others.'

Before I visited Willie Sneddon, I 'phoned and made an appointment. With a secretary.

That's what dealing with Willie Sneddon had turned into. Secretaries and appointments and meetings in offices.

Willie Sneddon was by far the most treacherous and dangerous of the Three Kings. Which was saying something when you considered that Hammer Murphy had not earned his nickname because of his joinery skills. But the thing that made Willie Sneddon more dangerous than anyone else was his brain. There were a handful of Willie Sneddons born in the slums of Glasgow every year or so: people who, despite the odds and the lack of stimulus, had the raw intelligence to clamber their way out of the gutter. More than half of them wouldn't make it: Britain's obsessive class-consciousness placing barriers in their way at every opportunity. The others would make it despite the odds stacked against them and become surgeons, engineers, self-made business magnates.

And a couple, like Willie Sneddon and Gentleman Joe Strachan, would use their brains to dominate and terrorize the city's underworld. Sneddon had been too small-fry to come to Strachan's attention; but, if Strachan hadn't disappeared when he did, then the paths of the two would, sooner or later, have come together. In a *this-town-ain't-big-enough-for-the-both-of-us* kind of coming together.

But the paths had not met, and Willie Sneddon had had a clear run at dominating the city's underworld, which he had, much to the annoyance of the other two Kings, Murphy and Cohen. They had divided the city up equally, except that Sneddon's share had been more equal than the others. He was the youngest of the Three Kings and had come much farther, much quicker, than the other two. And everyone knew that Sneddon's climb to the top wasn't yet over.

Like Strachan, Sneddon had been very careful to make sure that his only view of Barlinnie Prison was seeing it in the distance as he passed by in his Jaguar on the A8. He had had a few run-ins with the City of Glasgow Police, right enough, but hadn't picked up any indelible blots on his copybook. His relationship with the oily lawyer George Meldrum, and his open-handedness with brown envelopes stuffed with cash, had ensured that the only bars he ever looked through were the ones he ran or from which he extracted protection money. There was even a rumour that he was tight with Superintendent McNab, through their mutual membership of the Orange Order and the Freemasons or God knows what other *let's-do-a-funny-handshake-to-prove-we-hate-the-Fenians* secret society.

And Sneddon was rich. Almost inexplicably rich. He had more money than the other two Kings put together, more than anyone could fully account for. I, personally, never saw much of a difference between businessmen and gangsters, other than that I would probably trust a gangster's word more. Sneddon combined the callousness of a gang boss with the greed and acumen of a business magnate and that, I guessed, was what made him a different kind of animal in the jungle. The apex predator, as zoologists called such creatures.

Things were changing fast for Sneddon. He had re-invested the majority of his ill-gotten gains into legitimate businesses. It had all started out as front, but then Sneddon had seen that although the benefits were fewer and the profits less than his illegal activities, the risks were much, much lower. So now he ran a successful and perfectly above-board import business, an estate agency and three car showrooms, as well as having shares in a major Clydeside ship repair yard.

And he paid his taxes in full, on time. Scrupulously.

So now, Willie Sneddon – who was reputed to have once, in one of his more whimsical moments, boiled the flesh off the feet of one of his criminal competitors simply because this particular crook had made a remark about 'letting Sneddon stew' over a deal – now hobnobbed with lairds, ship-yard owners, Corporation officials and magnates.

But Willie Sneddon still, it was said, retained the services of Twinkletoes MacBride, his torturer-in-chief, and an entourage of Teddy Boy suited thugs including Singer, the ironically nicknamed mute. I often puzzled about how Twinkletoes MacBride – being big on muscle and cruelty and short on brains and subtlety – had adapted to the new commercial environment. Somehow, I now imagined him dressed in a bowler hat and pinstripe and carrying his bolt-cutters – used for removing toes of uncommunicative victims – in an attaché case.

Sneddon's secretary tried to put me off until the next day, but I piled on the charm and pushed my luck, saying it was an important and pressing matter but that it would only take up ten minutes of his time. She asked me to hang on while she consulted her boss and when she came back a minute later, she told me that Sneddon could see me in fifteen minutes.

The 'phone rang almost immediately after I hung up. It was Jock Ferguson.

'I've asked around about Donald Fraser. He's as kosher as a Tel Aviv butcher's. He deals with contract law, mainly. I wouldn't have thought he would be handling divorce cases.' Ferguson had drawn the obvious conclusion; I decided not to disabuse him of it.

'I think he's handling this case more as an obligement than anything else. A personal favour called in by a client. Did you find out anything else about him?'

'Nothing to find. Educated at Fettes in Edinburgh. In the Home Guard during the war. Dodgy eyesight kept him out of the regular army, apparently. His father was an officer in the Great War.'

'God, Jock, your intelligence gathering is a hell of a lot better than I thought.'

'Not really. One of the senior uniform boys here, Chief Superintendent Harrison, knew Fraser during the war. Fraser and Harrison are pals, apparently. So I'd say he's okay.'

'Fine,' I said. 'Thanks, Jock. That's all I wanted to know.'

'And how's your sniffing about the Empire job going? Anyone jump up and kick you in the teeth yet?'

'Not yet. But on that . . .'

'Here we go . . .' Ferguson sighed at the other end of the line.

'On that . . .' I continued, 'what do you know about Henry Williamson and John Bentley?'

'That's easy,' said Ferguson. 'Nothing. Never heard of either of them. Well, I know a couple of Williamsons – it's not that uncommon a name – but nobody connected to that world and certainly no one who would know Joe Strachan. And I don't think any of them is a Henry. I could ask around, I suppose, but then you might buy me another Horsehead pie, and I'm beginning to think they're named after their contents, not the name of the bar.'

'Okay, next time I'll make it an Italian meal . . .' I'd treated Jock Ferguson to a meal at Rosseli's before. In Glasgow that was as exotic as it comes and he had spent five minutes suspiciously poking around with his fork at his spaghetti. Forty minutes and two bottles of cheap Chianti later, he seemed to have developed an enthusiasm for Italian cuisine. Or as much of an enthusiasm as Jock Ferguson was capable of displaying: I could not imagine him ever throwing his arm around a waiter and bursting into *'O sole mio'*.

'Do you have anything on either of them?' he asked. 'So's I know where to start asking.'

'Well, I think Williamson was a war buddy of Joe Strachan's. In Number One, I mean.' I had just finished saying it when I heard at the other end of the line something as rare as an inside toilet in Dennistoun: Ferguson laughing.

'What's so funny?'

'A war buddy?' he said. 'Is that a polite way of saying fellow deserter?'

'I thought Strachan had a glowing war record,' I said. 'A war hero, his daughter told me.'

More laughter. 'Listen, Lennox, Strachan could sell any line of bull to anyone he chose. Do you know why everybody called him Gentleman Joe?'

'I've heard that he was a flashy dresser, and liked a few of the finer things in life. Mind you, coming from the Gorbals, toilet paper that doesn't leave newsprint on your backside counts as one of the finer things, I suppose.'

'Joe Strachan didn't dress flashy, Lennox. He dressed *well*. He knew what to wear and how, when and where to wear it. Like you say, he was one hundred per cent Gorbals, but he could pass himself off as anything, in any social circle. Believe it or not, it was actually what led the City CID in the first place to suspect him of having pulled off the Empire job and the other top-end robberies.'

'Oh? Why?'

'It was just by chance that a bank clerkess mentioned having served a tall, well-dressed, well-spoken gentleman a couple of weeks before the bank got hit. He had called in to cash a postal order but she had remembered that he had asked a lot of questions. Then, when they went over the other jobs, and prompted witnesses' memories, they remembered a tall, well-spoken, well-dressed gentleman having had some kind of contact a few weeks before the job.'

'Did he fit Strachan's description?'

'The description was slightly different each time, but there were enough similarities. It was by pure chance that it came out: no one thought anything of it because "gentlemen" don't commit crime. And do you know where Strachan learned his party trick? In the army at the end of the First War.'

'He saw active service?' I asked. 'I was told he volunteered as a fifteen-year-old . . .'

Ferguson snorted. 'Joseph Strachan was not the volunteering type. He was too young for most of the war but was called up at the arse end of it all. But the last shot hadn't been fired, so young Strachan showed real initiative by taking some leave without burdening his superiors with organizing it.'

'So that was when he deserted?'

'More than deserted . . . Strachan had this ability: to mimic voices, accents, mannerisms, that kind of thing.'

'What's your point . . . that Music Hall's loss was armed robbery's gain?'

There was a short silence and I could imagine Ferguson making an impatient face: he was not used to being inter-rupted. 'Anyway, he could pass himself off as anyone. Any class, any nationality: Scottish, English, Welsh. So when he deserted, he didn't just take a powder and lie low, like most would. Oh no, young Master Strachan also nicked a couple of subalterns' uniforms so he could pass himself off as an officer on leave. Fooled everybody. Spent six weeks running up mess and brothel bills.'

'Six weeks? I'm surprised he lasted that long. Passing your-self off as an officer with a put-on accent is one thing, but it's not just how you talk, it's what you've got to say about yourself.'

'Aye . . . I suppose you'll know all about that, Lennox.' Ferguson didn't attempt to keep the tone of contempt out of his voice. 'You having been an officer and gone to a fancy school yourself . . . So what are you saying? That Strachan would be bound to give himself away by using the wrong spoon or holding his bone china the wrong way or some crap like that?'

'I just don't see how a thug from the Gorbals could be that convincing as a public school-educated officer.'

'Well you're wrong. Like I said, that's why they called him "Gentleman" Joe: he could turn it on at the drop of the hat. You may just see him as a Gorbals monkey, but he was one smart monkey. He didn't just put on the accent, he knew the moves. He may have left school at thirteen, but everyone knew he was a clever wee bastard. When he wasn't shoving a gun in a bank teller's face, he was shoving his nose into a book. He was obsessed with knowing things. And they say that's why he got away with the officer act. He knew the right things to say at the right time. The rumour is that he also got to know the mutineer Percy Toplis and that was where he got the impersonating officers idea.'

'You seem to know a lot about Strachan's life story, Jock.'

'He was a bit of a legend with the older boys here. I think there was a fair amount of grudging respect, that kind of shite. But all of that went right down the pan when that constable was gunned down. So yes, it's not difficult to know a lot about Strachan if you're a Glasgow copper. Added to which I've had my ear bent non-stop by Superintendent McNab about him since those bones were dredged up.'

I thought for a moment about McNab's personal interest in Strachan. I was going to have to make a real effort to work around him, in much the same way as a pilot fish works around a shark.

'So if he was a First War deserter, how come he didn't end up in front of a firing squad?' I asked.

'I don't know too much about that, but I gather that he talked his way out of it. He was good at that, from all accounts. And the odds were in his favour: there were over three thousand sentenced to death, but only three hundred or so faced a firing squad.'

I nodded slowly as I processed the information. The British had been almost as keen on shooting their own as shooting the enemy in the First War. Most of those tied to a post and shot had been men with otherwise outstanding war records, whose nerves had been shredded and reshredded by an uncaring command that did not recognize battle fatigue. And many had simply been terrified children who had lied about their age to serve King and Country. One of the finer moments of the British Empire had been when it had shot a 'coward' who had just turned sixteen.

'There were rumours, apparently,' continued Ferguson, 'that Strachan maybe dodged a drumhead court-martial and firing squad because he volunteered to do reconnaissance work. You know, going over-the-top on your own at night and crawling around in the mud to find out what you could about the enemy disposition – barbed-wire, machine-gun posts, that kind of thing. Maybe that's where his daughters got that mad idea that he was a war hero. It was probably dangerous, all right, but you've got less chance of getting shot at night on your belly than tied to a post in front of a firing squad. Anyway, have you seen Billy Dunbar yet . . . the guy I gave you the address for?'

'Not yet.'

'Well I got the name of the witness we talked about. The van driver. But you're not going to get much out of him.'

'Oh, why?'

'Rommel got to him first. If you want to find him you'll have to go and play hunt the thimble in the North African desert. A German land mine sent his head in the direction of Tobruk and his arse towards the equator.'

'Great. Thanks for checking it out anyway. There's one other thing, Jock . . .'

'Oh, really, there's another thing you need from me? Why am I not bloody surprised?'

'I've got another name needs checking. Could you see if you've got anything on someone called Paul Downey? I think he's an actor. And part-time photographer.'

'Why the hell not? I've got nothing else to do other than pander to your every whim. Is this connected to the Strachan thing?'

'No, nothing like that,' I said. 'It's a completely different case. Someone's kid keeping the wrong company, that sort of thing.'

'And you say he's an actor?'

I shrugged. 'That's what I've been told. Or photographer, or both.'

'Okay, I'll check it out. But I'm warning you, Lennox, I'll be looking for a few *quid pro quos* for this. Next time I ask you for some straight information, I expect to get some information. Straight.'

'Fair enough,' I lied convincingly.

'And Lennox?'

'Yeah?'

'You've made a good job of keeping your nose clean of late.

Don't go sticking it back in the shite; it brings out the worst in you. You understand what I'm saying?'

'I understand, Jock,' I said. And I did.

My last business meeting with Willie Sneddon had been in a brothel and bare-knuckle fight venue he had acquired. He was nothing if not creative in combining enterprises. This place, however, was a completely different ball of wax.

The offices of Paragon Importing and Distribution were down near the Queen's Dock in a vast commercial palace of redbrick that had been soot-grimed a matt rusty-black. It was the kind of place the Victorians had built as a cathedral to trade, and reminded me of the huge ornate warehouses I had seen in Hamburg at the end of the war.

The office was huge and panelled in a polished exotic hardwood that made you think it would have been cheaper to paper the walls with five-pound notes. Sneddon sat behind a massive inlaid desk that could have been launched into the Clyde as an aircraft carrier. On the desk sat three phones: one black, one ivory, one red. The rest of the desk furniture looked antique and there was a small pile of books in one corner of the desk and a heap of files sitting on the blotter in front of Sneddon.

Sneddon himself was dressed in expensive grey herring-bone, a silk shirt and burgundy tie. I had never seen him dressed in anything that didn't look Savile Row. Willie Sneddon had the kind of physical presence that made you wary. He was none too tall and was stocky without being heavy: all muscle and sinew in a way that always made me think he had been woven from ship rope. That, and the ugly crease of a razor scar on his right cheek, told you that this was someone to whom violence came naturally and easily.

I wondered what his classy new chums would make of the razor scar.

'What the fuck do you want, Lennox?' said Sneddon in greeting. I guessed Dale Carnegie's *How to win Friends and Influence People* was not among the books on his desk.

'It's been a while,' I said sitting down without being asked. 'You seem to be doing very well for yourself, Mr Sneddon.'

He stared at me silently. His small-talk skills made Jock Ferguson look like a chatterbox.

'I wondered if you could help me,' I continued, cheerily undeterred. 'You used to be friends with Billy Dunbar. I just wondered if you know where I might find him? He seems to have dropped out of sight.'

'Billy Dunbar?' Sneddon frowned at me. 'How the fuck should I know? I haven't heard from him in over ten years. Billy Dunbar . . .' He paused thoughtfully. 'What the fuck do you want Billy Dunbar for?'

'A long shot. The police hauled him in and gave him a rough time back in Thirty-eight. Over the Exhibition robbery job. I just wanted to talk to him about it.'

Something flickered across Sneddon's expression in the small pause before he spoke. Whatever it was, I didn't have time to read it.

'Why?' he asked. 'Does this have something to do with Gentleman Joe Strachan being found at the bottom of the Clyde?'

'Well, yes . . . as a matter of fact it does.'

'And what the fuck has that got to do with you?'

'I've been hired to look into it. To make sure that was Joe Strachan they found.'

'And why the fuck shouldn't it have been Strachan? It makes sense, seeing as how it ties in with when he went missing.'

'Did you know Strachan?' I asked.

'Naw. Knew of him, of course, he was the big bollocks back then . . . but I never met him. Why do you think that it's maybe not Strachan they found?'

'I didn't say I thought that. I've just been asked to make sure. And I just wanted to talk to Billy Dunbar about it and thought you might have a more up to date address for him.'

'Leave Billy out of it,' said Sneddon. 'He was a good bloke. Someone you could trust. But he went straight fucking years ago and just wanted left alone. The coppers gave him the hiding of his life and he didn't tell them anything. I mean, they get handy with their fists a lot of the time, but this was different. What they did to Billy, and a few others, was nothing less than fucking torture. But there wasn't nothing for him to tell.'

'I see. So you don't know where I could find him?'

'How many fucking times do I have to tell you?'

I stood up. 'Sorry to disturb you, Mr Sneddon.'

Sneddon said nothing and remained seated. I made my way back to the door.

'You want my opinion?' Sneddon called across an acre of Axminster. I turned.

'About what?'

'About how the government could resolve the Cyprus crisis
... what the fuck do you think about, for fuck's sake? About
Gentleman Joe Strachan.'

'Okay ...' I said tentatively.

'Whoever it was they found at the bottom of the river, it
wasn't Gentleman Joe Strachan.'

'Why do you say that? I thought you said you didn't know
him, so what makes you think it's not him they found?'

'I took his place, Lennox. If Joe Strachan hadn't disappeared
it would be him sitting here, not me. He was a fucking legend
in this town. And the Empire Exhibition robbery is the kind
of job that every gobshite dreams of pulling off. Textbook stuff.'

'Except the fact that a copper was blown away,' I said,
trying to imagine what textbooks Glasgow criminals read.

'Aye ... that's where it all went tits up. Listen, Lennox, I
took over all of Strachan's operations after the war, or at
least the ones we knew about. That guy was all planning.
And brains. So I can put myself in his place – because I *have*
put myself in his place, if you know what I mean. So let's
say I'm Gentleman Joe ... there I am, I've just pulled off
three of the biggest fucking robberies ever, and, like you say,
the last one's left a copper dead. Even if the bobby hadn't
been killed, the coppers are going to be after you like shite
off a shirt tail. Matter of pride, you see: no copper wants his
patch to go down in history for the biggest job pulled successfully.

'So, like I say, there I am, having pulled this job, with a
stack of cash that doesn't need laundered and fuck knows
what else from the security van. But I've done a copper so I

am fucked as far as Glasgow's concerned. I've got three men with me on the job. Maybes it was one of them that done the copper, maybes it was me. Anyway, I'm the only name the cops are likely to have, so I divide up the loot, taking a bigger share for myself, because I've got to start somewhere new. Maybes one of the others kicks up about it, so I top him, dress him up in my clobber, shove the initialled cigarette case that I'm never seen without in his pocket and dump him in the river. If he isn't found, fine. If he is, the cops think that there's no point to keep on looking for me.'

'You've certainly thought this one through, Mr Sneddon,' I said.

'Aye, I have. I got my chance because Strachan dropped out. So aye, I've thought it through. Mainly because I've always had half an eye on the bastard resurfacing, but not in the way those bones did. But now . . .' He held his arms wide to indicate his surroundings. 'Now I'm putting all of that behind me. I'm a businessman now, Lennox. I've got kids who'll be able to take all of this over without having to take the shite the police have tried to give me over the years. So if Gentleman Joe Strachan comes back from the grave, then it's Murphy's and Cohen's lookout, not mine.'

'You're that sure that he's not dead?'

Sneddon shrugged. 'Like I said, I never met him. Didn't know him. But what I knew *about* him makes me think he was too slippery a shite to end up topped by one of his own. Too slippery and too dangerous. By the way, I don't think Billy Dunbar ever had anything to do with him either. So you're barking up the wrong tree there as well.'

'Well, thanks for your time, Mr Sneddon,' I said. 'Like I said, I just thought you might be able to point me to Dunbar.'

'Well I can't, so fuck off.'

I left Sneddon in his palace of commerce, wondering if he concluded meetings with the Rotary Club in the same way.

Glasgow had three main railway stations, each a gargantuan Victorian edifice: Queen Street, St Enoch's and Central Stations were all within walking distance of each other but divided the nation's destinations between them. If all roads led to Rome, then all railroads led to Glasgow city centre. Each of the stations was connected to its equivalent in London, binding the two most important cities in the British Empire together: Queen Street ran the service to King's Cross, St Enoch's to St Pancras, and Central Station ran the Euston connection. And each station had a huge, grand hotel attached to it.

My offices were directly across Gordon Street from Central Station and the dark, grandiose mass of the Central Hotel that was stone-fused into it. The Central Hotel was the kind of place where you were more likely to bump into a movie star or minor royalty than the average Glasgow punter; which was ironic, given that I was going to question a movie star about his bumping into minor royalty. The Central Hotel had had personages as stellar as Winston Churchill, Frank Sinatra and Gene Kelly under its roof; not to mention Roy Rogers and Trigger. Trigger, apparently, had had a suite to himself.

The receptionist 'phoned up to Macready's suite and I was asked to wait until someone came down for me, so I cooled

71

my heels in the hotel lobby. At least I was cooling them on expensive marble.

When I had telephoned from my office to arrange the meeting, I had spoken to a young woman with an American accent and enough frost in her voice to make the Ice Age seem balmy. She had been expecting my call, obviously having been prepped by Fraser.

I had just sunk up to my armpits in red leather and was reading a newspaper when I heard the same frosty tone. When I looked up I found myself in the full frigid glare of a Nordic goddess of about twenty-five . . . and thirty-six-twenty-four-thirty-four. Her pale blonde hair looked more natural than permed and the full, deep-red lipsticked lips accentuated the Prussian blue of her eyes. She was dressed in a grey business suit and white blouse and was all curve and legs so long I was surprised when they stopped at the ground. I found myself staring at her figure. She found me staring at it too and the frost in the pale blue eyes dropped a few degrees more.

'Mr Lennox?' she asked, with only slightly less distaste than if she had sunk a stiletto heel into dog droppings.

'I'm Lennox,' I said, and somehow resisted adding *and I'm your slave forever.*

'I'm Leonora Bryson, Mr Macready's assistant.'

'Lucky Mr Macready . . .' I smiled a smile a wolf would have thought uncouth and fought my way out of the red leather armchair.

'Follow me, Mr Lennox,' she said and turned on her heel.

She had made it sound like a command, but the truth was

72

that following her could easily have become my second favourite pastime. She had a narrow waist which emphasized the swell of her thighs and ass. And I use swell in every sense of the word. I was disappointed when we reached the elevator and the lift man slid the concertina door open for us to enter. He was a stunted little Glaswegian with a drawn, dour face, but he held my gaze for a split second as Miss Bryson entered the lift. Oh, I know, pilgrim, I thought as we exchanged the look. I *know*.

When we got out, Leonora Bryson led me along a labyrinth of corridors lined with expensive wood panelling. I wasn't worried about finding my way back: I would simply follow the trail of drool I was leaving behind. The doors to the rooms we passed were so widely spaced that you could tell that these were the hotel's suites. Stopping at one of the doors, she swung open a hundred pounds of oak without knocking and we stepped into a room so big that just a Glasgow mile and a half away it would be expected to house three families. That was the thing about Glasgow that had always struck me most: not just that there was a huge chasm between rich and poor, which was something you found in just about every British city, but that Glasgow seemed to do it on a bigger, louder, cruder scale. Wealth here was un-Britishly ostentatious and brash as if trying to out-shout the deafening poverty all around it. I was no Red, but, despite old Uncle Clem's very British post-war welfare revolution, sometimes the injustice of it all really got to me.

There were two goon-types in the sitting room of the suite: big sorts with loud suits and louder shirts and Marine-style crew-cuts. Obviously the security sent over by the studio. They looked as out of place in Glasgow as it was possible to look and I would have sworn I could see their Californian tans fading as I watched. A man who was easily as tall and broad as the goons stood up as we entered. In a quiet and friendly but authoritative tone, he asked the goons to leave us alone. My Nordic ice maiden led them out.

'Mr Lennox?' John Macready switched on the one hundred watt smile that had beamed from the publicity photograph. I shook his hand. 'Please sit down. Can I get you a drink?'

I said a Scotch would be fine but a Bourbon would be better.

'I didn't know you were an American, Mr Lennox.'

'I'm not. I'm Canadian. It's just that I prefer rye.'

He handed me a wrist-straining hunk of crystal filled with ice and whiskey.

'Canadian? I see ... I couldn't quite place your accent.' Macready sat down opposite me. He had been meticulously tanned, tailored, groomed and manicured to the point of artificiality; an unreality compounded by the fact that he was preposterously handsome. He turned down the wattage of his smile. 'I know you've been hired by Mr Fraser. I take it he has told you everything.'

'He's told me all I need to know about the blackmail, if that's what you mean, Mr Macready.'

'And the photographs? He showed you those?'

'I'm afraid he had to.'

Macready held me in a frank gaze with no hint of embarrassment. 'I take it you know what it could mean for my career if these photographs were to be made public?'

'The very nature of the photographs means that they can't be made public. Any newspaper or magazine that printed them, even with strategically placed black bars, would be prosecuted under the Obscene Publications Act. But that isn't the danger. A newspaper can print that they are in possession of the photographs and describe their contents in broad terms. It then falls on you to deny the allegations, which you can't, because – although they are unpublishable – they are fully admissible in court as evidence in a libel trial. And, it has to be said, in a criminal prosecution, too. You are aware that the acts depicted are illegal under Scots law.'

'Under American law as well, Mr Lennox.'

'Yes, but the Scots have an *enthusiasm* for prosecuting these kind of cases. Presbyterian zeal.'

'Trust me, I know all about that, Mr Lennox. Macready isn't a stage name: I'm of Scottish descent. My father and grandfather were both elders of the Presbyterian church in West Virginia.'

'Does your father know about . . .?' I groped around for an appropriate noun, but it remained out of my grasp, somewhere between *inclination* and *problem*. Macready picked up on my discomfort and gave a small, bitter laugh.

'My father has never discussed it with me, nor I with him, but I know he knows. Despite my war record, my acting achievements and the wealth I've accumulated, all I see in my father's eyes when he looks at me is disappointment. And shame. And, as you've pointed out, Mr Lennox, my sexual preferences make me a criminal, for some reason. But let me make this absolutely clear to you: I am not in the slightest ashamed of who and what I am. It is my nature, not a criminal trait or sexual perversion. I wasn't *turned* into what I am because someone fiddled with me as a kid, and it's not because I suffer from an unbounded libido that one gender cannot contain. Incidentally, that last description applies to one of your own swashbuckling heroes.'

'But the studio ...'

'The studio knows about it. Has done for years. They fret about it all right, but that's got nothing to do with some skewed sense of sexual morality. All they care about is the impact it would have at the box office. On the bottom line. Trust me, Hollywood has a much more *liberal* view of the world than Fayette County, West Virginia ... or Scotland. The fact that I am homosexual is an open secret in Hollywood circles, Mr Lennox. But it is kept well out of view of the queue outside the movie theatres in Poughkeepsie or Pottsville or Peoria. What and who you see on the screen as *John Macready* is a falsehood ... but it is a falsehood that moviegoers have to believe in.'

I thought about what Macready had said.

'I'm not here to judge you, Mr Macready. Frankly, I don't care what anyone gets up to behind closed doors so long as it doesn't harm anyone else. And I agree that there are far better ways for the police to occupy their time. But you are a Hollywood star and the other party is the son of one of Scotland's most prominent aristocrats. This is a serious situation.'

I paused and took a sip of the whiskey. It was a rich, aged bourbon and I guessed it hadn't come from the hotel's stock. I was four city blocks and a million miles away from the Horsehead Bar.

'The other party in the photographs ... you haven't mentioned this to him?' I asked.

'No, not yet. I've been advised not to, but I think he has a right to know.'

'I would stick to the advice you've been given, Mr Macready. The ... *prominence* of the young gentleman in question is possibly something that could work in our favour. I really don't see the press being allowed a free rein by the powers-that-be. It's entirely possible that they would be stuck with a D-notice.'

Macready shrugged at me.

'A D-notice is a banning order issued by the government to block stories that might damage the national interest.'

'Nothing like a free press,' said Macready with overdone irony as he sipped his bourbon.

'Well, it's something you might end up being grateful for.'

'If so, isn't that exactly why we should be telling *the other party*? That way we might get the whole damn thing stopped before it gets started.'

'I think we should keep our powder dry on that one. It's something we may have to resort to. But it would be a gamble: it could be that they could decide that he's simply not important enough for them to issue a D-notice. In which case, he would be as well and truly screwed as we would be.'

The phrase was out before I thought it through, but Macready didn't seem to have picked up on it. I took another sip of the bourbon and it breathed on an ember somewhere in my chest.

'What is the big deal with Iain, anyway?' asked Macready, giving *the other party* his name for the first time. 'I knew he was some kind of aristo, but I didn't know he was *that* well connected . . .'

'His father is one of the big Dukes up here. And he's a cousin – God knows how many times removed – of the Queen. The Queen's mother is a Scot, you see. Which makes him, no matter how far down the food chain, minor royalty. Royalty is big here, Mr Macready. It's symbolic. It's funny, I'm investigating another case that goes all the way back to Nineteen thirty-eight, when they had a big exhibition here in Glasgow to celebrate the Empire. Well, the Empire has all but gone and that makes the monarchy all the more important. Us Canadians hang on to it to prove we're not Americans. Yet. The Brits are clinging on to it because it's all they've got of the past. If the British lose their monarchy, they'll have to face up to the thing they fear most.'

'Which is?'

'The future. Or maybe even simply the reality of the present. So the monarchy is fast becoming a national treasure, like Stonehenge. And just like Stonehenge, it serves damn-all present purpose but it's nice to look at and allows you to wallow in the past. And you, Mr Macready, have just taken a leak on Stonehenge, as far as anyone else is going to be concerned. So, like I said, I think we'll keep *the other party* out of it for as long as we can. They might just throw you to the wolves.'

'Okay. But what now?'

'I try to find the guy who's got the photographs and use my simple charm to win him over and get the negatives. But first I need to ask you a few questions ...'

And I did.

Leonora Bryson showed me back to the lift when we were done. I made the move we were both expecting me to make, but she told me she was busy in a way that suggested she would remain busy for the rest of the century. Undaunted, I gave her my best philosophical *some other time* response but resolved not to give up. Some women were worth more effort than others. And I had three weeks.

CHAPTER FIVE

I went back to my office for an hour or two and tied up the loose ends on a couple of the divorce cases I'd been working on. It was mainly paperwork: the sad, sordid bureaucracy of marital disentanglement. Or extramarital entanglement. Or both. I trudged through the usual statements corroborating the evidence of a hotel manager, chambermaid or anyone else who would confirm that they had seen Mr X in bed together with Miss Y. Of course, it was all a put-up job – with me doing the putting-up for some divorce lawyer – and the witnesses were always twenty pounds better off after signing their statements. Divorce in Britain was a complicated and particularly seedy business. In Scotland, which had its own divorce laws, it was given exactly the same kind of turn of the Presbyterian screw that I had discussed with Macready.

Thinking about it, it was ironic that I was now investigating how someone had accomplished the same kind of set-up I regularly put together. Except this time it had been Mr

X and *Mr* Y, and at least one of them had not been party to the set-up.

By the end of the afternoon, I had everything I needed to tie up, tied up. I was left with just the three jobs on the books: the next day's wages run, Isa and Violet's job and the John Macready case. And between them, they would take up all of my time.

I made a couple of calls to those in the underground know and asked them if they knew a Henry Williamson. None did. I don't know why that name, more than the others on the list, had stuck with me. Maybe it was because he was connected to Gentleman Joe Strachan's First War record, which still remained a puzzle: why would his daughters believe Strachan had been a war hero when, according to Jock Ferguson, he had been anything but?

It was about seven by the time I got back to my digs, having eaten at Roselli's, as I often did on the way home. I had the upstairs floor of a large villa on Great Western Road. It was basically a family home that had been subdivided and Mrs White, my landlady, lived downstairs with her two daughters, Elspeth and Margaret.

Mrs White – Fiona White – was a very attractive woman. Not in the same knock-your-eye-out way as the redoubtably configured Leonora Bryson, but she was even beautiful, in a careworn and weary sort of way. She had bright green eyes that should have sparkled, but never did, above Kate Hepburn cheekbones. Her hair was dark and cut conservatively and she dressed with taste, if without imagination. The reason Mrs White always looked careworn and weary was because of an unfortunate brief encounter during the war between a German torpedo and a British destroyer on convoy escort duty. The result had been that, within minutes, the destroyer was lying, broken, at the bottom of the Atlantic, taking all but a handful of its officers and men with it.

When I had first moved into my digs, it had seemed to me that the White family still waited for husband and father to return from duty, philosophical about the delay in the same way Brits had become philosophical about all delays and shortages. But Lieutenant George White slept an even deeper, darker sleep than Gentleman Joe Strachan; he was never coming home.

I was comfortable in my accommodation, other than that I had never brought a female guest to my rooms. It was pricey, I suppose, but I had become attached to the little White family. Most of all, I had long harboured a desire to become biblically attached to Fiona White.

The attraction, I knew, was mutual, but grudging on her part. Call me finicky, but when a woman is filled with self-loathing because she finds herself attracted to me, it tends to dent my ego. The truth was, and it confused the hell out of me, Fiona White tended to bring out the gallantry in me. Which was highly unusual, because, generally, an act of gallantry for me would be to ask the young lady to remind me again of her name before we did the dirty deed in the back of my Austin Atlantic.

There were a lot of things about me that were complicated: my relationship with women wasn't one of them. Or maybe it was.

I found that whenever I looked at Fiona White, I felt something that I didn't feel with other women. I wanted to protect her, to talk with her. Just to be with her. To watch her laugh. Strange feelings that did not necessarily involve unbuttoning my fly.

Perhaps foolishly, I had made my feelings known to her. I had been in a particularly sentimental mood, having handed over a large amount of money – something to make me misty-eyed at the best of times – to someone for no good reason other than I felt they deserved it more than me. So, giving my shining armour a final polish, I had knocked resolutely on Mrs White's door and asked to speak to her. Sitting with her in the small kitchen of her flat, I had done all the talking . . . about what the war had done to us both, about how I felt about her, about how I wanted to put the past behind me – behind *us* – and how we could perhaps repair the damage in each other. To help each other heal.

She had sat quietly listening to me, a hint of the sparkle that should have been in the green eyes, and when I had finished my declaration of affection she had held my gaze and, without hesitation, given me notice to quit my lodgings.

I had taken that as less than a maybe. I had, of course, tried to talk her round, but she had remained resolutely silent, simply repeating that she would be obliged if I quit my lodgings within the fortnight, as the Brits referred to two weeks. I had been, I have to admit, more than a little dejected. And that in itself told me something about my feelings towards Fiona White. Hard though it was to believe, I had occasionally encountered some women who actually managed, somehow, to find me totally resistible. But this stung.

It had been the day after when I heard a soft knock at the door. Mrs White came in and, standing awkwardly and stiffly, proceeded to tell me that I need not look for new lodgings, unless I had found some already, and that she apologized for having been so brusque. I was relieved to hear it, but the way she delivered it was so impersonal that I felt I should have been taking down minutes. She went on to explain that, while she appreciated that what I had said had been well intentioned, there was no way she would be entertaining the idea of a *gentleman friend*.

As she spoke, there was a breathlessness in her delivery and I could see the neck above the white collar of her blouse blossom red. I was filled with the urge to rush over to her and kiss the bloom on her neck, but I decided to hang on to my lease instead. When she had finished she asked if I was in agreement and I had said I was and she shook my hand with the tenderness of a rugby-playing bank manager.

But it had been significant. I had known that what she was telling me was that she didn't want me to go, and her protestations that nothing could ever develop between us had rung less than convincingly.

Over the months since then, we had gradually moved to a situation where I spent the odd evening watching the television I had bought, but had suggested was better kept downstairs, together with Fiona White and her daughters. I had arranged the odd excursion to Edinburgh Zoo or the

Kelvingrove Art Galleries, again always with Fiona chaper-
oned by her two daughters.

I was playing the long game.

In the meantime, there was the usual itch that had to be
scratched and scratch I did, as I always had, but with more
discretion than before. I had always sensed that Fiona White
had me measured as a bit of a bad sort, based on the flim-
siest of evidence: like the fact that on one occasion the police
had banged on her door in the middle of the night and
dragged me away in handcuffs, or the time that a young lady
with whom I had recently parted company turned up and
created something of a scene. I therefore did my very best
to make sure that my liaisons were kept as out of view as
possible.

The one major difficulty this presented was the fact that
I had guessed Fiona White had always taken mental note of
the occasions when I had remained out all night. So, after
our heart to heart, I made sure I never stayed away overnight,
unless I had given my landlady advance warning, explaining
that I had to go away on business. Which it hardly ever was.

Coming home after being with a woman was not something
that troubled me, to be honest. It was the difference between
men and women, I supposed: women wanted you to *remain*
after intimacy. For the average Scotsman, this was rather like
being asked to hang around a football stadium for three hours
after the game had ended. What they really wanted to do was
get out as quickly as possible so they could get drunk with
friends while giving them a summary of the match highlights.

I prided myself on being a little more considerate and

sensitive than that, and certainly more discreet, but I did have a habit of finding a reason for getting home. The fact that I usually stayed at least as long as it took to smoke a couple of Players put me up in the ranks of hopeless romantics and continental lovers.

Having said that, I found the idea of waking in the morning with Fiona White on the pillow next to me was a whole different proposition. And somehow a perplexing one.

So, when I returned that evening at seven, instead of going straight up to my rooms I knocked on the Whites' door and sat with them watching television. Fiona White smiled when she answered the door to me: a small porcelain gleam between the freshly applied lipstick. She smiled more these days. She asked me in and I sat with her, Elspeth and Margaret and watched *The Grove Family* on television, balancing a cup of tea on the sofa's armrest. All around me were the signs of my increasing encroachment: the television set itself; a new standard lamp; and, in the corner, the Regentone radiogram that I had bought for fifty-nine guineas and had claimed was too big for my rooms. It all made me feel at my ease and itchingly restless at the same time. If anyone had stepped into that living room, it would have looked like a perfectly normal domestic scene with all of the essential elements of a perfectly normal family.

I was deliberately, inch-by-inch, easing myself into the gap left by a dead naval officer. I had no idea why I was doing it: it was certainly true that I liked the kids, really liked them, and my feelings for Fiona White were deeper than any I had felt for any woman, except perhaps one. But if I had felt sorted out enough, adjusted enough, to make a fist of a normal life, then why hadn't I already left Glasgow behind and all of the dreck I'd mired myself in and, at long last, taken that ship to Halifax Nova Scotia?

My domestic idyll was interrupted by the ringing of the telephone we shared in the small hallway at the bottom of the stairs that led to my rooms. Fiona White answered it and then called me to the 'phone, a mildly disapproving frown on her face.

'Hello,' I said once she had gone back into the living room, closing the door behind her.

'Lennox?' It was a voice I didn't recognize. It sounded like a Glasgow accent, but not as strong as most and a little bit fudged with something else.

'Who is this?'

Only Jock Ferguson and a few others had my telephone number here. Anyone who wanted me knew to 'phone my office, or find me in the Horsehead Bar.

'Never mind who I am. You're looking for information on Gentleman Joe, is that right?'

'You're very well informed. And quickly informed for that matter. Who told you I was interested in Strachan?'

'Are you looking for information or not?'

'Only if it's worthwhile.'

'There's a pub in the Gorbals. The Laird's Inn. Meet me there in half an hour.'

'I'm not going to meet you at short notice at The Laird's Inn, The Highlander's Rectum or The Ambush in the Heather. Just tell me what it is you have to tell.'

'I'm not going to do that. I want paid.'

'I'll send you a postal order.'

'You have to meet me.'

'Okay. Tomorrow morning, nine sharp, at my office.' I hung up before he had a chance to protest. I dialled Jock Ferguson's home number.

'What the hell is it, Lennox? The football's about to come on. The international.'

'I'll save you and Kenneth Wolstenholme the trouble, Jock. Scotland will lead by one goal until the last fifteen minutes and then snatch defeat from the jaws of victory by letting three goals in in quick succession and you'll spend the next two weeks saying "we was robbed" – like everyone else. Listen, Jock, who did you tell I was asking about Joe Strachan?'

'Nobody. I mean, just the few other coppers I had to ask for information, like I already told you. Why?'

'I've just had a call trying to lure me to the Gorbals, if you can use *lure* and *the Gorbals* in one sentence. He said he knew I was looking for information on Strachan and offered to sell me some.'

'You're not going, I take it?'

'As you Glaswegians are fond of saying, I did not come up the Clyde in a banana boat. I've told him to call at my office tomorrow at nine. I doubt if he'll show. I just wanted to know if it could have been someone you had spoken to.'

'Maybe your clients have been talking.'

'No. I thought about that but don't see it happening. Thanks anyway, Jock.'

I hung up and went back into the living room.

'You're not going out then, Mr Lennox?' Fiona White asked as I sat back down next to the girls.

'Oh . . . that? No. I'm sorry about that. It was a business thing, but I don't know how he got this number. I'll deal with it tomorrow.'

'I see,' she said and turned back to the television. I could have sworn there was a hint of a smile as she did so.

I was right to have suspected an ambush. I got up and headed into my office early, but as soon as I stepped out of the front door of my lodgings I was grabbed by the throat. Except it wasn't some thug that went for me but the lurking Glasgow climate. September was turning into October and something cold from Siberia, or worse still from Aberdeen, had moved into the city and collided with the warm air. Fog. And fog didn't linger long in Glasgow before it became thick, choking, yellowy-green-grey smog.

Glasgow had been the industrial heart of the British Empire for a century. Factories belched thick smoke into the sky, and the greasy fuming of a hundred thousand tenement chimneys combined into a single, diffuse caliginous mass above the city. And when it combined with fog, it turned day to night and took your breath away. Literally.

I didn't debate long about driving into the office. I generally took it that if I couldn't see my car from the door of my digs, then driving wasn't a great idea. The same went for the buses, which left the options of the subway, trolleybuses or trams. The trams were always the most reliable in the smog, so much so that queues of cars would trail along behind them as the only way of being sure to navigate through the miasma; although it often led to motorists finding themselves in the tram depot rather than where they thought they were going.

I walked along Great Western Road, keeping close to the kerb to make sure I didn't wander off into the middle of the street, and eventually found the tram stop. I could see the indistinct outline of an orderly queue at the stop and, as was always the case in Glasgow, this collection of strangers were chatting among themselves as if they had known each other for years.

I was about four feet from the end of the queue, which was about as far as you could see in the fog, when I felt something jab painfully into the small of my back. I was about to spin around when a hand clenched itself around my upper arm and dug in. The smog clearly had an accomplice, after all.

'*Don't* turn around . . .' I recognized the voice as the one I'd heard on the phone. The same odd mix of accent, but this time it was authoritative and calm. 'If you see my face, I'll have to kill you. Do you understand that?'

'It's not that complicated,' I said. In the smog you were deprived of much of your vision and your other senses became keener, it seemed. I puzzled as to why I hadn't heard him come up behind me.

'You should have kept our appointment last night, Lennox. Now, we're going to back away down the alley behind me and you're going to keep nice and quiet and nothing untoward will happen to you.'

Untoward. The vocabulary and the accent were both all over the place. 'All I want to do is to talk to you. No one need get steamed up or hurt.'

'I'm assuming that *is* a gun you've got in my back,' I said, 'not a rolled-up copy of *Reveille*. Let me see the gun or I'm not doing anything.'

'Nice try, Lennox. I lift the gun and you make a grab for it. I tell you what, I'll pull the trigger and you watch a bit of your spine and maybe a chunk of liver fly off into the fog. Would that convince you?'

'That would do the trick, for sure . . . but on reflection, I think I'll take your word for it.'

It was more than ten years since the end of the war, but there were still vast quantities of guns circulating, particularly in Glasgow. The hard thrust I felt in the small of my back didn't feel like a bluff, and my new best friend had the kind of quiet confidence that came from experience, so I decided to play nicely. Or at least play nicely for as long as it looked like I'd be able to walk away from our encounter.

He pulled me backwards and the vague outline of the tram queue was swallowed up again in the fog. We were in a side street now that was little more than an alleyway and he steered me backwards twenty yards or so before swinging me around until I was kissing brick. There were cobbles under our feet: Glasgow-black and slick, but which sounded under my heels. But not his. Like when he had come up behind me, he seemed to move silently.

'Lay your hands flat against the wall, level with your head.'

I did what I was told, but tried to measure, from the sound

of his voice, how far back from me he now stood. If he wanted to shoot me in the back of the head, now would be the time.

'You told me on the telephone last night that you had information worth paying for,' I said. 'I have to tell you I find your sales technique a little pushy.'

'Keep the wisecracks up, Lennox, and we might just seal the deal here and now.'

'Pushy but persuasive,' I said, still trying to measure the distance. I decided this was probably a no-sudden-moves-situation. 'Okay, friend, what's this all about?'

'You're sticking your nose into this Strachan business. I want to know why.'

'I'm naturally curious,' I quipped, and he quipped back by slamming a fist into my kidney. The impact jarred my cheek into the wall and drove every drop of air out of my lungs. I dug my fingers into the wall as I gasped in the tarry, damp fug. He gave me the time to recover.

'I'll ask you the same question, Lennox, but if you smart-mouth me again, you'll end up pissing blood for a month. Got me?'

I nodded, still incapable of speaking and sucking air into tortured lungs.

'You're going to drop the whole Strachan thing, you got that? You're going to walk away from it for good. If you don't, you'll end up at the bottom of the Clyde yourself. Now, I want to know why you've been asking about Joe Strachan. What's he to you?'

'Work,' I said through tight teeth. 'That's all. I was hired to.'

The pain in my side was intense and nauseous. My pulse throbbed hard and sore in my head. This guy knew what he was doing but I knew that if I played along and didn't do anything stupid, I'd probably walk away from this.

But the truth was that this guy was pushing my buttons. All the wrong buttons. The kind of buttons that made me want to play anything but nicely. The kind of buttons that stripped away ten years of civilian life and took me back to a place no one wanted me to be.

'Who hired you?' he asked, forgetting to give the r a celtic roll. Whoever he was, he was working hard at hiding it.

I let go a long gasp, clutching my side where he had hit me, and started to bend sideways.

'I'm going to be sick . . .' I leant away from the wall and down, my hand braced against it. I heard a muffled step backwards. He was probably trying to work out if I was genuine or making a move. I leaned deeper and began retching. I could see his shoes: tan suede with soft soles; the reason I didn't hear him behind me. His feet were planted square and resolutely: there was nothing tentative about this guy. If I made a move he'd be ready for it.

But I made it anyway.

I heaved against the wall with the hand I had been resting on it and thrust myself at him with the loudest scream I could manage: it was he who had to worry about attracting attention, not me. I saw he was about my age and well built, and definitely not Gentleman Joe, ghost or otherwise. Fixing my attention on the gun, I didn't have a chance to take in his face. He moved swiftly to one side, anticipating my lunge, but I swiped at him with a fist that skimmed his jaw. He swung a foot that caught me across the shins and I went sprawling on the cobbles.

I rolled as soon as I hit the ground, depriving him of an easy target, but he didn't fire. Instead, as I struggled to get up, I saw the gun arc through the smog in a vicious slash at my temple. I took most of the power out of the blow by blocking it with my left forearm and made an unsuccessful grab for the pistol with my other hand, at the same time slamming my heel upwards into his groin. I missed but caught him in the belly and he doubled. When it comes to a fight with a gun, possession is more than nine-tenths of the law and I made another grab for it. Instead of pulling against me, as most people would do instinctively, he pushed into me as I pulled and slammed the butt of the gun into my cheek, using my own force against me. We had obviously gone to the same finishing school. I felt something wet on my cheek and felt the world take a brief but perceptible wobble.

He staggered back to his feet and I saw him raise the gun to take aim. I was halfway to my feet too and dived to one side, again rolling several times before leaping up and running. I had lost all sense of direction in the smog, but as there seemed to be an upward incline beneath my feet, I guessed I was actually heading further up the side street, away from the main road. I was hidden in the smog now. But so was he, and, unlike mine, his shoes made no sound on the cobbles.

I sprinted blindly a few yards then stopped, pressing myself against the wall. I eased forward slowly, making as little sound as I could. I found a bricked-up doorway, pressed myself into it and waited for the first shot to be fired, hopefully in the direction of where I had been, rather than where I now was. But there were no shots.

I had only managed a swift look at his face, and when I had seen it, the features had been twisted into a snarl. I had gotten just enough of a view to see that he had dark hair and a hard, angular face. I was also pretty sure I had seen an ugly scar on his forehead. He wasn't someone I had seen before.

I kept pressed into the recess of the bricked-up doorway, straining to hear any sound. In the smog, at the best of times, you can feel isolated, detached, as if someone had switched off the world and nothing existed beyond the four or five feet you could see. But I wasn't alone: there was another wanderer out there, hunting me with a gun. At any second he could burst into my tiny circle of awareness and it would be down to who reacted quickest. By the same token, he could just as easily have been halfway to Paisley by now.

I waited, not moving, straining the smog with every sense and ready to spring at anyone or anything that came out of it. Nothing. I wiped my cheek with the back of my hand and saw it smeared red. I started to think about the man with the gun. About his fake accent and his handiness with his fists and a gun. If he had been a gangster, then he was one who'd had the kind of army training you only got in the commandos or the like. Three minutes became four, became five. I guessed he had slipped away, aware that coming looking for me in this murk was as dangerous for hunter as hunted. But I waited a minute more. He had been a cool one all right; the type that tends to have plenty of patience.

I was just about to start making my way back to the main street when I saw him. He just appeared in front of me, as if he had suddenly coalesced from the fog itself. He was more a shape than anything else and he didn't see me pressed into the doorway.

He was moving slowly, scanning the smog-filled alley with his automatic, as if it were a torch. My doorway hiding place was just outside the arc of his vision. I slipped my hand into my jacket pocket, forgetting it had been months since I'd gone to work with a spring-handled leather blackjack in it. This was the kind of opposition you didn't want to go up against with your bare hands. I weighed up my options, but in that split second of indecision, his form was swallowed up again as he moved further up the alleyway.

Waiting a few seconds after he passed, I crouched down, undid my laces and slipped my shoes off. Then, carrying a shoe in each hand, I moved as swiftly and as silently as I could back down the alley towards Great Western Road, leaving my dance partner still searching further up the alleyway. But I promised myself that we would dance again.

And the next time, I would lead.

I was properly shod by the time I got back to my digs. In the murk, Mrs White would not see me come up the path from the lounge window and I had hoped to slip unnoticed into my rooms to get cleaned up. As luck would have it, she opened the front door just as I got to it.

'Mr Lennox . . .' she said, shocked by my appearance. 'What on earth has happened to you?'

'This damned smog,' I grumbled. 'Pardon my language . . . I slipped on the kerb and smacked right into a lamppost.' It was a perfectly credible excuse: there would be dozens of genuine accidents fitting that description that morning.

'Come into the kitchen,' she commanded, steering me with a firm hand on my elbow. 'I'll have to have a look at that.'

I was pretty groggy and went along with what she suggested. Pulling out a chair from the kitchen table, she eased me down into it. I winced as she did so.

'Are you hurt elsewhere?' she asked.

'I fell after I hit my head . . . the kerb dug into my side. It's mainly my cheek though . . .' I hoped she bought it. Fiona White had seen me with various battle trophies, including on one occasion when they had been awarded to me by the City of Glasgow police. It was, I knew, her principal reason for wanting to keep her distance: all part of my qualifications as a *shady character*.

She made up a weak solution of antiseptic and boiled water and dabbed at the wound. I noticed the solution cloud pink when she dipped the gauze back into it.

'I think you might have to have this stitched,' she said, frowning. She came around in front of me and leaned in to examine me from that angle. Her face came close to mine and I could detect a faint scent of lavender and felt her breath on my lips. Her eyes moved to mine. She suddenly looked embarrassed and stood up in a businesslike manner; but there had been something in the look we exchanged. Or maybe there hadn't. I was sore and groggy and confused as hell about a lot of things, not least Fiona White.

'It'll be fine,' I said. 'If you have a sticking plaster, that'll do.'

'I really think you should have it seen to. It's in the same place . . .' She let the sentence die.

'As my scars? I know. They're all healed up now, Mrs White. A scrape isn't going to cause me any problems.' I smiled at her and was rewarded with a stab of pain from my cheek and a trickle of fresh blood down to my jaw line. She tutted and reapplied the gauze pad. She lifted my hand onto the pad to hold it in place while she took a roll of sticking plaster from a drawer and cut three strips from it.

'How did you get them? The scars, I mean?' she asked, awkwardly, as she used the strips to secure a fresh pad in place. I turned my head a little and she tutted again, pushing it back with two fingers. It was the first time she had ever asked me a personal question.

'I picked the wrong plastic surgeon,' I said. 'He said he'd done Hedy Lamarr's nose and Cary Grant's chin, but he'd only ever really done Clark Gable's ears.'

'Seriously . . .'

'They really are plastic surgery scars,' I said. 'They had to patch me up after I caught the tail end of a German hand grenade.' I didn't tell her that it would have been much worse, if one of my men hadn't taken most of the blast. My face

98

had been torn open, but they'd been able to put me back together again. His splashed-in-the-mud guts were beyond any surgeon's skill.

But the plastic guy who had fixed my face had done a pretty good job: all I had was a spider web of faint, pale scars on my right cheek. And my smile could look a little lopsided, because of nerve damage, but only in a way that made it look even more wolfish, as Leonora Bryson could fully attest.

While tea infused, Fiona White brought me a couple of aspirin and a tumbler of water. The talk became small and mainly about the smog and how it always caused trouble; but, as I sat there, a thought sunk heavy and sickeningly in my gut. I had lied to Fiona White about what happened, for the best reasons, and God knows that, on most occasions, I didn't have to have the best reasons to lie. But I didn't like lying to her.

That was not, however, the main cause for the feeling in the pit of my stomach. I had just evaded a very serious operator with a gun in his hand: the very same person who had 'phoned me at my digs the night before. And he had clearly been waiting for me, outside the house, knowing I would be heading in to see if he kept our specious appointment.

That meant he knew where I lived. And that, in turn, placed Fiona White and her girls in danger.

'Is something wrong, Mr Lennox?' Fiona White asked. 'Are you feeling worse? I really think we should see about getting you to a doctor.'

I shook my head. For a second I debated with myself about whether I should level with her or not. It would alarm her and would certainly end my tenancy, but she had a right to know.

'I need to make a 'phone call,' I said.

I stood up and walked through to the hall telephone.

While we waited for Jock Ferguson to arrive, I sat with Fiona White and told her exactly what had happened to me and why. For some reason I even levelled with her about the money being sent to Isa and Violet each year on the anniversary of the Empire Exhibition robbery, and told her that this was one fact that I was keeping from the police, *on client confidentiality grounds*. I also told her that I had another, very high profile case that I was working on that could cause all kinds of problems, but that my little samba in the smog certainly had nothing to do with that investigation.

She sat and listened to me quietly, her small, pretty hands folded on the lap of her apron and her face quiet and serious, but otherwise without any expression. I sat and listened to myself in amazement: I was the most secretive person I knew – I even kept secrets from myself – and I never talked to anyone about my work, yet here I was spilling my guts to my landlady.

I knew I should shut up. And somewhere deep inside, I was screaming to myself to shut up, but I wouldn't stop talking. I spoke fast and urgently and once I had given her the full background to what had happened, I told Mrs White about how I was now concerned that this man, and anyone he was associated with, clearly knew where I lived. I said I would pack a few of my things and move somewhere else, at least for the time being, but I would continue to pay my rent to her. I understood that she would probably want me to move out permanently because of the inconvenience I had caused her and I said that I would, of course, comply with her wishes, but in the meantime I wanted Inspector Ferguson to know what had happened and maybe get someone to keep an eye on the place and . . . I seemed to run out of things to say, or breath, or both. I punctuated it all with, 'I'm sorry . . .'

'Where will you go?' she asked in a tone that was impossible to read.

'I don't know . . . A hotel, probably. I'll be okay.'

'I see . . .' Still nothing to read in her voice or on her face.

The doorbell went. I made her stay where she was while I got it.

I was surprised that Ferguson had come alone. I introduced him to Fiona White, but they had met once or twice before, briefly, when she had answered the door to him on a couple of the rare occasions he had visited me at my digs.

I ran through everything with him.

'So it was your caller from last night?'

'Looks like it, Jock.'

'So, do you want to make a complaint of assault?'

'No. That could make things *complicated*. I just want to make sure Mrs White isn't troubled by this.'

'So you want me to post a guard outside the front door without there being a complaint on the books to justify it?'

'You could think of something, Jock. A prowler seen in the area, that kind of thing.'

'Lennox, you said this guy was armed. We can't have people running around Glasgow waving guns about.'

'True, I can see how that would lower the tone of the place . . .'

Ferguson gave me a look.

'Okay,' I said. 'I understand that. But before we start a manhunt, tell me why you're on your own.'

'What do you mean?'

'You know what I mean. Not even a beat bobby with you.'

He turned to Fiona White and smiled. 'Could you excuse us for a moment, please, Mrs White?' Then turning back to me: 'Let's go upstairs. I'll help you pack . . .'

My raincoat had taken the worst of the damage: there was a bad tear at the seam of one arm, and a sleeve and the back of the coat were smudged with tarry, black streaks where I'd skidded over the cobbles in the alley. My hat, one of my best Borsalinos, was still lying somewhere in the alley. Despite my suit being unmarked, I wanted to change it, along with my shirt, as you always want to do after you have been in a fight.

Jock Ferguson sat smoking in the lounge while I washed, changed and packed. Standing at the washstand, I looked at myself in the mirror. A faint discolouration haloed the sticking plaster on my cheek, but there was no swelling and I didn't look too bad. I guessed that I had bled enough to prevent serious bruising.

An odd idiosyncrasy of my personality was that I was a sharp dresser: I always bought the best clothes I could afford.

And often clothes I couldn't. I packed a dozen shirts, not wanting to have to come back to pick up more, and two changes of suit, four silk ties and half a dozen handkerchiefs. I also packed a brand new pair of brown suede shoes with composition soles, which were just the latest dab. I had decided to take a leaf out of my dance partner's book.

After I had my clothes packed, I called through to Ferguson to check he was okay and I apologized for the delay; he responded with something grunted. What I was really doing was checking where he was, and that he wasn't about to appear in the bedroom doorway while I took a copy of H.G. Wells's *The Shape of Things to Come* from the bookshelf and dropped it into my case. I then got down on my hands and knees and, stretching my arm under the bed, eased up two loose floorboards and reached into the floorspace. Taking the oilskin-wrapped bundle, I gave it another wrapping in an old shirt and dropped it into the case next to the book.

'Okay, Jock ...' I said when I reappeared in my sitting room, 'let's have it. Why are you flying solo?'

For the first time since I'd known him, Jock Ferguson looked ill at ease.

'I need to ask you one thing, Lennox,' he said firmly. 'Have you discussed your interest in the Gentleman Joe Strachan business with anyone else, other than me?'

'Ah ...' I said. 'I see you've followed the same line of thought that I have. The answer is no, I have another case on and I have been dealing with that since we spoke. I have discussed the Strachan business with no one other than you.' Of course

I had: with Willie Sneddon, but I knew that if Sneddon had wanted to frighten me off, it would have been more direct. I also knew that Sneddon kept his own counsel. In any case, I felt it best not to let Ferguson know that I'd been in touch with a King.

'That's what I thought . . .' Ferguson said glumly. He sat on the edge of the sofa, leaning forwards, his elbows resting on his knees.

'And you only spoke to your fellow officers about it, and then I get jumped and warned off. That's what's bothering you, isn't it?'

'It doesn't make sense . . .' He shook his head. 'I suppose I can understand you being warned off because there are officers who are so determined to find the rest of the gang . . . but waving a gun about . . .'

'Let's not get too ahead of ourselves, Jock. I really think that it is unlikely to have been a copper at all. There's always another side to every story. You suggested it yourself – my clients, Isa and Violet. Maybe they told someone that they were planning to hire someone to look into the discovery of dear old dad's remains. They told me that they had asked around and my name had come up. It could be that someone has simply done some two and two arithmetic.'

'And . . .' asked Ferguson, reading my mind.

'And Violet does have a husband who looks like he knows all the moves.'

'Name?'

'Robert . . .' I struggled to remember the married names the twins had given me. I had got used to thinking of them as Isa and Violet Strachan in my head. 'Robert McKnight. Mean anything?'

'Not offhand. I'll check it out. Discreetly. In the meantime I'd keep a low profile if I were you, Lennox.'

'I'll do my best. While I'm doing a Greta Garbo, can you have someone keep an eye on Mrs White? And give her a number to call . . .'

'Fair enough, Lennox. I'll come up with something. Probably a prowler, like you said. Just make sure you don't sneak round the back if you need to come back for anything. And Lennox . . .'

'Yeah?'

'You're really pushing it. Your luck with me, I mean. I could get my jotters handed to me if it was found out that I've covered up an assault with a firearm.'

'I appreciate it, Jock. If anything comes out of this that leads to a big collar, you can bet your name's on it.'

Fiona White was waiting in the hall, her arms folded and her face set hard.

'Is this really necessary?' she asked as I put my suitcases down in the hall.

'It's safer. I don't want you and the girls involved in this. I don't think anyone would dare show their face here again, but it would be best if I moved out.'

'I will keep your rooms for you, Mr Lennox. I'm assuming this is a temporary arrangement.'

'I would like it to be, Mrs White.'

The three of us stood awkwardly for a moment. Ferguson

handed her a card on which he had scribbled down his home number as well as the St Andrew's Square contact number.

'I'll arrange for the beat constable to check on you,' he said. 'But if you see anyone suspicious hanging around, 'phone me right away.'

'I'll ring with a contact number once I'm settled,' I added. She nodded abruptly. Ferguson and I carried the cases out to my car.

It was still as foggy as hell. Or maybe in hell they complained about it being as foggy as Glasgow. I dumped my bags at my office and sat at my desk until it got dark and I had to switch the lamp on. The other offices were emptying and I smoked my way through half a pack of cigarettes and contemplated, not for the first time, how crap my situation was. My face hurt like a son of a bitch every time I placed even the gingerest of fingertips on it, but from what I could see from my reflection in the broad blade of my letter opener, it still hadn't swollen. My side next to the small of my back still ached nauseatingly, but it was no longer a solo performance: all the wrenches and impacts of our scuffle in the smog were now singing in unison.

The darkening smog rubbed itself against my office window. I decided against venturing far to search for a hotel and was beginning to imagine the extra aches I would wake up with if I slept on the polished floor of my small office. Added to that, performing my ablutions in the toilet that was shared with the four other offices on my floor and the floor below did not appeal to me.

On an impulse I picked up the 'phone. I was surprised that the person I asked for took my call.

'Hi,' I said, failing to keep the weariness out of my voice. 'It's Lennox. Listen, I'm across the street in my office. I have a favour to ask ... could you meet me in the lounge bar in ten minutes?'

And, to my further surprise, she said she would.

Leonora Bryson was late. Which was fair enough. There was an etiquette to these things: a woman couldn't be seen waiting around in a bar for a man. You had to do the waiting. And women like Leonora Bryson knew that any man would wait for her, for as long as she wanted him to wait.

When she arrived in the lounge bar of the Central Hotel, she was again dressed in a formal skirt with a matching jacket and pale blue blouse beneath it. It was something that, on most women, would have looked almost drab, but on her it looked sexier than a bikini on Marilyn Monroe. She certainly attracted enough attention as she entered and I could have sworn I heard the marble bust in the corner give a gasp. I was waiting for her at the bar and suggested we take a seat at one of the tables. I asked her what she would like to drink. I was not surprised that she ordered a daiquiri, but was amazed that the Glaswegian bartender knew how to make it.

'You look like you've been in the wars, Mr Lennox,' she said, indicating the dressing on my cheek with a tilt of her daiquiri glass. There wasn't the same frost in her voice, but there wasn't any warmth either.

'This? Yeah, stupid really . . . I walked into something in the smog.' I neglected to explain that the something had been solid muscle with a gun.

'Yes, I know . . .' she said, suddenly animated. 'I've seen some pretty bad smog in San Francisco, but this stuff is unbelievable. I mean, it's not just dense, it's tinged *green*.'

'They colour it for the tourists. San Francisco . . . is that where you're from?'

'No . . . I'm from the east coast, originally. Connecticut.'

'Then where you were brought up was a heck of a lot closer to my home town than it was to Hollywood. I was raised in New Brunswick.'

'Really?' she said, with an interest so tiny that you would have needed the Palomar telescope set to maximum magnification to spot it. 'What is it you wanted to talk to me about, Mr Lennox?'

'I need somewhere to sleep tonight . . .'

The final syllable had not taken form before the temperature dropped a thousand degrees.

'No, no . . .' I held my hands up. 'Don't get the wrong idea . . . With the smog and everything, and my office just over the way, I wondered if you could swing a special rate for me here. Just for tonight. It's a bit rich for my blood normally but needs must . . .'

She appraised me with the glacial blue eyes and for a moment I killed the time thinking about what Rhine maidens and Valkyries might get up to in Valhalla. She seemed to make up her mind about me.

'Actually,' she said, 'we have a spare room at the end of

our hall. We had it for one of the studio executives, but he's flown home early. We have kept the booking open in case we needed it. I guess tonight we do.'

'I'll pay, of course . . .'

'No need.' She took a long, thin cigarette of a brand I'd never seen before from a specially made silver case. I held out a light for her the instant it met her lips. She took a draw and nodded a perfunctory thanks. 'It's paid for whether you use it or not. And, anyway, you're working for Mr Macready. Just tonight?'

'Just tonight.'

'Was there anything else, Mr Lennox?' She frowned at me over her sipped daiquiri, as if my presence was seriously compromising her enjoyment of it.

'As a matter of fact there was. How much do you know about why I've been employed by the studio? About Mr Macready's situation?'

'Everything,' she said blankly. 'I am Mr Macready's personal assistant. To do my job, I need to know everything that's going on, good or bad. I am how Mr Macready connects with everybody and everything around him.'

I was about to say he'd done some pretty enthusiastic connecting himself, but let it slide. 'Did you know about his . . . *tastes* before this incident?'

'Of course.' A little defiance now. And resentment.

'Where were you when Macready was at the cottage with his *friend*?'

'I was at the hotel. Not this hotel . . . the one up north. Up past that big lake. We were there for the shooting.'

'And Macready gave you the night off?'

'That's right. He was in the bar of the hotel drinking with Iain.'

'When I asked him about it, he said it was a spur of the moment decision to go to the cottage.'

'That's what he told me,' she said, holding me in a blue glacier gaze. 'Iain's family owned the estate we were shooting on and the cottage was one he used now and again. He paints, you see. An artist.' She said the word with disdain. 'Mr Macready said that Iain suggested they go to the cottage to continue drinking.'

'But as a guest of the hotel, Macready could order drinks after closing time . . .'

Leonora Bryson shrugged. 'I don't think drinking was what was on either of their minds. Why is this so important?'

'Have you seen the photographs?'

A split second of outrage, then the storm passed. 'No, Mr Lennox, I haven't.'

'I have. I had to. They were taken with some kind of hidden camera. In a wall void or something. I can't tell for sure because the other party . . . Iain . . . is not, I've been told, to be made aware of this *difficulty*. That means I can't examine the cottage. But it was an elaborate set-up. That means organization. Planning in advance.'

'And that doesn't fit with them going to the cottage being a spur of the moment thing . . . is that what you're saying?'

'Exactly. But that leads to the conclusion that his Lordship's – or is it his Dukeship's? – son and heir was in on the set-up. And that simply doesn't make any sense at all. He – and his father – have as much to lose as John Macready. More, probably.'

'So where does that leave you?'

'Tracking down the blackmailer. Paul Downey. Believe it or not, Miss Bryson, this city is a tough place to stay hidden in. And I've got the kind of contacts who can tell me exactly where to look.'

'So why haven't you spoken to these *contacts*? Shouldn't you be bumping into more mysterious objects in the smog, instead of sitting here?'

'It's not as simple as that. These contacts I have are, to be frank, criminals. If there's a crooked way of making a buck, then these guys have done it. With something as *delicate* as this, I have to be careful about what I say and to whom.' I noticed she had finished her daiquiri and beckoned to the waiter. 'May I get you another?'

'No.' When the waiter came over she ignored my protests and told him to put the drinks on her room bill. 'I'll ask reception to give you the key for the room.'

'Fine, thanks,' I said. 'I'll nip over to my office, if I can find it in the fog, and pick up my bags.'

'Bags?' She arched an eyebrow.

'I keep some stuff in my office.'

It was a lame answer and she saw through it. I could see her reappraising the wound on my cheek.

'Mr Lennox, I do hope that we can rely on you. I have to tell you that I was not in favour of you being hired. From what Mr Fraser told us about you, you have a lot of colour in your background. I wouldn't like to think that that colour could interfere with you sorting this mess out for us.'

'It won't. For your information, Miss Bryson, it is exactly that *colour* that could lead me to Downey and the photographs. May I ask you a question?'

She shrugged.

'What is it about me that you dislike so intensely?'

'I've not given you that amount of thought, Mr Lennox. But if you're going to push me on it, there isn't anything in particular I dislike about you. It's probably true to say that I dislike everything about you.'

I smiled. 'How wonderfully simple yet all-embracing.'

'I think you have made all kinds of judgements about John. You think of him as less of a man because of what he is. Well, I can tell you that John Macready is more of a man than you'll ever be. I can tell to look at you the type you are. Arrogant, pushy, violent. You use women and have no conscience about it. You had only met me for a few minutes and you tried your moves on me. Men like you make me sick.'

'I see,' I said and drained my drink. 'If I ask you for a reference after this job is over, would you mind awfully leaving that bit out?'

She laughed, but it was a twisted laugh full of distaste. 'And you think you're so funny. So smart. Well, make sure you're smart enough to sort this mess out, because I'm going to make sure you don't get a penny more until you do. Good night, Mr Lennox.' Turning abruptly, she marched out of the lounge.

I stood there, somewhat stung by her comprehensive character assassination of me.

But it didn't stop me watching her ass as she walked off.

I brought my cases over from my office and a porter carried them up to the room for me. I tipped him too much as I always tended to do when dealing with Glaswegians. They always chatted and joked with you, and the fact that they weren't doing it for the tip, just because it was in their nature, always made you tip more.

The room was a smaller encapsulation of the luxury I'd seen in Macready's suite and I decided, not for the first time, that I was definitely in the wrong business. Once I was alone, I locked the door and slid the heavy safety chain into place. Opening my suitcases, I took out the bundle and the copy of *The Shape of Things to Come* and laid them on the bed. I unwrapped the shirt and the oilskin from the bundle and took out the heavy, top-break Webley thirty-eight and the box of ammunition. After I'd loaded it, I thumbed down the safety, rewrapped it in the oilskin and shirt and put it back in the case. I spent more time with the copy of H.G. Wells's *chef d'oeuvre*. I opened it and checked the contents: the pages had been hollowed out and in it were tightly rolled fifty-pound notes and a small bag with a handful of diamonds.

This was my *Nibelungengold*. It had started off with the money I had made in Germany. I had been lucky to get out of the occupation zone with it: the military police had neither understood nor appreciated my spirit of private enterprise or my trailblazing in establishing post-war trading partnerships with the Germans. Then, while I had been in Glasgow, I had been able to add to my little trust fund significantly, given the fact that the people I had been working for were not the most assiduous bookkeepers. Between us, we had eased the taxman's workload significantly.

My move out of my digs, temporary or otherwise, had not been the main reason for me bringing my leather-bound trust fund with me: I had, for a long time, worried about the security of keeping it in my digs. I couldn't put it in a bank without the inland revenue taking notice, and carrying it around in a suitcase or keeping it in my office were not viable options either. However, since I had been doing the wages run, I had opened a business account with the commercial house who banked the wages cash. I had also rented a safety deposit box. I was due to do the run tomorrow, and I decided to deposit the gun and the cash in the box.

But I might just pick up the gun again after the run.

After I had hung up my suits, I locked both cases, the gun and the cash in one, shut them in the wardrobe and went back down to the bar. I spent an hour and a half smoking, drinking bourbon – which was good, but clearly wasn't of the calibre of the whiskey Macready had served me – and talked semi-drunken crap to the bartender. This was a better class of bar and bartender, so I made an effort to talk a better class of semi-drunken crap, and he did a pretty good impression of being interested. I had a great deal of admiration for bartenders and their unique skills.

I returned to my room before I started to see in plural, stripped down to my trousers and undershirt, washed my face, lay down on the expensive candlewick and smoked some more.

I must have dozed off. I woke up suddenly and had that wave of nausea you get when you've surfaced too quickly from a fathom of sleep. I sat up, swinging my legs off the bed, still not knowing what it had been that had woken me. My head was throbbing and my mouth felt furry. I heard it again: a knock at the door. Soft, but not tentative.

For a split second I thought about getting my gun from the case in the wardrobe, but elected for the sap that I'd slipped under the pillow. I couldn't see how my chum from the smog could have traced me to the hotel.

'Who is it?' I slipped the chain from its housing and placed one hand on the latch, while the other hung at my side, weighted by the sap.

'It's me. Leonora Bryson.'

I opened the door and she stepped in. She was in her dressing gown.

'What is it?' I asked. 'Is something wrong? Has something happened?'

She closed the door behind her and, unsmiling, pushed me back into the room. As I stood there, she unfastened the gown and let it slip from her shoulders. She was naked underneath. The natural detective in me guessed we weren't going to discuss the case again. Leonora Bryson's body was a work of art in a way that made Michelangelo's efforts look shoddy. Every part of her was faultlessly, firmly, shaped. I found myself staring at her perfect breasts.

'I don't understand . . .' I said, still failing to make eye contact. I perhaps should have stopped staring at her breasts, but, having been presented with them, it somehow would have seemed churlish or unappreciative not to: like being in the Sistine Chapel and refusing to look up at the ceiling.

'Don't talk,' she said, still unsmiling. 'I don't want you to talk.' She closed the distance between us and fastened her mouth on mine, pushing in with her tongue, making her command redundant. I was totally confused by what was happening, but decided to go along with it. I'm obliging that way.

She pushed me down onto the bed and began tearing at my clothes, almost frantically. There was something wild about her and it infected me. It was more than passion: as we made love, her eyes burned with something akin to hatred and she raked my skin with her nails, pulled at my hair and bit into my face and neck.

It was wild, passionate sex, but I couldn't help feeling that we could have done with a referee and a copy of the Queensberry rules at the bedside. After it was over, in the absence of smelling salts and a second in my corner to fan me with a towel, I lit a cigarette for both of us. She lay silent, smoking the cigarette before getting up abruptly, pulling on her dressing gown and leaving without a word.

I did nothing and said nothing to stop her leaving. Lying there dazed and confused, I guessed that I had just been used, and I had a pretty good idea why.

The thought made me feel dirty and cheap. Which is probably why I didn't stop grinning until I fell asleep.

CHAPTER SIX

Walking into a bank with a gun is a bit of a Glasgow tradition. Nevertheless, it made me nervous.

I had a hire arrangement with a garage at Charing Cross Mansions, who supplied the van, at a discounted rate, for the wages run each Friday. Picking the van up early, I turned up at the bank ahead of the usual time and asked to access my safety deposit box.

While the wages run was potentially a target for armed raiders, and the bank itself had been hit for cash on more than one occasion, I knew that the safety deposit boxes here were the safest in Glasgow. Not because they had thicker walls, bigger locks or better security than anywhere else; the reason was much, much more convincing than that: at least two of the Three Kings had boxes here. If you were to turn this place over, being caught by the police was the least of your worries.

I deposited the gun and the cash-stuffed volume of Wells in the box and went back up to the ground floor to meet up with Archie, the retired policeman whom I had hired to do the run with me.

As usual, Archie was waiting right on time, talking to MacGregor, the bank's Chief Clerk. Archie was fifty but looked older and walked with a slight limp: a souvenir of a falling through a factory roof while chasing some lead thieves. I assumed that the thieves had not been carrying the lead during their escape.

Archie was lean to the point of meagre and probably six-three, but a stoop took an inch or two off his height. An unruly horseshoe shock of black hair wrapped itself around his high-domed, bald head; he had large, watery spaniel eyes and continuously wore a tired, doleful expression. It had been this expression that had initially put me off giving him the job because it sometimes made him look lazy and unre-sponsive.

It had surprised me to discover that behind the dolorous mask was a mind sharper than you would expect from a Glasgow copper and a dry, dark Glasgow humour. He was also every bit as reliable as Jock Ferguson had promised. Jock had told me that Archie had always managed to give his superiors in the City of Glasgow Police the feeling that he was somehow taking the mickey, without them ever being able to put their finger on how he was doing it. That, prob-ably more than anything, convinced me to hire him.

Originally, Archie did the wages run with me to eke out his police pension and the money he made as a shipyard night watchman, but he had lost the watchman job, the unions complaining about his harassing their members. It was a universally accepted fact along Clydeside that almost everything that could not be nailed down, and most that was, was likely to leave a Glasgow shipyard under a fitter's raincoat or wheeled out in a barrow hidden amidst the throng of workers leaving the yards at shift-change.

Pilfering was endemic in the yards. Shipworkers' homes in Clydebank were famed for their eclectic décor: often tenement slum chic combined with ocean liner salon, complemented with a battleship-grey colour scheme. Archie, the ex-copper, had misunderstood his brief as night watchman and had managed to stop hundreds of pounds' worth of timber, paint and brass fittings from walking out of the yard. The management had not been able to forgive Archie for doing his job unacceptably well and he was let go. Since then, I had tried to give him whatever I could in the way of work, including the odd divorce witness job, and the Friday run was a regular fixture.

When I came back up to the main hall of the bank, Archie was talking to MacGregor, the Chief Clerk, who organized the run. MacGregor was the usual young fogey you found working in a bank – a twenty-five-year-old striving hard for middle age – and Archie made a point of befuddling him with humour at every opportunity.

Archie looked over to me with his Alastair Sim eyes as he signed the manifest log, his truncheon hanging from his wrist like a handbag.

'There's a bit of confusion here, boss,' he said, without a hint of a smile. 'Mr MacGregor here says the money is to go to the yard as usual, but I thought you said this week we were off to Barbados with it.'

'Ignore Archie, Mr MacGregor,' I said. 'He's having you on. Barbados has an extradition treaty, we're off to Spain.'

'This amount of money is no joking matter, Mr Lennox,' MacGregor said to me over spectacles pushed halfway down his nose, yet another misguided affectation of middle-class middle-age. 'You'll telephone as usual to confirm delivery?'

I said I would and signalled for Archie to stand guard on the street while I loaded the back of the van with the sacks.

It was the usual, thankfully uneventful trip: me driving, Archie sitting lugubriously with the mail sacks in the back. We delivered the wages to the shipyard office and I 'phoned MacGregor to confirm delivery. On the way back, Archie sat in the front with me.

'I know you've been hit hard by losing the watchman job,' I said. 'Listen, Archie, things have been picking up with the business and I could do with some help. It wouldn't be full time, not for a while at least, but if things keep going the way they're going, it could well become full time. You interested?'

Archie looked at me with his big, mournful eyes. 'Would it be the same kind of stuff that I've been doing for you lately?'

'Yes ... divorce cases, security work, missing persons. Wearing out shoe leather and knocking on doors, that kind of thing.'

The truth was I was already using Archie more and more for divorce cases. Divorce evidence in court always sounded better coming from a retired police officer, added to which Archie's perpetually gloomy demeanour seemed to give it added gravitas. There was also the fact that I got decidedly nervous in the witness box, something lawyers are wont to pick up on. Truth was I was worried that some bright young counsel would start to call my character as a witness into question. And my character, or at least my history, was best left unquestioned.

'I see . . .' Archie leaned back in the passenger seat and rubbed his chin thoughtfully. 'I was considering the chairmanship of ICI. . . but I suppose I could fit your jobs in. Do I get an expense account, superannuation and luncheon vouchers?'

'You'll get ten shillings an hour plus expenses. I'll leave your pension fund in ICI's hands . . .'

'I shall consult with the board, of course,' he said, hooking his thumbs in his waistcoat, 'but in the meantime you may assume my answer to be in the affirmative.'

'Good. I've got two cases on right now that I need help with. One of them is to do with Gentleman Joe Strachan and the Empire Exhibition robbery. Jock Ferguson said that you would probably have been in the force at the time.'

'Aye . . . I was that. I remember it well. Bad business.' Impossibly, his expression became more doleful. 'Very bad business.'

'What happened? I mean, how much do you know?'

'Most of what there is to know. Every detail, as did every copper in Glasgow. We had the whole story drummed into us over and over again. I take it you know all about the Exhibition?'

I nodded. 'I believe it was really something . . .'

'It certainly was. The Empire Exhibition was a big thing for Glasgow back in Thirty-eight,' Archie continued. 'The big thing. I was there, with my wife. They built the whole exhibition in Bellahouston Park, but you would not have believed you were in the middle of Glasgow. There were towers, pavilions, a freak-show, a funfair . . . Oh aye, and a giant model of Victoria Falls, a hundred feet wide. There was even an entire Highland village, complete with a castle and a loch. Aye, it was some undertaking. Even your lot – the Canadians, I mean – had a pavilion, with Mounties and everything. There were these women – they called them the Giraffe-necked Women – and everybody went to see them. They'd come from Burma and had all of these rings around their necks, one added a year, until they had necks a foot long . . .'

Archie paused, lost for a moment in memories, a faint wistfulness flickering disturbingly across his pall-bearer's countenance.

'Yep,' I said, 'really sounds like something.'

'It was right after the Depression, of course,' Archie said, 'and they thought it would do a lot of good for Glasgow, but the truth was Glasgow was about to get back to full swing anyway because of the war. And you couldn't afford to go into any of the pavilions . . . at least, not if you were an ordinary Glaswegian like we were. They charged you a bob just to get through the gates. Even the kiddies had to pay sixpence. It was all supposed to be about the future but it looked to the missus and me like a future we wouldn't afford. There were tearooms and the like, but the Atlantic Restaurant was beyond the reach of everybody except the seriously well-off. Like most people, Mavis and I spent most of the time walking around and looking at the pavilions from the outside. Do you know, we couldn't even sit down? They charged you tuppence for a deck chair, and your ticket was only good for three hours.'

We reached Charing Cross Mansions and the garage from which I had hired the van. I pulled up outside behind where I'd parked my Atlantic, and listened to Archie while he finished his story.

'The weather was shite,' he continued. 'The worst summer for rain anyone could remember, and in Glasgow that's saying something. The Exhibition was nearly a complete wash-out, literally. But it really was something. They said that it was the future, the way things would look. All these fancy build- ings. Like the ones they have in Hollywood.'

'Art deco.'

'Wouldn't know. Anyway, despite the rain, the exhibition took in a fortune in cash – at all of the attractions, the restau- rants and events and so forth – and the money was trans- ferred back to the bank in the city centre. The same kind of run as we've just done, so to speak, but in reverse. These boys had a reinforced van, though – armoured, like. There was some kind of arrangement where the armoured car picked up the exhibition takings on its way back along Glasgow Road from a textile wholesaler out at Paisley and then back to the main bank in the city centre. They had staff working the night shift there to lock it up in the main safe, instead of it being dropped into the night safe.'

'So there was more than the Exhibition takings in the van?'

'Aye. But how the robbers knew that was a mystery. The CID reckoned that the robbers had help or information somewhere along the way. An inside job. But all of the staff were interrogated and the CID came up with nothing. Anyway, the Exhibition had closed for the day and the van had just done the pick-up when it was ambushed by these armed men. Five of them. The driver and the guard played along, guessing that these boys meant business after one of the robbers gave the driver a doing, but there was actually a police office as part of the Exhibition. It was supposed to be empty at that time, but the young PC who had been on duty during the day had been held up for some reason.'

'Gourlay?'

'Yes, Charlie Gourlay ... he was on his way out of the Exhibition when he walked right into the robbery taking place. The driver of the van said in his statement that the tallest of the robbers let him have it with both barrels without a second's hesitation. Cold blooded murder.'

'Were you involved in the case?'

'No ... I was posted away on the other side of the city. But of course it was big, big news. A murdered policeman was seen – still is seen – as an attack on the whole force. Like I said, we were all of us dragged in and briefed and re-briefed about the robbery. I tell you, every policeman in the city was on the lookout for Joe Strachan. There were a couple of blokes got a real kicking because they fitted Strachan's description.'

'And they fixed on Strachan right away?'

'Aye. There had been rumours about the Commercial Bank job and the one before it. But I think there was more to it than that.'

'Oh?'

'If you ask me, someone somewhere got a tip about Strachan. I mean, we weren't looking for anybody else.'

'But Strachan didn't have a reputation as a life-taker, did he?'

'No . . . he didn't. No . . .' Archie shrugged and left his answer hanging. He turned down the corners of his mouth, which shifted his expression from lugubrious to funereal. 'I don't know all the ins and outs of it, of course, only having been a humble beat bobby, but from what I do know, Strachan didn't have any kind of record at all. No one could pin him with anything. He was a secretive type and made sure nothing incriminating could ever stick to him, so God knows what else he got up to. Maybe Gourlay wasn't his first murder. More than that, I don't know. You'd have to talk to someone who was in CID at the time. Or Willie McNab.'

'Superintendent McNab?' I laughed. 'He'd have my balls if he knew I was involved with this case. I gather that he and Gourlay were close friends.'

'Were they?' The massive expanse of Archie's brow creased. 'I didn't know that. But if you say so.'

'Did you ever come across someone called Billy Dunbar?'

'No, can't say I have,' said Archie after a moment's thought.

'Here's the last known address for him.' I handed Archie the address given to me by Jock Ferguson. 'That's a starting point. Could you see if you can track him down?'

'Is this me started, then?' Archie raised his eyebrows. 'When do I get my trenchcoat and six-shooter?'

'I think you're confusing Humphrey Bogart with John Wayne. Yes, this is a job. Keep a tally of your time and expenses. Just see if you can trace him. But try not to spook him. I just want to talk to him, okay?'

'I will move like a panther in the night,' said Archie.

CHAPTER SEVEN

I took the keys into the office and ran Archie home in the Atlantic. I went back to the Central Hotel to pick up my stuff, pausing in the lobby to use one of the telephone kiosks. It was all walnut, brass and polished glass and didn't smell of piss in the slightest. I 'phoned Mrs White and told her that I was in the Central Hotel but moving on, probably, that day or the next. She sounded genuinely relieved to hear from me and I asked her if everything was all right, which she said it was, but I could tell from her voice she was tired. I told her I would keep in touch and I hung up.

I rang up to Leonora Bryson's room, but got no answer. I had better luck when I tried John Macready's suite. I told her I was moving out and would keep in touch about progress, I also asked what Macready's movements would be for the next week, until he caught his flight. Her tone was as businesslike as usual and neither of us made mention of what had happened the night before: she because she was not alone in the room, probably; I, because the situation was so bizarre that I was beginning to doubt that it had really happened, or think that I had dreamt it.

After staying in the Central Hotel, I braced myself to come down in the world, and found a reasonably priced hotel down by the Gallowgate. It was more of a boarding house than a hotel and had a sign outside which declared: NO DOGS, NO BLACKS, NO IRISH. I had spotted signs like this in London and the South, but this was the first I had seen in Glasgow. I was greeted, or more confronted, by a small, rotund, balding bundle of hostility who introduced himself as the landlord. He had that speech defect that seemed to be particularly common in Glasgow, a slushy lisp where every fricative is distorted into something that sounds like radio interference. It was rather unfortunate, therefore, that his name was Mr Simpson. Or Schimpschon, as he introduced himself.

I restrained the instinct to dry my face with my handkerchief, or to ask if it was okay if I could keep *Nigger*, my black Irish Wolfhound, in my room, and followed Simpson up the stairs. When I answered his question about how long I would be staying, which I said would be a week, he stopped on the stair and turned, a suspicious frown creasing his porcine brow.

'You're no' Irischsch, are you?'

'What? Oh, my accent ... no, I'm Canadian. Is that all right? But I did spend a weekend in Belfast once ...'

My irony went over his shiny head by a mile.

'That'sch awright. Schscho long aschsch you're no' Irischsch ...'

The room was basic but clean, and I shared a bathroom

with four other rooms and there was a pay 'phone in the hall. It would do for a week or two, if needs be. I paid three days in advance, which Simpson took thanklessly and left.

With Archie on the trail of Billy Dunbar, I decided to dedicate myself to tracking down Paul Downey, the part-time amateur photographer who had done so well in capturing John Macready's good side.

I spent the first evening checking out the well-known queer haunts in the city centre: the Oak Café, the Royal Bar in West Nile Street and a couple of others. I decided to hold off on a trip down to Glasgow Green for the moment. Wherever I went, I was met with an almost universal suspicion, clearly being taken instantly as a copper out to trap homosexuals. I would have probably been less offended if they had thought I had been there cruising.

I tried to get around the suspicion that I was a cop by offering money for information, but that seemed to make things worse. I couldn't blame them for clamming up. As I had told Macready, the City of Glasgow Vice Squad – and police forces in Scotland generally – pursued homos with biblical zeal which, in itself, made me question the underlying culture. I never could understand why homosexuality was illegal in the first place: if consenting adults wanted to assault each other with friendly weapons out of the sight of children and horses, then I didn't see why that should be a police matter.

All the same, I avoided visiting the toilets while I was in the queer bars.

I was aware that somebody followed me out of the Royal. It was dark and the fog had come back, but nothing like as densely as before. Unlocking your car door is a prime time for an ambush, so I walked straight past the Atlantic, picking up my pace and taking a swift turn into the alley that connected West Nile Street with Buchanan Street. As soon as I was around the corner, I pressed into the wall and waited for him to take the turn. This time, just like I had promised myself, I was going to lead the dance.

I saw the figure hesitate for a moment, then turn into the alley. I leapt out and grabbed his coat, pulling it out and down over his shoulders and upper arms, transforming it into an improvised straightjacket. I swung him around, slammed his back into the wall and rammed my forearm up and under his chin, shutting off his windpipe.

I knew even before I got a look at his face that this wasn't the same guy from the other morning in the smog. It had all been too easy and, anyway, this guy was too small.

A pair of scared-wide eyes stared at me through uneven horn-rimmed spectacles.

'Please . . . please, don't hurt me . . .' he pleaded.

'Shit . . . Mr MacGregor . . .' I let go the bank's Chief Clerk. 'What are you doing following me?'

'I . . . I saw you in the bar. I know why you were there. I just know it.'

'Em . . . no, you don't, Mr MacGregor,' I said emphatically. 'I'm not that type of girl.'

'No, no . . . I know that, Mr Lennox. I know you were in there watching me. That's why I came after you. I promise

I'll never go in there again. Ever. It was my first time . . .' His fright turned to pleading. 'Well, my second time, but that's all, I *swear*. I *promise* you I won't do it again. Listen, I have money. I'll give it to you. Just don't tell the bank director. I know he hired you to check up on me . . . Or the police. Oh, please God no, not the police . . .'

'Is that why you came after me?' I pulled his coat back up over his shoulders.

'I saw you leaving. I didn't see you when you were in there, but I guessed that you had seen me. Please don't tell the bank, Mr Lennox . . .'

I held my hands up to placate him. 'Take it easy, Mr MacGregor, I wasn't in there looking for you. I had no idea that you . . . And no,' I said, reading the sudden change in his expression, 'I wasn't in there for fun. Let's get out of this alley before a patrolling copper takes us for a couple.'

He stepped back out onto West Nile Street. 'Come on, I'll give you a lift home,' I said. This was more than just an embarrassing moment: MacGregor worked for an important client and I could do without the complication. But it began to dawn on me that there might be some mileage in having the goods on MacGregor. He told me he lived in Milngavie and we headed out of the city centre and up through Maryhill.

'So what were you doing in the Royal?' he asked eventually, clearly still not convinced that he had not been the subject of my surveillance.

'I was looking for someone,' I said. 'A guy called Downey.'

'Paul?'

I took my eyes off the road and turned to MacGregor. 'You know him?'

'I do. Did. Not well. I haven't seen him in weeks. What do you want him for?'

'I can't tell you that, Mr MacGregor. I thought you said that was only your second time in that bar . . .'

MacGregor reddened. I was going to be able to milk this.

'Listen, I'm not interested in your private life, but I would greatly appreciate it if you could point me in the right direction. I really need to find Downey.'

'He used to go to the usual places, the Oak Café, The Good Companions, all of those places. But, like I said, I haven't seen him for weeks. You could try some of the steam rooms though. I think I heard someone say that Paul's friend works at one of the public baths.'

'Do you have a name?'

'I'm afraid not. No, wait . . . I think his friend was called Frank, but I don't know which baths he worked at. That's all I can tell you, Mr Lennox. Sorry.'

'It's something to go on. Thanks.'

We were passing through an area of flat, open country-side as we approached Milngavie. Off in the distance – a darker grey silhouette in the lighter grey of the fog – I could see something long and cigar shaped suspended from what looked like a gantry. I had seen it before, and more clearly. It looked like something Michael Rennie should have stepped out of in a science fiction movie and it had always puzzled the hell out of me. I decided to take advantage of having a Milngavie local in the car with me.

'Oh that? That's the Bennie Railplane,' MacGregor said in answer to my question. 'It's been there since before the war. There used to be a lot more of the track that it hangs from, but they took it down along with all of the railings and stuff for the war effort.'

'Railplane?'

'Yes. It was built in the Twenties or Thirties. It was going to be the transport of the future. It could travel at well over a hundred miles an hour, you know. But no one backed it and it never got more than the test track there.'

I thought about dreams of a future that never happened: the Empire Exhibition of Thirty-eight promising a cleaner, brighter Glasgow full of art deco buildings, with the Bennie Railplane connecting cities at superfast speed. What could have been. Like my wartime dream of me returning to Canada, making a proper life for myself. A lot of things had been killed in the war. Ideals and visions, as well as fifty million people.

I dropped MacGregor outside a bungalow in Milngavie which he admitted, a little embarrassedly, was where he still lived with his parents. He hesitated before getting out of the car.

'You won't say anything, will you, Mr Lennox?'

'What happened tonight stays between us,' I said.

'I'm very grateful, Mr Lennox. I owe you for this.'

Oh, I know, I said to the empty car as I drove off. I know.

In the absence of widespread indoor bathrooms, the Victorian Glasgow that exploded in population but not in area was faced with a major public health threat. The great unwashed of Glasgow really had been. The city's response to this problem was an array of public baths, swimming ponds, pools, Turkish baths and municipal 'steamies': communal laundries that were often attached to public bath houses.

In the Glasgow of the 1950s, and in the comparative rarity of the real thing, you could even have a 'sun-ray' bath at the Turkish Baths in Govanhill, Whitevale, Pollokshaws, Shettleston and Whiteinch. A sun-ray bath would cost you two bob; a combined Turkish-Russian and sun-ray bath would cost you four shillings and sixpence.

Bathing was segregated, the baths open between nine a.m. and nine p.m., with separate days for each gender at each venue.

Unofficially, there were set times when, if you were of a certain disposition, you could meet like-minded gentlemen in at least two of the bath houses.

I spent two evenings checking out the baths, asking if anyone knew Paul Downey or where I could find him, or if someone called Frank worked there. I was met at different locations with different responses, from the hostile and suspicious – as I had in the queer bars – to the unnervingly welcoming. But nothing took me closer to finding Downey; I could find no one who would admit even to recognizing the name.

Despite the knocks and hardship it had often endured, Glasgow was a proud city. And that pride was often given eloquent expression in the most impressive civic architecture in the most unlikely of locations. Govanhill Public Baths and Turkish Suite in Calder Street was a perfect example: a stately building from the outside, and Edwardian palace of ablution on the inside.

After asking a pool attendant, I was told that Frank was one of his colleagues and he was on lifeguard duty at the moment. The attendant sent me to wait in the gallery of the gents' swimming pool. I sat on the fire engine-red seats and watched the handful of swimmers in the water. Every splash resounded in the chlorine-fumed air of the white-tiled and deep red-beamed pool hall. You could have held an opera here, and not just because of the acoustics; the décor of this public bath house bordered on the opulent.

'You wanted to talk to me?' A large collection of muscles bundled into a white tennis shirt appeared beside me. In contrast to the bulging biceps and beefy shoulders, and despite being predictably square-jawed, the features of the face were fine, almost delicate. His fair hair was bristle-cut at the sides and back but long and thick at the top, and a dense blond lock had a habit of falling across his forehead and slightly over one eye. I had the impression, somehow, of a cross between some idealized Nazi image of Aryan manhood and Veronica Lake.

'I'm looking for Paul.' I said it as if I knew him.

'Paul who?'

'You know who . . . Paul Downey.'

'What do you want him for?'

'Just to talk. I know you know where he is, Frank. Where can I find him?'

Frank leaned in closer and drew his lips back from his

teeth. 'Why don't you just leave him alone? Didn't he promise that he'd pay the money back?'

Interesting.

'Maybe we can arrange easy terms,' I said. 'I just want to talk to him, that's all.'

'Anything you've got to say you can say through me. You'll get your money. And soon. I thought your boss accepted that.'

'And who, exactly, is my boss?'

Frank looked puzzled for a moment, then angry when he realized I wasn't who he thought I was.

'Okay, I'll level with you, Frank,' I said. He may have been a cream puff, but he had lots of filling and there was no need for things to turn nasty. 'I don't know what money you're talking about, but I guess from what you've said that young Paul owes the wrong kind of people money. That's not my concern. I'm on the supply side, not the demand. I've been hired to buy back certain photographs from Paul. I take it you know what I'm referring to?'

Frank shrugged his massive shoulders.

'Listen, Frank, if you know where Paul is, tell him to 'phone me.' I handed him a card with my office number on it. 'And tell him that he'll get his money, but we play this my way, not his. We're not prepared to mail that kind of cash into a Wellington Street PO box on the strength of good faith. And it would be good if you could point out to him that he doesn't get a single penny unless I'm totally convinced I've got everything: all the copies and all the negatives.'

'I don't know what you're talking about,' said Frank, but he took the card anyway.

Frank left the Govanhill Baths about half past ten. He stood outside on Calder Street for a good five minutes, checking the road in both directions, making sure I wasn't waiting to follow him – which I was – before heading off down the street to his tram stop. He was wearing a cheap but flashy belted raincoat and had pulled his hat down over his eyes, but there was no mistaking the shoulder to waist taper of a serious bodybuilder.

Fortunately for me, the other side of Calder Street was block after block of tenements; red sandstone beneath black soot. I had found a close, as the Scots called the open-ended entrance passageway and stair of a tenement building, and concealed myself in it while watching the bathhouse exit. Frank was a smart cookie, all right, and I found myself wondering if he had more to do with Downey's amateur photography club than just looking pretty.

He got on the tram heading away from the city centre and I walked around the corner to where I had parked my Atlantic. There was no rush: I knew where the tram was heading and I would catch up with it before its next stop. It was fortunate that I did, because Frank skipped off at the next stop and crossed the road. We were in a long arc of tenement-lined streets and I would have been conspicuous if I had stopped, so I drove on until I could do a u-turn out of sight. As I sat parked there, another green and orange Glasgow Corporation tram passed by, this time travelling towards the city centre. I waited long enough so that I came around the corner just in time to see Frank, in the distance, board the tram.

He was a *very* smart cookie.

I kept my distance, following the tram until Frank got off at Plantation, and started walking into Kinning Park. I dumped the car when it became the only vehicle on the streets and my walking pace progress, even in the light fog, would start to draw attention. I followed Frank on foot, my footfall silent because I was wearing my soft-soled suede numbers, and congratulated myself on following my alleyway chum's footwear tips.

Frank led me into a row of three-storey tenements and turned into one of the closes. I sprinted to catch up, to see which flat he went into, and reached the mouth of the close just in time to hear the downstairs flat slam shut. I doubted if Frank and Downey lived together openly – Glasgow's attitude toward that kind of thing made the Spanish Inquisition look tolerant – but I had put my money on Frank having wanted to tell his bestest ever friend all about my visit to the baths. I decided to give them some hello-honey-I'm-home time before I went knocking on the door.

I had noticed a call box at the corner of the street, so I headed back to it and called the lawyer, Fraser, on the out-of-hours number he had given me. I told him where I was and what I was doing.

'And you're outside now?' he asked. 'How sure are you that Downey is in the tenement?'

'I'm not sure at all, but I think it's a pretty safe bet. What

I need to know from you now is how you want me to handle this. If I go in there and Downey *is* there, and if the photographs and negatives are in there too, do you want me to promise the money and set up an exchange? Or do you want me to use *direct* negotiations to secure the negatives right now?'

'I don't approve of blackmail, Mr Lennox, no matter how it is couched. And I certainly disapprove most vehemently of anyone profiting from blackmail. I would like Mr Downey, as I mentioned, to be left in no doubt how seriously we take this matter. So I suggest you deal with this using your own, special, initiative.'

'Understood, Mr Fraser,' I said and hung up. As I stepped out of the kiosk, I slipped my hand into my raincoat pocket, just to check I had my own, special, initiative with me.

I decided to quell any naughtiness pretty quickly, should Frank get wound up, so by the time I knocked on the tenement flat door, I had already threaded my wrist through the leather loop of my sap.

I instantly recognized the boyish face at the door from the photograph Fraser had shown me. He was small and light framed and gazed at me apprehensively with his soft eyes. No trouble there.

'Hello, Paul,' I said cheerfully as I pushed past him and into the flat and checked the hall for Frank. 'How's the camera club?'

'Frank!' he shouted anxiously along the hall and his muscly boyfriend appeared through a doorway into the passageway and bounded towards me. He was a big boy, all right, so I swung my sap and caught him a textbook blow across the temple.

Frank's muscle bounced like rubber, first against one wall in the narrow hall, then the other, before he dropped.

'Say goodnight to the folks, Gracie,' I said as he hit the floor.

Paul started to scream and I slapped him hard to shut him up. I grabbed him by the throat and slammed him against the wall.

'It's playtime, Paul,' I said between clenched teeth. I was fired up. I had to be fired up because I hated what I was doing: Paul was no fighter and I saw nothing but raw terror in his eyes. Despite everything that I might have become, I had no appetite for picking on the weak. But this was business.

'Now,' I said slowly and menacingly. 'I'm going to let go your throat, but you make nice and quiet, like you're in a library, got it?'

He nodded furiously. Desperately.

'Because if you don't, you're going to wake up in the fractures ward. Are we *simpatico*?'

He gave a strangled yes and I let him go. Frank was making a rattling snoring sound when he breathed, so I bent down and checked him out. I put him in the position we'd been taught in the army and the snoring stopped. While I was down there, I retrieved my business card from his trouser pocket and tried not to think that he would probably have enjoyed me searching for it if he had been conscious.

'Is he dead?' Downey asked, his voice high and quivering. Nice line of work, Lennox, I thought.

'No. He'll be fine. He might not be as bright as he was, but, hey, that's brain damage for you. Now, listen. I reckon he's out for a couple of minutes tops. If he starts to come round while I'm still here, I'm going to have to send him bye-byes again, understand? And that could mean he'll spend the next fifty years pissing his pants and dribbling on his shirt. So, unless you're not a true Glaswegian and actually do have a fondness for vegetables, you've got two jobs to do. The first is to put those photographs into my hands, and I mean everything: every print, every negative, *everything*. The second thing, and this is going to be by far the more difficult, is to convince me that I *have* got everything there is to get. Because, if I'm not convinced, then I'm going to get tetchy with you and Veronica here. And if I find out, after I've gone, that I *haven't* left with everything, I will find you and your chum again, but next time I'll come with some friends, and we'll all have a *real* party.'

Again he nodded furiously and I knew from the look on his face that he would do exactly as I told him.

'They're in there . . .' He nodded down the hall to a closed door at the far end. I grabbed him by the shirt front and heaved him down the hall, tearing the shirt in my fist. He fumbled with the keys he took from his pocket and I snatched them from him.

'Which one?'

'That one . . .' he pointed and I saw how much his hand shook. I was beginning to get a bad feeling about this. Paul Downey just did not seem the type to mastermind this kind of blackmail scam. Nor did his boyfriend, for that matter, despite the muscles.

I opened the door and told Downey to put on the light, which he did, bathing the small room with red light. A darkroom, but my first inspection revealed it to be a swiftly improvised one. There was a table with developing materials and trays against the wall next to a small plan chest and a cupboard, and prints hung on clothes pegs from a makeshift drying line.

'Okay, Paul, hand them over.'

He opened the cupboard and took out a shortbread tin, all red tartan and photographs of Edinburgh Castle – the Scots were the only nationality I knew that bought their own tourist tat.

I tipped out the contents: prints of the photographs Fraser had shown me and a few more, plus a blue airmail envelope stuffed with strips of acetate. The negatives. But the Macready photographs weren't all he had in the box: there were two more sets of photographs, each partnered with a blue airmail envelope of negatives. I spread them all out on top of the plan chest. One set featured a prominent Glasgow businessman whom I recognized instantly, despite the fact he wasn't exactly showing me his best side in the pictures. An upstanding member of the Kirk involved in charity work, which he publicized widely. In the black and white images, he appeared as a bleached mass of pale flesh in between a thin boy whom I recognized as Paul Downey and another youth.

The third set troubled me. No sex, no illegal activity,

nothing that I could see would warrant payment of black-mail money. All the photographs were simple shots of a group of well-dressed men leaving what looked like a country house. The photographs had been taken from a distance and several were close-ups of one man in particular. The close-ups had been taken with a zoom lens and were grainy, but from what I could see the man looked in his fifties and vaguely aristocratic in a foreign sort of way, with a goatee beard and skin that was a tone darker than his companions, even in the black and white pictures.

'Is this everything?' I asked Downey.

He nodded. I took a step towards him. 'I swear!'

I looked again at the picture of the well-dressed, vaguely-aristocratic-vaguely-foreign-looking man.

'What's all this about?' I asked. 'Who is this?'

'I don't know,' said Downey. He was telling the truth: I could tell from the quiver in his voice and his obvious fear that I would not be convinced by the truth. 'I was paid to take photographs of these men. I had to hide out in the bushes. I was told to take photographs specially of the man with the goatee beard. I don't know what it was all about.'

'Who paid you?'

'A man called Paisley. But I think he was working for someone else, I don't know who. And I don't know why anyone would pay what he paid for these photos.'

'You've already delivered them?'

Downey nodded.

'So why. . .?' I nodded towards the prints and negatives.

'We thought we could maybe make some more money out

of them. There was obviously something important about these photographs and we thought there might be a chance to make a bob or two in the future.'

'Where were they taken?' I asked, leaving for the moment the fact that every time Downey said 'we' I got a funny feeling 'we' was more than him and Frank.

'The Duke's estate. The same place where we took the Macready photographs.'

I slipped the best of the close-ups into my pocket. Downey had now started to shake quite violently: the shock setting in. With some it takes all a battlefield can throw at them, with others a raised voice and the threat of worse.

There was a wooden chair in the corner of the darkroom and I told him to sit. It only took me a minute to cast an eye over the rest of the apartment, as well as checking on sleeping beauty in the hall. Truth was, I was getting a little worried about him and decided to make sure he came to before I left.

When I came back into the darkroom, I had an ordinary one hundred watt bulb that I had taken from the bathroom and I replaced the red light with it, flooding the small room with brilliance. I tipped out every drawer, tray cupboard and cubby-hole I could find, checking as I went. John Macready and his aristocratic playmate were clearly not the only subjects of Downey's artistic bent.

I decided to do some pro-bono work and gathered every print and negative I could find, other than the ones I had been contracted to deliver, placing them in an enamel developing tray. I tossed the other two sets in and started a small bonfire, that made sure Downey and his muscle-bound chum would not be making any more from fat Glasgow businessmen or foreign-looking aristos.

'Okay, Paul,' I said as the photographs and negatives burned and I hauled him back to his feet. 'I'll take the rest with me and that will be an end to the matter, unless you want me to come back, that is.'

He shook his head.

'But before I go, I want to know how you set it all up. The cottage and everything. It was an elaborate set-up. You plan it all?'

'I needed the money. I owe money and I have to pay it back. I can't now . . .' He started to cry. 'They'll kill me.'

'Who? Who will kill you?'

'I owe money to loan sharks. Local hard men.'

'So you came up with this scheme all by yourself?'

'No. It was Iain's idea.'

'Iain? Iain as in bent-over-obligingly Iain? Iain the toff in the photographs? Iain, the Duke of Strathlorne's son?'

'We used to be *close*. For a while. He needs money almost as badly as I do and he came up with the plan. He knew about Macready and he came up with the idea.'

'Why on earth would he need money desperately? His family own half the country, for God's sake,' I said incredulously. 'And anyway, doesn't he have as much . . . more . . . to lose than Macready if this all comes out? His family name . . . The connections . . .'

'Iain said that that was exactly why they would cough up. It would be such a scandal that they would pay anything to stop it coming out. And if it did come out, I don't think Iain would be that worried. It would destroy his father, more than him. And he hates his father.'

I regarded Downey. I guessed he was of Irish Catholic stock, brought up in Glasgow, which put you at the bottom of the social pile. And Iain, the Duke's son, was right at the top. In class-obsessed Britain, I couldn't work out how they could possibly have been 'close', as Downey had put it.

'It isn't that unusual,' he said, reading my mind. 'It's a different world. You should see the businessmen and toffs who hang around Glasgow Green looking for a bit of rough. I met Iain at a party in the West End.'

'Does he have copies of the photographs?' I asked, suddenly seeing a much more complicated task in front of me.

'No.' He nodded to the tin box that I had laid back on the table. 'That's everything.'

We were interrupted by Frank, who lunged into the door-frame, trying to focus his gaze on me. He made a clumsy charge and I easily sidestepped him, slamming my elbow into the bridge of his nose as he careered past. He hurtled into the table and sent the tray with the burning prints and negatives crashing to the floor with him. He wasn't out this time, but rolled over onto his side and cupped his busted nose, blood everywhere. He was finished.

Downey had started to shake again. I grabbed him by the shirtfront once more and pulled him towards me.

'Is our business with each other concluded, Mr Downey?'

'Yes,' he said in a quivering tone. 'You won't hear from me again, I swear.'

I pushed him against the wall again and he screwed his

face up tight. He knew he was going to take a beating, just to get the message across. I balled my fist.

'Just make sure you don't,' I said. I maybe should have slapped him around a bit, just to reinforce the point, as Fraser had asked for in his roundabout way. But I had my limits, I was surprised and pleased to discover, and I let him go. 'You better see to your girlfriend.'

We met at the Central Hotel, in a private dining room, at nine-thirty.

After I had left Downey, I had used the same call box at the corner of the street to get in touch with Fraser and Leonora Bryson. I told them both that I had all the copies and negatives and I had put Downey and his friend out of business. I didn't mention at that stage that I'd found out that Iain, the aristo in the pictures, had planned to be on the receiving end in more ways than one. I had decided I could tell them when we got together, which would buy me some time to think about what it meant.

John Macready was wearing a grey chalk-stripe, double breasted suit with a white shirt and burgundy silk tie that looked like they had just been hand delivered from Jermyn Street. The guy had style, I had to give him that. He sat smoking but stood up and shook my hand when I came in. Donald Fraser and Leonora Bryson remained glued to the upholstery. I had business on my mind, but Leonora was wearing a blue silk dress that looked like the silkworms had oozed it out directly onto her skin. Her hair was up and her throat bounded by a four tier pearl choker. She sat smoking and looking at me disinterestedly, or uninterestedly, or both. I couldn't help thinking about the night in the room upstairs and felt the urge to go over there and start tearing silk, but I guessed that would have contravened business meeting etiquette.

'Did you run into problems?' Fraser asked, indicating the plaster on my cheek.

'No . . . this is unrelated. Everything went pretty much as I thought it would.'

'You have the items?' Fraser asked me. I handed over the tartan tin.

'No . . . I thought I would bring you some shortbread instead. A souvenir of Scotland for our American guests.'

He looked at me blankly with his beady lawyer's eyes. As I didn't have a dictionary to show him the definition of the word *humour*, I decided to play it straight.

'They're in there . . .' I said, nodding to the shortbread tin.

'All of them?' asked Leonora.

'All of them,' I said.

'You're sure?' asked Fraser.

'I'm sure. Downey was too scared to hold back, and I saw the set-up for myself. All the negatives are there. And, just for good measure, I burned every other piece of film I could find.' I turned to the actor. 'It's over, Mr Macready. You can rest easy.'

'I appreciate that, Mr Lennox.' He smiled at me, but I didn't get the full one hundred watt business. 'I really do. If ever I can be of any help to you, please let me know. Mr Fraser, do you think it would be possible to give Mr Lennox a small bonus? After all, he really did sort this out very quickly for us.'

Fraser was caught totally off guard. He flustered for a moment, then reached into his jacket pocket and produced a juicily thick buff envelope.

'Your fee is in there, Mr Lennox. Four thousand pounds. Not bad for a few days' work. I trust you'll appreciate there's an element of hush money in there. You can never discuss this with anyone.'

'Obviously.'

'And we're paying you cash. No need to go through the books. I doubt if the taxman would believe it was the proceeds of just one assignment that lasted less than a week.'

'This means I won't have to convince him.' I held up the envelope before slipping it into my inside jacket pocket; close to my heart, where money tended to find a natural home. 'And don't worry about a bonus, Mr Macready . . . this is more than enough.'

In fact, it was the most I had earned in one go at any time. And three times what I'd earned in the whole of the previous year.

Macready rose to shake my hand again. The meeting was over.

'There is one more thing,' I said, not getting up.

'Oh?'

'As I discussed with Miss Bryson, it never did fit with me the way these photographs were taken, given that your visit to Iain's was supposed to be spur of the moment. When I asked you if you could guess how the photographs were taken, or where you thought the photographer could have concealed himself, you said that it was a mystery. Your guess was that they were taken through a window.'

'Yes . . .'

'The clarity and quality of the images suggested to me that they were taken somehow from inside the cottage. They were. There was a false mirror. Two-way. The camera and photographer were hidden behind them in the next room.'

Macready lit a cigarette and took a pull on it before answering.

'So you're saying Iain, or someone connected to the cottage or estate was in on it?'

'According to Downey, yes. It was Iain. He set the whole thing up to raise cash for some reason he can't tell Daddy the Duke about. Someone's leaning heavily on Downey for money and maybe Iain's under the same pressure. He guessed you would pay anything to stop the photographs falling into the wrong hands. In other words, anyone else's hands other than your own.'

'You've got proof of this?' asked Fraser.

'Downey admitted it to me. And trust me, Paul Downey has neither the brains nor the balls to come up with this on his own. Now, I can't really knock seven shades out of the son of a peer of the realm, but if you want me to talk to Iain, I'll do it.' I tapped the envelope in my pocket. 'And you have a little credit with me.'

'What do you think, Mr Macready?' Fraser asked. I could see the American actor was deep in thought. It was not a nice prospect, knowing that you had been deliberately set up and used.

'What would your advice be, Mr Fraser?' he said eventually and a little wearily.

Fraser made the type of face lawyers make to tell you that they're thinking and shouldn't be interrupted, because they're thinking at premium rate. 'I suggest we leave it, for the moment at least, Mr Macready. We have the photographs and the negatives, which can now be destroyed. It should be the end of the matter. And given the status and influence of Iain's father, it could be a lot more trouble than it's worth.'

'Sleeping dogs?'

'That would be my inclination,' said Fraser. 'For the moment, at least. Mr Lennox, may we feel free to call on your services in this matter, should we change our position?'

'Feel free, as I said.'

'I would echo Mr Macready's sentiments, Mr Lennox: you have dealt with this case with utmost speed and efficiency. I hope that I may retain your services in the future, on other matters.'

'It would be my pleasure,' I said and shook his hand, somehow managing not to add *you sententious little prick*. I find it's best not to insult people who hand you large sums of cash.

Leonora Bryson shook my hand too, with the warmth of an undertaker. That sure was one mixed-up lady.

CHAPTER EIGHT

I was pretty pleased with myself. With the Macready case out of the way, and with more cash burning a hole in my pocket than the average working Joe could hope to amass in a lifetime, I had a lot to be pleased with myself about.

I could now give my full attention to Isa and Violet's quest to find out who was sending them their annual dividend. The fact that the money always arrived on the anniversary, give or take a day or two, of the Nineteen thirty-eight Empire Exhibition robbery, seemed to scream out that it was their long lost paterfamilias.

The police, however, were absolutely certain that the bones they'd dredged up belonged to Gentleman Joe. Over the next few days, while Archie doggedly went from address to address trying to locate Billy Dunbar, I did the rounds and asked a few questions. I didn't expect to find out anything significant, but Glasgow's underworld was a tight-knit community. A village of thieves.

I was a great reader. I spent a lot of my time reading to try to understand how the world worked; mainly because my participation in it had only served to befuddle me. You get a lot of ideas from reading: some good, some bad. And a lot of stupid ones.

I had once read that physicists believe that the act of observing really tiny particles actually changes how they behave. The observer effect, they called it. I decided to apply the principle of observer effect on Glasgow's criminal classes: ask the right – or the wrong – questions in the right places, and things tend to start happening.

As I had ever since our brief encounter in the smog, I kept my eye out for the guy who had jumped me with the gun. I had no sense of anyone tailing me, but there again, nor had Frank when I'd tracked him back to his flat. If you knew what you were doing, it was easy to stay out of sight. And I had the idea that this guy knew exactly what he was doing.

I lodged a few hundred pounds from the fee Fraser had given me into my business account, but the rest I stashed in the safety deposit box. I was almost as stunned by my sudden fortune as I had been by Leonora Bryson's sudden amorous, if potentially homicidal, passion. Between one thing and another, I had more than eight thousand pounds locked away; more than enough to buy a house outright. To buy four houses in Glasgow. I now no longer had any reason not to go home to Canada. I could lodge the cash in a bank and wire it to Canada before the British inland revenue had a chance to sneeze.

But I wasn't ready yet. Something had happened to me during the war and I still didn't like who I had become. The folks back home would be expecting the return of the

Kennebecasis Kid: the idealistic, bright-eyed, enthusiastic youth who had taken a commission for the Empire. What they would get was me: the post-war, cynical Lennox who could be hired to slap frightened queers around. And that was me on a good day.

Jock Ferguson left a message for me at the boarding house to call him and, when I did, he informed me that he had checked out Robert McKnight, Violet's husband who played chauffeur to the twins.

'He's a car salesman,' Ferguson informed me. 'No known record.'

'What kind of car salesman?' I asked, as if they came in any discernible shades of character. 'Bomb-site used or gentlemen's Bentleys?'

'He works at the Mitchell and Laird Garage, up in Cowcaddens. Legit. They sell new or nearly new Fords, but I don't know if they're an authorized dealer or not. And they carry a big stock of second-hand cars, but it seems to be quality stuff.'

'I see,' I said, and remembered the Ford Zephyr with the Hire Purchase gleam to it parked outside my office. 'So he's clean?'

'Well . . . there is an interesting twist. Despite the name, the Mitchell and Laird Garage is actually owned by a trading company whose chairman just happens to be a certain William Sneddon.'

And there it was, the thing I had dreaded most: another of the Three Kings involved in my investigation. That made two, if you counted Michael Murphy's presence on the list of their father's associates the twins had supplied.

'But you know that doesn't mean anything really these days,' continued Ferguson. 'Willie Sneddon is still a crook and we're still after the bastard, but the truth is he's cleaned up his act. He has as many legit businesses as crooked ones. The Mitchell and Laird Garage just happens to be one of the legit ones. And that's where your boy works.'

'Yeah . . . my boy who just happens to be married to the daughter of one of Glasgow's most legendary crime figures. Tell me, Jock, was there ever any connection between Willie Sneddon and Joe Strachan?'

'None that I'm aware of. Sneddon came on the scene much later. Hammer Murphy though . . . I believe he was tight with Strachan for a while.'

'Yes . . . I heard,' I said gloomily. 'Thanks, Jock.'

Archie paid me a visit just before lunchtime, which I took as a hint and I treated him to a pie and pint in the Horseshoe. He downed the pint in seconds, his bushy eyebrows jumping with each swallow, and turned to me with a pained expression on his long face. It took me a couple of seconds to realize he was smiling at me.

'I'm like those Mounties of yours, boss,' he said. 'I always get my man.'

'Billy Dunbar?'

'The very same. I've run him to ground.' Archie dug around in his raincoat pockets, pulling out various scraps of paper, a crumpled handkerchief and a couple of bus tickets, all of which he dumped on the cramped space we had in front of us on the bar. Eventually he found what he had been looking for and his eyebrows once more declared their independence from the doleful face.

'Aye . . . here it is. This is where he lives now. He's changed address three times. From what I understand, he's straight now. Has been since his last stretch. That's why there have been so many moves: it's difficult to put a past like his behind you.'

'Tell me about it,' I said more to myself than to Archie. I looked at the address. It was a place in Stirlingshire. 'He's left Glasgow?'

'You know what it's like when one of these bozos decides he wants to go straight. It's like coming off the bottle – most go back to it, but if you want to stay dry, you stay out of the pub. My guess is that Dunbar needed to get away from everybody who knew about his past.'

'Good work, Archie,' I said. Nothing registered on his face but his eyebrows looked pleased. 'Do you want to come along for the trip? Chargeable time?'

'All right,' he said, frowning. 'But I'm worried what all that fresh air will do to my constitution.'

'I promise we'll keep the car windows tight shut and smoke all the way. Okay?'

Archie nodded dolefully. 'I'll be at the office at nine.'

Hammer Murphy, as I've already mentioned, did not earn his nickname because he was an accomplished handyman. Well, he *was* an accomplished handyman, and specially skilled with a hammer, but not in the putting-up-shelves sort of way. More in the smashing a business opponent's skull to pulp sort of way.

156

All in all, Hammer Murphy had always been the King I had done my best to avoid. Much in the same way as I avoided meat pies unless I was sure of their origin: Murphy owned a meat processing plant on the outskirts of Glasgow and the rumour was – well, more than a rumour – that Murphy had put some of his business rivals through the mincer. Literally. It was also widely suggested that Murphy obliged Handsome Jonny Cohen and Willie Sneddon by sub-contracting this function for them.

I mixed with a nice crowd.

I tried not to think too much about Murphy's meat plant, but when rumours started to circulate that a couple of likely lads who had particularly annoyed Murphy had gone through the mincer, tied up but still alive and conscious, then my appetite for his company diminished as drastically as my appetite for sausages.

You get the idea: Hammer Murphy was the most violent, volatile and vindictive of the Three Kings who ran Glasgow's criminal underworld, and someone to be avoided if at all possible.

The whole Gentleman Joe Strachan thing had taken on a bad taste for me as soon as Murphy's name was mentioned. Strachan seemed to have this split personality thing going on: there was this image of Strachan as almost the 'gentleman crook': a kind of Glaswegian Raffles, if you can stretch your imagination that far; the other image of him was of a cold, ruthless and often vicious gangster and life-taker.

The presence of Murphy's name on a list of Strachan's associates confirmed the latter for me. Now would have been a good time for me to have ducked out; to have taken enough to cover my expenses and tell the twins that Strachan was dead, and so were all of the leads as to who was sending them the cash. After all, I had had the windfall of the Macready case, which had been preposterously lucrative. So instinct screamed at me to drop the Strachan thing; to enjoy the freedom of the city's streets without having to do a two-step in the fog with a skilled dance partner. Unfortunately my hearing seemed to have deteriorated, and no matter how loud instinct screamed, I didn't seem to hear it.

So I placed the call I'd been putting off for more than a week. After speaking to a minion, I was put through to Murphy and the voice that came on the other end of the line was thick Glasgow accented and more abrasive than carborundum.

The conversation was brief and pithy, let's say. I had not realized that 'fuck off' could be used as a response to almost every question or statement, or even when you paused to take breath. It was only when I mentioned Gentleman Joe Strachan and that I was looking into the discovery of his remains that Murphy's curiosity was piqued.

'Do you know the Black Cat Club?' he asked.

'I know it.'

'Be there in a half an hour. Don't be fucking late.'

Murphy hung up before I had a chance to check my social diary. I knew the Black Cat Club, all right. I was a regular. A card-holding member. It was the kind of place you needed a membership, or a warrant, to get into.

I had discovered the Black Cat not long after I had arrived

in Glasgow. It was upstairs in an unimpressive-looking sand-stone block way down in the West End of Sauchiehall Street, past the Kelvingrove Art Gallery and where the address numbers ran into the thousands. Britain was full of clubs with names that were always synonymous with, but gener-ally avoided, the word 'Pussy'. There would be the usual ill-judged attempt at glamour and sophistication in the décor, and the lounge bar would be filled with corpulent busi-nessmen nervous that the police would raid the place and their names would end up in the papers. And of course, there would be the reason the businessmen didn't run for their lives or reputations: the hostesses, dressed in sham Hollywood style with impressive cleavages to compensate for their Glasgow accents.

The name of the game was that the hostesses would encourage the businessmen to relax and to ease their nerv-ousness by becoming drunk on over-priced and under-measured cocktails. The funny thing always was that visitors to these clubs seemed to lose their wallets with a frequency that defied statistical laws. Anyone fool enough to suggest theft usually found themselves face-first on the street outside. Most kept quiet and tried to work out the best way to answer their concerned wives at home when they asked, 'When was the last time you saw your wallet, dear?'

There were probably three or four clubs like that in Glasgow, and I had no doubt that The Black Cat had started out as exactly that kind of place. But there was a funny evolu-tionary process behind such establishments. The Black Cat probably started its metamorphosis by accidentally hiring a piano player or a combo or a chanteuse who was a cut above the usual knocking-shop standard; my guess is that when word got around, clients started to come to listen to the music rather than test cheap bedsprings with some pneumatic hostess. And when profits went up and police raids and pay-offs became fewer, the management booked more and even better jazz acts.

Sure, there were still hostesses, but they confined themselves to serving drinks that, while still expensive, were not extortionate, and any business between hostess and customer would be conducted discreetly and on a *freelance* basis. I had had the odd dalliance with a couple of the hostesses myself, but those had been strictly non-commercial in nature.

When I arrived at the unassuming green door with a small black cat painted above a peep hole, I was greeted with a brusque nod of recognition from a doorman with yard-wide shoulders. The fact that he nodded at all was an impressive accomplishment, given that, as far as I could see, he had no neck to speak of and his thick, Teddy Boy-quiffed, bullet head seemed to have been fused directly into the mass of his shoulders.

I went upstairs and was enveloped in a blue fug of cigarette smoke. The club was busy, with the usual mix of earnestly non-conformist types with chin beards and roll neck sweaters, trying to live the Beat lifestyle they'd started to read about in art magazines. Except they lived in Glasgow, not San Francisco or Manhattan. There was also a smattering of the usual suspects with the sharp suits and the hard look that told you that, even if you didn't recognize them as known faces, it was better not to bump into them and spill their drinks. And there were still the businessmen, but of a different type. This version would listen to the music as earnestly as the Beat types, with God knew what going through their heads about who they should have become instead of who they were.

Don't get me wrong, the décor and general atmosphere was still a Glaswegian painter and decorator's concept of chic and cosmopolitan, and the environment was only slightly less sham and shoddy than the usual hostess joint, but the music and the dimmed lights lifted the tone way above the expected and gave the place an ambiance that daylight and silence would rob from it.

Martha, one of the hostesses I'd played catch-me-tickle-me with, was working the bar. She was a medium height Gene Tierney type, with dark hair, green eyes and an impressive repertoire; we exchanged a few lines before she told me that Murphy was waiting for me in a private room at the back. She frowned as she told me, in the way everyone frowns at the idea of Hammer Murphy waiting for you. She told me when she finished and asked if I wanted to come out to play, but I told her I couldn't tonight. Even though I could. It puzzled me that I found myself thinking of Fiona White and I began to seriously worry that if I got any deeper involved with her I might catch a bad case of fidelity.

There was a Savile Row suit stuffed with muscle and latent violence in the back room. I was surprised to see Murphy was on his own – not that Michael 'Hammer' Murphy was someone who needed protecting, but he usually kept a couple of psychopathic goons on hand just for show.

'Hello, Mr Murphy,' I said. 'Thanks for taking . . .'

'Shut the fucking door . . .'

I shut the door and sat down opposite him.

'Is fucking Strachan fucking dead or not?'

Murphy was not one to stretch his adjectival or adverbial vocabulary. He was a small man in height, but in every other way he projected a giant malevolent presence. He was still sporting the Ronald Colman moustache that he had the last time I'd met him and his hair was expensively and immaculately barbered. But that was as Hollywood as it got: Murphy was an ugly bastard, that was for sure. He was the only man I had ever encountered whose face looked like a deadly weapon. His nose had been broken so often it had given up all ideas of symmetry or where it should really be on his face and the small eyes were set deep into the type of padded flesh that comes from frequent exposure to fists. The man was all violence. He seethed with it. Murphy made you feel threatened just by sitting still.

'I don't know,' I said. 'And that's the truth. There are as many people convinced he survived the Empire Exhibition robbery as there are others who believe those were his bones at the bottom of the Clyde.'

'Who's fucking paying you to find out?'

'Now you know better than that, Mr Murphy. I really can't say, Mr Murphy. You know where I stand on client confidentiality.'

'Aye, I suppose . . . And I fucking respect that about you,

Lennox, I really fucking do. And I really want to save you the fucking embarrassment of betraying some cunt's faith in you ... so, here's an idea: why don't I get a couple of the boys to smash your fucking kneecaps to fuck so's you can't fucking stand anywhere on client confidentiality or fucking fuck all else.' He paused for a moment's sarcastic reflection, then wagged his finger. 'I tell you what, just to keep your fucking honour in one fucking piece, we'll do your fucking ankles and elbows as well.'

'Isa and Violet, Strachan's twin daughters. That's who hired me.' I did not for a moment feel embarrassed about folding instantly. My father had always told me to find something you were good at and make a career out of it. To say Murphy was *really* good at threatening physical violence, would be like saying Rembrandt was quite good at drawing.

'What the fuck do they want to know for?'

'They just want to know if their father is dead or not.' I left it at that, skipping the bit about the cash dividend every anniversary of the Empire Exhibition job. Murphy was big on aggression and violence, and certainly had a kind of animal cunning about him, but he was no Einstein and I gambled he would settle for my half-truth.

He was about to say something when the door swung open. I reckoned this would be the goons now and my joints began to itch. But it wasn't. A tall, dark-haired man walked in. He had a Cary Grant cleft in his chin and was almost as preposterously handsome as John Macready. I recognized him instantly.

'Hello, Jonny,' I said as I stood up and shook his hand. 'How's it going?'

'Fine, Lennox . . .' said Handsome Jonny Cohen as he came in and sat down next, but not close, to Murphy. 'Just fine. And you?'

'Can't complain,' I said, trying not to look too relieved at his arrival. It hadn't seemed to surprise Murphy and I guessed they had arranged it. But I got the feeling that Cohen had arrived a little too early and it all became clear to me: Murphy had wanted to threaten and, if necessary, beat as much out of me before Jonny arrived. But Murphy knew Jonny and I were close, even if he didn't know why. What I couldn't get was why Murphy had summoned Cohen at such short notice.

'Can I get you a drink?' asked Cohen.

'We're not fucking here to fucking socialize,' said Murphy. 'Forget the fucking drink just now and let's get down to fucking business.'

'Business?' I asked. 'I just came here to ask about your involvement with Gentleman Joe Strachan . . .'

'That *is* business, Lennox,' said Cohen. 'Joe Strachan still casts a long shadow in Glasgow. Michael here 'phoned me to say you wanted info about Strachan.'

Michael . . . I had had no idea that things were getting so cosy between them. Of the other two Kings, it had always been Willie Sneddon that Jonny Cohen had seemed to favour, often bringing Murphy to the point of reopening the gang war that the Three King Deal had been brokered to end. Now the Catholic and the Jew were on first name terms.

'I don't get it,' I said. And I didn't. 'What's it to you, Jonny?'

'Michael, me and Willie Sneddon have run things in this town almost since the end of the war. We had our problems, as you know, but there's been no trouble between us since Forty-eight. And that peace has proved very profitable for us all.'

Aye,' said Murphy with a sneer. 'More profitable for Willie fucking Sneddon than either of us.'

Then I saw it: Jonny Cohen fired a warning look across at his thuggish new best pal, as if Murphy had contravened an agreement they had made before meeting me. So this was what the old pals act was about. Willie Sneddon was coming out on top, as he always did with any deal, and Cohen was keeping the lid on Murphy's resentment. But it was much, much more dangerous than that. Sneddon, the Kingpin of Kingpins, was easing himself out and into legitimate enterprise. And criminal nature abhors a vacuum.

'Anyway, as I was saying,' continued Cohen. 'The three of us have done all right for ourselves. Things have been pretty good, all in all. But not one – not for a single minute during all of these years – did we stop looking over our shoulders to see if Strachan was going to make a reappearance.'

'You wanted me to tell you about Gentleman Joe,' said Murphy with a sneer. Or maybe he was just smiling. 'I'll fucking tell you. We all have our little tricks to keep everyone in fucking line. You're really pally with that fucking monkey of Sneddon's . . . the cunt with the boltcutters . . .'

'Twinkletoes MacBride? I wouldn't say we're pally . . .'

'Well he cuts toes and fingers off. Jonny here has Moose Margolis who boils your balls for you. I have . . .' Murphy thought for a moment. 'Well, I have *me*. The fucking point is this . . . we all make a big show to scare the shite out of people. Keep the fucking rank and file in line.' Murphy leaned forward, resting his elbows on his knees and fixing me with those small, hard eyes of his. 'Well, Gentleman Joe Strachan never did any of that. No show, no flash. But if you offended him, even if you didn't mean it, you were fucked. He'd make no big deal about it, but the next fucking thing you'd know is that the one who'd crossed him would just fucking disappear off the face of the earth. No show, like I said. Nothing. And that, my friend, was the scariest fucking thing of all.'

Jonny Cohen picked up the story. 'Every job he was involved in, every one of his men, where the cash went or what was planned next . . . no one ever knew anything about it. He was before my time, Lennox, but from the very first job I ever pulled, from the moment I got my foot on the ladder, I knew all about Gentleman Joe Strachan and his army of ghosts.'

'Christ, Jonny,' I said. 'You're getting lyrical in your old age.'

'No . . . really, that's what they called them. Strachan's ghosts.'

'And there was only one who anyone could put a fucking name to,' said Murphy. 'If you can call it a name . . .'

'The Lad?' I asked.

Murphy nodded. 'So you've heard about him. He was called the Lad because it was like he was serving a fucking apprenticeship with Strachan. There wasn't anything this wee fucker wouldn't do for Gentleman Joe. And it was like Joe was training him up to take over.'

'You know what this "Lad" looked like? Or do you have

any hint of what his real name might have been or where he came from?'

'Naw,' said Murphy. 'There was this one feller, going way back, fucked if I can remember his name. Anyways, this cunt starts fucking blabbing in the boozer one night about how he nearly got a job with Gentleman Joe and starts going on about this evil wee fucker they called the Lad. That's how everybody found out about him. If this bastard hadn't got fucking pished, we wouldn't even know this much.'

'Let me guess, this guy who mouthed off ... he disappeared?'

'Off the face of the fucking Earth,' said Murphy.

'No body ever found,' said Jonny Cohen. 'The thing is, Lennox, when they fished those bones out of the river, it was the first time in years that we didn't feel we needed to keep looking over our shoulders for Strachan. But if that wasn't his bones, then God knows where he is and what he's got planned ...'

For a moment, I thought about what they had said. 'But that was nearly twenty years ago, Jonny. You can't seriously think he's come back now? If he ever showed his face in Glasgow he'd have a noose around his neck inside of a month.'

'You're forgetting Strachan's "Lad",' said Jonny. 'His heir apparent. If there was one thing Strachan was a master at, it was planning ahead and biding his time.'

I shook my head. 'I still don't get it.'

'It's fucking simple,' said Murphy. 'You're looking into this for his girls who, incidentally, have fuck knows how many half-brothers and -sisters spread around the fucking country.

Anyway, you do your job for them. That's fucking fine and fucking dandy with us. But we will give you a thousand each if you can give us a name, an address or even a fucking face for the Lad. You point us in the right direction, and we take it from there. You also end up two grand richer.'

'And Willie Sneddon isn't playing?'

'You want to fucking know something? Sneddon's the one who's always had the most to lose. But now he doesn't give a flying fuck. He's too busy becoming the Chamber of fucking Commerce's man of the fucking month.'

It struck me that if anywhere was going to have a *Chamber of Fucking Commerce*, it would be Glasgow.

I shrugged. 'It's no skin off my nose to point out this guy, whoever he is, but I really don't think I'm going to get within a country mile of finding out who he is.' I paused for a moment.

'What is it?' asked Cohen.

I shook my head. 'No ... it's nothing. It's just that the morning after I started asking around about Strachan I had a brief encounter with a heavy and a thirty-eight in the fog. And this guy was good. Professional. He wanted to scare me off looking into Strachan's disappearance.'

'So why couldn't it be Strachan's lad?'

'Too young. I mean it could be, but it would make him only seventeen or eighteen or thereabouts at the time of the robberies. Too much of a lad. Especially to work as an enforcer.'

'When I was eighteen I could malky any bastard that got in my way.' The pride was apparent in Murphy's voice.

'I'm sure you could,' I said. 'I don't know . . . it just doesn't feel right.'

'Yet you say this guy was after you to put the frighteners on and get you to drop the Joe Strachan thing?' asked Cohen.

I thought about it for a moment. It was a stretch with age, but I hadn't gotten that good a look at the guy. He could have been five years older. Three years older. It would be enough.

'I tell you what,' I said. 'If he is the Lad, then I'll serve him up to you on a platter, with pleasure.' Then I added, just for clarity: 'But I'll still take the two thousand.'

CHAPTER NINE

To say that Glasgow was a city of paradoxes is like saying the North Pole can be chilly. Everywhere you looked, everything about the city seemed to contradict itself and everything else. It was a bustling, densely populated, fuming, noisy, brash industrial city; yet, if you travelled fifteen minutes in any direction, you found yourself in vast, empty landscapes of moorland, hill and glen. It was a city defined by its people, and its people were defined by Glasgow: yet, that same small distance away, the Glaswegian identity gave way to a different type of Scottishness. In the direction Archie and I drove, it became increasingly a Highland identity.

The country estate on which Billy Dunbar worked was remote and dramatic, covering mountains, pasture and the odd salmon-stocked loch. I enjoyed getting out of the city and into this kind of landscape whenever I could, and had often driven up past the shores of Loch Lomond and stopped off at some lochside tea shop. I did have my contemplative moments – when I wasn't peeping on adulterous spouses, slapping people about or hobnobbing with gangsters.

As I drove, I thought about my meeting with Handsome Jonny Cohen and Hammer Murphy. Before I left, I had asked Murphy about his younger days when he had worked with Gentleman Joe Strachan. He hadn't been able to tell me much, but if he had omitted the word 'fuck' and all its derivatives, it would have taken half as long to tell me. But the picture I had come away with was of a Joe Strachan whom Murphy had been, and remained, incapable of understanding, as if he existed on a completely different criminal plane. Murphy had done a few jobs for Strachan, but they had always been in connection with something else that Murphy had never known about, like working on one corner of a painting without being allowed to see the whole canvas. This is, of course, my analogy. Murphy had described it as 'being kept in the fucking dark and knowing fuck all about fuck all that was fucking going on'.

It took Archie and me several stops at remote petrol stations and post offices before we found our way to the estate office. *Mr* Dunbar, we were told by the tweedy spinster type we found in the office, was the deputy head gamekeeper. Eyeing us with that kind of keen suspicion that only comes from a long lifetime's experience of virginity, she asked us the nature of our business with Mr Dunbar. I decided to christen her Miss Marple.

I told her that we were insurance agents and had papers for Mr Dunbar to sign. What kind of insurance we could be selling a gamekeeper beat me, other than perhaps cover against pheasant-related injury; but she seemed satisfied with the explanation and told us he was not on duty that day but we could find him at his cottage on the estate, to which she gave us directions.

I was grateful it wasn't raining because, as Miss Marple had explained, Dunbar's cottage was up a lane on the estate and we had to hoof it. At one time, every square yard of Scotland had been covered with an impenetrable blanket of trees: the Great Caledonian Forest. Some time in the distant past, long before Scottish history took a brighter turn and became the Dark Ages, the forest had been chopped, burned and stripped away for firewood, building materials, or simply to allow space for animals to graze. It had taken a couple of millennia, but the ancient Scots had managed to denude the majority of the Scottish landscape and turn it into peaty bog. Now, as Dr Johnson had once quipped, a tree in Scotland was as rare as a horse in Venice. Mind you, comedy had come a long way since the eighteenth century.

Notwithstanding the efforts of the troglodyte pre-Glaswegians, the estate we walked through was punctuated with dense clumps of mixed trees and a carpet of late afternoon sun-dappled autumn orange and red lay under our feet. It was exactly the kind of Scottish scene that you found on shortbread tins like the one that I had relieved Paul Downey of.

We reached the cottage after about ten minutes. It was small, stone-built, with a neatly laid out garden to the front and a pen with snuffling pigs to the side. A mound of raked-up autumn leaves smouldered and smoked in one corner.

A short, broad-built man in his mid-fifties came out of the

cottage just as we neared it. He was dressed in a dark brown jacket of a tweed so rough it looked as if it had been woven from bramble, and a checked tweed flat cap that didn't quite match the jacket. He had a shotgun broken over his arm. Tess of the d'Urbervilles did not, as I thought she might, come skipping out of the cottage after him.

The short man stopped as he spotted us and watched us suspiciously as we approached.

'Can I help you?' Despite the bucolic attire and setting, there was still a dredger bucket full of Glasgow in the accent.

'Hello, Mr Dunbar,' I said. 'We're here to talk to you about Gentleman Joe Strachan.'

He froze for a moment as the name from another life collided with him. He cast an eye back to the cottage, as if to check there was no one in the doorway behind him.

'You police?'

'No.'

'No . . .' he said, eyeing me from top to toe. 'You dress too expensive for a copper. Your pal, on the other hand . . .'

'I got this suit in Paisley's on the Broomielaw, I'll have you know . . .' Again, Archie's eyebrows left his expressionless face behind to indicate his hurt indignation as he looked down at his shapeless raincoat and the baggy suit beneath.

'This is a lovely setting, Mr Dunbar,' I said as disarmingly as I could. 'Who's estate is this?'

'It's one of the Duke of Strathlorne's estates,' he said irritatedly. 'If you're not police . . .'

'The Duke of Strathlorne?' I echoed. I was beginning to wonder if there was any part of Scotland he didn't own.

'If you're not police,' Dunbar repeated, 'then what's the deal? You work for one of the Three Kings?'

'No, Mr Dunbar,' I said, maintaining my friendly tone. My conviviality was prompted in part by the way he nestled the still broken-breeched shotgun in his arm. 'Although I have helped Mr Sneddon on several occasions. You used to know Mr Sneddon, didn't you?'

'Aye, I know Willie. Nothing wrong with Willie Sneddon. Doing all right for himself is Willie. Willie got me this job.'

'Really?' I said without much interest. But I *was* interested: Willie Sneddon had claimed not to know anything about Dunbar's whereabouts.

'Aye . . . The last assistant gamekeeper just upped and left. Didn't even give his notice. Willie found out about it and put me onto this number.'

'That was good of him, Mr Dunbar. Mr Sneddon likes to take care of people, as I know myself,' I said. By the way, my name's Lennox. And this is Archie McClelland. We're enquiry agents. We just want to ask you a few questions about Joe Strachan.'

'I know fuck all about Joe Strachan. You've come a long way to learn fuck all.'

'We just want to talk to you, Billy. You were quite an operator in your own way back then. There's maybe something you know that could help us.'

'Help you what?'

'Listen, could we . . .?' I nodded towards the cottage.

'No. My wife's in. I've got fuck all to say about fuck all. So fuck off.'

I decided against correcting his grammar. Pointing out double-negatives to someone with a double-barrelled is never the best idea.

'Did you know that they found Joe Strachan's remains?'

Now that, I thought, hit a nerve. Dunbar looked taken aback, then a little confused, then he returned to suspicious hostility. All a little overdone, perhaps. 'No I didn't. And I couldn't care fucking less.'

'Didn't you read it in the papers?' asked Archie.

'Oh, it fucking talks . . . Naw. I didn't read nothing.'

There you go again with the double negatives, I thought. 'He was dredged up from the bottom of the Clyde,' I said. 'They reckon he's been there since Thirty-eight.'

Dunbar smirked. A knowing smirk. 'They do, do they? Well whoopee-fucking-doo. Now, if you don't mind, I've got work to do.'

'I thought you were off today,' I said. He took a step towards me.

'I'm getting fed up with this. I have had nothing to do with all of that shite since my last stretch in Barlinnie. You say Joe Strachan's dead, fine, Joe Strachan's dead. I haven't heard the name in ten years, and I don't want to get involved with whatever you're up to.'

'All we're up to is finding out information about Joe Strachan, nothing else,' I said. 'No big deal. We're not looking to solve the crime of the century or recover stolen cash or settle scores. We're working for Strachan's daughters, who want to get to the bottom of what happened to their father, that's all.'

'Well you're looking in the wrong direction,' he said. 'Listen, I did ten years in Barlinnie: ten hard, hard years of getting fucking birched for any excuse, dodging the old queers and keeping away from the mad bastards and trying not to turn into one myself. I was twenty-two when I went in. I lost the best years of my life and I knew from the first day that I never wanted to go back to that, so I went straight. I came out in Thirty-seven and I'd only been out a couple of months when the polis picked me up and beat the shite out of me because they thought I'd been in on the Empire job. Broken nose and jaw, cracked ribs, four broken fingers on my right hand.' He looked down at the hand of the arm looped under the shotgun, as if examining the long-healed injury. 'One of the coppers fucking stamped on it. It's never been right since. I told them then that I knew fuck all and that's what I'm telling you now.'

'Why did they pick on you?' asked Archie.

'A copper was dead. That was all the reason they needed. Every name they had was pulled in. The bastard who stamped on my hand was a pal of the dead cop.'

'McNab?' I took a wild shot.

'Aye . . .' Dunbar looked surprised. 'Willie McNab. He became a big shot in the CID afterwards. Anyway, the other reason they picked on me is the job I did ten years for . . . they suspected that Joe Strachan had planned it, but couldn't prove it.'

'Had he planned it?'

Dunbar looked at me as if I had said something stupid. 'If

Joe Strachan had planned that job, I would never have got caught.'

'Did you do jobs with Strachan?' I asked and got the look again. 'Okay, did you *know* Strachan?'

'I knew him all right. Not well, but I knew about him. He was beginning to make a name for himself in the Twenties. Even back then the polis were desperate to nail him. There were a lot of big jobs being put down to Strachan. Not just robberies but frauds, blackmail, housebreakings ... The coppers could never prove it was Strachan.'

'But if he had that scope of operation, he must have had a regular team.'

'Aye, that's as maybes. But who they were was anybody's guess. That was another reason the coppers picked on me. *Because* I had kept my nose clean after prison. The theory they had was that Strachan either picked men without criminal records, or, if it was someone with form, told them not to do any other jobs than his and to keep their noses clean and their mouths shut between jobs. You know, the coppers never recovered a single fucking penny from any of the Triple Crown robberies? Not a single banknote was ever traced. That means Strachan must have had his laundry and distribution all planned out well before. But I'm only telling you what every other bastard knows. Like I told you, I know fuck all else. You could have saved your coupon.'

Dunbar referred to the petrol coupon it would have cost to make the trip up from Glasgow. Petrol rationing had ended five years before, but the expression had lingered.

'Okay,' I said resignedly. 'Thanks for your help anyway.' I

handed him a card. 'That's my office number if anything should occur to you.'

'It won't.'

'Fair enough,' I said wearily. 'Mr Dunbar, I hope you know we weren't trying to tie you into anything or anything like that. Our interest is quite simply to let a family know if the body recovered from the Clyde is that of their father, that's all. I'm sorry we disturbed you.' I handed him a five pound note. 'That's for your time. I have to say there would have been more if you had been able to help.'

I lifted my hat an inch and turned, leaving Dunbar staring at the fiver in his hand. Archie followed me, looking disappointed, which really didn't signify anything in Archie's case.

'That's that, then,' he said.

'Not quite. He has something to tell us. Something he really wants to tell us. And I think I already know what it is, but I want to hear it from him. That's why I've left my number.'

'Wait!'

'Yes, Mr Dunbar?'

'I was telling you the truth, I didn't have anything to do with the Empire robbery or any other Strachan job. And I've never seen Strachan since before I went to prison.'

'But?'

'But I've got some information that will cost you twenty-five pounds.'

'That all depends on what it is,' I said, but started to walk back towards Dunbar, making a show of taking my wallet out.

'It's about the body at the bottom of the Clyde.'
'You can tell me who it was?'
'No. But I can tell you who it wasn't . . .'

CHAPTER TEN

Dunbar reluctantly agreed to my request that his wife make us all a nice cup of tea and we could sit and discuss the information he had. Dunbar was certainly no matinee idol, and from the frugality of the cottage's interior, he clearly didn't have two pennies to rub together, so I was expecting his wife to be homely.

I was in for a surprise. Mrs Dunbar, who greeted us with a hostile glare and a grunt when we introduced ourselves, would have needed a team of Hollywood's finest plastic surgeons and cosmeticians to get her even within sight of the outermost suburbs of homely. Hers was the kind of ugliness that one normally took pity on, but my brief exposure to her personality relieved me of that burden. I could understand now why Dunbar had been so reluctant to admit us and I promised myself to bring a scythe and a polished shield the next time I visited the cottage.

'So, Mr Dunbar,' I said after his wife left the room: we were clearly not going to get a cup of tea. 'So, what is it you have to tell me?'

'Money first.'

'No, Billy, I'll pay you afterwards. I know you're going to tell me that it wasn't Gentleman Joe at the bottom of the Clyde. I knew that from your reaction when I told you about the remains right at the start. So you don't have much to bargain with, other than telling me *how* you know. But I promise you you won't be short changed, so spill some beans.'

'I volunteered for the army when war broke out, but they wouldn't have me: my age and my record went against me. So I ended up working here, on this estate, for the Duke. With so many men away at war, he was so short staffed he would take on anyone.'

'I know,' I said. 'The hell of war . . . making do with only three under-butlers must have scarred him for life.'

'Don't talk about His Grace that way. He did his bit in the war. And he's been good to me. If I hadn't found this place, I'd probably have had no choice other than to go back on the rob.'

'Okay, Billy, don't bust a lung. Just tell me your story.'

'Well, during the war the Duke was hardly ever here. He was one of the top commanders in the Scottish Home Guard. And he got me into it. The Home Guard, I mean.'

'Great . . .' I said. 'So you could guard railway stations and that kind of thing?'

'Well, no.' Something dark clouded Dunbar's expression, as if he really didn't want to go into what he was about to go into. 'Did you serve in the war?'

'Yes. Canadian First Army. Captain.'

'Canadian First, eh? You fellows had a rough time of it, all

181

right. I know what you must think of the Home Guard. A joke. Old men with brooms instead of rifles, unfit for duty boys guarding libraries and church halls?'

'No, as a matter of fact that's not at all what I think.'

'Well, for the first time in my life, my criminal record worked for me, not against me. The Duke called me up to the big house and I was interviewed by him and three other officers. They told me my *special* skills could maybe be useful.'

'In the Home Guard?' I tried to keep the incredulity out of my voice.

'In the Auxiliary Units.'

Now that took me aback. I reappraised Dunbar. He was a tough enough looking nut all right and it wasn't that incredible.

'What are the Auxiliary Units?' asked Archie.

'Officially they were members of the Home Guard,' I explained. 'Especially in places like this, where there are a lot of men used to working in the open and with a knowledge of the terrain. But they had special training and duties. Didn't you, Billy?'

'We was called Auxiliers. Or *Scallywags*. Like Mr Lennox said, we was officially attached to Two-Oh-One Home Guard Scotland.'

'But I thought all the Scallywags were based along the south coast of England,' I said.

'Aye, most were, but there were Scallywags in every part of the country. We was a special unit up here. You see, the Highlands were so fucking empty of people that they were worried that the Germans would drop agents and paratroopers into the Highlands in force to cause shite up here while the invasion took place somewhere else. A sort of Arnhem in reverse.'

'It was preparation for the invasion that never came,' I explained to Archie. 'Forget everything you think of when you think of the Home Guard. These guys were highly trained assassins and saboteurs, but you would never have known. Farmers, doctors, teachers, postmen . . . game-keepers. If the invasion took place and ended in occupa-tion, the Scallywags were to kill anybody who could be of use to the Nazis.'

'There's still explosives ammunition and guns hidden,' said Dunbar. 'We was to create as much fucking mayhem as possible. We was to be issued with seven weeks' rations if the invasion happened. The powers that be reckoned that after two weeks of action, we'd all be fucking dead.'

'This is all very interesting, Billy,' I said, 'but what has this got to do with Gentleman Joe Strachan?'

'I was getting to that. We was sent to Lochailort, way up in the middle of fucking nowhere on the west coast. It was where all the special units got their training. This wee fucking Highland village full of Beaverette armoured cars and machine gun posts all over the shop. The navy base there was where we was trained. You have no fucking idea the things they taught us. How to cut throats so that the fuckers dropped without a sound, how to make homemade bombs and them flame fougasses.'

'What's a fougasse?' asked Archie.

'A big fuck-off improvised incendiary. Five or ten-gallon

barrels of petrol buried or hidden with a detonator attached. Some could be as big as fifty gallons. Anti-tank and personnel carrier stuff. Torches everything and everybody to fuck. I saw three of our boys burn to death in training when one of those fuckers went off accidentally. Anyway, we got all of this training. Hand-to-hand combat. Defendu, have you heard of it?'

'Defendu . . . the Fairbairn system? Yes, I've heard of it,' I said. 'In the Canadian army we had Arwrology, which was pretty much the same thing.'

'Aye. Defendu was invented by that bloke that designed the commando knife. But if you came from Glasgow you didn't need to learn Defendu, we already had *fuck-you*.' He laughed at his own joke. I made an impatient face.

'Anyway, we was there for six weeks solid training, then back for another six. There was all kinds of brass hanging around the place, from every secret outfit you could imagine. We was under the command of the Special Operations executive, but there were commandos, Special Air, Special Boat brass, and others from units that I'd never heard of. It was during our second stint at Lochailort that I saw this officer, a major, with a group of others. One of the other officers this bloke was talking to was His Grace, who was a colonel. The officer I saw was one of ours . . . I mean he was Special Operations. And the other officers including His Grace was all attached to Scallywag training.'

'Joe Strachan?'

Dunbar looked surprised that I'd jumped his conclusion.

'I found out quite a bit about Strachan,' I offered in explanation. 'Do you think he was genuine? I mean a real officer and not just passing himself off as one?'

'You was in the army, you know what them special bases are like with security. Naw, if Joe Strachan was wearing a British Army major's uniform in that camp, then Joe Strachan was a British Army major.'

'Aw, come on . . .' Archie snorted. 'A Glasgow hoodlum like Strachan an army major? I thought you had to be an officer and a gentleman, not an officer and a gobshite . . .'

I held up my hand to stop Archie. He stopped, but his eyebrows protested for a few seconds more.

'Could you have been mistaken?' I asked Dunbar.

'Maybe. But I got a really good look at the fucker. I did one of them double takes. I mean, everybody's supposed to have a double, aren't they. Look at Monty. If this bloke wasn't Gentleman Joe, he was his bastarding twin.'

'I'm not being funny,' said Archie, 'but it maybe *was* his twin. You say Strachan's daughters are twins, and twins run in families . . .'

'Naw,' said Dunbar emphatically. 'Joe Strachan maybe became a man of mystery, but he was born in the Gorbals and there are no fucking mysteries or secrets there, when you're crammed into a tenement with four families on each fucking floor. Strachan had two sisters and a brother. No twin. I'm fucking telling you, I saw Gentleman Joe Strachan as large as life and twice as fucking ugly, swanning about with a bunch of top brass and crowns on his shoulder boards.'

'When was this?'

'Forty-two. Summer of Forty-two.'

'You tell anyone else about this?'

Dunbar looked at me contemptuously. 'After the hiding I took in a police cell because they thought there was the slightest fucking chance that I might know something or someone that could lead them to someone else who might know more about Joe Strachan? Naw ... I kept my mouth shut. Nobody knows what I saw. Until you, that is.'

There it was. Gentleman Joe hadn't, after all, slept the deep, dark sleep. Of course, it didn't mean he was still alive. If he had been attached to Special Operations, then he could be sleeping the dark sleep at the bottom of some canal in Holland or river in France. But even that thought – Joe Strachan as an officer in SOE – didn't make the slightest bit of sense.

Dunbar had told us what he had to tell us and small talk, even expletive-laced small talk, was not his forte, so it was time for us to leave. As I got up a thought came at me from out of nowhere; or at least from somewhere deep in the back of my brain where it must have been taking slow form during my chat with Dunbar. Actually it was more an image than a thought. For some reason the picture I had retrieved from Paul Downey came to mind.

'Are you around most nights, Billy?' I asked. 'I have a photograph I'd like to show you. I think there's a good chance, given what you've just told me, that it could be the only picture in existence of Joe Strachan. Can I come back and show you it?'

'Aye ... I suppose,' said Dunbar grudgingly. 'But I usually go to the pub on my night off.'

'I'll not be back for a day or two, but it'll only take a few minutes, Billy,' I said. 'And I'll make it worth your while. Oh, and there's one more thing before I go – and this has got nothing to do with Strachan – it's just something I'm curious about because of something that came up recently. Do you know the Duke's son, Iain?'

'Aye, I know him all right.'

'What's he like?'

'He's a wee shite. Nothing like his father. Absolutely nothing like. A fucking waster.'

'And?'

'And what?'

'Come on, Billy, we both know he's a shirt lifter.'

'Listen, I'm not going to say anything that could harm his father. God knows His Grace doesn't have to seek his trouble with that wee bastard already. Whatever dirt you're after, you'll not get it here.'

'Fair enough, Billy, but tell me what you can. Believe it or not I'm trying to protect, not damage, the family name.'

'Iain is so different to his father that you sometimes wonder if His Grace is his father at all. They don't look alike, they don't behave alike, they don't have the same values.'

'With the greatest respect, Billy, you're just a gamekeeper here . . . how do you know all this?'

'Everybody knows it. Everybody knows everything about everybody else. When you work for a family like this, in a place like this, there are no fucking secrets.'

'Iain has a cottage on the estate, is that right?'

'Aye, he calls it his studio, the wee prick. He thinks he's fucking Picasso or some shite.'

'And he entertains there?'

'Aye.' Dunbar eyed me knowingly. 'He *entertains* there all right.'

'Have you ever seen anybody odd hanging around the cottage?'

'You're fucking joking, right? When have I *not* seen someone odd hanging around. There are always oddballs and freaks up there. The artistic set, Iain calls them. Artistic my arse.'

'No, I mean anyone other than that lot. You've been around, Billy, you know the type, anyone who looked like they might be trouble.'

'Can't say I have, why?'

'Duke Junior's got himself into a little trouble, that's all. I've been trying to sort it out, for his father's sake, so to speak.'

'Right, well that's a different fucking story ... if there's anything I can do to help, just give me the fucking word ...'

'Thanks, Billy, I'll bear that in mind. But it looks like it's all sorted out now in any case.' I stood up from the table. I took out my wallet and peeled off twenty-five pounds. I could see Billy's eyes light up and I knew that it was double what he'd been expecting, but I kept peeling until I had put fifty on the table.

Spread the wealth, Lennox, I thought. Spread the wealth.

*

'You do know, you've maybe just been taken for a ride,' said Archie helpfully, once we were on our way back to Glasgow. 'I tell you what, if I tell you a lot of shite about how I saw Adolf Hitler in a bookie's in Niddrie, will you give me fifty quid?'

'No, because it's obviously not true: Hitler would give himself up to the Israelis before living in Niddrie. I saw the look on Dunbar's face when I told him about the body in the Clyde. I knew there and then that he didn't believe it was Strachan's.'

'So, you actually believe Strachan is hob-nobbing with the upper-crust and been made an officer in the army? "Here you go, Strachan, old boy, let's forget all about that minor unpleasantness of the policeman you murdered, and the fact that you were a deserter in the First War, and we'll all go and have some tea and tiffin in the officer's mess"?'

'Leave the sarcastic wit to me, Archie. I know it doesn't make any sense, but I believe Dunbar saw what he said he saw.'

'Listen, boss, I don't want to tell you how to do your job . . .'

'Heaven forfend, Archie.'

'. . . but you all but waved that cash in front of his face. He obviously felt he *had* to tell you something. And that bollocks about Strachan being an officer was the best he could come up with at the time.'

'No, Archie. The best he could have come up with would have been to say he saw Strachan at that bookie's in Niddrie you saw Hitler in, or on a street in Edinburgh or a railway station in Dundee. The thing that makes me believe he's telling the truth is exactly that it is so unbelievable. Dunbar's been interrogated by the police so often in his life that he knows that if he's going to tell a lie, make that lie simple and credible. You know that.'

'So where does that leave us? Where do we go from here?'

'Well, I've got a few names I want you to check out, from the list Isa and Violet gave me. Watch who and where you ask though, Archie. In the meantime, I'm going to have to make a couple of visits I've been putting off.'

I met Fiona White for tea at Cranston's. We sat in the Art Nouveau tearoom and ordered tea and salmon sandwiches. She was wearing a smart outfit that I hadn't seen her in before and what looked like a new hat. I also noticed that she was wearing a deeper shade of crimson lipstick and more make-up than I'd seen her wear before. I was flattered by the effort.

'How are your new digs?' she asked, a little awkwardly.

'Very exclusive,' I said. 'I have to be constantly careful that I don't bark, talk in brogue or tan too deeply.'

She made a puzzled face. A pretty, puzzled face.

'It's okay,' I said. 'It'll do me in the meantime. It keeps me dry, unless I get too close to the landlord when he's talking.'

'I see,' she said. 'There's been no one around the house. No one suspicious, I mean,' she added. 'I've noticed the local bobby keeping an eye on us, but there really hasn't been anything to cause me any concern.'

'I'm glad to hear it. I'm sorry that you've been inconvenienced by all of this, Mrs White.'

'Fiona ...' she said in a quiet voice that cracked halfway through the word. She cleared her throat. Her face reddened. 'You don't have to call me Mrs White. Call me Fiona.'

'In that case, you don't have to call me Mr Lennox.'

'What shall I call you then?'

'Lennox. Everybody does. I'm sorry you've been inconvenienced, Fiona.'

'It's no inconvenience. But the girls have missed you around the house.'

'Just the girls?'

For a second, I got a hint of the frosty defiance I'd been accustomed to. Then it melted.

'No, not just the girls. Why don't you come back to your rooms? I don't think there's any danger.'

'You didn't see the guy who jumped me. There's something going on with this Strachan thing that I don't understand. But I'm beginning to get ideas and those ideas tell me that there are some very dangerous people involved. I don't want to place you or the girls at risk.'

'Listen, Lennox, I've thought about what you said to me, about how you felt. I'm sorry if I seemed a little ... *unresponsive*. I said the things I said because I meant them. Or at least I meant them when I said them. It's just that ... I don't know, just that I'm not the kind of woman you're used to. I'm not experienced with men or sophisticated in any sense. When I married Robert, I thought that was it. I saw my entire life ahead of me; how it would be. That's what I thought I wanted back then. Then, when he was killed, it wasn't just that I'd lost him, I'd lost myself. What I had decided I wanted to be.'

'I know you're not going to believe this, Fiona, but I know exactly what you mean. A lot of us lost our way during the war, became people we didn't know we could be. Didn't want to be. But that's the hand we were dealt. All we can do is make the most of it. Nothing can bring your husband back and nothing can take away the things I did in the war. But we can try to move on. To find some kind of happiness.'

'I think you should come back.' Fiona looked down at the tablecloth. 'I can't promise you anything, say anything will change. But I would like you to come back.'

'I want that too, Fiona, but I can't. Not yet. I have messed up so many things in my life, but I'm damned if I'm going to mess this up. I'll be back as soon as I am sure I'm not going to bring a lot of trouble home with me.'

'But for all we know, the man who attacked you still thinks you live at home. If anything we're in more danger without you being there.'

'This is more than one man. And they're clever operators and they know I'm not there any more. I'm just hoping they haven't traced me to where I am now.'

'The police . . .'

'Can't help me. At least not officially, and I think I've squeezed the last drop of goodwill out of Jock Ferguson. Listen, it'll be over soon and I'll come back.' I laid my hand on hers. It tensed, as if she was going to pull away, then relaxed. 'Then we can talk.'

*

I went back to my office to finish up a few things before heading back to my temporary accommodation at the boarding house. I was just taking my raincoat off the coat rack when someone swung open my office door without first knocking. I turned and my heart sank. I suddenly realized that not conceiving of anyone worse than Hammer Murphy to share my company with only highlighted the limits of my imagination.

The man in front of me was six foot three and in his early fifties. He had broad shoulders and a brutal, cruel face. He was, as he had been every time I'd encountered him, dressed with precise and totally unimaginative neatness. In tweed. He decided to take the weight off his brogues without waiting to be asked. Like not knocking on a door before entering, waiting to be invited to sit down was something that Detective Chief Superintendent Willie McNab did not do.

I decided it was best if I sat too. I preferred to have something substantial like a desk, or a continent, between me and McNab. I watched the door, waiting for some burly Highlander in an off-the-peg Burton suit to come in after McNab: one of the privileges of rank was that you didn't have to do your own beating of suspects. To my surprise none came.

'To what do I owe . . .?' I asked McNab.

'You know exactly why I'm here, so don't piss me about.'

'I tell you what, Superintendent, just so's we're clear, why don't you spell it out for me?'

'You've been sticking your nose into this Strachan business. You ought to know by now that I get to hear everything that goes on in this city, and anything that's of special interest to me, I find out fast. What have you found out?'

'Nothing of interest to the police,' I said.

'Who are you working for?'

'Sorry. Client confidentiality.'

'Oh aye, client confidentiality.' McNab nodded sagely, as if appreciating the concept. 'Do you know why *client confidentiality* and *the shite* are very similar?'

'I'm sure you'll enlighten me.'

McNab did six foot three of standing up and leaned across the desk, bringing his face close to mine.

'Client confidentiality is like the shite because both can be knocked out of you in the cells at St Andrew's Square.'

I found it interesting that McNab and Hammer Murphy, although on opposite sides of the criminal justice fence, had the same approach to my professional ethics.

'You know something, McNab?' I said. 'I don't think so. A year or two ago you could maybe have gotten away with that, but I don't play in that end of the playground any more. I'm a respectable businessman.'

'You reckon?'

'I reckon. But that's not the only reason I don't think that will happen. You've come up here on your own and without due cause to arrest me, so why don't you tell me the real reason you're here? I'm sure it has to do with Strachan, but there's something odd in the ether.'

Despite the assurance with which I said it, I was surprised when McNab did sit back down. He took out a packet of Navy Cut and lit one. After a moment's thought, he offered me one.

'No thanks,' I said, more because I was taken aback by the

offer than anything else. 'I want to be able to speak tomorrow morning. What's the deal, Superintendent?'

He took off his trilby and threw it onto the desk.

'Lennox, you and I have had our moments. I don't like you and you don't like me. But one thing about you that I've noticed is that every time I've tried to get information from you, you've risked a beating or jail time by telling me where to go. So I suppose you have your own code of ethics, no matter how bollocksed-up they may be. You know I dug the dirt on you from your time in Germany after the war. That German black-marketeer who ended up face down in the harbour, for example. The one the Military Police suspected was your business partner . . .'

'Is there a point to this character analysis, McNab?'

'I don't care what happened in Hamburg, but I care what happens in Glasgow. Joseph Strachan murdered Charlie Gourlay. He gunned him down in cold blood and I want to see the bastard swing for it.'

'But he's dead, Superintendent. Officially, legally dead.'

'You don't believe that shite any more than I do. That wasn't Joe Strachan at the bottom of the Clyde. I can't prove it, but I know it. Strachan was too clever to be caught, and he was too clever to be topped by one of his own team.'

'So whose bones were dredged up?'

'I don't know. But they weren't Strachan's, I'll tell you that. Listen, Lennox, I've been a copper in this town for nearly thirty years. I've dealt with some of the hardest, most vicious bastards ever to foul the Earth with their presence. I've put a noose around the necks of over a dozen men: from kiddie-fiddlers to professional killers, from psychopaths to razor gangs. I've seen every type of fiend and monster you can imagine. But Joe Strachan is out there in a league of his own.'

'Is he?' I decided to play dumb. 'From all of the "Gentleman Joe" crap you hear, and the way he's idolized by every crook in Glasgow, you'd think he was some kind of folk hero.'

'Do you know, we don't have a single photograph of him on record? Or his fingerprints? He was questioned a dozen times but never arrested, far less charged. But do you know why we kept bringing him in? Glasgow criminals back then weren't the brightest or most capable of villains. The basic principle was to batter the fuck out of something until you got money from it. Most of the stuff we dealt with was razor gang stuff, or small time robbers getting caught because they didn't have the basic brains to plan a job properly. Things have changed. Now we've got your pals, the so-called Three Kings. Things have become organized. And do you know who started that? Who gave them the idea for that? Joe Strachan. But he was much, much better at it than they are. He didn't try to control everything, to make every protection gang pay him protection, the way Sneddon, Cohen and Murphy do. Strachan assessed the risks and the rewards. He only went for the big hit, the big money. And he picked only the very best for each job.'

'All of this I already know,' I said.

'Aye? Well what you probably *don't* know is that some people talked: a handful of disgruntled crooks whose noses were put out of joint because Strachan didn't pick them. One of them was already a paid informant. All of them turned up dead. Or presumed dead. Never a body to be found. No traces.'

'Strachan killed them?'

'His enforcer did. Someone else with no record. A name we never got. All we got from our informant was that this enforcer was young, and a protégé of Strachan's. Strachan only ever called him the Lad. His apprentice. He may have been young, but he kept everyone who worked for Strachan in line. Like I said, he was a cool and professional killer. From the little we got, we know that Strachan treated him like a son.'

'Hammer Murphy worked for Strachan for a while . . .' I kept the dumb act going.

McNab laughed. 'No way. Murphy was building his own wee empire with his brothers. They did jobs with Strachan, but not for long. My guess is that Strachan realized what a psychopath Murphy was and stopped using him because he was unstable. And that meant unreliable. If there was one thing Strachan demanded from his teams, it was reliability.' McNab paused to take a long draw on his cigarette. 'Who hired you to look into this, Lennox?'

'Now, Superintendent . . . you know I'm not going to tell you.'

'It would be in your best interests.'

'What . . . to avoid a beating?'

'No. Listen, Lennox, sometimes you've got to put the past behind you, along with your personal feelings about people. Sometimes people who would never have thought it possible have to work together.'

'What are you proposing?'

'I know you've been tapping Detective Inspector Ferguson for information. That's a dripping tap I can turn off permanently. But, for the moment, I'm going to do nothing. I'm also not going to put a man on your tail, twenty-four hours a day, following your every move and visiting every client we see you make contact with.'

'That's good of you, Superintendent. I'm guessing there's a *quid* for your *quo*?'

'I retire in two years, Lennox. I've bought a place out in Helensburgh and me and the wife are going to move out there, away from the city, after I leave the job. I want to have a quiet, peaceful retirement. But I'm not going to be at ease if I know that Joseph Strachan is still out there, enjoying life without paying for murdering Charlie Gourlay.'

'Then why not just accept that that was Strachan at the bottom of the Clyde?'

'Because I know it wasn't. And, like I said, I'm pretty sure you know it wasn't.'

This was a surprising conversation. It was about to become even more surprising. Ferguson took an envelope out of his pocket and dropped it onto my desk.

'There's four hundred pounds in there, Lennox. That's almost exactly what a City of Glasgow police constable earns in a whole year.'

I picked up the envelope, more to convince myself it wasn't an hallucination.

'You want to *hire* me? Or is this from the City Police's snout fund?' I asked incredulously. Why was everybody so keen to throw cash at me all of a sudden . . .

'This isn't informer cash. It's my money, not the Force's. Yes, I do want to hire you. I have spent nearly twenty years trying to bring Strachan to justice. As much as I hate to admit it, I need someone like you, someone who isn't a police detective and who can get to information that I can't.'

I tossed the envelope back onto the table in front of him.

'I can't.'

'You won't, you mean? Listen, Lennox, you help me out on this, and I'll make sure that there are doors stay open to you in the City of Glasgow Police long after I retire.'

'Okay, listen. I would help you, but there could be a conflict of interest.'

'You mean whoever's hired you already?'

'Something like that.' I sighed, this was complicated and confusing. I was having a conversation that I never would have envisaged myself having with McNab. 'Okay, here's the deal. I've been hired by Strachan's daughters to confirm or otherwise that that was Gentleman Joe who was dredged up.'

'I don't see the conflict of interest,' said McNab. 'You can tell them that and point me in the right direction. I know you've had a lot of shady stuff in your background, but I also know that you're the kind of man who wouldn't sit still and let someone get away with murder, whether it's a policeman's murder or not.'

'It would be a mistake to overestimate my nobility, McNab. But from what I've heard about Strachan, yes, it wouldn't upset me to see him caught. But we have different furrows to plough, Superintendent.'

'Give me something, Lennox.'

Again I paused, struggling with where I was with this.

'Okay, like I said, I am looking into Strachan's disappearance for his daughters. I had only made a couple of enquiries, barely putting my head above the parapet, when some guy jumps me in a foggy alley and tells me to lay off. Now this guy could handle himself, I mean really handle himself. Not like a street thug, more like a commando. It gets me thinking, if Strachan is dead, why am I getting serious professional advice to drop it?'

McNab's broad face lit up with something. I was telling him what he wanted to hear. I decided not to tell him that my dance partner had stuck a gun in my back.

'Then . . . and don't ask me how I found this out, because I'm not going to tell you . . . but then I get an account from an eyewitness who swears he saw Strachan during the war. In the summer of Nineteen forty-two, to be exact.'

McNab looked as if an electrical charge had just run through him. 'I knew it! I bloody knew it! Where?'

'Now don't get too excited . . .' I tried to inject a cautious tone. 'The rest of this doesn't seem to make a lot of sense, so just hear me through. This eyewitness, whom I tend to believe, said that he saw Strachan wearing the uniform of a major up at Lochailort. My witness reckons that Strachan was involved in the training of Auxiliary Units.'

I could see the electricity drain from McNab. 'That can't have been Strachan,' he said.

'That's what I thought to start with too, but don't dismiss it. I found out about Strachan's less than glorious service in the First War. He regularly went AWOL, wearing officers' uniforms and made an embarrassingly good job of passing himself off as an officer. You know yourself that he probably passed himself off as some plausible upper-class type to carry out reconnaissance of the locations of each of his major robberies. So Strachan being seen in an officer's uniform isn't that big a leap.'

'But you said he was at Lochailort. There's no way anyone, even Strachan, could have bluffed his way in there without the right papers and without others knowing exactly who he was and from what unit.'

'That's where I get stuck. And that's where we could do a little *quid pro quo*. I can't gain access to that kind of information; but you can.'

'I don't know, Lennox. There's only so much the City of Glasgow Police can get out of the military. Especially about places like Lochailort, that are still subject to the Official Secrets Act.'

'You've got a better chance than me.'

'And what do I get in return?'

'A call. If I find that Strachan is alive, and if I discover where he's hidden himself, I'll stick a couple of pennies in a pay 'phone. You probably won't believe this, but I've already cautioned my clients that if I do find Strachan is alive and well, I would be compelled to do my civic duty.'

'Just make sure no one gets a five-minute start, Lennox. Or our new found chumminess may falter.' In a gesture of purposeful ceremony, McNab used two fingers to push the envelope across the table towards me. I pushed it back.

'Like I said, Mr McNab, civic duty. Keep your money.'

McNab paused for a moment as if assessing me, then shrugged and pocketed the envelope as he stood up.

'Can I use your 'phone?' he asked, but had already spun it around to face him and lifted the receiver.

'Superintendent McNab here,' he said after a moment. 'I'm clocking off. Anything come in before I head home?'

He sighed as he listened to the answer, then took his notebook from his coat and scribbled into it.

'No rest for the wicked, I guess,' I said after he hung up.

'I've got to go,' he said. 'There's been a murder. Some nancy-boy out in Govanhill . . .'

CHAPTER ELEVEN

After McNab left, I tried unsuccessfully to get a hold of Jock Ferguson. He was on duty, the desk sergeant who answered the 'phone told me, but was out on a call.

Of course it could, I tried to convince myself, be a pure coincidence. But how many 'nancy-boys', as McNab called them, could there be in Govanhill? And like Glasgow Corporation buses, coincidences tended to come along in threes. Maybe Jock Ferguson had been called out to another case, but I couldn't stop the reel on the scene playing in my head: Jock Ferguson standing over the body and suddenly remembering, probably the instant McNab arrived, that the name of the deceased just happened to be the same as one of the names I asked him to check out for me.

I decided to grab the bull by the horns and drive over to the tenement. On the way over I would have to do a lot of quick thinking on how I was going to explain my interest, but without bringing Hollywood stars or minor royalty into it. I had just put on my hat and coat when I checked myself. Of course, that had not been Paul Downey's flat; it was Frank, the muscle-bound pool attendant, whose name was on the rent book. Maybe it was he who had been murdered, which meant I had some time before flat-feet plodded along a trail that would lead them to Paul Downey. But, pedestrian as they were, the CID would eventually make the connection, and Jock Ferguson would make another.

For once, I was grateful for the smog. It had come back with a vengeance and I decided to take the Underground to Kinning Park and hoof it the rest of the way. I walked past the end of the road, but the fog was too thick for me to see the far end and whether or not there were police cars parked outside. Walking past the street end, I turned into the next, which ran parallel to Frank's, and walked almost to its end before cutting through a tenement passageway and into the communal back court.

The communal court was a vast rectangle, fringed by tenements on all sides and punctuated by small, squat wash-houses and clusters of trashcans and heaped rubbish. The demarcation between each tenement's section of yard was marked by low railings, most of which were broken.

It was the kind of place the Black Death would have been happy to call home.

The court was overlooked by the backs of tenements on both streets, as well as the blocks at either end that connected them into a stretched rectangle. Not that there was much overlooking being done: the fog had dimmed the light from the windows to vague glows in the gloom and the far end of the rectangle was completely obscured. As I crossed the court, stepping through or over the railings I came to, I guessed I was pretty well concealed. The fogged air of the yard carried a rank smell and the cobbles beneath my feet felt slimy and I had to concentrate on not losing my footing. A sudden noise halted me when I was about halfway across and I froze for a moment, then realized it was something scuttling around in the trashcans. I continued my progress across the court: if I had calculated right, I would be directly opposite the tenement I'd followed Frank to. I listened for a moment but could hear no voices anywhere near, so I guessed the back court was empty behind Frank's, but I didn't want to take the risk of bumping into a copper taking a leak or having a crafty smoke.

As I drew closer, I could have sworn the air became denser and suffused with the smell of burning.

When I could see the tenements opposite more clearly, I angled my approach to take me towards the tenement next to Frank's and the acrid tinge to the air intensified. I could just make out, further down and behind Frank's tenement, a scattering of black-silhouetted objects. And voices. Many voices. I crept closer until I reached the first object: a scorched and blackened armchair that was still warm to the touch, despite having been doused in water.

Finding my way back to the neighbouring tenement close, I crept along the porcelain-tiled passageway towards its opening onto the street. I pressed my back to the tiles as I grew close to the passage's mouth, easing my head around to check out the street. I pulled back quickly: there was a copper about ten feet from me, guarding the next close which led to Frank's tenement. It had only been the briefest glance, but I had also been able to make out a large red Bedford fire engine parked out front, its crew talking and smoking. I'd also caught sight of a row of black police Wolseleys parked at the street end.

So that was that. The murder McNab had been called to *was* that of either Frank or Paul Downey. Fantastic. I wondered how long it would take Jock to make the connection. After that, whichever of the couple had survived could tell the police that I had slapped them both around and threatened to come back with my pals for a real party. And, if they took my fingerprints, they would find a veritable constellation of matching dabs in the flat.

Just half an hour before, McNab had been taking me into his confidence, something that was generally as conceivable as Dwight and Nikita having a slumber party together, and now it would be a matter of a day or so before he took me into custody. Nice going, Lennox.

What confused me was the presence of the fire brigade and the tossed-out furniture. The good news was that if there had been a fire in the flat, then there was a chance that my fingerprints would not be recoverable.

I heard voices as someone came out of the other tenement passage; I recognized one of them as belonging to McNab. He was talking to his subordinate about various arrangements, none of which gave me any insight as to which of my pals was now deceased or how he met his demise. I decided to get out of the area before I added another circumstance to the circumstantial case against me. I moved quickly and silently along the passage and into the back court again. This time I headed straight across, wanting to distance myself from the murder scene as quickly as possible. The fog seemed to have thickened on the way back and I found I'd lost my bearings. Halfway across, I could no longer see either wall of tenements, but pressed on, reckoning that if I kept on going straight, I must eventually manage to reach the opposite side.

What I did manage was to walk straight into a collection of trashcans, knocking one over, its lid rattling on the cobbles. The noise echoed in the court, but not as loudly as I would have expected, muffled as it was by the blanket of smog. I stood still and silent for a moment. No voices, no dogs barking, no police whistles. I again set blind course through the fog and eventually washed up against the sooty sandstone shore of the tenements opposite. I couldn't see a passageway out onto the street again, but knew that if I moved along the tenements in either direction, I'd find one soon enough. The only problem was that I had to edge past the windows of the lower flats of the tenement until I reached the passage. Again I moved as quietly as I could, crouching as I passed an illuminated window.

It was the window that wasn't lit up that was my undoing.

I heard the sounds of a struggle: someone gasping for breath and grunting. For a moment I couldn't place where it was coming from, then I realized the sounds were issuing through a hole in the cracked window. I stood up and looked through the grimy glass, into the gloom inside. It was the usual tenement kitchen-cum-living room and the only light was the glow from the open door of the range, used for heating and cooking. The glow picked out the edges of a huge woman stretched over the rough kitchen table, leaning her elbows on it. She was hugely overweight and naked to the waist, the huge pale moons of her breasts swinging and the fat on her arms quivering with every lunge of the small, thin man behind her. He was balding, with strands of black hair pasted over his pale pate, and a Groucho Marx rectangle of moustache twitched beneath his thin nose with each impassioned thrust.

It was the same sort of thing as when you inadvertently see some unfortunate take ill in public and vomit in the street. You don't *want* to see it, but no matter how much it repulses you, once you've looked, you can't tear your eyes away. I froze.

Jack Spratt and his wife were clearly trying to keep as quiet as possible, probably because there were kids sleeping in the tenement flat's only other room, but the fat woman moaned:

'Lover boy. . . oh lover boy . . .'

I rammed a fist into my mouth and bit down hard, but still my shoulders shook uncontrollably.

'Oh Rab . . . you're my lover boy . . .'

Move, Lennox, I told myself. For God's sake move.

Then, in a moment of heightened passion, the skinny little man gave forth:

'Senga! Oh . . . *Senga!*'

Despite the danger of my situation, something over-rode my survival instinct and the fist stuffed in my mouth, and the laughter I'd been trying to contain threatened to explode. Something high-pitched and strangled sounded in my throat.

It was loud enough for the fat woman to hear. Looking up, she saw me at the window, let go a shrill scream and clutched her arms to her massive bosoms in a ludicrously inadequate effort to conceal her nakedness. The small man saw me too and, disengaging himself, charged towards the window, thankfully pulling his braces back up over his shoulders.

'Pervert!' he shouted in a high, shrill voice. 'You fucking pervert! Peeping Tom! Peeping Tom!'

I made a run for it, along the wall, hoping I would find the passageway out. Meanwhile, lover boy had swung open the window and was screaming for the police at the top of his voice.

Well done, Lennox.

I heard shouts and a whistle; the sound of more trashcans being toppled and I could see, somewhere at the other side of the court, torch beams stabbing the fog ineffectually. I ran on, hoping I didn't trip over anything else in the fog. I was not too concerned about the stumbling coppers behind me, but I knew that if someone actually had the brains to think it through, a car sent around the block, even at smog-driving pace, could catch me when I came out of the passage and onto the street.

I found the passage and sprinted along it and out onto the street. I reckoned at this time of night and in this fog, there would be few cars around and I ran straight out onto the road. I found the tramlines and ran, concentrating only on the small pool of awareness I had in the fog and keeping in the centre of the tramlines. I reached a curve and a TRAM

PINCH warning sign, just discernible on the periphery of my vision, told me I was now out of the side street and on the main drag. Still no ringing bells of a pursuing police Wolseley. And now it would be useless in the fog.

I ran on for a hundred yards more, then slowed to a trot, then a walk, then stopped, leaning over to catch my breath, my hands braced on my knees. When I had recovered enough, I straightened up and stood silent in the smog and listened. Nothing.

The only problem I had was that I now had no idea where I was. Suddenly, a vast shape loomed at me out of the smog, a monster with two burning embers for eyes, rattling towards me. I leapt to the side, lost my footing and fell, rolling on my side and out of the way of the tram that trundled past, the driver shouting some obscenity through the window, but not applying the brake to check that I was all right.

The tram was swallowed up again in the smog. I stood up, dusted myself off and picked up my bashed trilby.

'Bollocks,' I muttered. Then, as I found my way back to the pavement, I suddenly thought about Senga and Lover Boy, and burst into laughter.

This time, the smog was persistent. It had lurked all night and was pressing against the windows of my boarding house room when I woke the following morning. My tumble in the street was now playing vigorous accompaniment to what had been the decrescendo of the bruises I'd picked up in the alleyway. I headed into the office early, again taking the tram and not risking driving in the murk.

When I got to the office I tried to get Leonora Bryson by 'phone at the Central Hotel, but was told she and Mr Macready were in Edinburgh for press interviews. I was luckier with Fraser, the lawyer: I told him we had to meet urgently and for some reason he insisted that we didn't meet at his office, so I suggested Central Station in half an hour.

Despite my only having to cross the street to the station, Fraser managed to get there before me. There is a kind of protocol to sitting in railway cafés: if you are just having a cup of coffee, it should always be with a cigarette and you should hunch over your coffee and look miserable, as if the train you are waiting for is scheduled to take you to the final of all destinations. Fraser was breaching this etiquette of gloom. He was sitting with his straight back to the counter, facing the station concourse, his beady eyes alert. He spotted me coming and took his briefcase from the chair next to him. I ordered a coffee at the counter from the glummest man in the universe, carried it over and sat next to Fraser.

'This is not the ideal place to talk about what I want to talk about,' I said, casting an eye over the other patrons who might be within earshot.

'I thought our business regarding these photographs was concluded, Mr Lennox,' he said.

'So did I. I got a visit from the police the other day. We're *cooperating* on another case. While he was there, my contact let slip that he was dealing with a murder in Govanhill.'

'I would imagine that's not a particularly rare or noteworthy event . . .' Fraser frowned.

'Maybe so, but this murder was at the address I recovered the photographs from.'

Fraser looked shocked for a moment, then leaning forward, lowered his voice to the level I'd been speaking at. 'Paul Downey?'

'That I don't know. The flat was rented by his friend, Frank. I'll probably find out later today which of them is dead.'

'My God . . .' Fraser thought for a moment, then said conspiratorially, 'Is there anything, *anything* that can link us and the Macready business to that address?'

'One of the reasons I'm expecting to have the identity of the deceased today is because I'm expecting the police to call. I asked one of my contacts if he knew anything about Paul Downey. If it's Downey who's been murdered, then they're going to want to know why I was asking.'

'But you can't tell them, Mr Lennox!' Fraser looked around the café and lowered his voice. 'You know how sensitive this whole thing is. I have to say that I think it was very careless of you to ask the police about Downey.'

'It was a calculated risk, Mr Fraser. And the calculation didn't include Downey or his boyfriend turning up dead. As far as telling the police about the background to it all, I'll do my best to keep Macready out of it. But the police tend to take a poor view of murder and my neck is allergic to hemp, so if push comes to shove, we're all going to have to level with them . . .'

'After all we've been through, Mr Lennox, that would be most unfortunate. I'm afraid we would have to disavow all knowledge of you working for us. After all, we paid you in cash.' Fraser's beady eyes turned cold behind his spectacles. 'And I can assure you that all of the photographs and negatives have been destroyed. So there would be nothing to back up your claim that we employed you.'

I smiled. 'Well let's hope it doesn't come to that, because then I would have to spill every bean in the pot, including the fact that after I ran Paul Downey to ground, I only gave the address to two people . . . you and Leonora Bryson. Then it would boil down to a simple case of whom the police are more likely to believe. And I have a track record with them.' I failed to add that that track record just might work against me. 'And, of course, you would have to gamble that I didn't hang on to a couple of the negatives, as insurance against just such a sticky situation as this. Added to all of which is the fact that it takes a lot of balls to lie to the police when it relates to a murder inquiry. And, no offence, I don't think you've got them.'

'Well, as you say, let's hope it doesn't come to that.' If I had ruffled Fraser, he was hiding it very well. 'And I don't see that it should. I mean, this is all coincidental. An unfortunate coincidence admittedly, but a coincidence none the less. Let's be honest about it, it can be a very dark and dangerous world that these *people* inhabit. I would not be at all surprised if it turns out that one of them murdered the other during some kind of fall-out.'

'It could be. But if there's one thing I have noticed about coincidences, it's that they have a nasty habit of coming back and biting you in the ass.'

'So what do you suggest we do?'

'Sit tight for the time being. Like I said, I should know more later today. In the meantime, instead of threatening to throw each other to the wolves, I suggest you and I both try to think of ways to limit the damage if the police do ask questions.'

'Any suggestions, Mr Lennox?'

I paused to take a sip of the coffee I'd been nursing and immediately regretted it. I wondered if whatever was in my cup had come up in the same dredger bucket as the mystery bones.

'The police aren't bright, as you know, but they have so much experience of lies that they can spot one a mile off. Our best strategy is to tell them the truth. Just not the whole truth. The studio wants to protect Mr Macready's reputation. Well, I suggest that we tell the police absolutely everything that happened, including about the photographs, but we say that it was a woman he was *in flagrante* with. If any of it leaks out, then it only enhances his reputation as a ladies' man.'

'And if they ask the identity of the lady?'

'Then we say only Mr Macready knows that; he wouldn't tell even us. But if pushed, you could say that Macready told you that it was the wife of someone very important. You Brits are so respectful of your establishment that it may just prevent the police digging. In the meantime, Macready will be on a plane to the States on Monday. The City of Glasgow Police are not going to extradite him back to get a name. Anyway, the police are also great ones for applying Occam's Razor to everything: they look for the simplest explanation, mainly because it is usually the easiest. I'm hoping that they won't look at my involvement too hard.'

Fraser considered what I had said, nodding slowly. 'Yes . . . yes, that all makes sense. I'll go along with it. But there is one question I have to ask, Mr Lennox, and I'm sure you'll understand the reason why I have to ask it . . .'

'The answer is no,' I said predictively. 'I did what you asked me to do in your roundabout way and put the frighteners on Downey. And I admit I gave his chum a bruise or two, but that's as creative as I got in interpreting your instructions. When I left them, both Frank and Downey were very much alive.'

By the time I left the station, the fog had thinned to a grainy mist that faded Glasgow to monochrome – not something that took a lot of effort – rather than obscuring it. I crossed Gordon Street and went up the stairwell to my office. I had locked the door and half expected to find Jock Ferguson or even McNab waiting for me at the top of the stairs. They weren't, so I unlocked my office door and stepped through.

I was back in the war.

The speed of thought seems to me the most unquantifiable thing: faster than the speed of sound, even the speed of light, even if Albert says it ain't so. But what happened to me as I stepped through the door of my Glasgow office took me instantly back to a place where you killed without thought or lost your own life.

He had been behind the door and when I came in he hooked his arm around me from behind and dug his fingers into my eye and cheek, pulling me sideways and down. If I had not been taught the same dance steps, that would have been the end of me, but without having to think it through, I knew a knife was heading for the side of my neck. I caught his forearm with a knife-hand blow. It had enough strength to block the blade, but not much else. I stepped sideways towards the knife, counter to instinct, trapping his arm between my shoulder and the wall. His hand still dug into my face and his thumb was trying to seek out my eye socket. I brought my other hand, which still held the keys, down and back and into his groin.

He gasped and the grip on my face loosened. I grabbed his knife hand and slammed it against the wall. My brain registered the shape of the knife: the long, slender, deadly but rather beautiful profile of a Fairbairn-Sykes. I was in trouble. Big trouble. Only one of us was coming out of this alive. He clung on to the knife, so I kept his knife hand pinioned to the wall with my left hand while slamming my right elbow into his face, five or six times within a couple of seconds. I had enough of a look at his face to see an old, ugly scar on his forehead and recognize him as the guy who had jumped me in the alley. Except this time there was no chat.

His nose burst and there was blood all over his face, but he didn't pay any attention to it. It was something that I always found hard to explain to anyone who hadn't experienced this kind of combat: it takes a lot to hurt you. Shock and a gallon of adrenalin blocks sensation until it's all over. Then it hurts.

I knew I had to deal with the knife. I aimed a blow at his wrist with my Yale key, the only weapon I had, but my attacker brought his knee up into the small of my back and pushed me forward. He was a strong bastard all right and I lost my grip on his wrist and spun around to face him. He held the knife flat, face-up, textbook style. He slashed at me. Again, he wasn't trying to stab me, like some street thug would do. He was looking for the quick kill: a slash across my thigh, neck or forearm to sever the femoral, brachial or carotid artery. Then you just step back out of harm's way and watch your opponent bleed out in seconds. Textbook stuff.

I rolled over the top of my desk. Every time he came at me, I moved around the desk, keeping it between me and him, like we were playing a childhood game of tag. I felt something wet on my hand and looked down to see blood blooming on my shirt cuff and the back of my hand running red. He'd got me, but on the wrong side of my arm. I needed a weapon. By this time I had done a full circuit of the desk and he was now behind it, where I usually sat. The only thing I could grab was the hat stand behind me. I held it in front of me, stabbing at him like a *retiarius* gladiator with a trident. He made a move to get around the desk so I jabbed the base of the hat stand at his face and it jarred as it hit bone. One of his eyes had all but closed, swollen from one of the blows with my elbow and I could tell his vision was compromised. I jabbed again, this time slamming into his chest as hard as I could. My captain's chair caught the back of one of his legs and he fell backwards into the window, smashing the glass. I pushed again, forcing him through the window. He grabbed the window frame on either side with both hands to stop himself falling through, dropping the F-S knife as he did so.

He gave me the look. The look that says 'I give up'.

Still, I kept the pressure on his chest with the hat stand.

'Okay,' I said. 'Who do you work for?'

'Forget it, Lennox. Just call the police and let's get this over with.'

Like me, he was trying to catch his breath and this time there was no attempt at a half-assed Glasgow accent. He spoke with an English accent, beautifully modulated, received pronunciation. I wondered for a moment if the BBC Home Service had an elite commando announcer unit.

'What's this? Name, rank and serial number stuff?' I jabbed him again and the bloodied fingers of one hand slipped from the window frame. He scrabbled to regain his grip.

'Okay, Commando Joe, I'm only going to ask this one more time: who sent you? Joe Strachan? Where is he?'

He laughed as heartily as he could manage, blowing a bloody bubble from one nostril of his shattered nose.

'Or what? You going to kill me in cold blood.'

'Something like that. So tell me . . . where's Joe Strachan?'

'You honestly think you're going to get anything out of me? I'm telling you nothing, Lennox, and no one else is going to make me talk.'

'You haven't met Twinkletoes McBride,' I said. 'He's an associate of mine, and he didn't get his name because of his skills on the dance floor. So talk before I call him around with his bolt cutters.'

A smile I didn't like spread across his busted and bloody face. 'You know something, Lennox? I don't think you're in any state to call anyone. You're doing nothing, Lennox. In India, they used to have a saying, *he who rides a tiger may never dismount.* You can't reach my knife without letting go of the hat stand; you let go of the hat stand, I get to the knife first. Whatever happens, we go another round.'

'You didn't win the last time,' I said, 'and you had the element of surprise.'

'But you're bleeding, Lennox. Nothing that can't be patched up, but you're weakening. I doubt you'll even be able to hold me off with this thing for much longer. All you can do is stand there and shout for help and hope someone comes.'

'You know something, you're absolutely right. It's a conundrum, but I tell you what, I have an answer to it.'

'Oh yes?' He kept that arrogant smile on his face. 'And what would that be?'

'That you shout for help ... On the way down.'

I thrust forward with all of what was left of my strength. The smile went and the one unswollen eye widened in the bloody mask of his face as he scrabbled to keep his grip. I pushed again and his bloodied fingers slipped from the window frame. He toppled, screaming, out of the window.

*

I heard a screech of tyres and a woman's shriek. I went to the window and looked down into Gordon Street where he lay smashed on the deeply dented roof of a taxi.

It was, I thought to myself as I stepped back in to call the police, one way to catch a cabby's attention. More effective than whistling.

CHAPTER TWELVE

Pushing people out of third-floor windows, apparently, contra-venes some Glasgow Corporation bye-law, so I spent most of the next two days in the company of the police.

The first night was spent in the Western General, with a boy in blue sitting guard at my side. For my own protection, Jock Ferguson less than reassured me.

Despite the fact that I was perfectly capable of walking, I was confined to a bed, but not in the ward, instead ending up in a room on my own. My guess was that the police had insisted on it.

I was in good hands. If you are going to have a stab or slash wound, my advice would always be to try and arrange to have it in Glasgow. Glaswegian hospitals have an unpar-alleled experience of stitching up knife, razor and bottle-inflicted injuries. I even heard of a guy admitted with multiple wounds from a machete. Why a Glaswegian would have a machete was beyond me; I was pretty sure I hadn't come across dense patches of jungle or rainforest during my time in Glasgow.

The wound to my arm was deep. A doctor who looked twelve and reddened every time I called him 'Sonny' told me that they had had to stitch muscle as well as skin. I could expect some nerve damage, he told me, as if it had been my own silly fault.

I gave a formal statement under caution to Jock Ferguson, witnessed by my uniformed nursemaid. I followed exactly the advice I had given Fraser and told the police the real sequence of events, describing my him-or-me struggle and how it ended with him falling through the window. Except I omitted to mention that it had taken me several shoves to get the bastard through, or that we had chatted for a while before he caught his taxi.

My heart sank when McNab joined us, squeaking a chair across the hospital floor. A professionally dour-looking detective stood behind him, at the door, with a briefcase in his hand. Not carrying your own things was obviously another privilege of rank.

McNab read through the statement I had dictated to Ferguson and signed.

'Funny thing is,' he said, pushing his hat up and away from his eyes, 'that we have witnesses who report glass falling into the street some time before the victim fell.'

I didn't like that word. Victim.

'Could be, Superintendent. We were smashing into everything.'

'And there were bloody handprints on the frame of the window, as if the victim had tried to hang on to prevent himself from falling.'

There it was again. That word.

'He grabbed at it as he fell. In fact, that was when he dropped the knife. But his hands were too bloody to get a grip: that's why he fell.'

'Mmm. I see.' McNab nodded to the detective behind him who handed him a roll of white cloth. Unwrapping the cloth, he revealed the knife. It had an evidence tag on it. And some blood. Mine. Flecks of it had stained the cloth.

'This knife?'

'That's the one.'

Now, after the adrenalin of the fight had left my system, draining every last ounce of energy from me, the sight of the blade that had sliced into my flesh made me feel sick.

'Aye . . .' said McNab contemplatively. 'This would be a commando knife, would it not?'

'A Fairbairn-Sykes Fighting Knife, yes. Standard commando issue. The Canadian special forces were armed with a variation of it, the V42 Stiletto. An inferior version of it.' I nodded to the knife and again felt my gut lurch. 'What you have there is the world's best close-quarters combat knife. And the guy who jumped me was an expert with it. Who was he, anyway?'

Jock fired a look at the Superintendent that wasn't returned. 'We don't know. Yet.'

'Let me guess, no ID?'

Jock Ferguson shook his head. 'No ID, no driving licence, no labels or tags on his clothing to say where he came from . . . no cards, letters, chequebook.'

'You any ideas?' asked McNab.

'He wasn't local, I know that. He pretended to be, to start with, but he was English. And officer class. Listen, I was fighting for my life. It really was him or me. Am I going to be charged with his death?'

'You've killed a man, Lennox. That's a pretty big thing.'

'I've killed plenty, Superintendent, but back then it wasn't such a big thing at all.'

'Well, we'll have to submit a report to the Procurator Fiscal and you remain under caution. The evidence does seem to point to self-defence, like you said. But you can expect a lot of close attention over this. Some back alley razor gang killing is one thing, dropping well-dressed officer types onto the Gordon Street taxi rank is something else. You know the press is all over this?'

'I can guess. How are you handling the "mystery man" aspect?'

'We're not. We're just saying that the dead man has yet to be identified.' McNab turned to the detective at the door. 'Why don't you get a coffee in the canteen, Robertson. Five minutes.'

After the detective had left, leaving me with McNab and Ferguson, I eased myself up on the bed. A copper like McNab reducing the number of witnesses to an interrogation was something that brought out the suspicious and nervy aspects of my character.

'Listen, Lennox,' said McNab, 'I know you don't go much for my way of doing things, and you know what I think about your involvement with the so-called *Three Kings*, but this is the hardest city on the face of the planet and you have to be hard to police it. But this whole thing you're involved in is way beyond my ken. And I do not like things occurring inside the city boundary but outside my ken. It attracts unwanted interest.'

'Such as?'

'Special Branch.' It was Jock Ferguson who answered. 'What took place between you and our mystery dead man was text book SOE or commando stuff. It's even been suggested that he was some kind of intelligence man.'

'British Intelligence have taken to assassination attempts on Her Majesty's loyal subjects? I doubt it. And if they did, it would have been done more discreetly than that.'

'Well, it was professional enough for it to look like something *specialist*,' said McNab. 'And that means Special Branch are treading on my patch. And I don't like anyone treading on my patch.'

'But I take it you've told them that we all know what the link is? Gentleman Joe Strachan. That guy began by trying to warn me off the Strachan case, then he tried to remove me personally and permanently. This isn't anything to do with the Empire robbery any more ... it's to do with whatever happened *after* the robbery. During the war.'

'I still can't buy that story about Strachan being an officer,' said McNab. 'And God knows I want to believe it wasn't him we found at the bottom of the Clyde. But it just doesn't make sense. He was a criminal on the run. And wanted for a policeman's murder.'

'That's all true. But Isa and Violet seem convinced that their father was a war hero of some kind, while the official records show he was a deserter, an officer impersonator and paybook fraudster. But there *are* rumours that he traded off a spot in front of a firing squad for dangerous reconnaissance patrols. He also seemed to have regular contact with someone from his army days called Henry Williamson, who doesn't seem to be connected to anything criminal in Glasgow.'

'What are you getting at?' asked McNab.

'I really don't know. There's something nagging at me about it all. Let's face it, there have been more than a few times we've seen the words *with military precision* used in headlines about robberies since the war. The one thing compulsory army service did was give your average crook the kind of discipline and training to make them all the more efficient at carrying out hold-ups.'

'Hold on a minute . . .' Ferguson laughed. 'Last week we had a raid on a diamond merchant in the Argyle Arcades: one man with a fake pistol. He was caught because he thought the jeweller had activated some kind of automated dead-bolt on the door. What really happened was he kept pulling the door instead of pushing it. This despite the fact that there was a big brass doorplate engraved with the word PUSH. We're not up to our eyes in master criminals or commando raiders yet, Lennox.'

'All right,' I said. 'But you do know what I'm talking about. My point is that what if Strachan was ahead of the game . . . what if he came out of the First War with skills, and maybe contacts who could have helped him plan better, more efficient robberies and other crimes.'

'Leading up to the Triple Crown and culminating with the Empire Exhibition robbery?' asked McNab.

'Well, that's the other thing. What if the Empire Exhibition robbery wasn't the end but still the means to an end?'

'I don't get you.'

'What if Strachan had something even bigger and better planned? Listen, here's the way we've always seen it: Strachan puts together three huge robberies with an eye to becoming the sole King of Glasgow, but a copper is killed and things become too hot for Strachan, so he takes the cash and a powder and drops permanently out of sight, yes? Then a tangle of bones dressed in his clothes and with his monogrammed cigarette case is hauled up from the bottom of the Clyde, so all that changes. Now we have a fall-out amongst thieves, which is what you lot were putting together, where one or maybe all of Strachan's accomplices realise their until-now genius boss has put a rope around all of their necks. So this one or all of the gang kill Strachan, take his share and dump him in the river.'

'It makes sense,' said McNab defensively. Thinking is something policemen find hard work and hate it when their labours are picked apart.

'Sure it makes sense,' I said. 'And it still might be the case, but we've got this witness who *swears* it was Strachan he saw in Nineteen forty-two, at Lochailort, and in an army major's uniform.'

'Bollocks,' said Jock Ferguson. 'I still think that's shite.'

'Well, just for a moment, pretend it isn't. Let's say that

that really was Strachan, and he was there, fully accredited, as an army major. How could that come to be?'

'It couldn't,' said McNab.

'Now play along, Superintendent. Let's take Strachan's presence as an absolute fact. How could he have achieved that?'

'Well . . .' Ferguson pulled on the word thoughtfully. 'We know that he had experience of passing himself *off* as an officer. And doing it very well.'

'Which means it's entirely conceivable that he was seen dressed as a major . . .'

'But Lochailort was one of the most secure military installations in the country. It would take more than a uniform, a plum in your mouth and an authoritative demeanour to get in there.'

'Exactly.'

'Which is where the whole thing falls down,' said Ferguson.

'Let's go back to the Triple Crown robberies. What if they were only a means to an end? From what I've been able to find out, Strachan would disappear for months on end. Just drop out of sight. What if he had spent months, years, establishing another identity elsewhere? Maybe more than one. What if his plan had been to use the proceeds from the Triple Crown robberies to fund something else, somewhere else?'

'Like what?' asked McNab.

'Maybe just a different life somewhere else. The quality of life he imagined he deserved. Or maybe the proceeds were to be reinvested in another job: something even bigger than the Exhibition robbery . . . a mail train or gold bullion or the Crown bloody Jewels, I don't know. But then, two things happen. One, things don't go to plan during the Exhibition robbery and a copper is killed, so if Strachan's plan was to use the money to become Glasgow King Pin, then it's a complete wash-out. Two, Hitler invades Poland and everything is turned on its head. The whole of the country is on a war footing and pulling any big jobs becomes ten times more difficult. But I suspect something else happened. I'm not sure what, but I suspect that maybe Strachan's officer act was part of whatever identity he set up for himself and somehow fantasy and reality fused and he ended up roped into some real unit.'

'Have you heard of Fairy Tale Frankie Wilson?' asked McNab, dully. I shook my head. 'Inspector Ferguson here has come across him, haven't you, Jock? He's a compulsive little bastard. A compulsive thief and a compulsive liar. We call him Fairy Tale Frankie because he can't keep it simple. When he's trying to lie his way out of something, he keeps tripping up over his own lies, so he keeps inventing new, more outrageous lies to cover up. Before you know it his lie about why he had a jemmy in his pocket becomes a full-scale epic with a cast of characters that would send MGM into bankruptcy. But you just have to keep on listening, because it's so bloody entertaining. I have to tell you, Lennox, even Fairy Tale Frankie couldn't come up with anything as ridiculous as you're suggesting.'

'You could be right.' I shrugged. 'But we're not dealing with the usual Glasgow criminal type here. And you can't deny that that was no ordinary thug who jumped me in my office.' I shook my head irritably as other thoughts crammed in. 'Why are there no photographs of Strachan, anywhere? I'm telling you, he was planning his disappearance for a long, long time. This is no fairy tale, Superintendent. This is a whole new ball of wax.'

After McNab left, I smoked a couple of cigarettes with Jock Ferguson and talked the thing to death some more. We were interrupted by Dr 'Sonny', who gave me the all clear to go. Archie was waiting for me downstairs and shook hands with Jock Ferguson when we arrived.

'Look after him.' Ferguson managed to make it sound like an order.

'I'll keep him away from windows,' said Archie dolefully.

I said goodbye to Ferguson, latching on, as casually as I could manage, something that I had been relieved had not yet raised its head.

'By the way, Jock, what was all that about a murder case the other night? Govanhill, I think it was McNab said.'

I had put the question as conversationally as possible, but it still sounded clunky.

'Why you asking?' he asked, but with no more suspicion than usual.

'Just curious.'

'We think it was some kind of fairy killing. A pool life-guard called Frank Gibson who was well known in those circles apparently.'

'How was he killed?'

Jock Ferguson looked at me suspiciously.

'Like I said, just curiosity.'

'Morbid bloody curiosity. He had his throat cut. From behind. Whoever did it set the flat on fire. The whole tenement nearly went up with everybody in it. Why the hell would he set the place on fire after he'd killed Gibson?'

I shrugged to signal the limit of my curiosity, but I was thinking of the burnt furniture thrown into the back court. The answer, I felt, was obvious: fire wipes out evidence. I thought too of all of the other envelopes stuffed with negatives. Maybe Downey and Gibson had been pulling the same stunt with God knows how many others. And where was Downey now?

The kind of business I was in called for discretion. A low profile. Showing my guest the window had gotten me onto the front pages of the *Bulletin*, the *Daily Herald*, the *Daily Record* and the *Evening Citizen*. The *Glasgow Herald* confined me to page four. The *Bulletin* had a photograph of my office building with my window boarded up, and an arrow indicating the route taken by my guest to the street: just in case the *Bulletin*'s readers were unfamiliar with the workings of gravity.

Archie had the papers in his car when he came to pick me up. Archie's car was pretty much as you would expect from Archie: a black Forty-seven Morris Eight into which he seemed to have to fold himself like a penknife. We didn't talk much as we drove across the city and down to the Gallowgate. My mind suddenly filled with the fact that I had killed a man; that my actions, not for the first time, had ended a human being's existence. I told myself that I had not had much choice in the matter. The truth was that I had had some.

Archie clearly sensed I was not in the mood for chat and we drove in silence back to my temporary lodgings. The door opened without being knocked and we were greeted sullenly by Mr Simpson. My landlord's demeanour had shifted from suspicious to outright hostile.

'I've chchread all of this schhhite in the papers. People being flung out of windowsch. We've got windowsch here. You're that Lennochsch, aren't you?'

'I am,' I said and noticed my bags, packed, sitting behind him in the hall. 'But I've committed no crime. I was the victim of the attack, not the perpetrator. So your windows are safe.'

'I don't want no trouble. No trouble. You'll have to go.'

'Would it help if I told you I thought the guy had an Irish accent?' I asked, deadpan. When he didn't answer, I leaned past him to pick up my bags. He flinched as I did so and I gave him a wink.

'Top o' the mornin' t'yah!'

'Where now, boss?' asked Archie, once we were back in the car. His voice remained dull but there was a twinkle in the large hang-dog eyes.

'Great Western Road,' I said. 'But stop at a phone box on the way so I can warn my landlady.'

The world had turned on its axis a few times since I'd last spent a night in my digs, but I had somehow expected to pick up where I had left off; and specifically where I had left off my tearoom conversation with Fiona White. But things had moved on without me, somewhat.

The telephone had been engaged and I hadn't been able

to warn Fiona White that I was on my way back. And when we pulled up at my digs I noticed two cars I didn't recognize parked outside. The first was a dark grey Humber. It had no police markings and the driver and passenger were in civvies, but it could not have looked more like a police car if it had flat feet. I felt the distinctly novel emotion of being pleased to see a police car outside my home: Jock Ferguson, or maybe McNab himself, must have arranged it. The second car was a black three- or four-year-old Jowett Javelin PE. Too flash for the police.

Lying in my hospital bed, I had played the movie of my return home in my head: Fiona White would be all nervously-contained agitation when I arrived. She would have read about the Defenestration of Gordon Street, but it would be clear she was glad to see me, and see me in one piece. A nervous little smile would play across her lips and I would have the almost uncontrollable urge to still it with a kiss. Instead I would let her fuss around in the kitchen and make Archie and me some tea.

After Archie left, we would settle into the routine of before, drifting slowly towards whatever it was we both wanted our relationship to become.

But I could tell as soon as she answered the door that my sudden and unannounced return perturbed Fiona White. She looked startled and awkward and almost hesitated before admitting me and Archie.

I didn't like him as soon as I set eyes on him. The main reason was, for a second, I thought I recognized him, then realized he could not be the person I took him for, because the person I took him for was dead. The face was not the same, of course, there was just a strong family resemblance to the picture on the mantelpiece above the fire. The picture of the long dead naval officer.

'You must be the lodger . . .' he said smilelessly as he stood up when we entered the living room. Tea for two with best biscuits on the coffee table. He was tanned and dressed too lightly for Glasgow and had a just-arrived-from-abroad look to him.

'You must be the brother-in-law . . .' I said flatly.

'We've been reading all about your . . . *escapades*. I must say that I'm not happy about you staying here at Fiona's. Do you know that I was accosted by a policeman when I arrived here?'

'Really? Well, you see, they've been told to challenge anyone who has a suspicious or dodgy look to them. And I don't really see what my rental arrangements with Mrs White have to do with you.'

'Well, as my sister-in-law and with my brother no longer here, I feel an obligation to Fiona and the girls' welfare.'

'I see,' I said. 'And it's taken ten years for this sense of obligation to grow on you?'

'I've been away. Abroad. Working in India. But now that I'm back, I think it's fair for you to know that things may change around here.'

'I see,' I said. 'Do you take the same size slippers as your brother?'

He looked stung but I knew he didn't have it in him to take it further.

'That's quite enough from both of you,' said Fiona. 'James,

I am quite capable of organizing my own affairs. Mr Lennox, you've had quite an ordeal. I'm sure you want to get some rest. I'll fix something to eat about six, if you want to join us.'

I stared at her for a minute. 'Sure,' I said. 'My pleasure.'

I nodded to Archie and we headed up to my rooms. I was tired and pissed off and really wanted to smack the sneer off the smug bastard downstairs. But in the meantime I had bigger fish to fry.

'I think your landlady is going to have to buy a bigger table,' said Archie.

'What are you talking about, Archie?'

'If both of you are to get your feet under it.'

'Oh yes, very funny.'

'You okay here, chief? I can hang around if you want.'

'No, Archie, that's fine. I'm going to take a spin up to Billy Dunbar's tonight to show him that photograph, but I can fly solo on that. You take the night off.'

I lay on my bed, smoking and aching. After about an hour I heard the front door open and voices. I went to the window and saw James White walk out to the Javelin. He turned and waved to Fiona and then looked pointedly up at my window. I looked pointedly back. The sight of him, his middle-class stability and his likeness to a long dead junior naval officer gave me a bad feeling in my gut. I had a vision of Fiona White's future and no matter how hard I looked, I couldn't see me in it.

I washed and changed. Suit, shirt, underwear, everything. It was something about hospitals I could never understand:

you came out of them smelling of carbolic yet you always felt dirty. I went downstairs at six and had a meal of fish, peas and potatoes with Fiona and her daughters. I tried to chat as much as I could but the truth was I was still pretty shaken up by what had happened in my office. Fiona frowned when she saw me take some prescription pills with my meal; the bandage and dressing on my arm was concealed by my shirt sleeve and she did not know how badly I'd been injured, if at all. But the other thing that nagged at me throughout the meal was the smug presence of a dead man's brother.

After we finished, I helped Fiona take the dishes through to the kitchen but she told me to sit. The girls settled down to watch television and I closed the kitchen door.

'Are you okay with this, Fiona?' I asked. 'I know that reading about what happened must have been a shock.'

She stopped washing the plate she was working on and leant against the edge of the sink, her back to me, and looking out of the kitchen window to the small garden at the back.

'This man. You killed him? I mean it wasn't an accident?'

I was about to say it was a little of both, but the infuriating thing about Fiona White was that she brought out the honesty in me. 'Yes, I killed him. But it was in self-defence. He ambushed me in my office and tried to cut my throat. He was the same guy who jumped me in the fog.'

She turned to me.

'So it's safe for you to be back here?' She made it more of a statement than a question.

'That's not one hundred per cent certain,' I said. 'I don't for one minute think that this man was working on his own.

236

But I can't imagine whoever was behind the attack risking anything so . . . so *visible* again. Anyway, it looks like we have serious police protection now. But there is still no way I want to put you and the girls at risk. I can find new accommodation for the time being . . .'

'No,' she said, but as if she had to think about it and without emphasis.

'It's not always going to be like this, Fiona,' I said. 'Things have got all mixed up. I thought this kind of thing was behind me. I guess I was wrong.'

'You don't have to explain,' she said. 'But you know I can't be part of that world. I can't bring the girls into that kind of world.'

'Of course not,' I said. 'But that's what I'm trying to put behind me. Things will get better, like I said.'

'I know they will,' she said and smiled.

But we both knew my fate was sealed.

It had still been just within banking hours so, on the way back from the hospital, I had had Archie stop off at the bank. News of my adventures had obviously reached the bank and when I walked in it was the kind of entry that you would expect a gunfighter to get walking into a Western saloon. MacGregor himself dealt with my request to access my safety deposit box. He was overly chatty but nervous, as if making a conscious effort to avoid the word 'window' or any reference to catching a taxi. I was glad I had the goods on him, otherwise I reckoned I would have already lost the bank job. As it was, my knowledge of his sordid private life would do little to save me if the board of governors set their minds to get rid of me.

But there again, they maybe liked the idea of their cash being guarded by a life-taker.

I had taken the Webley from the safety deposit box and had tucked it into the waistband of my trousers. I knew that if McNab found out I was walking about his town heavy with an unlicensed gun, the recent thaw in relations would turn out to have been a false Spring. But if someone tried to kill me again, I wanted to have more than a hat stand in my hand. When I had gotten back to my digs, and after my pleasant exchange with James White, I had put the Webley under my pillow.

It was about eight-thirty when I put my jacket and hat on, went down to the hall telephone and 'phoned Isa. We arranged that I would meet her and Violet the next day.

I knocked on the Whites' door and told Elspeth to tell her mother that I would be out for the evening. When I drove off, I was relieved to see that the dark grey Humber stayed on point outside the house, instead of following me. But I guessed my outing would be noted and radioed in.

Before I headed up north and into the country, I stopped at a telephone kiosk and called Murphy.

'You heard what happened?' I asked.

'About you throwing that cunt out the fucking window? I believe it may have come to my fucking notice. I thought you was supposed to be discreet? So who was he?'

'The same guy I told you and Jonny Cohen about. The one who jumped me in the fog.'

'So what are you telling me, that you want your fucking money?'

'No. Maybe. I don't think so. Listen, I'm not at all sure that this guy was this so called Lad of Strachan's. Unless Gentleman Joe sent him for elocution lessons, that is. He was English.'

'Aye? Fucking reason enough to throw him out the window.'

'Listen, Mr Murphy, could you tell Jonny Cohen about this? I've got to look into something else, and it might just tell us whether Strachan is alive or not. I'm also going to try to find out if this guy *was* the Lad or not.'

After I hung up, I drove out of Glasgow. The sky was heavy and dull but it felt good to get out of the city and into an open landscape. I guessed that there would be no one in the estate office at that time of evening, allowing me to dodge any encounter with the sexually repressed, tweed-clad Miss Marple. When I reached the estate, however, I found the gates closed and padlocked.

Running through the rough map of the place I had in my mind, I headed further on up the narrow ribbon of country road. A high dry-stone wall running along the side of the road marked the border of the estate. Eventually I found a lane that led to a disused entry, but this had been bricked up. At least the Atlantic was off the road and reasonably concealed, so I decided to risk my suede loafers and houndstooth suit by climbing the wall. I dropped down the other side into a mulch of old fallen leaves, twigs and branches. Ahead of me was a dense swatch of evergreens that the late evening light failed to penetrate, but I reckoned that if I walked straight ahead and managed not to break an ankle, I would come out onto the path that had led from the estate office to Dunbar's cottage.

I really didn't like the walk through the forest. I found myself listening to every creak, rustle and bird cry, my heart in my mouth. There was nothing to fear here and now, of course, but I'd taken many such walks through woods just like this, and back then there were things more deadly than squirrels and rabbits hiding in the foliage.

Ten minutes later I came out exactly where I thought I would, although it took me a minute to get my exact bearings on how far up the path I was. I looked around and found a largish rock by the side of the path. Its shape was reminiscent of a curled-up cat sleeping, or maybe it was just me who would see that. The point was it was distinctive enough for me to recognize and I moved it so that it sat out on the path. On the way back, all I had to do was find the rock, turn left into the woods and head arrow-straight towards the boundary wall.

It was beginning to get dark, even out here beyond the gloom of the trees. I didn't know why I was doing it, but I slipped the Webley out from my waistband, snapped open the breech and checked the cylinder was full before snapping it shut again and tucking it back into my waistband. I also checked my inside jacket pocket to make sure the photograph was there.

It took me another fifteen minutes to reach the cottage. There were no lights showing and no sign of life, so I guessed that my luck had run out and that no one was home. I went up to the door anyway and knocked, but there was no reply. I stood there for a moment debating whether I should leave the photograph and a note, asking Dunbar to 'phone me if he recognized the man in the photograph. I decided against it. It was my only copy of the photograph and I had to be careful with it: it could, after all, connect me to a burnt-out tenement flat and a dead queer.

I cursed the waste of time coming all the way up here for nothing and turned resignedly from the door. Before I retook the path, I went to one of the cottage windows, cupped my hands to blinker my eyes and peered through the glass. As I did so the memory of my last experience peeping through a window came to mind and I hoped with a laugh I would not catch Dunbar and his ugly wife in flagrante.

I stopped laughing.

I snatched the Webley from my waistband and moved back to the door. It was unlocked and I pushed it as wide as it would go, scanning the room as I entered, ready to fire at anything or anyone that moved. It was empty, except for what I had seen through the window. I moved into the kitchen. Empty too. I came back into the main room.

It was becoming difficult to see in the gathering gloom, but I dared not switch on a light. This was a place and a situation I did not want to be seen in. I said a silent prayer of thanks that I had parked my car where I had, out of sight.

Billy Dunbar lay on the floor of the cottage, in front of the settee. His throat had been cut and the wound gaped like a clown grin. I could just make out in the dim light a bloom of dark crimson staining on the rug beneath his head. His wife lay on the other side of the room. Same story.

I pressed the back of my hand against Dunbar's forehead. Stone cold. I reckoned he had been dead for at least an hour.

I stood silently in the middle of the room, touching nothing, listening for the sounds of anyone approaching on the path, trying to think what the hell this all meant and what I was supposed to do about it.

I thought of going for the police, but I was outside the City of Glasgow and I would find it difficult to explain my complicated involvement to some hick in a uniform who would have trouble with the most basic concepts: like it really wasn't a good idea for first cousins to marry.

I had no idea about the social life of gamekeepers, but I decided to get as far away as possible, as quickly as possible, in case someone else from the estate decided to drop in for a drink or to exchange beauty tips with Mrs Dunbar.

Backing out to the door again, I took my handkerchief and swabbed the handle, the only thing I had touched, clean. I checked up and down the path. No one. Just to be on the safe side, I gave the window I had peered through a good wipe down too.

I put the gun back in my waistband and ran down the path, back the way I had come. After a couple of hundred yards I eased the pace to a trot. It was getting really dark now and I could easily lose my footing. I remembered where I was now: the path took a sudden bend to the right and I would have another half mile to the 'cat' stone.

I was fully around the corner before I saw them: a group

of three men. The man in the middle turned and saw me and said something to the other two. Instantly I knew I was in trouble. Instead of coming up the path at me, the other two moved quickly off the path and into the fringe of woods, one on either side. The man in the middle stood still and watched me, his hand reaching inside his short, dark coat. I made a run for the cover of the woods to my left, trying to penetrate them as deeply as I could before the guy who had taken that side could outflank me. I was making a hell of a racket, but at this stage, distance and cover were the most important advantages to gain. I had elected for this side of the path because this was the direction the car lay in. If I had gone the other way I would have been at their mercy for longer.

I was running blind now and my chances of getting a foot caught on a root or tripping over a rock in the dark were too high. I stopped dead and stood stock still, straining the night for any sound. Nothing. But I knew that all three were now in these woods. Again the name of the game would be to outflank me. They would guess that my car was somewhere out on the road and I would be heading back to the perimeter wall. I listened some more. Still nothing.

I don't know what it was about the three men on the path, but I had known instantly that they were Dunbar's killers. Again it was something that I had picked up in the war, something I couldn't analyse or explain: you just learned to tell whether the figures you had spotted in a landscape were combatants or civilians, even if they were vague figures, sighted from a distance. It was a predator's instinct to recognize another predator.

And these guys had been predators.

More than that, there had been something about the man in the middle. He had been older than the other two. About my height. And there had been something about his bearing that, again from a distance, made me think of some kind of foreign aristocrat.

I was pretty sure I had his photograph in my pocket.

I took the revolver from my waistband, crouched down and waited. They were good all right, but not too good. I heard one of them far off to my left and a little ahead of me. He was moving quietly, but the sound of anything more than a crawl was difficult to hide in a forest at night. I guessed that he was about fifty yards off. My guess was that his compadre would have taken the same measure on the other side. Their boss, I reckoned, would wait until they were fifty yards into the woods and then come in to take the middle way. A triangulated search. I moved as low and silently as I could and advanced several yards to my right. There was a depression in the ground, not much of one, but it had been formed between root balls and it allowed me to crawl along beneath the profile of the forest floor.

Somewhere to my right, something made a noise and suddenly the dark was split by three beams of light. Their torchlight converged on the same spot and a small deer that darted off deeper into the forest. The torches went off, but they had been on for long enough for me to get a rough fix on their positions. I had been right about the search pattern.

These guys were good. Professional. My main problem was that the point from which the light behind me came suggested that their boss was going to walk right into me.

The meagre light made me nostalgic for scuffles in the Glasgow smog and I inched back into the woods, trying to find an even better place to conceal myself. I picked up a rock and threw it as hard as I could into the dark. It didn't travel as far away from me as I wanted before striking a tree. The torches came on again and focused on a point ten yards off. Not finding a Scottish Red Deer or a Greater Canadian Dumbass where they expected, they began to scan the forest and the beam of one torch passed directly over me. If I hadn't been in the depression I would have been spotted for sure. The two flankers kept their torches on, constantly scanning and keeping me pinned down, but the guy behind me switched his off. My guess was he was on the move. In my direction.

I inched even further back. Eventually I found what I was looking for. A sprung tree had pulled itself up by the roots and a tangle of thick root, fibrous tendrils and clots of earth gave me a curtain to hide behind. In the other side was a thick fallen branch, the diameter of a small tree trunk. All thoughts of preserving suede or houndstooth forgotten, I slipped in behind the exposed root ball and hunkered down. I eased back the hammer on the Webley. Again I was back somewhere I didn't want to be, but when it came to my life or someone else's, I would make sure it was someone else's. One of the searchers' torch beams swept close over my head again and I sunk deeper. Shaking some of the soil from a root, I used it to darken my face, just in case I was caught in torchlight.

I didn't hear him until he was almost on top of me. He had been moving almost silently and much more quietly than the other two. He stopped in his tracks, standing on top of the ridge, no more than three feet from my head. So close I couldn't even ease round to take aim at him. If I moved, I'd have to shoot him. If he turned on his torch, he'd see me through the tangle of roots. I held my breath. This was insane: I'd already killed one man and now I was probably going to have to kill three more if I wanted to survive.

He moved on. But he did so so quietly that there was no way of me knowing how far. I stayed motionless. What this meant was that they were now all behind me, and between me and the perimeter wall and my car beyond. But by the same token, the way back to the path was clear. I turned slowly around in my hiding place and eased myself up to look behind me. I ducked back down when I found myself staring at the silhouette of the older guy's back, only a few yards further on. Peering over the ridge I could see as he turned sideways. It was so dark that it was impossible to see him clearly, but again I got the impression that I was looking at the man whose picture was still in my pocket.

I was looking at Gentleman Joe Strachan. I was sure of it.

CHAPTER THIRTEEN

I waited a full five minutes after the older man had been swallowed up in the dark before I made my way back towards the path. It was only a matter of time before they started to sweep back in my direction again.

As soon as I had the path under my feet I sprinted along it in the dark, again having to ignore the risk of stumbling over something. I slowed down when I thought I was close to where I had left the 'cat stone', but everything was so different in the dark. I slowed to a walk and realized that I must have come too far and turned back, cursing the lost time. If my pursuers had worked out that I'd gone for the path, they'd catch up with me any moment.

I found it. Again, it looked totally different in the dark and no longer reminded me of anything feline, but I recognized it from the position I'd left it in. I set off back into the woods, heading in a straight line at right-angles to the path, just as I had planned. This time I really did have something more than squirrels and rabbits to worry about and I kept my pace steady but slow and quiet, crouching low with my knees slightly bent and my gun held ready.

What had taken me ten minutes on the way in took half an hour on the way out. Eventually I found the wall and recognized the mulchy bed of leaves and twigs where I'd landed. That meant that my car was directly behind the wall. I was just about to scramble up the wall when I checked myself. These guys were good. Really good. What if they had worked out that I must have come by car and one of them had checked the road around the estate? Admittedly, that was a lot of road to cover, but they would know it wouldn't be too far from Dunbar's cottage.

I could climb over the wall and drop straight into an ambush.

I decided to follow the wall about ten yards further on and climb over as quietly as I could. When I was on top of the wall, I checked to see if I could see the car, but I had chosen too well and it was concealed by bushes. I eased myself down and took the gun from my waistband again. As I edged towards the car, I could see the back of it begin to emerge. I stopped. I had been right. A figure stood by the car, watching the wall next to it with his back to me. It took me a few seconds to work out he was on his own. My guess was the other two were still searching the woods for me. I could see he was younger, leaner and shorter than the older man I'd seen in the woods. He had something in his hand. Not a gun. For a moment I thought it was a large knife but, as I crept closer, I could see it was a baton, like a policeman's truncheon. They hadn't expected me to be armed and I hadn't realized that I had had an advantage. But I decided not to risk it. Turning the gun around in my hand and holding it hammer style, I crept forward until I was right behind the goon by the car.

I let him have it hard on the back of his skull, then twice more on the way down when I didn't really need to. He was out cold, but all of the tension and adrenalin of the chase in the woods took over and I rolled him onto his back and fixed his face for him. I guess I only hit him three or four times, and not with all my strength, but it cost him several of his teeth and his sense of smell. I wanted the others to find him and see what happened when you went Lennox-hunting but you didn't make the kill.

I went through his pockets and took everything he had, not taking the time to look at it but stuffing it into my jacket pockets. When I was finished I got into the car. I was shaking: my hands, my legs. That was how it got me. It wasn't the scares, it was the adrenalin and the testosterone and what-ever the hell else your body flooded with. And it never got me at the time, only after.

I had it now, I had had it after the fight in my office, and I had gotten it regularly during the war.

I eventually found the ignition with the key and drove off.

I got back to my digs about nine-thirty. The Javelin was back, parked outside. I could have just gone in and gone up to my rooms, or I could have played who's-the-gooseberry in Fiona's living-room, but I didn't have the stomach for it. Once I'd opened the floodgates like I just had with the goon on the country road, I generally found that I was too quick to get handy again. And I really, really wanted to get handy with that smug little shit.

I headed down Byers Road and along Sauchiehall Street. Something gnawed at me as I drove: maybe the real reason I hadn't gone home and stood my ground was that I knew, deep down inside, that Fiona would be better off with James White. Brother of her dead husband, dull but reliable type, the kind of steady Joe that I could never be. Maybe it was simpler than that. Maybe it was just that I was no good for Fiona. Or just no good.

I got the same curt nod of recognition from my neckless chum on the door. No meeting with Hammer Murphy this time: I was at the Black Cat to get wet and set about it with great alacrity at the bar. The funny thing about good jazz is that it slows down your drinking and I turned my back to the bar, leaning my elbows on it cowboy style, and listened to the trio who were doing something mellow with a baroque piece; taking the mathematics out of it and playing with its rhythms. When they finished I turned back to the bar and inadvertently nudged the guy next to me.

'Why don't you watch what you're doing?' he whined, making a big deal of holding his drink up as if I'd spilled some of it, which I hadn't. He was a big guy, and I could see that he had had a few, but I could tell at first glance that he was no fighter.

'It was an accident, friend,' I said. 'No harm done.'

'You spilt his drink . . .' One of his buddies decided to chip in. But over his shoulder. 'You should buy him another one. And it was a malt.'

'No, I didn't spill it. And like I said, just an accident.'

'You calling me a liar?' The big guy, emboldened by his friend's support, turned to me, square on, but still holding his glass. I sighed, put my drink down and faced him.

'Look, I didn't spill your drink, and it was an accident. But here . . .' I slapped his hand up and the entire contents of the glass splashed over his shirt, jacket and some on his face. 'Now your drink *is* spilled,' I said as if explaining arithmetic to a five-year-old. 'And that *was* deliberate. And yes, I'm calling you a liar. And I'm calling your mother a filthy whore who took sailors up the ass. Yours too, by the way . . .' I leaned to one side, smiling, and addressed his chum as if I didn't want to offend him by leaving him out. 'Now if either of you two queers are man enough, which I doubt, not to take that, then I'll happily put the pair of you in hospital. And trust me, you've picked the wrong night.'

Glaswegians are as pale-complexioned as it is possible to be, yet I could have sworn both of them turned an even whiter shade.

'Do we have a problem, gentlemen?' Neckless the doorman was beside me. Buzzer behind the bar, I reckoned.

'I don't think so,' I said cheerily. 'These two gentlemen and I are just going outside for a stroll, aren't we?'

'Listen, I don't want any trouble . . .' The big guy now looked scared. The doorman wouldn't care what happened between us if we took it outside.

'Lennox . . .' I felt a hand rest gently on my shoulder and

got a blast of perfume. I turned and saw Martha. She smiled nervously. 'No trouble, Lennox, okay? Why don't you and me sit down over here and have a drink? On the house. These boys didn't mean any harm.'

The two guys next to me were now turned back to the bar, doing the don't-make-eye-contact-with-the-psycho thing. Neckless backed off a little and I let Martha lead me across to the table. I noticed her nod to the barman and our drinks followed us quickly.

I sat and glowered at the two guys at the bar for a while longer, but eventually the jazz started to soak into my bones and dissolve the tension in my muscles.

'You've got to watch that temper of yours, Lennox,' said Martha. 'It could get you into bother.'

'Wouldn't be the first time,' I said, easing back into my chair. I stopped watching the two guys at the bar, mainly because they were breaking all the laws of probability and never casting a glance anywhere on my side of the room. The next time I looked up, they were gone. 'Anyway, I wasn't looking for trouble. Those guys all but picked a fight.'

'But the way you go at people . . . the way you lose control . . . it isn't right, Lennox.'

'You think I'm ready for the psycho ward, Martha?'

'I'm not saying that. I just think you should ease up a little. Someone's going to end up hurt. Bad.'

'It wouldn't ever come to that,' I said, trying to tuck away in some dark corner of my mind the image of the goon I'd left on a country road with few teeth and a lifetime of mouth-breathing ahead of him. I smiled at Martha. She was pretty

and, despite her job, she was a good kid. There was something about her, about the architecture of her face and the
high cheekbones that reminded me in a vague way of Fiona
White. 'Enough of the gloomy talk,' I said. 'Let's have another
drink . . .'

I drove Martha home. Which was quite an accomplishment
given the amount of bourbon I'd consumed. For a lot of the
way I was confused by the sudden presence of so many dual
carriageways in Glasgow, but managed to resolve the problem
by keeping one eye shut while I drove. Martha had had a few
as well, but I'd left her pretty far behind. When we got to
her place she made me some of that coffee that came out
of a bottle and you mixed with hot water. It tasted like crap
but started to do the trick.

Martha's place was in a newish building with shops on
the ground floor and flats above. We had only ever tangoed
in my car so this was my first time there and I was surprised
at how tasteful it was. The furniture was the Modernist type
of thing that was coming out of Denmark and she had a
few Impressionist prints in cheap frames on the wall. A
small bookcase was filled with book club novels and there
was a two-month-old copy of *Vogue* on the coffee table, to
be seen as much as read, I guessed. The place screamed of
someone trying to break out of the rut they were stuck in
and the bright, stylish, cheerful flat depressed the hell out
of me.

We talked for a while and I drunk more coffee, but the
booze in my system was messing with my visual recall and

Martha began to look more and more like Fiona White to me. I moved in, as we both had known I would, and experienced a lack of resistance that would embarrass an Italian general. We ended up on the floor and her dress became a crumple around her waist. What followed was unlovely and almost brutal and I eased off when I saw a touch of fear in her eyes. I became more gentle and kissed her, but with my eyes closed it was still Fiona White and not Martha I had under me.

Afterwards we smoked and she was quiet. I apologized for being so rough and asked if we could see each other again.

'I'd like that,' she said, and I was disappointed to see that she meant it.

It was about ten the next morning when, accompanied by Archie, I arrived to meet the twins at Violet's home in Milngavie. I had decided against conducting our business in my office because I felt the boarded-up window behind my desk might just have been a little off-putting for clients: a reminder, as it was, that I had added a new option in how you could leave my office.

There were also the fact that when I had called by the office first thing that morning to pick up a few things, there had been a reporter from the *Bulletin* hanging around the building. Fortunately he was without a photographer and was slow on the uptake. He had asked me if I was Lennox and I told him, in a broad Glasgow accent, that I wasn't. It was only when I said I was from the City Corporation Licensing Authority and was there to find out about taxis making unauthorized pick-ups that he stopped nodding absently and began to look suspicious.

Archie and I took my Austin Atlantic and drove up to Milngavie. On the way I noticed again the cigar-shaped profile of the Bennie Railplane sitting forlorn in its distant field, hovering over a huddle of sheds, like a discarded prop from a Buck Rogers featurette.

I gave Archie an update of where we were with things, including my suspicion that the man in the photograph was Gentleman Joe himself, and that he was behind the attempt on my life in my office. He asked me how it had gone with Billy Dunbar and I told him I hadn't had a chance to make the trip, after all. I didn't really know why I lied to Archie; maybe it was the fact that he was, at the end of the day, a retired copper. The fact that you'd stumbled on a double murder but hadn't reported it, or the fact that you had pulped some gangster's face by pistol-whipping him with an illegally held firearm, were the kind of things you didn't volunteer to coppers, retired or otherwise.

Violet McKnight lived in a detached Nineteen-thirties bungalow, with the obligatory attic conversion above and the obligatory small square of manicured gardens out front. Milngavie was Glasgow's hadn't-quite-made-it middle class suburb: a sprawl of identical bungalows set out with the imagination of a vegetable allotment.

I noticed that the Ford Zephyr, still gleaming its Hire Purchase gleam, was parked in the driveway, and when we rang the doorbell we were admitted by Robert McKnight,

Violet's husband. He beamed a car salesman's smile at us, letting it flicker only momentarily when he saw I was not alone. McKnight was shorter than I had expected him to be, but the shoulders were as packed as I had seen from above. He had a broad, handsome face, but his nose had been busted at some point and had not been professionally set, giving it a twist to the right. The effect was off-putting: even when he was looking at you straight on, you had the feeling he had already started to turn away.

He showed us into the living room, or *loungette* as they probably called it in Milngavie. Everything was new and immaculate and in what they called the Danish Style. It depressed me to realize I was seeing the kind of look that Martha had tried to emulate in her tiny rented flat and on a much smaller budget.

Isa and Violet were sitting on the sofa. I noticed that they sat almost pressed up to each other, as if physical contact between them was essential to comfort. I introduced Archie as my associate who had been working on the case with me, and the twins invited us to sit.

'We read all about it . . .'

'. . . in the newspapers . . .' they began.

'That was terrible . . .'

'Just *terrible* . . .'

'Tell us, Mr Lennox . . .'

'. . . was it to do with you trying to find out about Daddy?'

I smiled and dropped my hat onto the G-plan. 'I'm afraid it was. I have to tell you that I actually think that *Daddy* might have had more than a little to do with it.'

'You mean . . .'

'. . . Daddy is alive?'

'That's the information I've been given. Or at least he was still alive in Nineteen forty-two, according to one witness. Just the one, mind. But added to that single witness is the fact that the gentleman who took a swan dive from my office window had tried before to warn me off looking into your father's disappearance, and when I couldn't be warned off, he tried to retire me permanently from the case. And that means I am definitely on the opposite side of the fence from Joe Strachan. If I continue to work for you, that could be seen as a conflict of interests. And detrimental to my well-being.'

For once Isa and Violet said nothing but sat in identical silence.

'So you really do think that Joe is still alive?' asked Robert McKnight, the salesman's smile gone from his lips and replaced with a frown of equivalent insincerity.

'Looks like it. And that's why I wanted to talk to you both. As I said, I've taken this case as far as I can. As far as I am willing.'

'We quite understand . . .' said Violet.

'. . . given everything that has happened . . .'

'. . . but we want to be sure . . .'

'. . . that Daddy *is* alive . . .'

'The only way to be sure would be to find him,' I said.

'That's what we mean . . .'

'. . . would you find him for us, so that we can talk to him?'

'The short answer to that is no. I am in no doubt that if

I ever did succeed in finding your father, then I don't think I'd live long enough to tell you about it. And if I did survive the encounter, I would have to tell the police.'

They both opened their mouths to protest. I held up my hand.

'Listen, ladies, I warned you from the start that if I found out your father was alive, and where he was, then I could not withhold that information from the police. Now the police are all over this like a rash, and I don't want to catch it. If they ask me, right now, if I know the whereabouts of Joe Strachan, I can tell them with absolute honesty that I don't know. And that I don't know for absolutely sure that he is alive. If you want my advice, I think we should leave it like that.'

'But we want to talk to him . . .' they protested in unison.

'Let's face it, ladies, he has been sending you that cash every year for eighteen years. If he wanted to make contact, then he would have before now. If you ask my opinion, and I'm sorry to be so blunt, that money is guilt money. I think your father always planned to disappear, to leave you and your mother behind, whether or not a copper was killed during the Empire Exhibition job. I believe he has a completely new identity in some other part of the country, or the world: an identity he was probably setting up since before you were even born. The only reason he is making his presence felt here in Glasgow again is because I've been sticking my big nose in where it's not wanted.'

'So what do we do?'

'Accept that your father is alive, but not in a position to

contact you. Keep taking the money and keeping your heads down. That's my advice and it's advice I intend to follow myself. By the way, I think it could be a matter of your safety as well.'

The twins looked outraged.

'Our Daddy . . .'

'. . . would never do anything to hurt us!'

'Perhaps not, but I think there's a chance he could have got involved with a very dangerous group of people. More organized, better resourced and more dangerous than any criminal gang. And they look out for each other, as I found out to my cost.'

'What kind of people?' asked Robert.

'Military types. No, not even military types . . . more the "stay behind" guerrilla groups that were set up before and during the war. They were supposed to sabotage Nazi invaders, that kind of thing, but a lot of them were set up to deal with the Commies if the war should take that kind of turn.'

'That doesn't sound like our Daddy . . .' said Isa.

'Not like our Daddy at all . . .' added Violet.

'He wasn't political.'

'But you said that he was some kind of war hero in the First War?'

'He was . . .'

'He got medals for it . . .'

'He went behind enemy lines and everything.'

'But he was also nearly shot for being a deserter, isn't that also true?'

'That's all lies . . .'

'Lies . . .' echoed Violet.

'Listen, ladies,' I said as gently as I could, 'it's easy, very easy, to build up someone into a hero figure when they're not around. A lot that I have heard about your father, and everything I have experienced, leads me to believe he was or is a totally ruthless character. I don't think he ever did anything that wasn't in his own interest. I'm sorry, Isa and Violet, but I'm going to have to let this one go. And if I were you, I would do the same. This is one gift horse you shouldn't be looking in the mouth.'

'Could we talk to the witness you traced?'

'That would be difficult to arrange,' I said, without adding that we would need to hire a medium to arrange it. 'I'm afraid he's moved away. Permanently.'

Now for my big finale.

'There is something else . . .' I reached into my jacket pocket and took out the photograph. 'I know it's not a good photograph, and he will, of course, have aged since you last saw him, but can you identify this man for me?'

I felt a small electric thrill as I placed the photograph on the table in front of the twins. I watched their faces closely to catch the moment when they realized that they were looking at the father they had last seen when they were eight years old.

'Oh my gosh . . .' said Isa.

'. . . of course we recognize him . . .'

'. . . even after all of these years . . .'

I exchanged a meaningful look with Archie. I probably

looked smug. I felt smug and I felt I had every right to feel it.

'Yes . . . that's Mr Williamson, all right.'

My smugness came to an abrupt end.

'Sorry. . . what did you say?'

'You asked us if we recognized him . . .' said Isa.

'And we do . . .' said Violet.

'That's Henry Williamson, our father's friend.'

I picked up the photograph and looked at it. Henry Williamson. Gentleman Joe's non-crook friend and supposed First War buddy.

'You're sure?'

'Positive.'

I pocketed the photograph again.

The twins spent a couple of minutes trying to talk me into contacting their father for them, but I wouldn't budge and they gave in with amazingly good grace. I told them I'd keep half the cash they had paid me and handed them an envelope with the rest. They refused, saying that they felt they had put me at great risk and at the very least through a terrible experience and they insisted I keep the lot. We debated some more but they were steadfast and I was less so. When I walked out the door, I still had their cash.

Robert McKnight followed us out to my car.

'By the way, Mr Lennox,' he said. 'I think you're right. I keep telling the girls not to go digging into all of this shite. Like you said, if Joe wanted to get in touch he would have put a note in with the money. I know they're not happy, but

I wanted to thank you for what you've done, Mr Lennox. When they think about it, they'll be happy to know their Da is still alive.'

His eyes lit up with something when he saw my car. 'Is this yours? The Atlantic?'

'Yep.'

'Listen, Mr Lennox, no sales shite. I'd like to do something to thank you for everything you've done and all of the trouble you've been to. I can do you a really good trade-in . . . maybes even a straight trade . . . and get you something nicer.'

'That's good of you, Robert, but I'm happy with the Atlantic.'

'Maybes you are, but with those funny lights and everything . . . I'm telling you I would do you a favour. Not the usual shite, a *real* favour. I'd clear it with the boss and I know they'll be no trouble. Listen, I've got just the thing for you: a one-year-old Wolseley Four-Forty-four Saloon, Royal Blue. Hardly anything on the clock. Like new condition.'

'Like I said, I'm happy with the Atlantic.'

He placed a hand on my arm to halt me. I looked down at the hand but he didn't move it. 'Listen, this is a genuine offer. No bull. The Wolseley is going for eight-four-four. Actually eight hundred and forty-four pounds, five shillings and tenpence. I'll exchange the Atlantic and let you have it for two hundred and fifty quid.'

'Now why would you do that?' The deal made no sense, unless there was something wrong with the Wolseley or car salesmen had suddenly developed a passion for making losses. Or consciences.

'Like I said, to show appreciation. The girls . . . we all . . .

were shocked when we heard about what happened: that bloke trying to kill you. Call it a bonus. I've already cleared the deal with my boss. No catches.' He handed me a business card with the garage address and number. 'Why don't you come down and see it for yourself. I'll put a reserved sticker on it till you come.'

I looked at the card, then back at McKnight's face. It was empty of guile, of expression, yet somehow he still managed to look insincere. I wondered which boss it was – the showroom manager or Willie Sneddon – he had cleared the deal with, without anyone seeing the condition of my Atlantic.

'What would you give me for a Nineteen forty-seven Morris Eight?' asked Archie. McKnight switched his salesman smile back on.

'Why don't you bring it to the showroom and I'll cut you a deal.'

Archie shrugged. The three of us knew that Archie wouldn't be offered the kind of deal I'd just been offered. Nobody would. I just couldn't work out why I had been singled out for such gratitude. In fact, the generosity of others was beginning to trouble me; and the more it troubled me, the more I tried giving myself the same advice I'd given the twins: don't look a gift horse in the mouth. But the truth was I could buy the Wolseley ten times over, without McKnight's deal, because I had earned so much money, so quickly from tracking down Paul Downey and his photographs. The easiest money I had ever made.

And that troubled me almost as much as McKnight's offer.

*

I dropped Archie back at his house. He asked me if I wanted to come in for a cup of tea, but I said I had to get on. The truth was I had to pick up some of the pieces of my personal life, such as it was. I also had to have a discussion with my new best chums in Saint Andrew's Square.

Archie was about to step out of the car when I stopped him. I took the envelope from my pocket and counted out a hundred in twenties and handed it to him. As usual, his face retained its unchanging, slack-mouthed dolorousness, but his eyebrows looked like they were going on holiday somewhere on the top of his bald pate.

'What's this for?'

'A bonus. You've been a great help, Archie. I wouldn't have found Billy Dunbar without you.'

The muscles in his face twitched as if someone was running an inconstant electrical current through his cheeks. He was, I realized, attempting to smile.

'Thanks, chief,' he said.

'Think nothing of it.'

Before I headed in to the City of Glasgow Police headquarters, I drove past my digs. No Jowett Javelin.

I was surprised how easy it was to get to see Detective Chief Superintendent McNab without an appointment. McNab parked me in a disused office while he tracked down Jock Ferguson. I was even more surprised when McNab had a young, pretty woman police constable – something that I had always considered a contradiction in terms – bring a tray with three cups, a jug of milk and a huge aluminium pot of tea. I was a sucker for a uniform, so I made sure that I had her name and a telephone number I could get her on before McNab returned.

It was a scene that bordered on the surreal: McNab, Jock Ferguson and I chatting like a bunch of old women over cups of tea and digestive biscuits. I did most of the talking and told them almost everything I had, again skipping the details of my nature trek in the forest. I did tell them that I'd been to see Billy Dunbar, accompanied by Archie, a reliable witness to the fact that Billy and his wife were both breathing when we left.

One thing that I had been expecting was to be hit with my possible connection to the death of Frank Gibson, Paul Downey's muscular *innamorato*, but either Jock Ferguson hadn't made the connection between Downey and Gibson, or he had forgotten that I had asked about someone with that name.

I placed the photograph on the desk.

'I could have sworn this was going to turn out to be Gentleman Joe Strachan, but it's not. It's a guy he used to know. A friend of his called Henry Williamson. From what I've heard, he's straight, but I'm pretty sure the guy who fell out of my window was working for him.'

I stabbed the photograph with my finger. I hoped the emphasis would prevent them asking exactly why I suspected him of being the brains behind the attack. McNab stared at the photograph and frowned. It gave me a bad feeling. The kind of bad feeling you get when the husband of someone you've got playful with stares at the smudge of lipstick you've got on your shirt collar.

McNab picked up the phone on the desk and tapped at the cradle before sighing and walking out of the room without a word. Ferguson looked at me and shrugged.

McNab came back in and sat down, staring at the photograph.

'What's up, Superintendent?' asked Jock.

'I've asked Jimmy Duncan in records to come up and join us. He works part-time as a civvy clerk, but was on the force until three years ago. He was senior man when I joined as a probationer. There's not a face in Glasgow that he can't put a name to.'

We sat in expectant silence for five minutes, then a heavy-built man in shirtsleeves, wearing ugly health service horn-rimmed glasses and with a shock of white hair walked in. He may have been pushing sixty, but he had the look of someone you would not want to tangle with.

'What is it, Willie?' asked the retired constable-turned-filing clerk, as if the Chief Superintendent was still his probationer.

'We don't have any photographs of Joseph Strachan on file, do we? But you saw him, didn't you, face to face?'

'Aye, Willie, I did, but that was thirty year back and I didn't see him for long. Didn't talk to him or anything like that . . .'

McNab handed him the photograph. 'Is that Joseph Strachan. Or could be Joseph Strachan now?'

Duncan looked at the picture for a long time.

'I don't know, Willie . . . I really couldn't say. It really isn't a good photograph and people change a lot in twenty year.'

'I've been told that the person in the picture is called Henry Williamson,' I said. 'Does that name mean anything to you?'

Duncan looked at me as if I'd spoken to him in Albanian, then McNab gave him the nod that it was okay to answer.

'Naw . . .' He shook his head thoughtfully. 'I can't say that it does. Not as far as records is concerned.'

'What do you mean?'

'Well, there was a Henry Williamson who had dealings with us right at the beginning of the war. Involved in the Home Guard.' He looked at the picture again. 'But I couldn't say if this is him either. But again I only saw him the once and in passing. I had to drive Chief Superintendent Harrison over to Edinburgh for a conference about the Home Guard. Over at Craigiehall . . . you know, army headquarters.'

'Home Guard, you say?' Jock Ferguson chipped in. He didn't look up from his tea cup and I could tell he was trying to hide the question behind a curtain of casualness. I just hoped McNab had not seen through it as easily as I had.

'Aye, that's right,' said Duncan. 'Like I said, Chief Superintendent Harrison was the force liaison with the Home Guard. Of course he was just an inspector back then.'

Ferguson looked across at me, but without much of an expression. I got his meaning though. That morning I had been jumped in the fog, the only people who had known about my interest in Strachan had been Willie Sneddon, who was unlikely to have mentioned it to anybody, and the police officers with whom Jock Ferguson had made casual inquiries.

And one of them, as he had told me, had been Chief Superintendent Edward Harrison.

CHAPTER FOURTEEN

When I was leaving my digs in the morning, I bumped into Fiona White as she was coming out of her ground floor flat. Bumped into in the sense that I had the distinct impression she had been waiting to hear my footfall on the stairs before coming out.

It was a sad little exchange. I was still mixed up about her and the sudden appearance of her dead husband's brother, or substitute, or whatever the hell he was. She was trying to frame something that she had not fully thought through: some kind of reassurance, I guess, but we were both all at sea. After all, anything that there was between us had been, until then, unspoken – if you excluded my soliloquizing the year before. And that had done more to formalize whatever we had between us than anything else. She told me that *James* was just concerned, as the girls' uncle, for their well-being and there was not much else to be said. I said that it really was none of my business and that, I could see, stung her.

It was thus that our little stairwell exchange ended and I

headed out to the Atlantic, feeling like crap. Always a good way to start the day.

I got to the office in time to let the joiner and glaziers in. They took most of the morning to replace the window. I hadn't been allowed to repair it until then, but once the coppers had all of the photographs and fingerprints they wanted, I had got the go-ahead to replace the temporary boarding with new glazing. For the rest of the day, my office stank of putty, resin and the strangely lingering odour of workman sweat.

I took out a note pad and did a quick calculation of where I was with the money I had earned; none of it likely to come to the taxman's attention. It was a lot. A whole lot. The John Macready case had been ridiculously overpaid. It annoyed me that people giving me unreasonably large sums of tax-free cash brought out the suspicious side to my nature. It annoyed me intensely. But it did.

I was now officially off the Macready and Strachan cases. I had narrowly dodged taking a long sleep in a shallow grave in the forest and I had more than enough cash to do what-ever I should be doing with my life. Now, Lennox, I kept telling myself, is the time to leave well alone.

It appeared I was as deaf to internal dialogue as I was to instinct.

I found out from Donald Fraser that Macready and entourage were leaving town and flying back to the US the next day. I 'phoned Leonora Bryson and asked if we could meet for a coffee.

'I really don't see the point,' she said. 'Whatever happened between us, I don't want you to think that it means anything.'

'Oh, believe me, sister, you've made that crystal clear. But this is business. A little epilogue to my investigation, you might say.'

I could tell from her tone that she was unsure what to do; she eventually agreed to meet me. But in my office.

She turned up quarter of an hour later. She was wearing a less formal outfit that hugged her figure. I guessed that every man she had passed on the short walk across from the Central Hotel was now wearing a neck brace. She wore a silk patterned headscarf instead of a hat.

'So, Mr Lennox. What's on your mind?' She squeezed an impressive amount of boredom into the question. She should have looked at her watch to underline the point, but she didn't.

'It's more what's on my conscience, if I'm honest. I know this woman, Martha. She's a nice girl but I haven't treated her well.'

'Am I supposed to be surprised? Or interested?'

'Oh I think you should be interested. I've treated her badly because I've used her as a substitute for someone else. Someone I care about but, if I'm honest, I know I will never be able to be with. You said on the 'phone that what happened between us didn't mean anything. It did. It meant a lot. I have to tell you, there was a lot of aggression in there, sweetheart.'

Leonora Bryson stood up. 'I don't have to listen to this. I knew all along you were no gentleman, but this ...'

'Save the outrage, Leonora and sit down. Or I might just suggest to the police that they stop you getting on that plane tomorrow.'

She said nothing. Still defiant, still standing.

'The way I was with Martha . . . I realized it was the same way you were with me. I'm sorry, Leonora, I really am . . . I can't imagine what it must be like to be so much in love with someone you are with every day in life, but with whom you can never have any kind of relationship.'

'I don't know what you're talking about.' But she sat back down.

'You are completely, totally, insanely in love with John Macready. God knows any man on the planet should get down on his knees in thanks to have a woman like you worship him. But, let's face it, Mr Macready gets down on his knees for a whole different set of reasons. All that impressive equipment you've got there, completely wasted on him. He's blind to you. And he's blind to the fact that you would do anything to protect him.'

'You really are a small man, Lennox. A sordid, poisonous little man.'

'Fair enough,' I said. 'I'm not really the best person to defend my own character. But I don't like people getting killed when they don't deserve it. Frank Gibson, for example. You got the wrong guy there, didn't you? I don't know who it is you have working for you here, but you called them right after I 'phoned you from outside Gibson's flat. You couldn't rely on me getting hold of absolutely everything. There could have been another darkroom somewhere, more negatives, more prints. And you wouldn't let anyone damage the man you love. Get rid of the blackmailer and you get rid of the blackmail. But when your people got there, there was only Frank. My guess is that Paul Downey did a runner as soon as I left. Whoever you used has probably been on Downey's trail ever since.'

'What do you want, Lennox?' she said coldly. 'Sex? More money?'

'I have more than enough money, thanks. And, though I cannot believe I'm hearing myself say this, I'll pass on the sex. It's probably best anyway, at least until the Infirmary sets up a post-coital ward in its casualty department. Anyway, don't worry, I can't prove anything. The police maybe could, given time, but your secret is safe with me.'

She tried really hard not to look relieved. 'So what is it you want from me?'

'Three things. I can't see a striking woman like you cruising Glasgow's underworld in search of professional killers, so I want to know who did the stalking and killing for you.'

She remained silent.

'The second thing I want to know is if they have found Downey, and if so if he is still converting oxygen into carbon dioxide. If he *is* still alive, then I want to know where he is, or at least to find out where to pick up the trail.'

'And the third thing?'

'The third thing is the most personal, and I want an honest answer. Was the guy who left my office via the window here on your instructions? Did you pay someone to kill me?'

'No.'

'It would make sense. How could you know that I wouldn't blab about John Macready? Or that I had maybe pocketed a couple of keepsake negatives myself? After all, I know how much the studio is prepared to fork out to protect their star's reputation.'

'I thought about it, but no. The one thing that we all knew about you, whatever else seedy you've got going, was that you wouldn't cheat on a client. So no . . . whatever happened here has nothing to do with me.'

'Okay . . . I believe you. What about my other questions. Where did you get the hired help?'

'Fraser, the lawyer.'

'Fraser?' I failed to keep the surprise out of my tone. I'd been doing so well up until then with my omniscient detective act. The truth was I had not been at all sure I was on to anything at all.

'He knows people,' she said. 'From the war.'

'But Fraser was in the Home Gua . . .' The sentence died on my lips. I felt like throwing *myself* out of the window, I had been so stupid.

'And is Downey dead?'

'No.'

'Do you know where he is?'

She didn't answer but instead reached over my desk and pulled my telephone towards her. As she did so I could see the swell of her breasts in the cleavage of her silk blouse. I decided I was too quick to turn down offers and that a short spell in casualty would not have been that bad.

She spoke a few words into the receiver and scribbled

something down on my desk blotter. Her last words were to call the dogs off.

'They've tracked him down to this address,' she said. 'Nothing will happen to him. But if he ever tries to sell any photographs of John, I promise you, Lennox, I'll make a call across the Atlantic and I'll be giving my contacts two names.'

Standing up and walking around the desk, I stood over her and read the address. It was in Bridgeton. Poor bastard.

I grabbed Leonora by the flesh of her upper arm and hauled her to her feet, pushing her hard and fast across the room until her back hit the wall.

'I don't hit women, Leonora. Just one of these odd little quirks about me,' I said. 'But if you ever threaten me again, I don't care how many continents I have to cross, I'll come over and slap you senseless. Then, after that, I'll give the police every scrap of evidence I've got to see if they can pin anything on you. You got that?'

She nodded, but her eyes were clear of fear. She was a real piece of work, all right. I let go her arm.

'And let me be clear about this . . . if I hear that anything – and I mean *anything* – untoward happens to Paul Downey then, again, I will go to the police with everything I know. Now I may not have enough for them to make a case, but it will be one hell of a scandal and everything you've fought so hard to avoid coming out will be splashed across the news-papers.'

I backed off. I felt bad about the rough stuff, but I reacted badly when people threatened me. And, anyway, given my experience with Leonora, she probably considered it foreplay.

'Another bit of advice, Miss Bryson: when you get on that plane tomorrow, I strongly recommend you make sure it's a one-way ticket and never, ever set foot on British soil again. Got that?'

She straightened herself out before answering. She was trying to retain her dignity, but the truth was she had never lost it.

'You've expressed yourself very well, Lennox. But don't worry, I have no intention of setting foot in this shitheel country ever again.'

'One more thing,' I said as she was leaving. 'Not a word to Fraser. I don't want you tipping him off that I know about your little arrangement.'

She turned at the door and nodded curtly. Then she was gone.

I sat and stared at the window, out at the black stone and iron lacework of Central Station, contemplating what had just happened and the information I'd been given. The war had been over for ten years, but it still loomed large in everything, casting its shadow into every corner of life. I had forgotten, even when Jock Ferguson had asked the old retired copper about Harrison, that Fraser had been in the Home Guard.

I was considering my next move when someone walked into my office; just like McNab, without knocking. I considered getting a sign.

'Hello, Jock,' I said. 'I was just thinking about you.'

He came in and sat down opposite me. As he did so, I saw that he had noticed the address written on my blotter and glanced at it absently before tossing his trilby on top of it.

'Here's your photograph back.' He handed me an envelope. I had let him and McNab keep the picture of Joe Strachan or Henry Williamson or whoever the hell he was, but on the understanding that they copied it and gave me back the original. I had been relieved that they had not pushed too much to find out exactly how I'd come by it.

'You get anything on the guy in the picture?' I asked.

'Nope. He remains a mystery man. But I have some good news – and I have to point out that I haven't shared it with Superintendent McNab yet – I think I've tracked down someone who might be able to cast a little light on the matter.'

'Oh . . . who?'

'Stewart Provan.'

'Wait a minute . . . I recognize that name . . .' I scrabbled about in my drawer and found the sheet of paper the twins had sent me with the names that had been found on the note behind furniture. There it was, the fourth name on the list. 'How did you find him?'

'Pure chance. He's living under the name Stewart Reid now. Changed his name by deed poll. But with ex-prisoners, we get notified of change of names and residence. I got the name from old Jimmy Duncan, who you met the other day. Told him I wanted to track down anyone who was suspected of being an associate of Joe Strachan. He came up with Stewart Provan, which led to Stewart Reid.'

'Any form since the Thirties?'

'None. Like Billy Dunbar, he's gone straight.'

I nodded, not wanting to add that I could guarantee that Dunbar would never break the law again.

'And you have an address for him?' I asked.

Ferguson nodded indulgently and handed me a slip of paper with Provan's details on them.

'I appreciate this, Jock.'

Ferguson shrugged. 'Just don't let McNab know I've tipped you off. Having said that, what is it that's going on between you and McNab? It's almost like you're on the payroll. You're not, are you? I mean, he's not paying you snout money?'

'Don't be stupid, Jock. Let's just say the Superintendent has come to a greater appreciation of my finer qualities. Now, what do you reckon to this Home Guard connection? Do you really think that this Chief Superintendent Harrison tipped off whoever it was that came after me?'

'I don't know, Lennox, but *you* know that coincidences are pretty difficult things to believe in. But I can't believe a senior officer in the City of Glasgow Police would knowingly be involved with this kind of nonsense.'

I raised an eyebrow so much that Archie would have been proud of me.

'We're not all on the take or corrupt,' said Jock defensively.

'Not all, I'm sure. Anyway, thanks for the address, Jock.' I stood up. I wanted Ferguson to clear out. I had no idea how long the terrified Paul Downey would stay at the address Leonora Bryson had given me.

'You're welcome.' I could tell from his tone that he was a little put out.

'Sorry, Jock ... it's just I've got something to deal with. And it's urgent.'

I saw him down the stairs and out onto the main street.

I made my way around the corner to where I had parked the Atlantic and headed out to Bridgeton. I drove past the address three or four times, circling the block on either side, just to make sure there was no sign of the mob Bryson had set on Downey's trail. I needed to get Downey safe and secure before I dealt with Fraser.

I had a more immediate problem.

The address was in a tenement block that was little more than a slum, as were the blocks around it. I couldn't leave the Atlantic anywhere near. Mainly because, if I did, there would be little of it to come back to, but the other reason was it would stick out a mile in this part of the city and I had as much chance of getting to Downey unseen as if I approached waving a banner and beating a drum. I drove out for a half mile until I found the rail station and dumped the Atlantic in the car park, hoofing it back to the tenement. The exact numbers were difficult to sort out and I decided against knocking on doors and asking if anyone knew Downey. Even as it was, I thought I could hear the rhythm of jungle drums as I strolled past the tenements.

I could have staked the place out, of course, but it might have been hours before the spooked Downey would venture out. Or maybe he had already moved on. I stood at the corner, smoking and watching shoeless kids sail newspaper boats on the iridescently oily surface of rain puddles.

I had just decided to risk knocking some doors when I saw Downey at the far end of the street, carrying a large brown paper bag of groceries. He hadn't seen me and I ducked around the corner and waited for him to reach me.

I really did feel sorry for the guy. When he turned the corner, he looked as if he had walked straight into the Grim Reaper himself, which was pretty much who he thought I was. He started as if he was about to make a run for it but I grabbed his arm and hauled him up against the wall. He dropped the grocery bag on the cobbles.

'You killed him!' he shouted. 'You killed Frank! You're going to kill me!'

The kids playing in the gutter stopped playing and watched us, but with a dull curiosity that suggested they had seen it all before.

'Stop shouting, Paul,' I said in a calm, even voice, 'or I'm going to have to slug you, and I really don't want to do that. I'm not going to hurt you and I didn't hurt Frank.' I frowned. 'Well . . . okay . . . I *did* hurt Frank, but it wasn't me who killed him. And I'm not connected to the people who did. Got that?'

He nodded furiously, but in that *I'm-too-scared-to-listen* way.

'Paul . . .' I said patiently. 'You need to understand what I'm saying. I'm not here to hurt you. Believe it or not, I'm here to help you. To make sure you stay safe. Do you understand?'

He nodded again, but it had sunk in this time. Now his expression clouded with suspicion. I let him go.

'I want to help you, Paul . . . to put an end to all this mayhem and fix things so that you can stop running. But first of all I need to talk to you so that I can try to understand what's going on better. Can we go up to your place?'

'I'm staying with a friend. We can't talk there.' Again his look and his tone were laced with suspicion.

'Okay . . .' I picked up the groceries and handed them to him. My car's parked at the station. We can talk as we walk . . .'

I had given Downey his groceries to carry as an encumbrance, or at least an early warning, if suddenly dropped, that he was going to make a run for it. But as we walked he listened to everything I told him, including how my involvement had been simply to retrieve the photographs and negatives of John Macready. I lied by telling him that I suspected Frank had been killed by people working either on Macready's behalf or on behalf of the Duke to protect his son. The truth, of course, was that I knew damned well that it had been Leonora Bryson and the lawyer Fraser who had organized the killing.

We got back to the car and I told him to get in, which he did, but only after casting an anxious eye around us. I did a bit of casting myself and got in after him. He sat there, small and slight and clutching his now crumpled grocery bag, more child than man.

'Why did you get into all of this business, Paul?' I asked. 'You're just not cut out for it.'

'It was Frank's idea to start with. Then Iain came up with this plan to fleece Macready. I never thought people would start getting killed. I never knew that Frank . . .'

He broke off and started to cry. I looked the other way, out of the window, embarrassed. And trying to avoid getting angry with him because he had embarrassed me. He stopped after a while.

'Listen, Paul,' I said. 'I don't think this is all just about the

Macready photos, either. I think you ended up in possession of something valuable and dangerous and you didn't even know it was valuable and dangerous.' I reached into my jacket pocket and pulled out the envelope Ferguson had given me. I took out the photograph and handed it to Downey.

'You remember this?' I asked. 'I think your life is in more danger because of this photograph than the whole business with Macready. I believe this is someone who has made a great effort never to have his face or anything about him recorded, anywhere.'

'Who is he?' asked Downey.

'I am pretty convinced that this is someone called Joe Strachan, although everybody seems to want me to believe it isn't. Everybody wants me to think it's someone called Henry Williamson, but I don't know if he ever existed. What I can't work out is why the people who have lied to me about it, lied to me about it.' I thought back to the twins' reaction, or lack of it, to the photograph when I had shown it to them.

'The name means nothing to me,' said Downey. 'I don't know anything about this man except I was given a description of him and told to try to get a picture of him.'

'By this man you say hired you? The man who called himself Paisley?'

'Yes.'

'How did he find you?'

Downey looked afraid. Or more afraid. 'I didn't tell you everything,' he said and looked as if he was expecting me to hit him.

'It's all right, Paul,' I said. 'You can tell me now.'

'Mr Paisley turned up when we were setting up the camera in the cottage. You know, the way Iain had asked us to do so we could get pictures of him and Macready. Somehow Mr Paisley knew all about what we had planned. He said he would make sure that the police got to know what we were up to if we didn't do as he asked. He also told me that he knew all about my betting debts and who I owed the money to. He said he could make that all go away, that he could square everything with the loan shark and he wouldn't come after me any more for interest.'

'He seemed well-informed.'

'He knew everything. He said we could go ahead with our plan and we would end up keeping anything we made instead of handing it over to the shark.'

'He didn't ask you for a cut, for a percentage?'

Downey laughed. 'It would have been small change for him, from what I could see. He arrived in a huge Bentley and his clothes were very expensive.'

'He was alone?'

'Yes.'

'And you went along with him, just like that?'

'Yes. Even with the clothes and the car, you could tell he was someone you didn't want to mess with. He looked hard. And dangerous. He had this scar on his cheek, like he'd been in a razor fight.'

'Right or left cheek?'

Downey thought for a moment. 'Right. The other reason we didn't kick up was it seemed easy money. We were on the estate anyway and Mr Paisley said that the man I was to look out for should turn up in the next few days.'

'And all you were to do was to take a photograph of him?'

'That's all. The best I could manage. Mr Paisley said that we would be paid well, but if we ever talked to anyone about it, we'd end up dead. Do you think it was him who killed Frank?'

'Honestly? No, I don't think so. Tell me, Paul, is there any chance that the man you photographed spotted you? Knew that you'd taken his picture?'

'No. Or at least I don't think so.'

'No, nor do I,' I said, remembering how difficult it had been, even with years of army training and combat experience, to give him and his goons the slip in the woods.

'What happens now?' he asked.

'You have to disappear for a while. And not to where you were. The people who are after you now wouldn't take long to track you down. I'm going to take you out of town. We'll find you somewhere to hide out. But you hide out, is that clear?'

'Clear.'

Largs was on a narrow strip of coastline squeezed between the sea and a massive shoulder of rock known as the Haylie Brae, which rose precipitously behind it. It was a dismal day and the rain started to come down in sheets, turning everything into sleek shades of grey.

Before I drove all the way down the Ayrshire coast to Largs, I had not made any 'phone calls or asked anyone for help or advice. Not even Archie. I had no idea why I had picked Largs, which was a good thing: no one else could put together a logical sequence that would lead them to my random choice. Although I supposed there was some logic to it: I had had it in the back of my head that a coastal resort was ideal for anonymous and by-the-night accommodation and I had had a vague notion to make for one of the many guest-houses that lined the promenade. The only thing that concerned me was that most Largs guest-house landladies exercised the kind of discipline and adherence to regulation that made the average glasshouse sergeant-major look easy-going. And two men booking a room off-season, particularly when one of them was Downey, could end up attracting the attention of the police.

After the war, the British had developed a renewed passion for caravanning, which had started to gain some popularity in the Thirties. Now there were caravan parks springing up alongside any seaside resort or on Highland estates, where holiday-makers could enjoy the experience of sitting in cramped conditions looking out at the rain, instead of sitting at home in cramped conditions looking out at the rain. I suppose I understood it in a way. The trips abroad so many had been obliged to take in the previous decade had probably blunted the nation's wanderlust.

I had gotten the idea as we approached Largs along the ribbon of coast road. Between Skelmorlie and Largs a large open field, backed by a curtain of cliff, had been converted into a caravan park. A drive led to a cabin that bore a sign telling you that it was the 'reception office'. Half of the field beyond was occupied by ten to a dozen identical two-tone cubes arranged in ranks, looking out over the sea to the hulking grey mass of the Isle of Arran. On the other half of the field, next to the identical caravans, was a largely open space, populated by two boarded up, larger caravans. I guessed one side of the park was for visitors bringing their own vans, while the other was for caravans to rent. Across from the 'reception' shed was a largish, red-sandstone villa.

I told Downey to stay put in the car while I went into the park's office cabin. There was no one there, but a sign above a large hand-bell, the kind ye olde worlde town criers would use, instructed me: IF NOBODY'S HERE IT DON'T MEAN A THING, PICK ME UP AND GIVE ME A RING.

So I did.

A minute later, a woman in her early thirties came across from the villa, hurrying as much as her tight pencil skirt and high-heels would allow. She had light brown hair and pale grey eyes and a smile that told me I could be her special guest. That made things easier and I flirted as I booked in. I explained that the caravan would be occupied mostly by my young friend, who had been ill and needed the sea air to recuperate.

'We get a lot of that from Glasgow,' she said, nodding gravely but keeping her eyes on mine. 'So, will you be staying at all yourself, Mr Watson?' she asked, reading the fake name I'd entered into the register. 'I'm Ethel Davison, by the way.'

'I hadn't planned to,' I said, hamming up the wolfishness

as I shook her limp hand. 'But maybe I should keep an eye on my friend.'

'We'll look after him. I'm here all of the time and my husband is here when he's not at work. He works nights,' she explained helpfully.

'I wouldn't worry too much about my friend. He has a pile of books and really wants solitude as much as the sea air, which is why I chose your site. It really is a lovely spot you have here,' I said, and looked appreciatively out of the cabin's window to the sea, just as a beer lorry rattled past the road end.

I gave her a week's rent in advance, which she was delighted with. 'If your friend needs to stay longer, that's not a problem at this time of year,' she said. 'Or if you wanted a caravan for yourself, we could do a special combined rate . . .'

I smiled and told her it wouldn't be necessary, but I really would make sure that I checked on him regularly. Probably in the evenings.

After she showed me where the communal toilets and washhouse was, she took me over to the caravan. Like the others, it was cream on top and black below, with flat flanks but a belly swell at the front and back. Inside it was clean and still had a smell of newness. There was a horseshoe of seating at one end and she demonstrated how it folded down into a bed. I could easily have encouraged her to demonstrate some more, but Downey was waiting in the car and I had a lot of business to deal with.

Once I had gotten Downey settled in the caravan, I drove into Largs and picked up provisions for him, as well as half a dozen cheap paperbacks. Warning him not to set foot anywhere further than the toilet block, I told him I would check on him regularly and left him to it.

I 'phoned Willie Sneddon's office from the post office in Skelmorlie but was told that he was out and would not be back that day. I tried him at home, but his wife told me he would not be home until later that evening. Telling her who I was, I said I would try to get hold of Mr Sneddon later. I thought about cruising a few of his places to see if I could find him, but decided to leave it for now.

I had other business.

The address Jock Ferguson had given me was in Torrance, an uninspiring small town to the north of Glasgow and a couple of hours from Largs. Stewart Provan's house was a substantial looking, stone-built bungalow that small Scottish towns were full of: statements that the occupiers were financially comfortable but without imagination or ambition. It was the architecture of mediocrity. I guessed that, in Provan's case, it was a statement of anonymity.

He answered the door himself. He looked in his early fifties but I'd already worked out that he would be sixty at least. He was dressed in flannels, a Tattersall shirt and a navy cardigan – the uniform of Britain's lower middle-classes – but his face didn't quite fit. No scars, no broken nose, no cauliflower ears: just a lean hardness that told you this was not someone to mess with. I thought I detected his shoulders sag a little when he saw me on the doorstep and an expression of resignation on his face. Not for the first time, I felt as if my arrival had been expected.

'Yes?' he said, and cast a glance past me, down the path and to where my car was parked on the street, as if he was looking to see who was with me.

'Mr Provan? I'd like to have a word with you, if you don't mind.'

'Here? Or . . .' He nodded towards the car.

'Here would be fine, Mr Provan,' I said, trying to work out who he thought I was who would take him away in a car. Not the police, I reckoned.

'I take it you know what this is about?' I decided to milk it a little.

'I know. I've been expecting you. Ever since the bones were hauled up. You'd better come in.' He stood to one side, with even more of a resigned sag of the shoulders. I stepped into the hall and past him.

I was hit with such force that I flew forward and halfway up the hall, coming to rest face down on the floor, having sent an umbrella stand flying and scattering its contents all over the floor.

From the explosion of pain, I reckoned he had kicked me in the small of my back. He was on top of me in an instant, his knee pinioning me to the floor, pressing down on the exact same point on my spine that he had kicked. He looped his forearm under me and used it as a choking bar on my throat. My air supply was shut off and I knew I had seconds before the lights went out. Finding his hand, I seized his little finger and yanked it forward, hard. I knew I'd dislocated it, but he knew I only had seconds left and he ignored the injury. I twisted the finger round hard and he found it impossible to ignore. He eased the pressure off just enough for me to twist my shoulders sideways and throw him off balance. I slammed him into the wall, then again, and managed to get free enough to ease up on one knee. My hand fell on a robust walking stick that had spilled from the stand; grabbing it, I swung it blind but hit my target. I swung round and hit him again, this time across the side of the head. The stick didn't have enough weight to put him out, but another couple of blows dazed him enough for me to get to my feet.

I snatched the Webley from my waistband and levelled it at him. He was slumped on the floor, half propped-up against the wall, and he gazed up at me with a strange look. Like some kind of resigned, contemptuous defiance. It was that look that told me all I needed to know. He thought I was his executioner.

'Wife?' I asked. I knew there was no one else in the house, or they would have come running because of the racket we had made.

'Dead. Seven years.'

'You're alone?'

He nodded. 'Just get on with it.'

'You think Joe Strachan sent me, don't you?' I said.

'Ghosts can't send killers, can they?' He laughed, low and bitterly. 'I thought he would do it himself. Like the others. I knew it was him. I always knew it was him.'

'I'm not who you think I am,' I said.

He frowned as he watched me ease the hammer back on the Webley and tuck it back into my waistband. I could see he was unsure what to do, so I left my hand resting on the gun butt.

'Who are you then?'

'A mug. A mug who was hired to clear up the truth about Joe Strachan, but I think I was maybe really hired just to muddy the waters. Now, I'm not here to kill you or take you for a spin in the trunk of my car, and I'm not a copper. So can we maybe relax a little?'

He nodded, but I left my hand on the gun. It was beginning to dawn on me that I really had struck gold.

'This is a nice little place you've got here,' I said. 'It must have set you back a bob or two. I take it this was all bought with the money from the Empire Exhibition robbery?'

Provan wiped blood from his nose and laughed again. Bitterly. I guessed it was the only way he knew how to laugh.

'I didn't get a penny from that robbery,' he said. 'Not a penny.'

'But you were one of the team?'

'Who the fuck are you, anyway?'

'Lennox. Like I said, I'm an enquiry agent. I was hired by Strachan's kids to find out what happened to their father.'

'Kids? Which kids?'

I frowned. 'What do you mean, which kids?'

'Gentleman Joe was one for the ladies. There are Strachan bastards all over the shop.'

'These ones are legitimate. His twin daughters.'

Provan looked at me as if weighing up the truth of what I was saying. 'Can I get off the floor?'

'Sure,' I said. 'But no more funny business. I'm no threat to you and I'd like it to be mutual.'

'Fair enough.' He got up. 'You all right?' he asked and nodded to my hand. I looked down: there was blood on the back of it. I guessed our little tussle had popped a stitch or two on the knife wound. I decided I really should think about a different line of work. Maybe Bobby McKnight could get me a job selling used cars.

'I'll live. Incidentally, that was a present from a commando type who had been sent to *dissuade* me from pursuing my enquiries. I guess that was who you were expecting to turn up.'

'Come through to the kitchen.' Provan led the way. 'I think we could both do with a drink.'

On the assumption that the sun was above the yardarm somewhere on the planet, I agreed and followed. Provan took two tumblers that looked more suited for milk than whisky down from a kitchen shelf. He told me to sit at the kitchen table. The kitchen was a widower's kitchen right enough: bachelor Spartan but with sad, faint vestiges of a past-tense femininity.

'Blended okay?' he asked me as he reached into a cupboard.

'The way I feel, wood alcohol would do the trick.' I rested my unbloodied hand on my wounded forearm. I would have to go back to the hospital. When I looked up, it was into the black eyes of a sawn-off shotgun. He must have kept it as a reminder of his previous life. I'd heard that Max Bygraves still kept his carpentry tools. It was good to have a trade to fall back on.

'Okay, Lennox, just lay both hands flat on the table.' Provan spoke authoritatively, but without heat. 'There's no reason for anyone to get hurt, but I don't want you getting any ideas about taking me into the police or delivering me up to Strachan, if he really is still alive.'

'Do I still get the whisky?'

Provan smiled, but it looked wrong on his face, as if he was out of practice. He kept the sawn-off trained on me but poured us two massive belts with his free hand.

'I reckon you're on the level,' he said after taking a slug without wincing, which was impressive: my first sip of the cheap blended whisky had shrivelled up every sphincter muscle in my anatomy. 'I read about you in the papers. Was that the fella . . . the one who took a dive from your window?'

'That was him. And if it hadn't been him, it would have been me. He wasn't taking prisoners. Listen . . .' I leaned forward and he refocused his aim on me. I made a placating gesture. 'Take it easy. Like you said, no one needs to get hurt. What I was going to say is that I need your help here. There's no way I can force you to tell me, and there's no way I can prove to you that I won't repeat what you tell me to the cops, other than my word that I won't. But the more you tell me, the more likely I am to be able to bring this thing to an end.'

Another bitter laugh. 'You don't stand a chance, Lennox. You're lucky that you survived the attack on you. You won't be so lucky the next time. I won't be so lucky the first.'

'So what are you going to do?'

'I don't know. To begin with I thought I'd run. Run and hide. Get the lawyer to sell this place for me. Then I decided there was no point in running, they'd just find me. I'd made up my mind to stay put and just take what was coming to me. But then, when you turned up, it was like a survival instinct took over . . .'

'Yeah,' I said. 'I noticed. Can I smoke?'

'Yes, but move really slow. This thing has a hair trigger and I don't want to have to redecorate.'

I took his point and eased my packet of Players from my jacket pocket and offered him one. He shook his head.

'Tell me what happened,' I said after I'd lit the cigarette and snapped shut my lighter. 'Everything, starting with the robbery.'

'Why should I?'

'Because it would help me, and helping me might just help you. This has gotten very personal with me and I want to make sure it's Strachan, if that's who's behind it all, that gets what's coming to him. And if he does, you don't, if you get me.'

'I get you. What do you want to know?'

'You said the others . . . what others? And what happened to them?'

'Johnny Bentley, Ronnie McCoy and Mike Murphy. They were the other members of the outfit. We did the Triple Crown robberies together.'

'What? Hammer Murphy was part of the gang?'

'No. This was another Michael Murphy. Hammer Murphy wouldn't have anything like the brains or finesse Gentleman Joe needed from us all.'

'I see,' I said. I had undergone the unpleasantness of

Murphy's company for no good reason. 'So what happened to them?'

'All dead. One by one, over the years. Bentley died in a car crash and McCoy was killed by a hit and run driver. Mike Murphy disappeared on the night of the share-out and my money is on him being dead too.'

'So none of them slipped off quietly in their sleep, that's what you're telling me?'

'The police wouldn't connect their deaths because they had no idea they were all part of the Exhibition Gang, as the newspapers took to calling us. And anyway, whoever did them took his time: there was five years between Bentley and McCoy's deaths and six between McCoy's and Murphy's. And that left me.'

'So you think it was Joe Strachan who killed all three?'

'Not necessarily. I don't even know if Strachan *is* alive. There was another member of the outfit, you see.'

'The Lad?'

'You know about him?' Provan looked genuinely surprised.

'All there is to know, which isn't much.'

'Well, if it isn't Strachan, then it's the Lad who killed the boys.' By now Provan had drained his tumbler in a few gulps but the whisky hadn't seemed to have any effect on him.

'I suppose I had better start with what happened at the Empire robbery . . .'

CHAPTER FIFTEEN

It seemed that we were settling down for a long account, and I don't like guns pointing at me. It's a prejudice based on their habit of going off, even when the person holding the gun has had no intention of firing it. During the war, I had seen too many men killed or wounded by their own side, just because someone had been forgetful with a safety catch or had been waving their weapon around carelessly. I communicated my prejudice to Provan and reminded him that he was loath to redecorate the wall behind me and he agreed to put the shotgun down, provided I kept my hands where he could see them. He sat down opposite me at the table and started on his memoirs.

'I suppose you remember the Exhibition?' he asked.

'Before my time. I only came to Glasgow after I was demobbed. But I believe it was quite something.'

'Aye. It was. They poured tons of cash into it. They were trying to prove something; just what it was they were trying to prove is beyond me. Maybe it was that Glasgow had taken such a kicking in the Depression and they thought that trying to convince us all that everything wasn't all messed up after all and we weren't going to spend the rest of our lives in squalor. The other thing was that everybody knew back in Thirty-eight – aye, well everybody except Neville Chamberlain, that is – that Hitler was going to keep stirring the shite until it spilled out into another war like the Great War. All this shite about the Glory of the Empire ... I think they were trying to kid us on that everything was going to get better and stay the same at the same time. That we would always have colonies and dominions with Glasgow at the heart of it all.

'Whatever the reason, they built this entire fake world on Bellahouston Park. Most of it looked like that H.G. Wells film, *The Shape of Things to Come*, while the rest of it looked like bloody Brigadoon or some bollocks like that – some kind of imaginary, romantic Scotland with a loch, a castle and a Highland village. Anyway, Joe Strachan had read up all about it right at the very beginning when it was just being planned. He worked out that there would be thousands in workers' wages every week and even more in cash takings from the public. That was his big thing – his special gift – he could always see where the big money, the best takings, could be. No one else had his eye for it. He gathered us together and talked us through the Triple Crown.'

'You, this guy Murphy, Bentley, McCoy, and the so-called "Lad". What was his name?'

'I don't know. I never knew his name, never knew his face. And when you ask if Murphy, Bentley and McCoy were there, I know now that they were, but at the time they could have been anybody. None of us knew anything about the others. We all knew what Strachan looked like and he knew our faces, because he had recruited us, but he made us meet up at the old Bennie Railplane track, up by Milngavie.'

'Why there?'

'It was abandoned but somewhere we could all find. I also think that Strachan liked a bit of drama. If there was one thing he did have going against him, it was that he was a flash bastard. Anyway, there was this disused building that had been part of the original station they had built. We were told to turn up there, fifteen minutes apart. When we did, there was this guy on the door with a balaclava hiding his face.'

'The Lad?'

'Aye. That's how he was introduced by Strachan later. Anyway, he was armed and gave each of us a balaclava to wear before we entered the building.'

'So *he* saw your faces?'

'Aye. But we never saw his and we didn't see each other's. Strachan said that it meant no one could identify any of the gang, other than Strachan himself, if they got caught. And it was made clear that it didn't matter what prison we were locked up in, if we fingered Strachan, we wouldn't last a month.

'So, anyway, we all gather there, wearing these balaclavas and calling each other by an animal name: I was Fox and the others were Wolf, Bear and Tiger. Load of shite, but that was the way Strachan ran things. Like it was the fucking army. And we couldn't complain, because it worked. Strachan then set to going through what we were going to do. He had four smaller robberies planned, but these were just practice runs, and to get funds to finance the bigger robberies. All he told us about these bigger robberies was that the first two would be the usual type of job, but on a much bigger scale than anyone had ever seen. But the third was going to be something so different, so unexpected, that they wouldn't know what had hit them and the police wouldn't know where to start looking. Oh, there was one thing we did know about each other – that none of us had any kind of serious form that would make us suspects.'

'Did he tell you then that it was going to be the Empire Exhibition?'

'Naw. I got the feeling that the first four jobs were more than practice or to raise funds. I think he was testing us out, to see how we worked as a team; to see if he could trust us. It was only after that that he gave us the details of the Triple Crown. But there was a lot more weird stuff. Every time we met, it was up at the Bennie Railplane, and every time we had to turn up at different times so that we didn't see each other without our masks on. I really didn't see how we could keep it up. Even with the test jobs, we were all masked up and in the back of a van. We were told that anyone who took his mask off and let the others see his face would be shot there and then. And if you knew Gentleman Joe Strachan, you'd believe it. It was then that it started to dawn on me: the real reason for the masks and the codenames and not being allowed to talk to each other. Strachan and the Lad were tight; they knew each other; the rest of us were useful if we did what we were told, but if we started to talk to each other, we could maybe plan a double-cross. Divide and fucking conquer, that's what it was.

'But we were happy. We got a big slice each from the practice jobs and we had all seen how Strachan's planning worked better than any boss we'd had before. And we knew that if we pulled off the Triple Crown, we'd never have to work again. But like I said, it was all pretty weird. For three months we had to meet up every Tuesday night and Strachan would drive us up into the fucking wilds and make us do all of these exercises and combat practice. Again, like in the army. Anyway, one night we were disturbed by this gamekeeper, who obviously thought we were night-time poachers. He approached us, waving his shotgun at us, but Strachan put on his army officer palaver and before you knew it this poacher was tugging at his forelock and calling him sir. But the Lad had been on lookout and, while Strachan was talking to the gamekeeper, the Lad came up behind him, completely silent, and cut his fucking throat. In the bat of an eye and without breaking his step.'

'I see . . .' I said, casting my mind back to a more recently deceased gamekeeper with a slashed throat. 'What happened to the body?'

'We took it back in the van. What happened to it after that I don't know: Strachan and the Lad disposed of it, I suppose. But on the way back, Strachan stripped the body and left the keeper's shotgun and all the clothes that weren't blood-stained by the side of this fast flowing stretch of river. I said to Strachan that it didn't make sense, that no one would believe that the gamekeeper had gone for a midnight dip in a dangerous stretch of river, never to be found. In any case, I says, it's not like the sea . . . anyone drowned in the river would be washed up somewhere downstream.

'Strachan says to me that that doesn't matter. That the less sense it makes the more of a mystery the gamekeeper's disappearance will be. Country people love a mystery, he says, and they'll make up all kinds of stories about the game-keeper running off with a woman or crap like that. No one will think about it being a simple murder because he disturbed someone in the woods.

'After that, things got tense. Me and the other boys had been shaken up by the way the Lad had done the gamekeeper in cold blood. I started to think that maybe the loot from the big jobs would only be split two ways and the rest of us could end up taking a nap at the bottom of the Clyde.'

'Did you do anything about it?' I asked.

'I'll get to that,' Provan answered me impatiently. 'So we do the first two of the big three and everything goes to plan. But there's no talk of a divvy-up of the takings. We're told we have to wait until after the Exhibition Robbery. Then, says Strachan, we'll get everything that's coming to us.

'But one of the other guys slips me a note. It's got the address of a pub in Maryhill and a day and a time we're to meet. Strachan is such a twisted bastard that I worry that it's a set-up to test our loyalty or security or God knows what. But I go along anyway. I stand in the pub like a fucking lemon because I've got no idea what he looks like and he's got no idea what I look like. I'm just about to leave when this bloke comes up and asks if I'm Mr Fox. I say I am and he tells me that he's Mr Bear. Turns out he's Johnnie Bentley. He tells me that he gave the same note to Mr Wolf and Mr Tiger, but he can't tell if either of them are there yet.

Half an hour later we goes up to this fella sitting on his own nursing a pint. Right enough it's Mike Murphy. Ronnie McCoy sees the three of us together and works out we're his furry workmates. We leave the pub and sit in the bus stance for two hours talking everything through. Turns out that the other two have the same thoughts I did and reckon that we're going to get shafted by Strachan and the Lad.'

'So you decide to do some shafting yourself?' I asked.

'Not there and then, but we meet four or five times after that. We had to be careful because there was no way of knowing if Strachan had his Lad following us. Christ knows we would never have been able to recognize the bastard. Anyway, we agree that after the Exhibition Robbery, we'll deal with the pair of them. Problem is that we have no idea when and where we're supposed to meet to split up the cash, but we guess it's going to be the Bennie Railplane, so we agree that, whatever time we're given by Strachan, we'll all turn up, tooled-up, fifteen minutes earlier.

To start with, we agree that if we can just make sure that we get our fair share, as Strachan promised we would, we'll leave it at that. But we have to see the Lad's face so's we know who to be looking over our shoulders for. But then Johnnie Bentley says about the gamekeeper and how there's no chance that Strachan or his masked monkey will let us get away with holding them up. So eventually we agree that we have to kill them both. It was a big step. Not one of us was a life-taker, not like them other two, and it would be murder. You hang for murder. Anyway, it all became academic after what Strachan does during the robbery.'

'The copper?'

Provan nodded. 'Strachan only gives us the full details on the day of the Exhibition job. Nothing's last-minute though, somehow he's been able to train us up, to prepare us for it in bits. Like a jigsaw puzzle. Then everything comes together when he tells us how it's going to go down. The bastard was good, I have to give him that. If he hadn't been a villain, he'd have made a good general.'

I decided not to tell Provan about the supposed sighting of Strachan in officer garb during the war.

'The only fly in the ointment is that he tells us on the day of the robbery that we're to split up after the robbery and stay low for a week, then we meet up at the Railplane. So we're sitting in the back of the van, masked up and tooled up, but we can't arrange to meet to discuss our next move, because the Lad is sitting right there next to us. We arrive at the Exhibition site at Bellahouston, just when it's closing. It's a Saturday night so the Exhibition is closed the next day and the armoured car will be picking up the whole week's banked takings. We go in through the entrance opposite Ibrox Stadium. Strachan's driving and he tells the gateman that he's got an urgent delivery for Colville's Steel, who had a pavilion. There's a bit of argy-bargy and we hear Strachan tell the gateman that that's fine if he isn't going to let him in, it's no skin off his nose but he'll need a note of his name because Colville's are going to go spare. The gateman's an old codger with bottle-bottom glasses and although he's looking straight at Strachan, he can't give a description later.

'Strachan even has that planned to the last detail: we come in the Ibrox gate because Strachan knows exactly who's on duty at what gate and when. God knows how, but he did. We get in and we drive up the main boulevard of the exhibition. I can't tell you how weird it was . . . all of these futuristic buildings and fountains and towers. It was like pulling a job in ancient fucking Egypt or on Mars. Anyway, there's nobody there now except staff and they're beginning to leave. We turn into the avenue that leads to the amusement park restaurant and park up, tucked in the shadow of the Palace of Engineering, where we have a clear view of the main drag. We kill the lights and wait. Strachan balaclavas up like the rest of us and, right on time, the security van comes up the main boulevard, heading for the exhibition bank office.

We wait till it makes the pick-up and is on its way back, then Strachan pulls out and blocks the way and we're out and got the van surrounded. The security men inside are shocked but not too worried, because they're inside an armoured car, until Strachan shows them that he has a grenade in each hand. He tells them to get out of the van or he'll start rolling pineapples under it. They know that the van's not armoured underneath, and even if it doesn't kill them, they're going to lose legs or balls or both, so they get out. The Lad gives the driver a hiding, really quick but really thorough, just to prove we mean business, and the other guy opens up the goodies for us. We've got the armoured car open and the cash sack transferred to our van all inside fifty seconds, just as Strachan timed it.

'Then this copper turns up. He's just a kid in a uniform that's too big for him, but he comes running over with his truncheon in his hand. I mean, I've got a sawn- off, Murphy's got a sawn-off, Johnnie Bentley's got a Lee-Enfield rifle and Strachan and the Lad have both got army revolvers. And this kid comes running up clutching fifteen inches of fucking wood. So Strachan shoots him. One shot, right in the fore-head. No warning. No shouting for the copper to stop. Fuck all. Then Strachan turns back to us as if nothing's happened and tells us to get in the van.

We do what we're told but we see Strachan and the Lad over by the security car men, who we've got spread-eagled on the ground. They tell the security men that they'll have to kill them because of what they've seen and take aim at their heads. It's all show, but the security men believe it and us sitting in the van believe it because of what we've just seen. Strachan says he'll let them live, but if he hears that they've told the police anything useful, they'll be getting a visit. Ten minutes later we've dumped the van, transferred the cash into the back of Strachan's car, and we're dropped, one at a time, at different places in the city. I end up in the Gallowgate, stuffing my balaclava into my pocket and standing completely fucking dazed, wondering if what happened really happened.'

'What did you do?'

'The only thing I could think to do, and it was totally against Strachan's orders to lie low: I went to the pub where

Johnnie Bentley had arranged our first meeting, hoping that the others would have the same idea.'

'And had they?'

'Aye. If a copper had come in he would have sussed us right away. Four of us as white as fucking sheets, whispering to each other and looking as if we already had an appointment with an executioner. We talked as well as we could. This really changed everything. Strachan had put a noose around our necks and the only way we could dodge the drop in Duke Street would be to turn King's Evidence. Now we all knew that Strachan would have worked that out too, so we had no choice. We either went straight to Saint Andrew's Square and spilled our guts, meaning we'd dodge the hangman but spend thirty years each in the Bar-L, or we kill Strachan and his psycho Lad.'

'So no choice, in other words.'

'Instead of turning up at the usual intervals, we all go to the meet at the Railplane a full hour ahead of schedule, and together. We don't have the weapons we had for the robbery 'cause Strachan was supposed to dump them in the Clyde after we split up, but Johnnie has a Great War Luger that he brings along and I have my own sawn-off. Strachan turns up half an hour after us and we get the drop on him. But there's no money with him. We've got him at gunpoint and the bastard just laughs at us. He tells us that he knew we'd try to pull this so he's stashed the cash where no one knows about it except him. Stalemate. Johnnie tells Strachan that he's going to torture him, shoot his balls off one at a time, but Strachan knows we're not made of the same as him. He could do that kind of thing, but not us. We're fucked. We can't kill Strachan because if we do, we'll never get the money and, anyways, we're all a bit squeamish about committing murder and Strachan knows that. The bastard knows everything.

'So we're just standing there shouting at each other 'cause no bastard knows what to do next when we realize that the Lad'll be there at any moment. So Johnnie, who's kind of taken everything over, sends me out with the shotgun to wait for him arriving. No squeamishness about killing now. We all know that the apprentice is an even greater danger than the master, if you know what I mean, so I'm ready to blow the fucker's head off if he turns up. So I'm outside and don't know what the fuck is happening in the hangar and by now it's getting dark and there are no lights at the site. I'm standing there in the dark with the Bennie Railplane above me and only four shells for the shotgun.

'I see the shape of someone coming my way from the main road. More of a silhouette than anything else but I can tell from his build that it's the Lad. But I have to wait till he gets really close. A sawn-off is useless at anything more than a few feet. He's still far too far away when all hell breaks loose inside the hangar. There are a whole load of shots fired and Johnnie and Ronnie come running out, shouting for me to make a run for it. Johnnie's shouting "He's dead, he's fucking dead", but I don't know if he's talking about Strachan or Mike Murphy. The Lad starts running away too and I chase, firing one barrel at a time, but just for show because there's no way I could hit him, but I guess he's unarmed and I don't want the bastard coming after me.

'End of story? Four men run off in opposite directions, never to meet again, without a penny from the robbery in their pockets. Three of them are going to have to keep running. Who's dead in the Railplane hangar? It could be Joe Strachan, it could be Mike Murphy, it could be both. All I know is that years later I read that Johnnie Bentley and then Ronnie McCoy meet with tragic accidents.'

'You never saw them again?'

'Naw. We all did a disappearing act. I even used a fake name for a while, but after a time I thought it was safe and, anyway, I met the wife and had to get married under my legal name. But I never heard another word from the others and I didn't go looking for them, so I'm stuck not knowing if it was Strachan or Mike who'd been killed.'

'The body . . .' I said. 'Surely the police found a body?'

Provan shook his head. 'Not that I heard about. And believe me, I checked. Every day, all the papers.'

We both fell silent for a moment.

'And where did you get the money for this?' I gestured vaguely to indicate the bungalow we sat in.

'I pulled a few jobs on my own. A couple in Glasgow and a few in Edinburgh. I'd learned a lot from Gentleman Joe and I decided that all of my jobs would be big takes. Strachan always said that robbing fifty quid carries the same risk as fifty thousand. When I had enough to keep me going, I gave the business up. Went straight. Even got a job for appearances' sake and actually did well for myself.'

'That night, when the Lad approached the Railplane site

... he won't have had a balaclava on then. Did you get a look at him?'

'No. Or not enough to ever recognize him again. Like I said, it was as dark as a coon's arse that night and he didn't get close enough for me to get a decent squizz at him. But he was young. Younger than I thought and a lot younger than me.'

I took another few sips of the whisky but decided not to drain the tumbler, unless I wanted to see dual carriageways through Glasgow again.

'What are you going to do now?' I asked.

'Believe me, Lennox, I'm open to suggestions.'

'Do you have a car?'

'Aye. In the garage.'

'Then I suggest you get packed. Right now. And get in your car and drive. Lock this place up, empty your bank account and drive. South. England. Don't tell me where, just go. And I suggest you stay there for a few weeks, or until you hear that this is all over.' I handed him a business card. 'Telephone me every Monday morning at ten a.m. I'll tell you what the state of play is. Call yourself Mr French when you call and if you hear anybody's voice but mine, hang up. Got it?'

He nodded, but had a strange expression. Not suspicious, more confused.

'Why are you helping me?' he asked.

'It's Bob-a-Job week and I'm a Boy Scout. By the way, you owe me a shilling. I don't know ... I think you've been punished enough for your involvement in the robbery. You didn't get anything out of it and you've spent the last eighteen years looking over your shoulder. And whether it's Strachan or the Lad or someone else, whoever's behind all of this mayhem has made it all very personal with me, like I told you.'

'Well,' said Provan. 'It's appreciated. Sorry about . . .' He nodded to my blood-stained hand.

'That's okay. I don't feel like I'm me if I'm not bleeding or bruised. Anyway, it's a souvenir from my encounter with my commando window cleaner.' I nodded to the kitchen sink. 'Do you mind if I clean up?'

'No problem. I've got a first aid kit if that helps.'

I took off my jacket and rolled my shirt sleeves up. My right sleeve was sodden with blood. I eased up the dressing and saw that two of the stitches had popped, as I'd suspected and the wound gaped slightly at one end. I took a fresh pad and bandage from the frowning Provan and patched myself up as well as I could.

While I cleaned up, Provan packed a couple of holdalls for himself. He saw me out, locked the bungalow's door behind him and shook my hand.

'Thanks again, Lennox,' he said.

'Don't thank me yet. Like I said, keep driving until you're the only one with a Scottish accent, then drive some more.'

'Will do.' He waved and headed into the green-painted wooden garage.

I sat in the Atlantic for a moment and considered my next move. I knew who I had to see. I'd known it for some time now. My guess was that if I didn't see him, he'd come visit me. And there was Fraser, the solicitor, with whom I had an account to settle. But I decided that before I did anything, I'd have to visit the Casualty Department and get my wound stitched up again. Then I'd visit a sign painter and get the lettering on my office window changed to 'Lennox. Enquiry Agent and Human Tapestry'.

I could have sworn the whole car shunted sideways. The blast sideswiped the Atlantic and I felt the same stunned paralysis that I'd got during the war every time a shell or a grenade had gone off that little bit too close to me. And as the scars on my face attested, they had gone off too close. I ducked down and hugged my knees and a shower of green painted wood clattered down on the car. After it subsided I turned and looked out of my cracked side window. The garage was gone, along with a lot of Provan's car. And Provan. I could make out something barely recognizable as a human shape blazing like the rest of the car.

Instinct took over and I sped off, taking the first turning off Provan's street, hopefully before the neighbours who were coming running from their homes spotted my car or, worse still, my licence plate.

I cursed as I drove. I still didn't know exactly whom I was cursing, but I cursed colourfully and loudly. Once I was in open countryside, I pulled over to the side of the road and checked the Atlantic for damage. Nothing much, apart from the cracked window on the driver's side. I brushed what fragments of green-painted wood were left on the roof and bonnet and drove off at speed.

Into Glasgow.

*

I was left waiting in the Western Infirmary's Casualty Department for four hours before a doctor deigned to see me. He tutted and sighed until I glowered at him with sufficient menace to change his attitude. Then he and a pretty nurse stitched me back up. I smiled at the nurse while the doctor worked. It is one of the paradoxes of being a man, or maybe just of being a Lennox, that you can be battered and bleeding, you can have just seen someone blasted and burned to death, you can have the most dangerous villains hunting you down, but somehow you still take time to make a move on pretty nurses.

Like the suicidal spawning journey of wild salmon, it was one of the wonders of Nature.

I called Fraser from a pay 'phone in the hospital.

'We need to talk,' I said firmly.

'I've been somewhat expecting your call, Mr Lennox. I agree, we do have to talk. I do so hope we can resolve matters between us.'

'In that case you'll understand that I'd like to meet somewhere public. The Finnieston Vehicular Ferry, tomorrow morning, the first sailing at six-thirty, if that's not too early for a lawyer.'

'I'll be there. I'll bring a small bonus for you, Mr Lennox, just as a goodwill gesture. I don't see that we need to rock the boat.'

I wondered if Fraser was making a joke about the ferry, but decided that that kind of humour would be more alien to him than a little green man from Mars. I hung up.

I went to the hospital canteen and had a coffee, more to

wash down the antibiotics I had been given to fight infection than anything else. I noticed my hand shook as I held the cup and the image of Provan's burning silhouette kept pushing its way to the front of my mind.

After I'd calmed down a little, I made my way out to the car park. There were two men waiting at the Atlantic. One was a wiry, hard-looking Teddy Boy. The other was sitting on the wing of my Atlantic and I was seriously worried about permanent damage to the suspension. He stood up as I approached and the Atlantic bounced.

I knew them both.

'Hello, Mr Lennox,' said the giant, in a baritone that bordered on the bottom of the human hearing range. 'We've been *re-quest-ed* to *furr-nush* you with *conney-vey-ance* to see Mr Sneddon.'

'I was kind of expecting that, Twinkle,' I said. 'I see you have Singer with you. Hello, Singer.'

Singer nodded. Which was all he could do. I thought of quipping 'I see I'm in for the silent treatment', but joking about Singer's affliction was something I never did, for some reason I didn't fully understand.

Singer was mute. He was also the meanest, most vicious life-taker you could encounter. But I owed him: he had saved my life once and, as far as I could tell, he had some kind of regard for me, as did Twinkletoes. I liked Twinkletoes. He was a great one for self-improvement and worked tirelessly at improving his word-power, mainly through study of the *Reader's Digest*. The funny thing was that, despite this,

313

Twinkletoes managed somehow to speak English, his native tongue, as if it were a second language.

This endearing image of Twinkletoes was the one I tried to keep at the forefront of my thinking as he escorted me into the back of the Jaguar they had parked behind my Atlantic. The alternative image was of the psychopathic torturer who handed you your toes one by one while reciting 'This Little Piggy'.

I looked back at my Atlantic. I had stashed my gun in the boot before heading into Casualty.

'Need to get something, Mr Lennox?' asked Twinkletoes.

'No . . .' I said thoughtfully. I just had to play this hand with the cards I'd been dealt. 'No, it's okay, Twinkle.'

Singer drove and Twinkletoes sat in the back with me, which meant I was squeezed into one corner.

'Still doing a lot of work for Mr Sneddon, Twinkle?' I asked conversationally.

'*Oh cunt-rare* . . .' said Twinkle. 'That's French for on the contrary, by the way . . . Mr Sneddon is currently in a process of commercial *diversy-fey-cation*. But he's finding other things for me to do and I'm still on full pay, but.'

'That's good . . .' I said, hoping this trip fell under the category *other things*. I watched out the window. We were heading for the docks. Maybe Sneddon's corporate office, which would be a good sign. But we took several turns into the quayside and were soon surrounded by the black hulks of quayside warehouses. Not so good.

Twinkletoes fell silent and stopped smiling. Which was worse. We pulled up at a warehouse shed and Singer got out, opened the doors, then drove inside. It was dark inside and it took me a while to adjust to the gloom. Twinkle got out, walked round to my side and hoisted me out by the arm. I was frogmarched past some empty office compartments, through double doors and into the vast hall of the main warehouse area. It was completely empty except for the heavy steel chains that dangled like jungle creepers from the roof, and for the single tubular steel office chair in the middle of the space.

Willie Sneddon, dressed in a sharp suit as always and with a camel coat draped over his shoulders, was sitting on the chair. He nodded across to Twinkletoes and a train hit me in the kidneys.

'Sorry, Mr Lennox,' said Twinkletoes genuinely as I vomited up my breakfast. And my spleen. Yellow dots danced in front of my eyes and I was only vaguely aware of being dragged across the floor and something cold and hard being wrapped tight around my wrists. I was suddenly hoisted up and my feet left the ground. It took me a moment or two to realize I was suspended by one of the chain hoists I'd seen dangling from the roof. I felt a trickle of blood run up my arm to my shoulder. There go my stitches again, I thought, and wondered if it would be better to get a zip fitted the next time.

Sneddon shrugged off his camel coat, stood up and came over to me.

'Now *this*,' he said with an irritated tone, 'is *exactly* the kind of shite I've been trying to put behind me.'

'If there's anything I can do to help you put it behind you,' I said through my teeth, 'just let me know.'

315

'And that,' he said wearily, 'is the kind of wisecrack that makes you a pain in the arse.' He nodded to someone out of my sight behind me, presumably Twinkletoes. Another train hit me in the soft part of my back. It was Twinkletoes.

'I've given you a lot of work over the years, Lennox. I know that you think you're too good to work for me or Cohen or Murphy any more, but this shitty little business you run . . . it wouldn't have got off the ground without us. And I've always treated you fair, haven't I?'

'Generally speaking yes,' I said, trying to focus on his face and ease the pain in my arms. 'But I have to say that this current little *tête-à-tête* is stretching both our working relationship and my arms from their sockets. So why don't we cut to the chase?'

'Fair enough,' said Sneddon. 'You know why you're here?'

'I'm just trying to get to the bottom of this Strachan thing, is all. And I know you have more to do with it than you've admitted. I know who you are. I mean, I know who you *were* . . .'

Sneddon looked past me again and jerked his head towards the door. 'Go wait outside with Singer, Twinkle.'

'Okey-dokey,' said Twinkle behind me, somewhat mournfully. 'Sorry, Mr Lennox . . .'

'It's okay, Twinkle,' I said, still taking short breaths. 'I know it's just business.'

'Okay. . . *enlighten* me,' said Sneddon, after we were on our own.

'I can't prove any of this . . . and you've got to understand that I don't want to prove any of this. All I want is to know who's been trying to kill me and why.'

'Go on . . .'

I groaned a little first. My shoulder sockets hurt like hell and I still felt sick from Twinkletoes' punches. His half-heartedness about beating me up hadn't been transmitted to his fists.

'Let's go back to the Empire Exhibition robbery in Nineteen thirty-eight,' I said. 'It was the biggest raid in Glasgow history. One of three robberies, all record breakers. I am now one hundred per cent certain that it *was* Gentleman Joe who pulled them all off. Gentleman Joe and his band of anonymous merry men. But that copper got killed and everything went to hell. Four of the gang get the wind up, but Strachan and his apprentice, the so-called "Lad" keep running everything by the book. From what I've been able to find out, it was the Lad who did most of Strachan's enforcing but, like the rest of the gang, his identity was kept well hidden from everyone.'

'Get to the point, Lennox.'

'Let's say Strachan was the shooter. Killing that copper put a rope around everyone's neck. So there was an argument. Before he died, Stewart Provan told me that the gang split up after the raid and arranged to meet up a week later at the Bennie Railplane hangar. The three reckon they're going to be double-crossed by Strachan and the Lad, so they do a bit of double-crossing themselves. Emotions are running high because of the murder and shots are fired. Strachan or one of his crew ended up dead. My money has always been on Strachan, because the bones they dredged up fit with a taller man. So he takes the deep, dark sleep at the bottom of the Clyde and no one gets to know where the money is. Except that doesn't make sense, because Strachan's wife and twin daughters get a grand apiece, every year on the anniversary of the Empire Exhibition robbery. So my guess is someone *did* get to the money. The whole pot. And kept it stashed nice and safe over the war years.'

'And who do you think that someone was? From what you're saying, it sounds like I was right and Gentleman Joe survived,' said Sneddon.

'Not necessarily. There was a member of the Empire Exhibition team who was even more of a ruthless son of a bitch than Strachan. The one they called the Lad. He sits tight. Maybe does his war service, while all the time he knows that when demobilization comes he'll be sitting on a gold mine. Enough money to . . . well, what could he do with money like that? He could set himself up in some far-flung part of the world, but keep looking over his shoulder, or he could build a power base that would make him the one to be feared. The one whom others look over their shoulders for. So that's what he does. He becomes the richest, most powerful organized crime boss in Glasgow. You're the King of Kings, after all, aren't you, Mr Sneddon? You had the viciousness and the ambition all along, but now you had the working capital. It was you: *you* were the Lad. And you know all about the money the twins get every year because you send it, don't you?'

I grinned. I was a smart guy. I had it all figured out and I had to go and prove I had it all figured out. I was so smart that I'd talked my way into an early grave. Sneddon didn't call for Twinkletoes. He would do this himself. No one could know what I knew.

'And what makes you so sure of that?' he asked in a quiet, calm voice.

'I came to you to ask where I could find Billy Dunbar, and during our talk, I tell you that I'm looking into Joe Strachan's disappearance. The next day, I'm jumped in a foggy alley by someone who tells me to drop the whole thing. The only people I suspect of having dropped me in it are the police: I never, for a second, think that it might have been you. Then I see Billy Dunbar who spins me an elaborate line of bull that just might be true. But he lets it slip that you put him onto the gamekeeper's job because you knew about the vacancy. You knew about it because you created it when that gamekeeper stumbled on you, Strachan and the others practising for the Exhibition job.'

Sneddon laughed. It was something I'd never seen him do. 'You know, Lennox, you're really something. You really want to rush headlong into an early grave, don't you?'

'Maybe I'll get some peace there,' I said. It wasn't a wisecrack.

'Go on,' said Sneddon.

'My guess is that you killed Strachan when you went back to the hangar, and probably Mike Murphy too. Then you hunted the others down, ending with a bomb in Stewart Provan's car today. But back to Dunbar ... you and Billy Dunbar are old mates, and Dunbar doesn't have two pennies to rub together, so you concocted the whole Strachan as an officer crap. You knew that I would have found out about

Strachan's gimmick of impersonating officers at the end of the First War, and how he could pass himself off as anyone, anywhere. It was wild enough for me to swallow it. In the meantime, you hire some officer-type ex-commando to scare me off and when that doesn't work, you tell him to kill me.'

'You think you're such a clever cookie, don't you, Lennox?' said Sneddon.

'I was just complimenting myself on that very fact.' My voice was dull now. I was exhausted. And I knew that I was going to die.

'Why do you send the money to the girls, Sneddon?' I asked. 'I can't believe you have any kind of conscience. Sending that cash exposes you, so why?'

He smiled. I didn't like that. Not one bit. He came around behind me. I was going to get it in the neck, or the back of the head. I looked up at the chains: there was nothing I could do. At least it would be quick.

Suddenly I was on the grimy floor, coils of chains cascading down on me. Sneddon had unhitched the gear, releasing me. He was round in front of me again. He pocketed his gun and sat back down on the chair. Twinkletoes burst through the factory door.

'Everything all right, boss?' he asked, looking across to me. 'I heard some *cacko-phoney*.'

'Everything is fine. Twinkle. Mr Lennox and I have sorted out our misunderstanding. Wait outside, we'll be out in a minute.'

'I don't get it . . .' I said, for once out of wisecracks. I eased the chains from around my wrists.

'No you don't, Lennox. You're right: I was "the Lad", all right. Joe Strachan taught me everything I know.'

'So you *did* take part in the Triple Crown robberies?'

'There are some things I'm not going to admit to. Some things that are locked up tight for good. You draw your own conclusions. But know this, Lennox. I didn't kill Joe Strachan. Yes, it's me who sends the twins the cash every year. You've asked why, and I'll tell you. I send them the money because they're my half-sisters.'

'You're Strachan's son?'

'I tracked him down. I don't fool myself that I wasn't one of the many bastards that Strachan had fathered. I found out later that my Ma had been a real looker when she was young. And Joe Strachan always had an eye for the ladies. They have a thing going and she gets knocked up. She dumps me as soon as I'm born and I end up being raised in an orphanage. That's where I learn that you've got to be top fucking dog or you're nothing at all. It took me an age to find my Ma and then Gentleman Joe. I took a length of lead pipe along to our father–son reunion, but things turned out all weird. I swear he was nearly in fucking tears when I told him I was his son. He just had the twin girls, you see, and Strachan was full of that crap about passing something on. A son to inherit the empire. So yes, I was the Lad. But he didn't call me that because I was his apprentice, I was his son. So when I told you I took over his wee empire,' said Sneddon, 'that's exactly what I did. I inherited my father's estate.'

I eased myself painfully to my feet and rubbed at my

wrists. 'Let me guess,' I said. 'You're going to tell me I got everything else wrong.'

'How do you know that?'

'Well, everything seems to fit: you tell Dunbar to spin me that line about seeing Strachan during the war . . . a smoke-screen. And then you hire an ex-commando to warn me off, but when that fails, you tell him to kill me. But then there's something that doesn't fit.'

'What's that?'

'That old razor scar of yours. A distinguishing mark, you might say. There's a frightened little queer called Paul Downey who specializes in dodgy photography. He's persuaded to do a blackmail job to pay off a loan shark when suddenly a knight in shining Bentley turns up and offers him a simple job, nothing illegal on the face of it, and in turn he gets an unreasonable amount of money. This rich knight calls himself Mr Paisley and he's a flash dresser but has a razor scar on his right cheek, just like yours. By the way, I guess that you inherited your father's taste for expensive tailoring. So you are the Lad, *and* you're "Mr Paisley"?'

'It's your story, Lennox. Go on . . .'

'So there's these two facts, added to the fact that I'm still breathing, that screw up my theories. Why would you pay someone to take photographs of some guy who we all think is Strachan, if you know for sure Strachan is dead?'

Sneddon took out a gold cigarette case and offered me a smoke. I took it. He lit us both up. 'So what's your take on it now?'

'I don't know why,' I said, 'but you needed to convince

yourself that Joe Strachan was dead or not. You got a tip-off that he was going to be up meeting with the Duke of Strathlorne on his estate and you know that Downey's going to be up there because you own the loan shark, and therefore the loan, that Downey had to pay off. You knew about the whole John Macready blackmail thing.'

Sneddon shook his head. 'It was a mad fucking idea. They were never going to get away with it. But when I heard that they were using a cottage on the estate, it was too good an opportunity to miss.'

'It was you who told George Meldrum to recommend me to the lawyer Fraser, wasn't it?'

'Aye. I knew you'd clear it up in no time and they'd pay you over the odds. I needed that whole thing tied up before someone found out about the photographs I hired Downey to take.'

'So you didn't put anyone else on it. You weren't behind the killing of Downey's boyfriend and the fire at the tenement?'

'No. I couldn't put anybody onto that. And I had no need to have them killed. You were my man on the case, even if you didn't know it at the time. But then you got yourself involved with the twins and finding out who was sending the money. You've brought all of this shite down upon yourself, Lennox. Don't blame me.'

'I'm not. But I'm asking you for some straight answers.'

'Then ask.'

'Okay . . .' I reached into my jacket pocket and took out the photograph I'd gotten from Downey. 'In that case, in the name of Christ and all that's holy, will you please, *please* tell me ... is this man your father, Gentleman Joe Strachan, or not?'

Sneddon took a long, slow pull on his cigarette and smiled maliciously as he let the smoke go, savouring my frustration.

'Yes.'

CHAPTER SIXTEEN

'You were right about us all meeting up at the Bennie Railplane,' said Sneddon. 'And about everybody being worked up about the dead copper. We weren't supposed to talk to each other, see each other until the meet. But the other three had got together and had planned out their own wee play. I reckoned Joe and me were to get it there and then, but there had been coppers at Maryhill Station and I had to take the long way round, meaning I turned up late.

'They must've had Joe at gunpoint in the hangar, because, as I was getting close, I heard gunfire and people shouting. One of the bastards had been lying in wait for me. I was going to get two barrels in the face, but I was too far away. I wasn't armed, so I made a run for it. They fired a couple of shots at me but couldn't risk any more. The coppers were running around all over Glasgow and there was always the chance some gamekeeper would think there were poachers in the area. I went home, got tooled up and got Billy Dunbar to come back with me. When we got there they had gone.'

'So who was dead if it wasn't Strachan? Mike Murphy?'

'You see,' said Sneddon, 'that's the thing . . . I had expected to find Joe's body, but there was nothing. Not Joe, not Mike Murphy, nobody. But there was blood. A lot of it. Someone had taken a breath stopper, there was no doubt about that.'

'So you didn't get the money after all?'

'Aye, I did. Joe must have cottoned on to the fact that the others were likely to turn on us. They got nothing. I got sent a postcard, through the fucking Royal Mail, believe it or not. He had balls, did Joe. He must have posted it on the way *to* the robbery. He must have known even then. Anyway, this card was posted in Glasgow but it was a postcard of Largs, down on the coast.'

I tried not to shudder at the mention of the exact location where I'd stashed Paul Downey.

'This postcard had a picture of the Pencil on it,' Sneddon continued. 'You know, the monument to the Battle of Largs when we kicked out the Vikings or some shite. There was nothing written on the card, but I knew that Joe kept a boat down there at the marina next to the Pencil. He had it under a different name, so the coppers didn't know about it or could search it. I was the only other person who knew about it and the identity he kept it under.'

'Henry Williamson . . .' I volunteered. Sneddon stared at me in amazement.

'I have my moments,' I explained.

'Anyway,' continued Sneddon. 'I went down to the boat and right enough, stuffed under a bench inside, were two suitcases full of money. So much money I sat there shaking. Shaking like a fucking leaf.'

326

'All of it?'

'Half of it. And not just half of the Exhibition job, half of all the Triple Crown robberies. I sat there and counted it all out. I reckoned it was the safest place to do it.'

'That was a lot of money.'

'Just like you said, enough money to change your fucking life forever. You know, Lennox, no one has ever known about that money. Now you do, and I don't know what to do about that.'

'You had your chance a minute ago.'

'I could still shut you up for good.' Sneddon sighed. 'You won't talk. You know that it would end up fatal for you. But, more than that, you still think you're some kind of colonial fucking officer and gentleman. You've been rolling around in the shite like the rest of us, but none of it seems to stick to you. You won't tell because it would go against your code.'

'I wasn't aware I had one,' I said. 'What do you think happened to the other half?'

'At the time I had no idea. I thought that maybe Joe had stashed it somewhere else to halve the risk, and maybe the others had tortured it out of him, but I doubted that. He would have spat in their fucking eye and taken a bullet first. I just assumed that he had hidden it somewhere good and the bastards never got it. But then, as time went on, I began to wonder if he had survived the shoot-out in the hangar and had taken the other half for himself and was hiding out somewhere.'

'But you did kill the other three, didn't you?' I asked. 'Bentley, McCoy and Provan, who you blew up today.'

'As a matter of fact, I didn't. I don't give a shit whether you believe me or not, but I didn't. I wanted to. I wanted to hunt them down, one by one, and kill them slow. But you have to remember that no one knew who I was. I had all of this cash and started to build my little empire. Vengeance had to take a back seat. Bear in mind no one could connect me to a robbery in which a copper was murdered. I couldn't put my head above the parapet.'

'So it was Strachan?'

'When I read about the first, then the second death, I began to put it all together. Then Billy Dunbar told me about seeing Joe during the war. He also told me that he'd seen Joe hob-nobbing with the Duke of Strathlorne. What Billy didn't tell you is that he saw Joe twice more, after the war. Both times on the estate meeting with the Duke. I worked out that Joe had been living off his half of the proceeds of the robberies and had set up this identity. Or stolen it, I suppose you could say. Every time the Duke has special guests, he arranges a shooting party, so Billy got advance notice of them coming. I told Downey in turn.'

'Mr Sneddon,' I said tentatively. 'Do you know about Dunbar?'

'Know what?'

I told him about my second trip up to see Dunbar, about finding him and his wife, about my chase through the forest, about recognizing the older man from the photograph. Joe Strachan.

Sneddon looked stunned by the news.

'Billy was a good bloke. A good friend.'

'Your father killed him. Your father killed a lot of people, some of them innocents who just got in the way.'

'Listen, Lennox. Joe Strachan is exactly the person I described to you. All of that was true. I saw him in action, up close. If I had stayed with him, I'd have turned out the same, maybe worse. I've done a lot of things I'm not proud of: doing that gamekeeper was one of them. But now, I'm trying to put that all behind me. Joe Strachan was no father to me. He used me like he used everyone else. Like he used my ma. It's because of him I ended up in that fucking orphanage and everything that happened to me there. The only reason he left me that cash was because he didn't want to kill me if he could avoid it. But if he felt it was necessary, he would have put a bullet in my head the same as everyone else. If you think I was trying to find dear old daddy out of sentimentality, then you're wrong. I needed to know if he was out there or not. So I could stop looking over my shoulder.'

I nodded. Sneddon had used the same expression that Provan had used. Right before he was flambéed in his Morris Minor.

'So what are you saying?' I asked.

'If you do or say anything to link me to the Empire Exhibition robbery, I'll make sure you're dead within the day. Other than that, I don't care what you do. If you bring Joe Strachan down and can do it without involving me, then you do so with my blessing.'

I lost count of the number of times Twinkletoes apologized to me on the way back to the hospital car park.

'It's okay, Twinkle. Like you said, it was just business. Nothing personal,' I assured him, while struggling with the concept of how having someone ram their fist halfway through your internal organs was less than personal.

I decided that I should check my wound before I drove out of the hospital car park. Although the gymnastics in the warehouse had made it bleed some, the stitches seemed intact and I decided against going back into Casualty. In any case, I had no idea how I would have explained damaging it again in such a short space of time.

I drove back to my digs. There was no Jowett Javelin parked outside and Fiona White came out when she heard me at the door.

'How are you, Mr Lennox?' she said awkwardly and formally. She was wearing a lilac print blouse and I could smell that smell of lavender from her neck.

'I'm fine, Mrs White. And you?'

'Just fine. I thought . . .' She frowned earnestly. 'Well, I thought I ought to let you know, we've agreed that James will come round once or twice a week to take the girls out. We decided that it would be good for them. And, to be honest, it gives me some time to myself. He is their uncle after all.'

'As I told you before, you don't have to justify yourself to me, Fiona,' I said. 'So long as you and the girls are happy.' I smiled wearily. I *was* tired. And sore.

'Right . . .' she said. 'I, er . . . I just wanted you to know that that is all there is to it. I get the idea that you perhaps thought there was more to it. That there was some kind of . . . em . . .'

'It's fine, Fiona, I get the idea. Thanks for putting me in the picture. It's important that we know where we all stand. Do you mind if I am equally unequivocal?' I asked.

'Of course not,' she said.

I pushed her against the wall more roughly than I had intended. She looked startled, frightened even, and she made a half-hearted attempt to push me away as I fastened my mouth on hers and kissed her the way I'd been waiting to kiss her for two years. And it was good. Boy, was it good. And she kissed me back.

When I let her go she was kind of slumped against the wall, staring at me. But she didn't slap me, she didn't scream, she didn't give me notice to quit.

'Like you said, I just feel it's important that we all know where we stand, Mrs White. Now, if you'll excuse me, I have to go and freshen up. It's been a tough day and I need to go out this evening on business. But I need you to know that I am happy to continue this discussion any time you feel like it.'

She said nothing and I left her standing there, leaning against the stairwell wall, and went up to my rooms to clean up. I heard one of the girls call to her and the door close as she went back into her flat.

I stopped off at a transport café on the way down to Largs and ate something that was described as a steak with the same accuracy as Hemingway was sometimes described as literature. The tea was strong enough to tan leather but it was hot and wet and it did something to revive me.

I called in to see Paul Downey and he just about jumped out of his skin when I opened the caravan door. I had brought some groceries and newspapers and sat and chatted with him for a while in that way that people who have absolutely nothing in common chat.

On the way out, the woman who owned the caravan park came trotting out of the sandstone villa. As she trotted, her breasts bounced unencumbered by support beneath her blouse and I imagined a brassiere hastily removed and stuffed behind a cushion before she had come out.

'Ah, Mr Watson,' she said breathlessly. 'Have you been visiting your friend?'

'I have, Mrs Davison. He's very much enjoying his stay here.'

'Oh that's good. I'm so pleased.' She moved in close to me and I got a lungful of cheap, overdone perfume. 'While you're here, could I offer you a cup of tea?'

I looked across at the villa. If I went in there, I knew no tea would be drunk. But she was attractive and her cheap perfume was working on me and the taste of Fiona White was still on my lips and I was messed up and confused and bruised all over from everything that had happened so I thought, what the hell?

'I'd love to, Mrs Davison,' I said and let her loop her arm through mine and lead me to the house.

'Please,' she said coquettishly. 'Call me Ethel . . .'

Do I have to? I thought. Do I really have to?

It was difficult to believe, but the Finnieston Vehicular Ferry had not, in fact, been designed by William Heath Robinson.

When I had seen it for the first time, it struck me as the most bizarre piece of navigational engineering I had ever seen: somewhere between the skeleton of a Mississippi riverboat and a giant, floating hamster cage. The reason for its unusual appearance was actually its ingeniousness. It could operate throughout the day and evening, whether it was high or low tide – and here the Clyde was tidal – because it had a steam-driven elevating car deck that could be adjusted to the exact height of the quay it docked at, irrespective of the water level at that time.

When I arrived at the ferry next morning there was no smog in the city, but a thickish fog skulked low on the river without the conviction to rise up over the banks and into the streets. The fog turned the improbable superstructure of the ferry into something even more black and gothic. Mine was the only car on the first crossing of the day and there was only a handful of foot passengers. Fraser boarded at the last minute and walked over to where I stood, looking down at the fog fuming on the dark surface of the Clyde.

'A rather gloomy crossing, don't you think, Mr Lennox?'

'Oh, I don't know. It beats crossing the Styx, I guess. But there again you would know more about that than I would, wouldn't you, Mr Fraser. It would appear that you have paid the boatman to take more than a few people across that river.'

'Listen, Mr Lennox, you have got the wrong end of the stick about all of that. This really is a bad business, a thoroughly bad business. Things have just gone far too far. It really is just too unfortunate.'

'Unfortunate? You pay me silly sums of money and I lead your killers to where Paul Downey is hiding out, except your boys aren't as good as you think they are and they kill the wrong pansy.'

'You don't understand . . .' For once Fraser wasn't full of cocky assurance. 'Things have got out of hand. I don't know . . . you think you *know* people, you think you understand where you are with them. That there's some kind of bond between you. Then someone comes along and turns the world on its head.'

'You're talking about Joe Strachan?'

Fraser turned from looking out over the water. 'Help me, Lennox. Protect me. I didn't know any of this was going to happen. Leonora Bryson asked me if I knew anyone who could follow up on the Downey thing and I put her in touch with Colonel Williamson. The deal was that if you found Downey, Williamson's men would double check that you had got all of the negatives. And they would perhaps be more *forceful* in making the point than you had been. I had no idea that Miss Bryson asked them to go further than that.'

'I was forceful enough. Downey and Gibson were no threat to you, or Leonora Bryson or John Macready. The truth is that Williamson, as you call him, was only too happy to oblige Leonora because he had a good reason to see Downey dead. He wanted to make sure there were no more copies of *this* photograph . . .' I took out the picture that had been my constant companion these last few days. 'This is Williamson, right?'

'Right.'

'Wrong,' I said. 'This is Gentleman Joe Strachan, armed robber, murderer and all round bad bastard of the first water.'

'I know,' said Fraser. 'Colonel Williamson persuaded me to put pressure on you to drop all other jobs so you could focus on the Macready case. It didn't take a genius to guess that what he really wanted was for you to stop looking for Joe Strachan. I worked it out from there. I couldn't believe it at first ... I've known Colonel Williamson since the war. And I couldn't work out how he could have got security clearance for the work he did during the war, based on a fictitious identity.'

'So how did you square that circle?'

'If there's one thing I'm good at, Mr Lennox, it's paperwork. And every life leaves a paper trail. When it comes to following documentary traces, I'm like a native tracker.'

'Let me guess: Henry Williamson isn't a fictitious identity.'

Fraser shook his head. 'No. He was a South African, educated at an exclusive boarding school in Natal. Parents both dead, no brothers or sisters, and any other kin distant both in terms of relationship and geography. He served as an officer in the Great War, then nothing much on record for twenty years, other than his being a shareholder in various companies and buying two properties: a townhouse in Edinburgh and a large country property in the Borders. Then, just before hostilities break out, he renews his commission in the army, but with a totally different regiment from the one in which he served during the Great War.'

'Let me guess again,' I said. 'He re-joined the army in

Thirty-eight? Right about the time of the Triple Crown robberies?'

'Exactly. You have to believe me, Lennox, I had no idea until then that the person I had known for all of these years was anyone other than Colonel Williamson.'

'So when did you meet him?'

'In Nineteen forty. He had been stationed at Edinburgh Castle and was moved up to Headquarters staff at Craigiehall, sometime between re-enlistment and Nineteen forty he had been promoted to full Colonel. He was put in charge of "special training" for hand-picked units of the Home Guard. I was selected to command a unit and, effectively, he became my senior officer. I tell you, Lennox, there wasn't a thing about the man that didn't ring true. There were even officers who remembered meeting him in France during the First War. How he managed that I can't imagine, and it was the one thing that I still have trouble with. I just can't reconcile that with him being a fake.'

'It's not that complicated. During the First War, Strachan was a deserter and an officer-impersonator, pretty much in the same way as Percy Toplis was. From what I can gather, he was a popular member of the officers' mess. There were bound to be others who would remember him, whether he used the name Williamson or not.'

Fraser nodded. 'I worked out that, at some point between Nineteen eighteen and Nineteen twenty-nine, the real Williamson must have died – probably murdered by his imposter, who stepped seamlessly into his life.'

'That's my guess too,' I said. 'After that, I reckon Strachan merely maintained the identity, without being too active within it. Although his daughters told me that he would disappear for long periods. Anyway, back to the war . . . what exactly were you and Strachan involved in?'

'Officially the only Scallywag units were stationed along the south coast of England, where everyone thought the German invasion would take place. But it was worked out that large deployments of paratroopers and amphibious troops could be dropped or landed in the more remote parts of the Highlands and Scottish coastline. So the Duke of Strathlorne was put in command of special operations training for Auxiliary Home Guard units in Scotland.'

'And after the war, you, Strachan and the Duke all remained tight in your little special forces club.'

'Something like that. I was proud of what I did, Lennox. You have no idea what we were trained to do. If the invasion took place, we were to carry out sabotage and assassinations. Any senior public official who collaborated with the occupation was to be eliminated: politicians, council heads, even police chief constables. We had hidden arms dumps all over Scotland and enough rations to last us seven weeks.'

'And what were you supposed to do after the seven weeks?'

Fraser laughed bitterly. 'It was the same arrangement as the Scallywag units on the south coast of England . . . they gave us all seven weeks' rations because they had worked out that we would all be dead before then.'

'And these arms dumps . . . have they all been cleared out?'

'No. Not at all. No one except the units themselves know

where the dumps are. It's the same all across Europe. The Duke is in contact with other organizations, including Gladio.'

'I see,' I said. I was beginning to understand.

'The danger is still there, Lennox. Except it's not the Nazis any more, it's the Soviets. And they ground the Nazi war machine into dust; how long do you think it would take them to sweep across Europe? The only defence we have is the bomb.'

'And the stay-behinds . . .' I said. 'So that *is* what this is all about. You and your Home Guard chums are still playing at soldiers. This isn't just about Strachan protecting himself, it's about protecting the Duke. Including protecting him from the kind of scandal his son was likely to cause.'

'That's about the size of it,' said Fraser.

'And Strachan – or Colonel Williamson – is in charge of security, is that it?'

'Something like that. He recruits men straight out of the army: commandos, paratroopers, that kind of thing. New blood.'

'I guessed as much,' I said, thinking about the new blood splashed all over my office and the taxi below.

'But of course,' continued Fraser, 'his loyalty to the Duke is phoney . . . everything he does is for his own purposes.'

The dark, grimy flank of the quayside and the brooding mass of the fifty-ton Stobcross crane loomed out of the fog and into view; the ferry was near docking.

Fraser reached into his coat and I did the same.

'Take it easy, Lennox, it's just this . . .' he said, handing me a fat envelope. 'There's a thousand pounds in fifty pound notes in there. I want you to have it, Mr Lennox.'

'Why is it everybody wants to shove vast sums of money into my lap? What's the deal? What do you want from me?'

'Like I said, I need you to protect me. Keep my name out of all of this. And more. I'm not so naïve as not to know that I am a marked man, so I'm going to disappear for a while. I'm taking my family with me. Somewhere out of the country. But I want to come back. I want it to be safe for me to come back.'

'I can't guarantee that,' I said, but pocketed the envelope. He owed me at least that much. 'But I intend to take Strachan down, one way or another.'

The ferry docked.

'Get into my car,' I ordered Fraser. 'And I'll tell you what we're going to do.'

CHAPTER SEVENTEEN

I had quite a bit of time to kill, so instead of going into the office, I went back to my digs. The net curtain twitched in the downstairs window as I opened the gate and walked up the path, but Fiona didn't come to the door as I came in, so I went straight up to my rooms.

In the bedroom, I opened the top drawer of the chest and laid the Webley in it. Reaching under the bed, I eased up the loose board and retrieved a box of shells for the revolver and a small leather roll-case. I unrolled the case on the bed and took out a hunting knife, still in its sheath and a set of brass knuckles. I laid these in the drawer with the gun and shells. Next, I found both my saps and laid them in next to the other weapons. They would stay there until tonight. I stripped off my shirt and examined the dressing on my arm. It was fresh and clean, but I would double bind it tonight, just to have that little extra support.

Back in the living room, I sat down at the bureau and wrote three letters: one to Jock Ferguson, detailing absolutely everything that had happened over the past two weeks and giving him the lowdown on a few other aspects of my colourful career. The second was to Archie, instructing him to take over my business. The third was a short note to Fiona White. I stuffed the money that Fraser had given me into the envelope for Archie. In with the letter to Fiona White, I placed my bank safety deposit box key and a letter of instruction to MacGregor, the bank's Chief Clerk, informing him that I had taken Mrs White into my confidence in *all* matters relating to my investigations and she was to have unfettered access to the deposit box.

Once all the envelopes were sealed, I put them all into a larger brown envelope, on which I had written: IN THE EVENT OF MY DEATH.

I had undertaken cheerier tasks.

I shut the envelope up in the bureau, but didn't lock it, then went through to the bedroom and lay on my bed, smoking. Maybe it was because I was trying to fill my head with anything at all other than the night that lay ahead of me, but I started to think about home. Thinking about Canada was something I tried not to do too much, but now I indulged myself. I thought about the 'Kennebecasis Kid' as I always called that self I had been before the war: young, idealistic, blissfully ignorant of the crap life can throw at you. Stupid, probably. I thought about the killing I had done and the killing I had seen throughout the war. About how it had changed me into something I didn't like.

All in all, I wasn't too proud of what I had become during the war. I wasn't too proud of most of what I had been up to since. It wasn't that I was ashamed of myself in the way I would have been if I had become a white slave trader selling virgins into prostitution, sold drugs to school kids or played hockey for the Montreal Canadians – but I'd piled up the sins all right.

But even with all of my erring, sinning, fornication, drinking, brawling and shoving ex-commandos out of third floor windows, I was a choirboy compared to Gentleman Joe Strachan. Another thing I knew about myself was that I was bright. I had smarts enough for two, but even there I was left in Strachan's shadow. He had made a career out of crossing, double-crossing, beguiling and confusing others with an ease and skill that was breathtaking. It was one thing I had found out about life, about people. We're not all the same. There were always the manipulators and the manipulated, the singular and the unremarkable.

I even wondered whether it was true, after all, that Sneddon was Strachan's illegitimate son, or if Gentleman Joe had somehow manipulated him, moulded him into the belief.

Maybe tonight it would be me who walked blindly into a trap of Strachan's design.

There was a knock at my door.

I hadn't heard anyone come up the stairs and I took my Webley from the drawer, draping a hand towel over the gun to conceal it. When I opened the door, Fiona White stood there, silent and awkward.

'Fiona ... come in,' I said. 'Excuse me for a moment ...' I went through to the bedroom and placed the gun back in the chest of drawers and pulled my shirt back on. When I returned, she now stood in the centre of the room, every bit as awkwardly as she had on the threshold.

'Is there something wrong, Fiona?' I asked.

'The girls are at school . . .' she said, as if I should understand what that meant.

And I did.

We spent the whole day together, mainly in bed, until the girls were due home from school. About noon, I made some coffee and she nipped down to her apartment to fetch some cold cuts for us to eat for lunch. She laughed and joked in a way I had never seen her before and the intimacy of it was even greater than the sex we'd had.

And, for a reason I couldn't understand, or maybe I could, it made me very sad. It could have been that I really did not expect to see the next day dawn, or that I knew that even if I did, no matter how we felt about each other, our paths lay in different directions. But I laughed and joked too and bottled everything else up tight: my sadness, my fear, my hopes.

She kissed me when she left. A long, lingering kiss and she smiled again in a way that showed me the girl she had been.

I ate with her and the girls and everything was business as usual, except for the infrequent lingering glance we exchanged when the girls wouldn't notice.

Fiona frowned, when I excused myself at eight-thirty.

'Something I have to deal with,' I explained. 'Business I need to tie up.'

Collecting my stuff from my room, I strapped the knife to

my right ankle, tucked the Webley into my belt, slipped the flat blackjack into my inside jacket pocket, the heavier one into one of my side pockets and the brass knuckles into the other.

That was the thing about a life of violence: it played havoc with your tailoring.

I parked the Atlantic in the city centre and hoofed it down to the waterfront, hoping that if I bumped into a copper, the fact that I was carrying a gun, knife, brass knuckles and two saps wouldn't strike him as suspicious.

It was beginning to get dark by the time I got down to the Queen's Dock. There was a night watchman just beginning his shift on the main gate and I walked past on the far side of the cobbled road, dodging the pools of lamplight. There was an open quay further along with several piles of crates to offer cover. I was over an hour early, but I reckoned Strachan would arrive ahead of time for his appointment with Fraser, just to scope out the location. I was applying the same logic that Provan and his buddies had applied eighteen years before. I tried not to think about how that had turned out for them.

Strachan pulled up in a glossy Triumph Mayflower. He was only ten minutes early and I was surprised, really surprised, to see that he had turned up alone.

I was impressed. Here he was on a gloomy Glasgow dockside, the Gorbals born and bred Joe Strachan, and he could not have looked more out of place. There was nothing about him that said Glasgow: he was as tall as me, and when he stepped out of the car without a coat, I could see that he was impeccably dressed as a country gentleman. The tailoring did not have the robust, shapeless and slightly tasteless look of typical British country wear; I guessed that his sports jacket and flannels were of Italian or French origin, which added to the vaguely foreign-aristocrat look I'd picked up from the photograph. And there was no doubt in my mind that he *was* the man in the photograph.

Strachan may have been in the back end of his fifties, but he had the physique of someone twenty years younger. This was no old man.

He stood at the end of the pier, watching the Clyde slide by inky and sleek in the dark. As I watched him, I wondered if Strachan was pondering on what it would really have been like to take the deep, dark sleep at the bottom of the river.

A second car arrived and I had to duck down behind the crates to avoid being picked up in the sweep of headlights. The car parked at the land end of the pier and Fraser got out. He walked right past my hiding place and as he made his way towards Strachan, I could see him glancing nervously about.

From my silent, shadowed hiding place I willed Fraser to stop looking around. He was sending a signal to Strachan as sure as if he had called 'Lennox! Lennox! Come out, come out, wherever you are!'

He reached Strachan and the two men shook hands, Fraser still moving stiffly and looking as rigid as hell. I couldn't hear what they were saying to each other but I just hoped to hell that Fraser was sticking to the script we had agreed in the car as we'd driven off the Finnieston Ferry. I'd told

Fraser to say I'd come to see him and I wanted to do a deal. I wanted out of the whole business and just wanted assurances that they would leave me alone. I told Fraser to say that I had told him I had a complete dossier on Strachan, including his new identity and the photograph Paul Downey had taken, and if anything happened to me it would automatically be sent to the police, so on and so forth. I told Fraser to drop in that I had an eyewitness stashed away to boot. The eyewitness they had planned to bump off.

It was all complete guff – other than me having Paul Downey tucked away in a Largs caravan park – and Strachan would know it, but it was all just something for Fraser to say until I got a chance to get the jump on Strachan. And without his goons to support him, although it was still going to be a dangerous play, it was going to be that much easier.

As they talked, Strachan gazed at the ground in concentration and nodded, as if taking in every syllable that Fraser uttered. Then, suddenly, he held up a hand as if telling Fraser to wait. He walked over to the Mayflower and opened the boot. He hauled a small, slightly-built man with dark hair out of the boot and to his feet.

Paul Downey.

I made a start but then checked myself.

'Good evening, Mr Lennox,' Strachan called out into the night, but not in my direction. 'As you see, I have your witness here.' The accent, like the tailoring, didn't have even the tiniest vestige of Glasgow about it. Cut-glass clear and modulated, the same way as my chum who took the window exit. 'When you told Mr Fraser here to call my men off the search for Downey, all we had to do was to follow you. You're really not as good as you think. Now, Mr Lennox, please don't be tiresome. Show yourself. I know that you are here.'

It was then that I heard them: the other two. I turned to see one beginning to search the far side of the pier, starting at the top and working his way towards the water. I heard his chum on my side, further back and nearer to where Fraser had parked his car, working his way through the stacks of barrels and crates.

I kept tight, but I was pissed. I was pissed at being hunted again by these bastards. I felt my anger boil in my chest. If I was going to die here, I wasn't going to be the only one.

'Mr Lennox . . . please.' He sighed and let go of Downey, who stood, his shoulders hunched, as if suspended by an invisible wire. Strachan now stood with Downey on one side, Fraser on the other. 'Do you know the Fairbairn-Sykes Timetable of Death, Mr Lennox?' He spoke loudly but did not shout. He knew I was somewhere on the pier. 'Standard issue for commando and SOE operatives. He reached inside his jacket and slipped something from his belt. Not a gun.

'Number One . . .' Strachan held the F-S fighting knife, the same type with which my attacker had been armed, to the inside of Paul Downey's arm, 'the brachial artery. Depth of cut, just half an inch. Loss of consciousness, fourteen seconds. Death, one minute thirty seconds.'

I could hear Downey sob; see his shoulders shake. With lightning speed, Strachan moved the knife to Downey's wrist. 'Number Two . . . radial artery. Depth of cut, only one quarter of an inch. Slightly slower action, however and a smaller target, so I've never gone for it myself. Loss of consciousness, thirty seconds. Death, two minutes.' He paused. 'Now, Mr Lennox, please show yourself, or my demonstration might become more *explicit.*'

I stayed put. If he was going to kill Downey, he was going to kill Downey. I just had to work out how to get the three of us out of there. I heard noises closer to me.

Strachan sighed again. 'All right, Mr Lennox. Do you know I've demonstrated these knife strikes more often than I can remember? All through the war. Now we come to the really quick kills. Number Three . . .' The knife flashed and was at the side of Downey's neck. 'The carotid. Depth of cut, one and a half inches. Loss of consciousness in just five seconds. Death within twelve seconds. Mr Lennox?'

The guy to my right was getting really close. I slipped the Webley from my belt.

'Now this brings me to my favourite of all strikes . . .' Strachan arced his arm up, again so fast that Downey didn't even flinch, and the blade of the commando knife was angled down resting just behind where Downey's collar bone would be. 'The subclavian. The gladiator strike. Depth of cut two and a half inches. Unconsciousness in two seconds. Death in three and a half. Like I said, my favourite of all cuts.'

With that, his hand arced again, the blade flashing in the dark. But this time it was away from Downey. It looked no more than a tap on the shoulder, but I could see the blade had sunk deep into Fraser's body and was pulled free in the same sliver of a second. The lawyer sank to his knees, without uttering a sound, a dark bloom soaking his white shirt. He toppled, face down, onto the pier.

'Now, Mr Lennox. I will give you this boy. I will let him leave here tonight to go on running and hiding and living in fear. But my price, Lennox, has to be you.'

I had a fix on the heavy searching on the far side of the pier and at that moment, the second goon emerged from behind the pile of crates next to me. His head was wrapped in bandages and from what I could see from his face, he wasn't going to be modelling knitting patterns. He was the goon whose features I'd rearranged the night of our nature trek in the woods.

'I'm here,' I said quietly and stood up. I shot goon two in the bandages. I heard the percussive crack of a bullet passing close to my head and I fired at the other goon before he could improve his aim. He took it in the belly and doubled up, dropping his gun and screaming.

I aimed at Strachan, but he pulled Downey in front of his body as a shield, holding the F-S knife at the youth's throat. And as I had just seen, he knew how to use it. There was no fear or panic in Strachan's movements, just efficiency.

The goon behind me was still screaming, so I went over and kicked his gun out of reach. Strachan did nothing while I checked on the other goon. The bandages around his head were soaked crimson. He'd used up all the oxygen he was ever going to use.

I walked back towards where Strachan held Downey.

'You all right, Paul?' I asked.

'I've wet myself,' he said tearfully. 'Please don't let him kill me, Mr Lennox. Please don't let him.'

'What about it, Strachan? You said you'd let the boy go in exchange for me.'

'That's not quite the bargain it was, Mr Lennox, considering you have that gun.'

'It's the only bargain you'll get. Let's face it, if you kill Downey, I'll kill you. Let him go and we can talk.'

'By talk, do you mean bargain?'

'If there's one thing you should have learned about me by now, Mr Strachan . . . do I call you Mr Strachan? Or Joe? Or Colonel Williamson?'

'Whatever you're most comfortable with.'

'Well, if there's anything you should have learned about me, it's that I'm pragmatic.' I turned my attention to Downey. 'Now, Paul, I want you to listen to me very carefully. If Mr Strachan here lets you go, I want you to run and keep running. No police. You tell nobody what happened here, ever. Do you understand?'

'Yes, Mr Lennox.'

'If you want to live without having to look over your shoulder for Mr Strachan, he'll have to be convinced that you're no threat to him. You forget what happened here and get as far away from Glasgow as you can, and don't come back. You got it?'

'Yes. I swear.' He turned his head as far as Strachan's grip would allow. 'I promise, mister. Honest.'

'Well, Strachan. What about it?'

Strachan let go his hold on Downey, who stood frozen for a moment, shocked and unsure what to do.

'Go, Paul,' I said and tried to keep the urgency from my voice. 'Run. And remember what I said. Tell nobody anything, about what happened here, about Fraser, about Strachan, and especially about me.'

He nodded furiously, staggered a few steps forward away from Strachan, then broke into a run.

'I suggest we tie this up quickly,' I said once we were alone. Behind me, the goon with the burst gut had stopped screaming and was now making the low, harsh snoring sounds that herald the way out. 'I'm guessing someone, probably the night watchman at the yard, maybe heard the shots.'

'So you really want to bargain?' said Strachan. 'I thought that was all bull. Well, I'll bargain. And I'll tell you, I could always use a man like you.'

'My job was to find out what happened to you. I was hired by your daughters. As far as I can tell, my business with them is concluded. And handing you over to the police isn't my concern. Although I have to tell you they offered a handsome bounty.'

'I'm sure I can recompense you for your loss. More than recompense you.'

'I was counting on that.' I smiled.

'Could we perhaps dispense with the artillery?' Strachan nodded towards the Webley.

'Oh, I'm afraid not. At least not yet. I'm not that green.'

'I can see you are indeed not, Mr Lennox. But as you say, time may be pressing. What do you want?'

'The truth. That's all. I think any business relationship

should be based on trust. So, I want to know, how did you manage to pull the whole Colonel Williamson stunt?'

'No stunt, Lennox. Henry Williamson is who I am. Who I became. I've lived this way for so long that Joe Strachan with his vulgar little ways is a stranger to me.'

'And the real Williamson?'

'Long gone. Let me explain something. Back in the First War, I saw the main benefit of class and privilege. The main benefit is that there is always someone to do things for you. The lower classes. And in a war like the Great War, they do the dying for you. That was the biggest benefit: keeping you out of harm's way. So, if I wasn't the part, I could play the part.'

'Your little excursions impersonating officers?'

'It started as impersonation, but then I found that I sank into it rather too well. When I was caught, I became an embarrassment to the army. The act I put on was so convincing that I kept it going throughout the trial. It really threw them. A cockney or a scouser or someone with a heavy Glaswegian accent – it was easy to put someone like that in front of a firing squad, but if you talked like an officer, then it was a bad show to put you against a wall. They knew I was putting it on, but they couldn't see past it, or hear past it. So when I was asked if I had anything to say before sentencing, I said that I did not want my family shamed by me being branded a coward ... as if my family would give a tinker's damn about me. I asked if, instead of facing a firing squad, I could be sent on dangerous missions over the wire. Missions where I would inevitably, eventually, die in action.'

'And they agreed to that?'

'As I said, they couldn't see past the bearing and the accent. I told them I would rather die fighting for my country than shot as a coward, which I was not. It was the out they were looking for and I was assigned to Battlefield Intelligence. Basically, I was ordered to crawl all the way over to the enemy's trenches and get as much information on their deployment as possible. So I did it. And they ended up giving me a medal for it.'

'How did you survive?'

'The first few times I did my duty and came back with accurate reports. They were used to direct our artillery on the best points in the enemy's lines. It was after that first artillery barrage, where they not only missed the points in the enemy trenches I had pointed out, but they missed the trenches completely, that I decided there was no point in risking my life for nothing. They had been sending me out with another ex-deserter, but he stood on a landmine, so I was left to do the intelligence gathering on my own.

'Command seemed to think that one man was half as likely to be spotted as two. So I would crawl out into the dark, halfway into no-man's-land, find a deep enough shell crater and have a few hours' sleep. Then, when I got back, I would give a made-up report. Made-up, but based on what I had really seen on the first few sorties. I just changed the positions, the numbers, shuffled around the regiments, that kind of thing.'

'And no one suspected?'

'Not for a long while, then a young intelligence corps

captain started to question me about one of my reports. He said I couldn't have seen the regimental markings that I reported seeing. Everyone else was convinced, but Williamson insisted he came with me on the next sortie. We went all the way over to the German lines, following the route I had taken when I'd really gone over. I guided him from cover to cover, and that convinced him that I really did make the trip each night. The problem was that he then insisted on coming on other sorties. The fool was going to get me killed. But it allowed me to become chummy with him, or as chummy as the chasm in rank and class would allow. I asked him all about his background, and he told me he was South African but had been sent to their version of public school. I did a bit more chat and got out of him that he had no close family left. He was about my age and size, and even looked rather like me, so I decided I'd kill him in no-man's-land, take his papers and all his marks of rank.

'I needed everybody to believe that Henry Williamson was still alive, in order for me to use his identity after the war, so I planned to tell command that he had been captured, not killed. I had it all planned out for the next time we went out into no-man's-land at night, but we were halfway across when the Germans sent up a flare right above us and we were spotted. They opened fire and Williamson was hit in the legs.'

'So the Germans did your job for you . . .'

'No. Not at all. I needed Williamson alive, so I carried him back to our trenches. And that was it. Suddenly I'm not a deserter any more, I'm a hero. Instead of getting a chest full of firing-squad bullets, I get a chest full of medals. And Williamson ...' Strachan shook his head in disbelief. 'Williamson became my bosom buddy.'

'Williamson survived the war?'

'He did. He wanted to keep in touch, so I encouraged him to do just that. He came up to Glasgow unannounced, thinking it would be a great surprise for his old war chum. I thought it was all very odd, given that he was an officer and a gentleman, but then he finds out that I'm known and feared as a gang boss. It turns out that he hasn't two pennies to rub together and no job prospects, so he asks me for a loan and if I could put any work his way. So I did. He was perfect for pulling scams, because no one suspects an officer and a gentleman. Turns out the real Henry Williamson was every bit as rotten to the core as I was; it was just that he used the advantages of class to hide it from the world.'

'Let me guess ... you convince him to teach you all the moves and manners, so you can form a double act?'

'I'm impressed, Lennox ... again. That's exactly what I did. All the time I'm getting every detail of his history from him – as the *typical gentleman's background*, of course. I found out where he went to school, who he went to school with, who the masters were, all of that. The beauty of him being South African was that he went to Michaelhouse in Natal, their version of an elite public school. It gave me social credibility without me tripping over "old school chums" here in Britain.'

'So then you do him in?'

'Sadly, yes. But not quite as you imagine. I had planned to, of course, but I actually caught him stealing from me.

Little amounts to start with, and items – like my favourite gold cigarette case.'

'Oh my God . . .' The penny dropped. All the way to the bottom of the Clyde. 'It was his remains they dredged up?'

'The police were absolutely miles off with the dates. I shot him in the neck and wrapped him up in chains and dumped him in the middle of the river. But that was in Twenty-nine, not Thirty-eight. I actually felt quite badly about the whole business, so I let him keep my cigarette case, as a gesture, so to speak. I had another case made, identical, by the same goldsmith. I have to say I never thought old Henry would ever be found, and certainly not after such a long time. But the fact that everyone thought it was me was an added bonus. Joe Strachan is dead, Mr Lennox. Now, can we remove ourselves from this sorry little tableau, before someone finds us here?'

'You're going nowhere, Strachan. Despite your phoney accent and ersatz refined manner, you're nothing but a common, low, Glaswegian thug. No matter what you do, you'll never wash off the stench of the Gorbals. Drop the knife or I'll let you have it now.'

'You disappoint me, Mr Lennox,' he said. The F-S knife clattered on the cobbles of the pier. 'You're not as bright as I thought you were. Tell me, what exactly are you going to do? You can't hand me over to the police. For a start, I'm dead, remember? Officially I've been at the bottom of the Clyde for eighteen years. And secondly, how are you going to explain your involvement with the deaths of Frank Gibson, Billy Dunbar and these poor unfortunates scattered around here?

No, Lennox, you don't have much of a choice in this. So let's do a deal. I know you won't talk, and I'll pay for your silence and my peace of mind.'

I sighed, and was surprised how weary my sigh sounded. We both knew where this was going; we both disbelieved everything the other said. The night was cooling and the wake of a ship that was now long passed broke against the pier. I kept my eyes fixed on Strachan because he was someone you kept your eyes fixed on, but I was aware of the shadowed shapes and distant navigation lights of ships and tugs sliding silently by, far out on the black Clyde behind him. Every journey comes to an end and this journey had been rougher than most, and it had brought me here: to the end of a Glasgow pier with the killers and the killed.

I looked at the man before me. Strachan must have been pushing sixty, but not in the way people were sixty in Glasgow. In Glasgow, sixty was elderly. Broken by hard work and harder living. Strachan's comparative youthfulness and fitness spoke of a life a universe removed from Glasgow. A life he was desperate to return to, unscathed and unsullied by everything that had happened. I thought of my own life here, in Glasgow, and a life left behind in Canada a wartime ago. The unfairness of it made me feel sick. Strachan had paid for his second chance with the pain and blood of others.

'So you just get to walk away?' I said eventually. 'And what about the trail of death and misery you've left behind you? I'm expected to let that all go? Just forget about the innocent people you've killed simply to preserve the fiction of your fake existence?'

'Like I said, Lennox, you have no choice. Let it go. Let *me* go. It'll make you a rich man. I'll organize it through Willie Sneddon.'

'He doesn't even know for sure you're alive. I don't think he's even sure that he really is your son.'

'Then it's time for a father–son reunion to put his doubts to rest. You know I'm right. You know everything I'm saying is right.'

'That's true,' I said and nodded respectfully. 'What you've said is all true. And do you know what the truest thing is?'

'What?' He was smiling now, knowing he had beaten me down with his logic.

'The truest thing you've said is that you're dead. As far as everyone is concerned you've slept the deep, dark sleep at the bottom of the river for eighteen years.'

'Your point is?' he asked, the smug smile still on his face.

'That this isn't murder.'

I shot him in the face. Right in the middle of his smug smile. My second and third bullet hit him in the chest and the life left him before he toppled backwards, off the pier and into the river.

'Sleep well, Gentleman Joe,' I said.

I used my handkerchief to wipe down the Webley before I threw it as far as I could into the dark.

I heard it splash, somewhere far out in the inky Clyde.

ACKNOWLEDGEMENTS

I would like to offer my heartfelt thanks to the following people for their help and support: Wendy, Jonathan and Sophie; my editor Jane Wood; Ron Beard, Jenny Ellis, Lucy Ramsey, Robyn Karney; Marco Schneiders, Ruggero Léo, Colin Black, Chris Martin, Larry Sellyn and Elaine Dyer.